Tales of the Wide-A-Wake Café

by

Curt Munson

STEVE, MAXEY, & FAMILY —

CURT MUNSON AND I BECAME
LIFE LONG FRIENDS BECAUSE OF OUR
EXPERIENCES TOGETHER IN VIET NAM.
AFTER WE GOT OUT, I DROVE TO ARKANSAS
TO BE IN HIS WEDDING TO JANIS.

I HOPE YOU ENJOY HIS BOOK
AS MUCH AS I DID.

Mike Krall
2012

First published by AuthorHouse 08/26/04

ISBN: 1-4140-6121-8 (e-book)
ISBN: 1-4184-5094-4 (Paperback)
ISBN: 1-4184-5095-2 (Dust Jacket)

Printed in the United States of America
Bloomington, Indiana

This book is printed on acid free paper.

Photo courtesy of the Edmond Historical Society.

Acknowledgements

Writing this book was one of the greatest privileges of my life. It began when I saw the photo of the waitresses taken in August 1940 for an ad that ran in the Edmond Sun newspaper. I obsessed about the things those women didn't know because they staggered me. They had never heard of Pearl Harbor, Midway, Guadalcanal, or any of the hundreds of touchstones of the world war that would later be associated with the worst and the best times of their lives. The years that followed that photo linked those women from a small insular community to the millions of others with whom they experienced World War II. That transformation from small town innocence to global connection was among the most awesome cultural phenomenon of all time, and more than anything in the world I wanted to make that same journey.

That is where the story tellers came in. This book is dedicated to the people who shared their memories with me. Including my mother, Imogene Munson, I interviewed dozens of people from Edmond who racked their memories for arcana and details. Oren Lee Peter's phenomenal memory was invaluable to me – from the cost of a streetcar ticket to the layout of the café itself. Lucile Peters spent hours with me from her hospital bed following surgery for a broken hip and told me about her experiences during the war, including being an inventory control specialist at Tinker Field – an occupation I immediately assumed for Janice Lookabaugh. .

Lee Nixon, of Lafayette, La. spent hours telling me stories of what it was like to be a waitress at the Wide-A-Wake as well as a co-ed at Central State College. Lee also attracted two marriage proposals on the same day, a story I modified for Clara.

Although too young for the Greatest Generation, Sandy and Roy Webb helped me recreate the geography of Edmond as well as understand what it was like to be a kid in this wonderful community. Dr. Clif Warren was the first to see my collection of short stories as the novel it is today. Tammie Gilliam read the manuscript (many times) and offered counsel and support. There were so many others.

At every point in the preparation of this book I sought the highest level of authenticity I could achieve. This extended to the clothing, music, prices, pay, and tips, and even what movie was playing on a particular night. That veracity extended to one of the "characters" featured in the book, the venerable Boeing B-17 Flying Fortress. In one scene, Janice and Teresa discuss combat damage suffered by an imaginary B-17 nicknamed "The Salty Dog." Although the damage is almost fantastic to read about, real B-17s suffered every one of the attacks I described before somehow bringing their crews back home. The legendary ruggedness of that aircraft was a key reason the men of the 8th Air Force loved and trusted their planes so very much.

My most ardent thanks are to my wife Janis. She read and re-read the manuscript endlessly, adding counsel as well as punctuation. When I wanted the best from Janice Lookabaugh, I had her behave as Janis Munson would have done. Others helped me; she is my muse.

Curt Munson
Edmond, Oklahoma
March 7, 2003

Preface

The Lookabaughs

The Lookabaugh Farm
Oklahoma County, Oklahoma
Thursday, August 14th, 1937
3:43 PM

I

Powdery dust rose in tiny cloud-like puffs behind her bare feet as Janice Lookabaugh ran across the grassless yard of the farmhouse towards her home. The dust was then carried immediately away by the hot wind that blew from the south all that summer. In a matter of moments, it began carrying away the evidence of her passing as her footprints were smoothed and the yard resumed its dry barren appearance.

Earlier, Janice had glanced up from the book in her lap when she heard the truck engines. After finishing her chores, she had escaped the August heat in the tiny farmhouse in which she lived with her parents, older sister, and baby brother to a nearby grove of cedars. Her grandfather had planted the cedars, long before she was born, to shield the house from the winds that constantly blow in Oklahoma. She was reading because she loved to, because her ninth grade year was about to start, and because she had a natural abhorrence to doing nothing. When she saw the trucks drive by on the dusty lane that ran along the southern edge of her family's farm, a large flat bed, and a one and a half-ton stake bed truck she'd seen before, she stood and began walking home. When they turned up the lane to her house, she began to run.

Janice arrived only moments after the trucks. The men who arrived with them were dismounting as she ran up the steps to the house's porch and burst through the front door, slamming the screen behind her.

"Momma," she called and then skidded to a stop when she saw her father peering through the window that faced the barn where the men had begun loading harness and tack onto the stake bed. Her brother, John Junior, was pushing a wooden locomotive her father had made for him on the tiny rug, and her mother, Marge, was seated on the horsehair davenport with a handkerchief clutched in her right hand. John Lookabaugh turned to look at his daughter, but said nothing.

"Why didn't you tell me?" she demanded.

"They're early," John replied, "they weren't supposed to be here 'til tomorrow. I planned to tell you and Karen in the morning. I could see no reason to upset you earlier'n I had to."

Janice had seen the trucks from the bank many times. The stock market in New York may have collapsed in 1929, but the depression had arrived on the farms of Oklahoma almost a decade earlier. John Lookabaugh had been a farmer all of his life. Since his return from the war, he had watched as the prices for wheat, corn, cotton and milk dropped lower and lower until finally, it was more expensive to produce them than to buy them from the farmers who did.

The pressure of his debts and the prices for his commodities made it impossible for John to continue in the work that had occupied his family since they had come to America. The only thing that made the Lookabaugh's different from thousands of other families that were driven from the land was their tenacity. Okies, as they were known, had begun moving off their farms to places like California or Chicago as early as the beginning of the 1920s. Whether it was delivering milk and eggs personally, or working part time as a carpenter or mechanic, John had done everything he could to retain the independence of his family farm. It hadn't been enough.

"Are we moving to California?" Janice asked with dread tingeing her voice.

"No," he assured her. "I've hired on full time at the brick plant. We're just moving to Edmond."

II

After the men from the bank left, Janice and her sister, Karen walked across the dirt yard of the home site to the door of the barn. Every tool, every piece of farm equipment, almost all of the tack and harness had been taken. Even the milking stools and buckets were gone.

"How are we going to milk?" Janice asked.

"Milk," Karen spat back at her, "you poor simple thing, hasn't it occurred to you that we don't own those cows any more?"

"It has occurred to me, Karen," Janice responded as though she were talking to an imbecile, a tone that never failed to infuriate her older sister, "but listen to them baying. The cows don't know who owns them, they just know their udders are full. They still need to be milked, even if we aren't going to benefit. I am not going to make those poor animals suffer. Come on, Daddy will be along in a bit, let's bring them up before he asks us to."

Grumbling with every step, Karen followed Janice to the wire gate and allowed the already waiting cows to enter the corral and then led them to the barn. The animals walked docilely into the stanchions as they had done morning and evening a hundred times before. Janice climbed the ladder to the hayloft and began throwing down hay that Karen spread out in front of the animals.

"Well ladies," Janice addressed the cows as she began locking down the stanchions, two upright bars through which the cows stuck their heads which were locked firmly into position with a lever so the animals would stand still for the milking, "I know you're going to be cranky with me for feeding you nothing but hay tonight, but we don't have any grain."

Janice then got down on her knees, pressed the side of her face onto the warm flank of the cow in the first stanchion, and began milking her directly onto the concrete floor of the milking bay. After complaining further for another minute or so, Karen yielded to the inevitable and walked to the cow in the second stanchion and did the same. As a sixteen-year-old, Karen hated it when something happened that made it look like she was obeying her younger sister.

With the exception of John Junior, who at age three was scarcely capable of understanding what the family was doing, Karen was the only Lookabaugh not upset to be leaving the farm. Unlike Janice, Karen despised the constant chores and requirements. Mostly, she hated the almost guaranteed poverty farming provided. She had been attending Edmond High School for two years, riding the bus 7 miles to town every morning. Karen's good looks had made her as popular as any of the "farm kids" at Edmond High was likely to be, and she looked forward to being able to spend more time with her friends after school. Before the girls had finished, John Lookabaugh walked into the barn, assessed what was happening and moved to the third cow and began milking without saying a word.

"We don't even have a bucket to carry water to wash the milk off the concrete," Janice observed, "this barn is really gonna' smell ripe by tomorrow afternoon."

"We won't be here then," her father observed without emotion, "let the bank worry about that."

III

Before dawn, John Lookabaugh rousted his family and while he and the girls milked the cows uselessly onto the concrete one last time, Marge Lookabaugh prepared breakfast for her husband and children. The family ate, cleaned the dishes and pans and then packed them into an already overloaded car they had borrowed from Marge's brother. As he drove away, John Lookabaugh didn't even look back at the house in which he had been born and with the exception of the three years he had been in the army, had lived his entire life. Marge sat quietly, holding John Jr. on her lap as tears flowed unchecked and unremarked upon from her eyes. In the back, jammed between boxes of clothing and household goods, sat the two girls. Karen looked straight ahead with the arrogance of youth, even forcing a small smile from the corners of her lips. Only Janice looked back at the only home she'd ever known.

"Well," she said practically, "that's that." She then turned to the front, opened the book she had in her lap and began to read.

Dedicated to my own Greatest Generation Heroes

and to the real Janis, who inspires

everything I do.

These stories are imaginary. Neither the principal
characters nor what happened to them are real except to
the extent that telling stories in a historical context requires.
To do that, real settings real names and events enhance the
authenticity. The Noes, two brothers, Eugene and Crawford,
and their wives, Essie Mae and Cleo, really existed and I have
included them since they owned the Wide-A-Wake Café, and
were known and respected by everyone in town. There are
others, but in no case have I tried to recreate their actual
lives. I only borrowed their names. Essentially everybody
else was inspired by a photo of the Café's staff that was used
in an Edmond Sun newspaper ad in September 1940. I made
them up - names, lives, everything. If the real people in the
photo weren't like the ones I wrote about, then for the most
part, that's their loss.

The story begins in the summer of 1940 in Edmond,
Ok...

Chapter One

Tommy

The Wide-A-Wake Café
213 S. Broadway, Edmond, Ok.
Friday: August 16, 1940
9:05 a.m.

I

$\mathcal{T}$ommy Morrison was on the third day of his leave when he entered the Wide-A-Wake Cafe. The cafe never closed, and was very rarely empty, but he'd timed his arrival, and most of the breakfast crowd had already gone. Two farmers were arguing about the price of cattle, and a roughneck was trying to out-coffee a hangover. Otherwise, there was a counterman pouring coffee into the roughneck's cup and two waitresses.

"Good morning, soldier," the older of the two waitresses, a woman just past 30 said to him.

"I'm a Marine," Tommy replied politely.

"Whoops," the waitress responded, "sorry, we don't get many uniforms in here. Good morning, MARINE!" she emphasized.

Tommy smiled and lowered his lanky five-eleven frame into a seat. The Wide-A-Wake Café was actually quite small, but the space inside had been carefully planned. Booth's lined two of the walls, with two square tables crowded into the open space that had once been a dance floor. A "U" shaped counter worming its way through the remaining area served many more diners than a straight counter would have allowed. Over the years, the owners, two brothers, Eugene and Crawford Noe and their wives Essie Mae and Cleo had covered the walls with photos of the truck drivers and customers who patronized the café. Open twenty-four hours a day, and located at the intersection of Oklahoma State Highway 77 and the famous Route 66 that carried travelers from Chicago to California, the Wide-A-Wake Café had used bright lights and attractive waitresses to encourage travelers to stop for almost a decade. Just to the north of the intersection, Edmond, Oklahoma's tiny business district was close enough for the town's bankers and merchants to drop in for coffee in midmorning, or for lunch. It was also within easy walking distance of the town's only high school, three blocks away, and Central State College, which was located four blocks to the east.

Tommy had sat in the cafe the previous day and worked out the table assignments. He hoped they were unchanged. He was in luck! The younger waitress, a girl still in her teens, grabbed a menu from a pile next to the cash register and a glass of water from a plastic tray and approached his table.

"Would you like some coffee?" she asked in a friendly but no nonsense voice.

"Please," Tommy responded. At nineteen years of age, Private Thomas Aubrey Morrison, USMC, hadn't yet acquired much of a taste for coffee, but its one most redeeming quality was that the cup would be refilled endlessly until he left the restaurant. He wanted an excuse to stay. Under the table, Tommy wiped his sweaty palms on the legs of his khaki uniform trousers.

After the waitress filled his cup, Tommy ordered the "Sunrise Special" even though his mother had made him breakfast only an hour earlier. His second meal of the morning was to be eggs to order (sunny side up), hash browns, toast, and bacon, all for twenty-five cents. Before the girl turned to go she looked at him and said, "I knew you were a Marine."

"Do you know any Marines?" Tommy asked.

"No," she said with exaggerated firmness as though it was the most unlikely thing in the world, but then continued with less assurance, "I – I saw a picture in Life Magazine."

"Oh," Tommy answered. Then without delay to prevent her from leaving he said, "What's your name?"

The girl looked at him over her shoulder, made an arch of her eyebrow as though she were examining a bug and responded, "Waitress," and left.

When she returned with his breakfast he tried to make amends.

"I hope you don't think I was being fast," Tommy explained, "but I'm from here and I'd have bet I'd know everybody. Are you new?"

"Not really," she replied, relenting from her no-nonsense response of a moment ago with a small smile that thrilled Tommy to his socks, "I went to county schools and didn't come to town 'til high school. I'll be a senior when school starts."

"If you're going to be a senior, you must have been in school when I was. I'm Tommy Morrison."

"I know," she responded, and returned to the counter where she busied herself by sweeping the already spotless floor.

By now the timeless boy-girl ballet that Tommy was trying to choreograph had attracted the attention of the counterman and the other waitress. Tommy detected the hubbub of some good-natured teasing directed at the younger girl

2

and by overhearing he gathered that the older waitress' name was Hazel and the counterman was Sam.

Finally, the roughneck stumbled out to his truck and the farmers left for their fields.

"Swan," Sam said in a clearly audible mock whisper once the other customers had departed, "I think he's a fine lookin' boy, what do you think, Hazel."

"Fine looking?" Hazel challenged way too loudly, "why heck Sam, even good looking, don't hardly do him justice. Ya' know what, I'd almost call him beautiful." Then turning to the girl she nudged her and added, "What do you think, Sweetie?"

"Shut up," the girl hissed at the others. Her demand only inspired further teasing, and loudly "whispered" comparisons of the young Marine's looks to those of Robert Taylor, the movie star.

Tommy felt the warmth of a blush crawling up his neck, but he couldn't help but smile. This was small town Oklahoma. There wasn't so much entertainment about that he could expect the girl's co-workers to let an opportunity for some fun at her expense pass them by and Tommy wasn't about to leave the restaurant just to avoid it. In the calculus of etiquette in the Southwest, this sort of teasing served as a kind of socially acceptable introduction. Tommy had lost an entire night's sleep thinking about this girl. If being teased a little bit helped him meet her, it only made him more determined to see it through. Besides, he'd just finished Marine Corps boot camp and sea school. Tommy knew he could handle a little teasing.

Listening to her voice as she tried to silence her co-workers sparked a confusing memory in Tommy's mind and he studied the young waitress for a moment, gazing at her from under a knitted brow. She was small and blonde, only a couple of inches over five feet tall, carrying the slender frame of a girl not quite yet a woman, but, Tommy noted with enthusiasm, possessing tremendous promise.

It was the girl's face, however, that had attracted Tommy the day before and then kept him awake all the previous night. Had it just been her features, she would have been no different from any of the pretty girls Tommy had known. It was her eyes that captured him. Large and blue, they looked at the world with intelligence, humor and a knowing confidence that Tommy found utterly captivating. As he studied her, the clouds finally cleared for him and Tommy almost slapped himself on the forehead. How could he have not seen it? Suddenly, the girl started in surprise as she heard her own name.

"Janice Lookabaugh," Tommy said loudly, "holy cow, I didn't even recognize you!"

3

"That's my name," she responded, and for a moment Tommy was afraid she was going to finish with, 'don't wear it out' but she didn't. "It took you long enough," she concluded.

While she was speaking, the girl crossed to the table with the Pyrex coffeepot. As she refilled his cup, Tommy said much more softly, "How can you blame me? When I left you looked like you were about 12 years old."

The girl stiffened. Realizing too late that he was saying the worst thing possible, Tommy grasped at the first straw that occurred to him in an attempt to redeem himself and added, "but you look wonderful now."

Once again, too late, he realized he was putting his foot even further into his mouth. "Oh good grief," was all he could think of to finish.

By this time, the out of control laughter of the eavesdropping Sam and Hazel proved infectious and Janice began laughing as well. As she did so, the too full pot in her hand shook and coffee spilled onto the tabletop. Both Tommy and the girl reached for the napkin dispenser to mop up the mess before it dripped onto his uniform trousers. Their hands bumped roughly and they knocked over the napkin dispenser, which promptly fell onto the floor where it was out of reach. Finally, Tommy determined to abandon the table before the inevitable flow of hot coffee reached him unchecked. As he stood, the girl was leaning in and their heads knocked together.

BONG.

Somewhat dazed, Tommy managed to finish standing, but Janice was off balance. She continued leaning forward as he forced himself more upright until their bodies were pressed together as though she was trying to push him back in to his seat.

Suddenly regaining her senses, and realizing what it looked like, Janice tried to straighten up, just as Tommy got his arms around her to keep her from falling.

Since nothing is quite as funny as an injury suffered by somebody else, Hazel and Sam were in conniptions of laughter by this time and even Tommy smiled sheepishly and began chuckling as his head cleared from the shock of the collision. Almost as a surprise, he realized he was holding the small blonde girl in his arms and they were more or less upright. He looked into her eyes.

"Would you care to dance?" he asked.

The laughter of Sam and Hazel started all over again, but Janice was mortified. She jerked the boy's arms away from her, and pushed them downward as though trying to throw his hands onto the floor and stalked away, even stamping her feet as she went.

It occurred to Tommy that despite this setback, things were going better than he'd hoped. He entered the restaurant just wanting to learn the girl's name and perhaps speak with her. Instead, she'd actually been in his arms. He could still almost feel the warmth of her body against his. From the look on his face as

4

he stood next to his table, the young Marine seemed to be having as much fun as Hazel and Sam. He didn't want to embarrass Janice, but he couldn't help it, and after resisting for a few seconds, he rubbed his forehead at the spot where they had collided, and laughed right along with the others. Unfortunately, Janice didn't seem to be enjoying their meeting as much as he had and by the time he got his check; the young waitress hadn't even spoken to him again.

With coffee, his breakfast had cost 30 cents. Tommy pulled a dollar from his small horde of bills and left it on the tabletop. He then walked out. Before he had even crossed the restaurant's small parking lot, the girl was at the screen door.

"Hey," she called to him, squinting into the morning sun, "you forgot your change."

"It's a tip," he answered.

"A seventy cent tip for a thirty cent breakfast? You must be crazy."

"I just want you to remember me," he answered.

"You can be pretty sure I'll do that," she said and touched her head where they'd collided.

"Well," he paused, "I do like to make a good impression." He squinted back at her through the glare of the sunlight reflected from the café's windows and held her gaze a moment.

"I get off at three-thirty," she responded as though he'd asked; then added, "The Cowboy From Texas" is playing at the Broncho Theater tonight." She raised her hand above her brow to shield her eyes from the sun. Tommy thought it looked a little like a salute.

"I don't see how we could live with ourselves if we missed that," he said and smiled.

II

Janice watched as Tommy Morrison walked away from the café. At the corner, he turned and waved back at her, then turned and walked east on Second Street until he disappeared from view. The girl stood where she was for a moment, even after she couldn't see him any longer, her arms crossing her stomach just under her smallish breasts. A smile played at the corners of her mouth. Then she turned and reentered the café.

"What did you say to him?" Hazel Nutt asked.

"I told him what was playing at the Broncho Theater tonight," Janice replied.

"What did he do?" Hazel persisted.

"He asked me to go," Janice admitted, the slightest hint of a lilt in her voice.

"Just like that?" Hazel asked, surprised.

"Just like that," Janice confirmed.

5

"Well, I'll be swan," Sam Abbot, the counterman interjected, "you been shooting down cowboys and roughnecks trying to cozy up to you in this place for a year now." Then as an aside to Hazel he suggested, "I guess some gals just like a man in uniform."

"It wasn't the uniform," Janice replied softly, "it was the boy inside it."

"Why do I have the feeling you know that boy?" Hazel speculated.

Janice smiled, and kept her counsel. Even if Hazel professed to understand, it would only be grist for future teasing. Tommy Morrison had asked her for a date, well, almost. Truth be told, she'd asked him for a date. But the outcome was the same. They were going to the movies together, tonight. She smiled again.

Janice knew that boy.

Chapter Two

Janice and Cynthia

The Wide-A-Wake Café
213 S. Broadway, Edmond, Ok.
Thursday, December 19, 1940
3:40 p.m.

I

*J*anice Lookabaugh groaned as she scanned the schedule posted behind the cash register in the almost empty cafe. Hazel Nutt was standing behind the counter wiping down its surface. She looked up from her work and chuckled.

"Lucky you," Hazel needled, "three shifts with ol' Crash Gordon in one week. What did you do to Cleo?" Cleo Noe wrote the schedules for the café every week as well as working many of the daytime shifts.

"I don't know, but it must have been awful," Janice replied as she shook her head in resignation, then added, "I was hoping you and I would be working together."

"We will after Christmas, but Cleo and Essie Mae are going to be out of town for a couple of days so they need you and me on different shifts. Cleo wanted to make sure the others don't burn the place down or make off with all the T-bones or something. Sorry, kid, you're just too valuable."

"Why do you call her that?" Janice asked, changing the subject.

"Crash?" Hazel asked and Janice nodded. Hazel chuckled.

"Well," Hazel began, "old high and mighty broke so many plates and glasses her first two months here I thought we were going to wind up serving the food on wax paper or something. I used to swear she was a saboteur sent here by Royce's café just to put us out of business. Why Cleo didn't fire her the first week, I have no idea. But here she is" Hazel changed her voice to imitate that of a carnival barker, "three years later, Edmond's most glamorous debutant and our very own little coed, Miss Cynthia Butler, still snooty and still thinking she is better'n the rest of us."

"Oh Hazel," Janice replied non-confrontationally, "you shouldn't say that."

"Why," Hazel demanded, "because it ain't true?" Janice looked away.

"Besides," Hazel added with the crooked smile that, to Janice, at least, could keep her comments from seeming too mean, "that nickname drives her nuts." Hazel paused for a moment before she continued. "I am happy for you, though. Who knows, in a week, you guys could be best pals. God knows you could use a little culture. Have fun, honey."

"Oh, shut-up," Janice pretended to snap at her friend but she couldn't keep from smiling as she did it, "anyway, it's my own fault," she admitted. "I told Cleo to put me on as much as she could during vacation from school. I could use a couple of bucks for Christmas gifts and who knows; maybe some of our customers will get the holiday spirit and actually tip every now and then."

"Let me know if it happens, and I'll break out the camera," Hazel responded, "we'd want proof of that." Hazel took a moment to wipe the bottom of a salt shaker before she continued. "Ya' know, I kept track one time - for a whole week. Made little tick marks on the back of my order pad to keep count of how many customers I waited on for five days. It was almost always right at 30 tickets a day and only twice did I have a dollar in tips. That's less than a nickel for each table." Hazel shook her head. "You know what they say, easy come, right?"

"Yeah, then easy go," Janice finished for her. "Hey, speaking of tips," Janice continued more upbeat, "did you hear about Clara?"

"Another boyfriend?" Hazel sniped.

"What's gotten into you today?" Janice demanded.

"OK, OK, I'm sorry," Hazel said contritely, "now, what about Clara?"

"Last Saturday night," Janice resumed, "Clara got almost five dollars in tips."

"Bullshit!" Hazel spat in dismissal.

"No, I'm serious. Tina told me," Janice affirmed.

"What are you talking about?" Hazel's tone making it sound like the very idea was beyond belief.

"That's what I heard. The place was full of drunks here on a hunting trip from Tulsa or someplace and she got five bucks in tips."

"That is hilarious," Hazel observed, "Clara, who falls all over herself for anything in pants, and those idiots gave her five bucks just to serve 'em coffee. Those guys missed a bet."

"That's not very nice," Janice said.

"That's probably the opposite of what those hunters were saying."

"Hazel, please."

"Oh well," Hazel retreated, "trust me to pick apart somebody else's good fortune."

"She was just lucky, that's all," Janice said.

"Let me tell ya' 'bout the facts of life, Janice, some people make their own luck," Hazel replied with an arch of her eyebrows.

"You're just impossible today," Janice concluded with a shake of her head as she gathered up her books and headed out the door. "Hey, I'm out of here. I'll see you at the Christmas party I hope."

"I'll be here," Hazel assured her, "I'm working that shift."

"Working?" Janice asked.

"Yeah, Jimmy thinks parties are a waste of time." Jimmy Nutt, a roughneck working the oilfields west of Edmond, was Hazel's husband. "The only way my kids can go is if I'm on the payroll. It's a little game Cleo and I have been playing for a couple of years now. The bad part is that if I leave Jimmy alone that long, he'll be loaded by the time we get home."

"Loaded?" Janice asked innocently enough but she saw the shock in Hazel's face as she realized she'd been indiscreet.

"Forget I said that," Hazel blurted out.

"Forgotten," Janice assured her and headed out the door for home.

Janice didn't really forget Hazel's reference to her husband's drinking. She wondered if Hazel's worry about Jimmy explained her behavior and the catty comments about Clara. The incident preyed on Janice's mind as she walked through the late afternoon cold towards her home several blocks from the cafe. Janice had hoped that Hazel was trying to open up a dialogue about her husband's drinking and its aftermath. The two women had skirted this issue for several months but Janice was reluctant to pry and Hazel was reluctant to talk. It was a perfect formula for disaster. Janice felt a chill in her bones that came from more than the relentless wind that blew from the north that bitter winter's day.

II

When Janice reported for work on the Monday following the break from school for Christmas vacation, Essie Mae Noe was still on duty. Generally, Essie Mae worked nights while her sister-in-law Cleo worked days. Neither was there for every shift, it depended on who the waitresses were. If Janice, Hazel Nutt, or Edna Pryor was on duty, the women felt confident they could be out of the café for that shift.

"Don't let the place burn, Janice," Essie Mae requested as she pulled on her coat.

"I'll try," Janice chuckled recalling Hazel's comment a few days earlier, "but be sure you tell Cynthia the same thing."

"You make sure she knows it too," Essie Mae said, smiling as she looked over the top of her glasses at the young waitress, "I have to go."

"Oh sure," Janice promised, "that's one thing about Cynthia, she always enjoys having me tell her what to do."

"Be strong," Essie Mae instructed her over her shoulder as she pushed her way through the door into the cold of the early dawn.

Cynthia Butler bustled into the café a few moments later. Janice smiled in spite of herself. Cynthia was wearing make-up, her hair was perfect, and somehow, even in the stiff one-piece jumper the waitresses all wore, she looked almost stylish. Janice hated to admit it, but she was envious of Cynthia, a thought that was never far from her mind when they worked together. If she'd needed to make a list of the reasons why, it would have taken a while, but looking that perfect at six in the morning would have been pretty high on the list.

"Good morning," Cynthia said, "are you about to go off?"

"No," Janice replied, suddenly on guard, "I - I just got here a few moments ago myself."

"You did?" Cynthia said in a voice that immediately made Janice think she must look as though she was just finishing an eight-hour shift.

"Why?" Janice asked.

"Nothing," Cynthia said, then after a momentary pause continued, "you just look tired is all."

"Thanks, Cynthia," Janice replied as dryly as she could, but almost unconsciously, she looked at her reflection in one of the windows to the café to reassure herself that her hair wasn't weird or something.

How does she do that to me all the time, Janice wondered. *She makes a comment right on the verge of rude, and now I'll be paranoid all morning that I have spinach in my teeth or something.*

It took several minutes before Janice realized that she was tired. She was working the early shift, she'd been up late the night before studying for finals which would start right after the Christmas break, and in truth, she was tired. Janice looked at Cynthia who was taking a breakfast order across the room. As if she could sense Janice's eyes on her, Cynthia looked up and saw her, then quickly averted her eyes. Janice considered if Cynthia could have just been making an observation that showed concern for her. In a moment she pushed the idea from her mind. Janice tossed her hair as she shook her head.

Even if I am tired, she concluded with a huff, *it was still rude of her to comment on it.*

III

The two girls actually worked fairly well together. Since they spent almost no time speaking to each other, they were perhaps more attentive to their customers. The hours seemed to pass quickly. The breakfast crowd kept the café humming along until about 9 or 9:30 a.m. After that there was the hour or so during which the café was never busy in midmorning, followed by the pandemonium of lunch. Cleo Noe was in the café during that part of the shift and the three women were engaged in an artful ballet of sorts as they managed to operate the restaurant without dropping trays or crashing into one another. By 2:30, the café was empty again. Janice swept the floor and then walked out back to take a short break.

Cynthia watched her go. *Well whoop de do,* she thought to herself, *there goes little Miss Perfect, everybody's favorite. Sweep the floor and then take your break like I can't handle a broom or something.* Cynthia paused for a moment when she realized just how stupid that particular complaint sounded, even to herself. *Good Grief,* she thought, *I don't know why I let her get under my skin so much? Somehow she manages to make me think everything I do is wrong.*

Cynthia could hear Carlisle, one of the cooks and the only other collegian working at the café out back bantering with Janice. Both of them were laughing about something. It reminded Cynthia how rarely the other employees took the trouble to just visit with her and she wondered if they were laughing about something she'd done.

"Well, hello there," the male voice said from behind her. Cynthia was startled out of her reverie. The man was a truck driver. Cynthia could see his rig parked at the side of the road across from the café through the front windows.

"Good afternoon," Cynthia replied, professionally.

"You're just about the best looking thing I've seen this side of Dallas – or maybe Houston too," the man continued.

"May I get you a menu," Cynthia replied. She was uncomfortable, but not unduly concerned. This sort of talk was part of the job.

The man walked over to the counter and put his thermos on the top. "I think I can see plenty I'm interested in without having to read a menu," the man answered. He leaned forward on the counter and leered purposefully into Cynthia's eyes. Cynthia backed away and grabbed the pyrex coffee pot from the heating element. "Coffee?" she asked.

"For now," the man said. Cynthia filled his thermos.

"Are we alone in here?" the man asked.

"The others are out back," Cynthia answered too hastily, as though in a rush to get the words out. Although she wasn't unduly afraid, the man was giving her the creeps. Cynthia decided to keep the coffee pot in her hand. She was convinced she had the guts to splash somebody with boiling coffee if she needed to.

Cynthia began to cross the small room to the cash register. The man moved smoothly to intercept her.

"You know," he began, "I pass through here pretty often, but I don't remember seeing you before. Are you new?"

"No," Cynthia replied stiffly, the man was now too close to her, and she didn't like it. Her fingers clenched on the coffee pot's handle. She moved sideways to try to get around him. He moved the same way.

"I can't believe that. I know I'd remember if I ever saw you before."

"I usually work a later shift," Cynthia explained nervously.

"Well maybe I could start going by here a little later in the day," the man replied with an unfriendly smile. His teeth were yellow, and he was at least fifteen years older than Cynthia. *Why doesn't he know better than to behave like this?* she wondered angrily.

"Maybe you and I could get together sometime?" the man suggested as he put his hand on Cynthia's arm.

"Sir," Cynthia demanded, "please remove your hand." Cynthia could feel the handle of the coffeepot as she tightened her grip, ready to swing.

"Hey, Henry," Cynthia heard Janice's voice from the doorway, "what are you doing handling the merchandise?"

The man immediately jerked his hand from Cynthia's arm as though he'd been burned.

"How do ya' like that," Janice continued lightly, "I turn my back for one minute and here you are trying to make time with another waitress."

"Well," the man replied, his attempt to match Janice's tone was unsuccessful. He was shocked and nervous and he sounded like it. All of the sinister elements of just moments earlier had dissipated. "I finally gave up on you. That Marine boyfriend could show up any minute and then I'd wind up fighting my way through town every time I pass through here."

"Switchin' your attentions to her won't help," Janice observed coolly, "one of our city cops has more than a passing interest in Cynthia there." It was an out and out lie, and Cynthia was surprised to hear how easily it came from Janice's lips. "He may be more of a problem for you than my boyfriend would be. You don't want to be getting a ticket every time you drive up to Route 66 do you?"

The trucker laughed ingratiatingly. "Now, now, Janice, we don't need nothing like that."

"OK, then you behave yourself when you're in here. Don't you make me call Cynthia's fella'."

Cynthia couldn't believe the change in the man. He had been horrible and menacing a moment earlier. Now he was docile to the point of being cowed, and by a girl he probably outweighed by more than 100 pounds. Janice walked easily to the cash register and rang up twenty five cents for the thermos refill. The driver paid quickly and almost ran across the street to his truck. He vaulted into the cab and the sound of his transmission gears being ground could be clearly heard as he pulled back onto Highway 77 going north.

"He didn't tip," Janice observed, feigning surprise.

Cynthia put down the coffeepot and sat down feebly in a chair at one of the two tables in the center of the café.

"Henry always tips," Janice continued.

The two girls had had their backs to each other. Cynthia started to put her face in her hands, but they were shaking so she returned them to her lap.

"I hope you don't mind my getting involved," Janice remarked turning to look at the other girl.

For some reason she couldn't explain, Cynthia replied, "I was handling it."

Janice snorted and shook her head behind Cynthia's back, "Yeah, I could tell. Judging from the way you were holding that pot it looked like old Henry was about to get a face full of coffee." Cynthia actually flinched as she realized how close she'd been to doing just that.

"Lunch counter Romeos are part of the job, Cynthia," Janice continued, "you have to be able to handle it. Everybody else in this place has had Henry's number for years. Guys like him are like dogs, they sense fear and close in for the kill. If you just josh 'em a little or invoke some mysterious boyfriend they turn into a puppy instead. We can't afford to run off all of our customers by hitting 'em on the head with a hammer or pouring coffee on 'em. They're the reason we have a job to begin with."

"I said I was handling it," Cynthia snapped, suffering more from the aftermath of being afraid than from anger.

"So you did," Janice acknowledged, shaking her head behind the other girl, "you're welcome."

Cynthia didn't reply. Her heart was racing and she was afraid to stand up for several minutes. The truck driver had scared her badly. Also, she was frustrated that Janice had deflated the man so easily. Finally, she was ashamed that she hadn't told Janice how much she appreciated what she had done. For the remainder of the shift Cynthia tried to think of a face-saving way to say something to Janice that would express what she really felt. Nothing occurred to her and by the time she left for home, the two girls hadn't exchanged another word.

Janice watched Cynthia walk away from the restaurant. She shook her head again and thought to herself, *I don't know why, but I never ever say the right thing to that girl!*

Chapter Three

Hazel

The Wide-A-Wake Café
Monday, December 30, 1940
5:57 a.m.

I

$\mathcal{I}$t was 5:57 a.m. by the six-sided clock outside the Wide-A-Wake Café when Hazel Nutt arrived, walking stiffly, just in time for her shift. Janice Lookabaugh, still working full time during the Christmas break from school, noticed the distress in the other woman's eyes.

She's taken another beating, Janice thought, *that rotten bastard.*

Hazel would never admit why she was sore, but occasionally, bruises would be visible on her arms or legs. In the beginning, Janice had been slow to figure out what was wrong. A man hitting a woman was so far from her life experience, it just never occurred to her. Nobody she knew had ever even mentioned a husband beating his wife. In the 1940s, women submitted to their husbands, and they kept their mouths shut.

As Hazel walked slowly by her, Janice arched her eyebrows at her co-worker. Hazel made a face and rolled her eyes with an expression that seemed to say, "I'm such a klutz," but Janice was having no part of it.

After the breakfast rush was over, Janice and Hazel stepped out back so that Hazel could smoke a cigarette.

"Are you OK?" Janice asked.

"Land sakes, girl," Hazel replied breezily, "other than freezing my butt off out here, I'm fine. I bumped into the bathroom door last night when I was trying to get to the john in the dark. I'm just a little sore. I feel sillier than I do hurt."

"OK," Janice responded. She didn't sound convinced. Hazel knew it, and the silence that bounced around the small area in which they were standing was deafening. Hazel puffed nervously on her cigarette until she couldn't stand what was unsaid any longer.

"I'm fine, I tell ya'," she insisted.

"And I said, OK," Janice replied, pointedly looking away from Hazel. This exchange was followed with a long pause as the two women studiously avoided making eye contact. It was agony for Janice.

Hazel Nutt was the first adult who ever treated Janice as an equal. Their friendship had started almost from the younger girl's very first shift at the café. As a practical joke Hazel had sent the naïve Janice to look for a spool of "chow line" in the storage building behind the café, an airless and stifling shed. Inside were containers of ever sort, paint cans, detergent, canned goods, and whatever dirt had blown in on the Oklahoma winds since the most recent annual cleaning.

Janice had spent ten minutes digging around in the sweltering old bin looking for the nonexistent line before it finally dawned on her that she was being had. Dirty, but not defeated, Janice had returned a few minutes later with a length of twine wrapped around a hand labeled card she'd lettered reading "Chow Line, 25 feet."

"Well," Janice had reported deadpan, "it took some doing, but there it is. That looks like the last of it though, you'll have to tell Cleo to order some more."

Hazel had brought the few customers in the café in on the joke and seeing it backfire on her caused them all to howl with laughter. Hazel loved practical jokes and having the tables turned had only added to her enjoyment. The two women had been fast friends ever since.

Because Hazel and Janice worked together often; in the manner of women, they talked about everything. Or at least Hazel did. Janice listened and Hazel talked, usually prefacing her tales with the cautionary, "Now let me tell you about the facts of life, kiddo."

The facts of Hazel Nutt's life centered around three things, her kids, her work, and her husband. In that order. Hazel loved her three kids, and spoke of them often. When she did, a softness came over her that was usually absent from her gritty discussions. Otherwise, her tales were about a life in which almost all of the lessons had been learned the hard way.

Hazel stopped going to school after the sixth grade and frequently referred to herself as dumb, but Janice knew it wasn't true. She may not have been educated, but in the human aspects of life, Janice came to realize, Hazel was a genius. In a hundred breaks in the small open area behind the café, Janice learned the facts of Hazel's life, of how to work with customers and bosses, about her kids, and even a few guarded facts about her husband. Because farm children were expected to learn about life by watching the livestock, Janice's own mother had never spoken frankly with her daughters about things like sex, pregnancy, labor, or the like. Hazel's nonstop chatter, including frequent allusions to sex which she usually referred to as "Hoohaw" had served to fill in some of the gaps in Janice's knowledge with earthy details based upon the older woman's own experience and the tiny amount of factual information Hazel actually possessed.

Janice loved her for it. Not only did frank talk make her feel like a grownup, but she was learning things about her own monthly cycles, labor, lactation, and a host of other things she'd have never heard from her mother. Sometimes Janice doubted the veracity of Hazel's advice: "Put a knife under the mattress when you're in labor, kiddo," Hazel had advised at one point, "and it cuts the pain in half." When Janice had looked incredulous, Hazel had affirmed, "I know it sounds crazy, but I'm telling you it works!"

It was on those rare occasions when Hazel spoke of her husband that Janice had her greatest concerns. To Janice, Jimmy Nutt was a dark and brooding character. Hazel's comments about him were usually guarded and cautionary, but there were some facts, Janice finally acknowledged, that just couldn't be ignored. They showed up on Hazel's arms and legs in the form of bruises or an occasional fat lip or black eye.

As the two women stood shivering outside the café, Janice waited for what seemed like an eternity for Hazel to continue, but she didn't. This time it was Janice who could no longer stand the silence. Their break would be over soon and the younger girl wanted to talk about Hazel's injuries before they had to return to work.

"Hazel," Janice began, "you don't have a bathroom. You've told me that yourself."

"It was the door to my bedroom. I was on my way to the outhouse," Hazel amended. Both women stood silently a while longer before Janice tried again.

"Tell me something," Janice requested.

"What?" Hazel responded, suspicious.

"How is it," Janice asked, "that somebody who can handle a tray with six glasses of water and two cups of coffee without spilling a drop in that beehive in there keep clanging into doors, cabinets, steps, and furniture in her own home every week or so?"

Hazel knew there was no real denying the point of Janice's question. She fell back on a technique she'd used many times before.

"I wish you could have know'd him when we was courtin'," Hazel finally continued in a voice so quiet she seemed almost to be speaking to herself. "He was so sweet. He didn't drink back then. The depression hadn't started, and everything seemed so grand. The sky was the limit. We were going places, kiddo." Hazel paused for a moment and shook her head slowly, a faraway look in her eyes. "I don't know where exactly," she admitted smiling ruefully, "but we wasn't gonna' spend our lives on some 40 acre poverty trap, I kin tell you that.

"Maybe if I could just keep from makin' him so mad, things'd be better, more like they was. When things aren't goin' so great," Hazel continued wistfully, "I think about what he was like back then and it all seems worth it somehow."

Hazel had used that same sentimental tone to deflect Janice's inquiries in the past. Janice bolstered herself by looking at the bruise on Hazel's arm, took a deep breath and plunged ahead.

"How long are you going to keep denying what's happening, Hazel?" Janice demanded.

Hazel didn't answer while she took a deep drag on her cigarette and then exhaled. Finally, she sighed and acknowledged, "It was my fault."

"How?" Janice demanded immediately.

"Oh … sometimes I just won't shut up. I just gripe, gripe, gripe, nag, nag, nag."

"What about?" Janice asked as soon as Hazel stopped speaking.

"Drinkin' mostly, but wastin' money too. It's always something with me," she finished waving her cigarette in a circle up by her head, trying to sound like she believed what she was saying. "He makes good money. We could make it just fine if he'd just get home with his paycheck every week. It's always something."

"So what you're saying," Janice responded calmly, "is that he drinks his pay, or wastes it in some other way, then when you complain he roughs you up." There was a hint of sarcasm in her comments by the end of the statement.

"No," Hazel answered, "not all of the time. He's really sorry whenever he does it. He'll be as sweet as an angel for weeks now. You just watch. He feels terrible about it."

"Hazel," Janice answered, "it used to be weeks, but now it's more often than that. You're hardly healed up from one beating 'til you're hurting from another one. That ain't right and you know it. It ain't safe either. What will happen to your kids if he ups and kills you by and by."

Hazel reacted as though she'd been struck, and the tolerance she'd shown for this invasion of her privacy was instantly gone. Her face showed that she was furious at Janice's suggestion.

"Janice," she snapped, "I am not going to talk about this anymore. Kill me indeed. He loves me. He told me so all night long. Why . . .I - I don't know what I'd do without him. Anyway, my kids and my husband are no concern of yours, so watch what you say. If you think I'd be friendly with somebody who'd talk that way about the man I love you're crazy." Hazel threw down her cigarette and stomped back into the Wide-A- Wake.

Janice ground out Hazel's still glowing ember under the toe of her white canvas sneaker and then followed the older woman back into the café. For the remainder of the shift they didn't exchange one word that wasn't necessary. At three- thirty, they both went home without saying good-bye.

Conversation between them was still strained during their next shift, but by Friday Hazel was feeling better and her natural ebullience and wit were back on display. She joshed with the truckers who stopped at the café, and teased Janice about her Marine boyfriend, surrounded by hula girls half a world away. Janice was glad to see her back in good spirits and when their shift ended on Friday, the two girls actually hugged goodbye for the weekend.

II

On Monday morning Janice awakened to the sound of pebbles bouncing off the window of her bedroom. When she was finally awake and oriented enough to know what was happening, she threw back the covers and walked to the window. She couldn't imagine a boy who would be doing this since everyone at school knew about her and Tommy Morrison. When she finally saw Hazel in the driveway next to her house she almost didn't recognize her.

Janice pulled up the window and whispered down, "What are you doing? Why didn't you just come to the door?"

Hazel was still looking down when she answered, "I can't Janice." With that she looked up, and in the glow of the street lamp the younger girl could clearly see the damage that had been done to her friend's face.

Janice did a double-take and then gasped, "Oh my God, Hazel! Hold on, I'm coming right now!"

Janice slammed down the window and dashed into the hall only to suddenly be face-to-face with her father, who was pulling the suspenders of his hastily donned trousers over his shoulder and standing in her way. He had heard her call out, but not the reason why.

John Lookabaugh, Janice's father, was a gentle bear of a man who finally lost his family farm in the ninth year of the depression. After he moved his wife and children to town, he found work making brick, rising quickly to watch supervisor at the plant just outside of town. Shocked at seeing his daughter about to dash downstairs dressed only in her nightgown he held up his hand and demanded, "What's wrong?"

Janice did a small head bob as she considered trying to just push past her father in her haste. It was a futile gesture, he simply took up too much room in the narrow passage, and after realizing she was going to have to explain to get him out of her way, Janice snapped,. "Oh for goodness sakes, Daddy, Hazel is hurt. Now make yourself useful or go back to bed!"

John Lookabaugh had two daughters, so he recognized an imperative when he heard one. First he got out of Janice's way, and then followed her as she raced down the stairs and outside where Hazel was supporting herself on the side of the Lookabaugh's 1938 Chevrolet.

Hazel's look shifted from Janice to her dad and her eyes filled with shame and concern. "Oh dear," she said, her voice sounding almost like a moan, "I didn't want to cause a commotion."

"Don't be silly," John answered, gently taking Hazel's arm, "we want to help you."

John and Janice helped Hazel into the house and onto a chair in the kitchen. After that, they were better able to assess her injuries. It was immediately apparent even to their untrained eyes that Hazel was hurt way beyond "toughing it out" was going to cure. John turned to get the first aid kit Marge kept in the cabinet above the refrigerator. Janice opened an ice cube tray and dumped its contents into a bowl.

"How did you even get here, Hazel?" Janice asked as she wrapped ice in a towel and held it to the other woman's cut lip.

"I walked," Hazel said as she grimaced from the sensation of the ice on her injured face. "When I got started I was too numb to feel anything, it wan't till the last mile or so that it got so tough."

"How far is it to your house?" Janice asked in amazement.

"Three, four miles, I guess." Hazel said through tightly clenched teeth as John put iodine on a cut.

John turned to his daughter, "Go get dressed honey and we'll take Hazel to the hospital."

"No, no," Hazel said as firmly as her cracked ribs and damaged lips would allow, "I'll be fine. Just let me rest here until its time for me to go to work."

"You're not going to be at work today," John said, "you're going to the hospital."

"I can't go to the hospital," Hazel insisted weakly, "I got to work. Just patch me up and I'll be fine."

"Hazel," John said gently, "if you was a calf that had got hung up in a barbwire fence, I'd know pretty much what to do, but I'm worried about the stuff I can't see. I'm afraid there's more here than I know how to fix. If we don't get you to a doctor, I'll probably wind up doing you more harm than good." John then turned back to his daughter, "Go on and get dressed, Janice, then we'll help Hazel out to the car."

Exhausted from her walk in the early morning cold, Hazel was simply too weak to resist. Once John and Janice were dressed they gently assisted Hazel to the Chevy and drove downtown to the doctor's clinic that was upstairs from the Broncho Theater. Although not staffed for 24 hour-a-day emergencies, John had called Dr. Wynn and he met them at the clinic. Following a brief examination the doctor called his nurse. After she arrived, her first actions were to shoo Janice and her dad out of the examining room.

John Lookabaugh spent the next hour sitting quietly on a chair outside the door to the examining room. Janice studied him through tear filled eyes as he sat clenching and unclenching his fists. It was something he did when he was worried or anxious. Janice had seen him do it dozens of times when they lived on the farm as he was facing the failure of his enterprise.

"Why Daddy?" she asked fighting to control her voice. "Hazel is funny, witty, smart . . . she works so hard to be a good momma, you should just see the lights that come on in her eyes when she talks about her kids. Why?"

John Lookabaugh's genius lay in using his hands. When Janice thought of him, images of her father working with his tools, repairing farm equipment or mending fences; helping a scared heifer give life to her first calf, or feeding a suckling piglet held tenderly in his arms using a bottle and nipple came easily to her mind. What he couldn't do, was use words with equal facility. In his mind's eye, John saw himself saying just the right thing, reassuring his daughter, making her understand that we all make choices and sometimes those choices are wrong and those errors have consequences. The anguish and confusion on his daughter's face was almost more than John Lookabaugh could bear. He felt hot tears come into the corners of his eyes. He knew he couldn't trust his voice. It occurred to him, that even if he were a man to whom words came easily, a few phrases or a platitude of some sort had no chance of having any meaning to his daughter on this day. Nothing worth saying came to him, he only answered, "Baby, I don't know."

Hazel was in the clinic for three days, on each of which Janice visited her on her way home from the café. On the fourth day, when Janice walked into the clinic, the bed was empty. A cold grip attached itself to her heart and she turned to the ancient nurse.

"Where is Hazel?" she asked, already dreading the answer she knew she was about to get.

"She went home," the nurse replied.

"HOME!" Janice demanded. "With her husband?"

"Well, yes," the nurse answered.

"Oh MY gosh," Janice spat out, "it was her husband that put her here in the first place!"

"Her husband visited her ever' night, he seemed to be really sorry for what happened."

"What happened?" Janice almost shouted. "What happened was he beat the hell out of her!" Tears filled her eyes. "Are you crazy, or was she? I tried to get her to press charges against that monster. How could she just leave with him?"

"It was what she wanted," the nurse explained.

"Baloney," Janice snapped back, as she turned her head to look at the nurse. The woman was so calm Janice was initially tempted to grab her shoulders and

21

try to shake some sense into her. The impulse passed and a numbing fog began closing out her other thoughts. Janice knew what Hazel had done was bad news, but her mind just wouldn't accept what had occurred. She walked slowly down the steps from the doctor's office with both hands on the rail. When she got to the dusty street below she looked North in the direction she knew Hazel and her taciturn roughneck had gone as though she might still see them, might still stop what she knew was going to happen.

Jimmy Nutt was not the sort of man who would abide the airing of his family's dirty laundry in public. Janice could almost see him in her mind's eye as he drove slowly towards their small acreage and tiny house, a fury burning behind the blackness of his eyes.

Janice stood forlornly in the street. When a car horn sounded behind her, she waved absently at the driver and then almost as though she were coming to, realized she was standing there blocking traffic like some village idiot. At that moment, she knew what she had to do. Without delaying long enough to think better of her decision, she began striding east on 1st Street on her way to the police station. She walked directly into Chief Pynchon's office. The Chief, unused to interruptions, looked up in surprise when Janice stomped into his office, centered herself on his desk, and pointed one finger at his face.

"Chief," she demanded, "Hazel Nutt gets beaten an average of two or three times a month. Her husband has now almost killed her. In the name of decency, lock him up!"

There wasn't so much crime in Edmond in 1941 that Chief Pynchon didn't know exactly what Janice was talking about. "Now Missy," the Chief began, "I had a real talkin' to with old Jim and I'd bet my Stetson hat that he won't be doing anything like that again."

"Again," Janice exploded, "what about what he's already done?"

"There hasn't been a complaint filed. Little Lady, you need to learn that there are things in this world that ain't none of your business."

"Maybe it's not my business, Chief, but it is yours!" Tears both burned and lit Janice's eyes. "He beats her more and more viciously and more and more often. He then apologizes and she forgives him. Hell, he has her blaming herself half the time and that's just crazy. Why haven't you done anything to stop him! What sort of law officer are you, anyway?"

"Young lady," the Chief warned, "you keep a civil tongue in your head. I won't accept that sort of talk in my office."

"Or what? Will you arrest me? Wouldn't that just take the cake? You'd arrest me for trying to make you prevent a crime, but you won't arrest Jimmy Nutt even after he's committed one."

"There hasn't been a complaint filed," the Chief repeated.

A steely calm came over Janice. She walked over to a stack of typing paper and tore a piece from the top. She then grabbed a pen from a set on top of the Chief's desk. Quickly, she wrote a few lines then handed it to the chief. It said:

"On January 14ᵗʰ, 1941, I, Chief Tom Pynchon, was warned that the life of Hazel Nutt was in danger, but I felt there were no actions required."

"Sign it," Janice ordered.

"You're hysterical," the Chief countered.

"I am not. I am perfectly calm. I have warned you about the commission of a crime and you have chosen to ignore it. I want you to sign that letter! If you won't, then arrest Jimmy Nutt."

"For what, Miss? For exactly what?" The Chief placed harsh emphasis on the last word. "His own wife, the alleged victim, won't swear out a complaint against him. Just exactly what would I arrest him for?"

"For Heaven's sake, Chief, isn't it illegal to beat a woman 'til you've broken her ribs, loosened her teeth, blackened her eyes, and created who knows what other injuries?"

The Chief looked coolly at the fiery little blonde. This impromptu interview had gone on far too long and he was getting nowhere.

"Have her swear out a complaint," the chief countered coolly, "I doubt we could do anything more than lock old Jim up for a few hours, but get her to do it. Then let's see what happens to her after he's released."

"Damn you," Janice responded. She hated herself when she cried, but this time it was lucky. Chief Tom Pynchon didn't take his personal dignity lightly, and her tears were a big reason Janice wasn't arrested, or at least thrown into the street.

"You go home," he said coldly, "I don't want to see you in here again. Do you understand me?"

Janice stood mutely and returned the chief's stare for several seconds before she finally turned to go. Her shoulders were heaving as she walked to the door. Before she left, she turned one last time, looked at the old man and repeated, "Damn you."

After she was gone, the Chief lifted the note Janice had written from his desk. He ignited a wooden kitchen match using his thumbnail. He used it to light the edge of the sheet furthest from his fingers. He held it until the heat of the flames forced him to drop the page into the large glass ashtray on his desk. When the fire finished consuming the paper, he stirred the ashes and dumped them into the trashcan on the floor. When he was finished he sat down, leaned back in his chair, and put his boots on the steel radiator under the window. For several moments he simply stared into space. Finally, he shook his head, swore, lowered his feet, rotated back to his desk and returned to the paperwork that had occupied him prior to the interruption.

III

Once school started again for the Spring semester, Janice resumed working the 3:30 until 10 p.m. shift at the café. Because Hazel worked days, the two friends still saw each other when the shift change occurred. They would trade wisecracks, or Hazel would tell Janice stories about her kids before she left for home. On Tuesday, February 11, 1941 Janice reported on time for work to discover that Edna was working with Cleo Noe.

"Where's Hazel?" Janice wanted to know.

"She didn't come in," Cleo responded, "and they don't have a phone."

"Did you call the Sheriff?" Janice demanded immediately, panic creeping into her voice.

"Don't be silly," Cleo responded, "if I called the Sheriff every time a waitress didn't show up for her shift, they wouldn't have time to do anything else."

"How many times has Hazel skipped work?" Janice asked, fearing the answer she knew she was going to get.

"Well," Cleo responded and then paused, "you know, except for last month when she was in the hospital, never, now that you mention it."

"He's done something awful," Janice said with finality. "I knew he would never quit. I told everybody." After the briefest pause, Janice continued, "Cleo, I can't stay." Without waiting for an answer, she turned and bolted out of the restaurant.

Janice ran the five blocks to her home and burst through the front door.

"Momma," she shouted between ragged breaths, "I'm taking the car." The keys were kept on a hook near the door that led from the kitchen to the driveway.

"What," Marge Lookabaugh replied in confusion. She had been standing in the living room awaiting the arrival home from school of Janice's little brother. She began walking towards the kitchen. As she walked she called out, "why aren't you working?"

"Hazel needs me," Janice explained. "I have to go to her house and get her."

"Wait, honey," Marge countered, "your father will be here soon. You can't go out there alone."

Janice ignored her. She had already opened the door to the kitchen, and a moment later was pressing the starter of the Chevy with her foot. Once the engine caught, Janice unconsciously waited while she counted to ten in her head to give the oil a chance to begin circulating just as her father had trained her. While she was waiting, Marge reached the kitchen door. She started down the steps when Janice put the car in gear and backed down the driveway.

"No, Janice, don't go," Marge called, but her daughter was gone, "you don't know what you'll find," she finished softly, speaking to no one.

IV

Janice had only the vaguest idea of where Hazel's home was located. She knew she needed to go out Kelly Avenue, one of the section line roads that ran north out of Edmond, and that her friend's home was about a mile north of a homestead known to everyone as Coffee Creek farm. Beyond that, she planned to just hope that the Nutt's name would be on their mailbox.

Dust boiled up behind the Chevy as Janice drove rapidly down the dirt road that Kelly Avenue became at the city limits. She wheeled the car around a school bus that was returning rural kids to their homes. Less than a mile after that, she found what she was looking for, a rusty metal mailbox with "Nutt" lettered unevenly on its side. She turned down the lane and a few moments later skidded to a stop on the hard packed and grassless yard of a small, unpainted, wood frame house.

"Hazel," she called as she leapt out of the car. "Hazel!"

The Nutt's old pick-up was parked near a shed behind the propane tank out back. There was a small fenced in patch near the side door of the house that Janice figured served as a kitchen garden during the summer. Janice skirted its edge, stepped up on the sagging wooden step and knocked loudly. "Hazel," she called out, "Hazel, it's me, Janice. Are you in there?"

The house was quiet. Janice tried the knob. She would have been surprised if a house in the country had been locked. The door swung open and Janice leaned into the kitchen.

"Hazel," she repeated, "it's me, Janice." The silent house seemed to mock her, but it felt strange to Janice, a weirdness that was almost palpable. It finally occurred to her that her feeling wasn't due to some strange aura, it was a smell, almost coppery, but it overlaid another that was harsher somehow. Something was terribly wrong.

"Hazel," she called out again, this time with less volume.

Janice heard a slight scraping noise coming from the front of the house. She followed the sound until she entered the living room. It was dark, but as soon as her eyes adjusted to the diminished light, she saw the body. Her hand flew to her mouth and she cried out. Face up in the middle of the front room, awash in a pool of congealed blood, feces, and the release from his riven stomach, lay a man. His releases combined on the floor to create the smell Janice had followed to arrive at this charnel house. The man's eyes stared vacantly at the ceiling, his mouth open in a macabre grimace as though he was still surprised at his fate. Janice had never met Jimmy Nutt before, but she had seen his shadowy form in the old pickup when he would come to the café to drive Hazel home. She knew this was him.

Janice stood frozen as she tried to absorb what she was looking at. The only dead bodies she had ever seen in her life belonged to her Uncle Frank, an oil field worker killed in a rig accident, and her grandmother, who died well into her 70s. Both had been in caskets at the time.

Janice heard the scraping sound again, and spun around to see Hazel propped more or less in a sitting position with her back to the wall. Although obviously alive, Hazel too was sitting in a pool of dark purple blood.

"Oh my God!" Janice cried as she crossed the room and knelt at Hazel's side. "What happened here?"

"I killed him," Hazel answered through clenched teeth. "I been thinking about it all day. Out of nowhere, he just decided he wa'nt goin' to work today and he wouldn't drive me neither. I don't miss work, Janice, we need the money too much. Of course we got to arguing and you know where that leads us. Not five minutes after the kids left for the school bus, he come after me. I was holding that knife and I just decided this was gonna' be my last day as his personal punching bag," Hazel stopped for a moment and regained her breath before she continued, "but before he could die, the bastard got me too."

"We've got to get you some help," Janice responded frantically, "let me get you out to the car."

"Oh hush, Janice," Hazel ordered. "I'm not going anywhere. Not in this life anyway." Hazel paused for several seconds while she seemed to gather her strength. "When I heard your voice a minute ago I thought I was dreamin' it. I'm so glad you're here. I've been lying here all day, praying I wouldn't die 'fore somebody came. I can't let our kids be the ones to find us like this, Janice. They'll be home from school anytime now. Promise me you'll go meet 'em. Don't let them come in here. They know who you are, they'll go with you, I talk about you all of the time. Take 'em back to town with you, find my sister, she'll take 'em in."

"I can't do that Hazel," Janice cried, "I passed the school bus over a mile back. By the time your kids walk all of the way here from the road it might be too late. We have to get you to a doctor, and we have to go right now!" Janice tried to lift Hazel's arm onto her shoulder, but Hazel's cry of pain was so great she quit trying to move her.

"Janice, listen to me," Hazel wheezed through gritted teeth, "Jimmy gutted me like a hog. I've been sitting here all day holding my intestines in and trying to keep enough pressure on to keep from bleeding completely out onto the floor. There ain't enough doctors in the world to help me now. The only thing," Hazel sat gasping for air for a long moment before continuing, "the only thing you can do for me now is go out there in the yard and keep my kids from coming in here."

"Don't ask me to do that, Hazel, we can still get you to a doctor." Tears were streaming down Janice's face. "You're alive right now, and if we get you to a doctor you'll stay that way."

There was another long pause while Janice cried softly into her hand. Finally Hazel continued, "Look at this room. It looks like a slaughterhouse." Her voice broke. "Swear to me, Janice, swear to me that this won't be the last memory my kids have of their daddy and me."

"Hazel we can't wait, we've got to go!" Janice sobbed. "You need a doctor." But Hazel had been right. She was dead the moment she finished speaking.

Janice stood and walked around the house opening doors until she found Hazel's bedroom. She removed the quilt and sheet from the bed and spread them over the bodies. She then returned to the room she'd identified as belonging to the children and gathered as many of their clothes as she could into a pillow case. They would need clean underwear and socks and whatever changes they had available in the days ahead. Janice carried the clothes into the kitchen where she pumped water into the sink and washed Hazel's blood from her hands and knees before finally walking out into the yard to wait for the children.

Chapter Four

Jimmy, Ruth, and Haley

The Nutt Family Home
Off Kelly Road, North of Edmond
Tuesday, February 11, 1941
4:33 p.m.

I

*J*anice watched as Hazel's children walked down the dusty road from the school bus drop-off. A boy, she knew to be Jimmy, aged 11 and his sisters, Ruth, age seven, and Haley, almost six. The children walked with their heads down. Jimmy kicked a stone with the toe of his shoe, walked to it and kicked it again as he went. Only Ruth carried any books. They were held together with a strap she had slung over her shoulder. Ruth was also the only child that seemed to be speaking and even from this distance, Janice could tell she was just prattling – part of the endless stream of talk that Hazel always mentioned when she described her to Janice. Just talking because that was what she did. When the boy saw Janice in the yard he stopped for a moment. Sensing his disquiet, Ruth fell silent and still and all three children observed Janice from a distance.

"Hello," she called to them, "I'm Janice Lookabaugh, do you remember me."

"From the café," the boy announced as though that alone made it so.

"Yes," Janice confirmed.

"I know who you are," the boy replied. "Are you looking for our folks? Momma gets off at 3:30, if she's not here yet, it won't be long."

"Actually, I'm here for you. Your mom asked me to take you to your Aunt Mildred's house," Janice informed them.

"Why," the boy asked. His eyes went to the truck parked next to the shed. "Where's my Daddy?"

"I'm supposed to take you to your Aunt's house," Janice repeated.

The two girls followed the conversation between Janice and their brother as though watching a tennis match, turning their heads to follow the speakers in turn. Janice didn't know what to do. She was afraid of lying to them, but not nearly as much as she was of telling them the truth.

"Why?" the boy repeated. He moved to place himself between the girls and Janice. It was a gesture of protection. Janice realized she was going to have to tell him what had happened or he would panic the younger kids and Janice would lose whatever control she had.

"Jimmy," Janice said, "can I speak with you privately?" She held out her hand. He wouldn't take it, but they did separate themselves from the smaller children.

"Jimmy," Janice began, "I have some very bad news about your parents."

"My momma's dead, isn't she?" he asked.

Janice nodded her head. "I'm sorry."

"I knew it when I saw you there," Jimmy continued. As he spoke his eyes were fixed on the ground near Janice's feet. "Daddy hates for anybody to be on this place but us." Jimmy waited a long moment before he continued, then he looked up at Janice with his head cocked slightly to the side, his eyes squinted against the setting sun, "He's been hitting my mommy for a long time. I have dreams sometimes that he's killed her. I knew he wouldn't let you be here if he was around. Where is he?" The boy was unnaturally calm. It was scary to Janice.

"He's with your mom," Janice answered gently.

For just a moment, Jimmy looked at the house as though expecting his father to come walking from it. Then as he realized what Janice had meant, he seemed to wobble and his little shoulders recoiled as though he'd been struck. He recovered almost immediately though and looked back at Janice for confirmation.

"Both of 'em? Are they both dead?" he demanded.

"Yes, Jimmy," Janice whispered, "I'm so sorry to be the one to tell you."

"How could that have happened?"

"I'm not sure, Jimmy," Janice hedged.

"Maybe somebody else did it," he suggested.

For a moment Janice considered letting him believe that. The potential for harm appeared even greater if she started lying, she realized, and she shook her head.

"No," she said, "they killed each other."

The boy didn't reply. He looked at the house. Finally he turned back to Janice. "Are they in there right now?" he asked.

"Yes."

"Can I see them?"

"No."

The little boy nodded his head sagely.

"I need your help," Janice continued, "with the little ones."

It was just the right tack. Jimmy squared his shoulders, looked Janice in the eye and nodded again, "I'm the man in the family now, aren't I?"

30

Janice nodded and the little boy turned to the others.

"OK, you two, let's get into Janice's car, we're going to have our supper at Aunt Mildred's house." He then led them to the Chevrolet where they all climbed into the back seat.

Even after Janice was in the driver's seat, she still couldn't drive because of her tears. She sat motionless behind the wheel as she struggled to get control of her emotions.

Finally, Ruth, the middle child, squeaked from the back seat, "When are we leaving?"

Jimmy reached up over the back seat and patted Janice on the shoulder. When she felt the reassurance of his small hand she breathed deeply, wiped her eyes and started the engine.

II

Janice followed Jimmy's instructions until he told her to pull over in front of a tiny white framed house on Edmond's northwest side. The house was only a few blocks from the house Janice's own family had lived in when they had first moved to town after being evicted from their farm. She turned in the seat to look at the children huddled together in the back seat.

"Stay here for a few moments," she told them, "let me go make sure she's home.'

Janice walked up the sidewalk, crossed the narrow porch and knocked on the door jam. A few moments later, Mildred Price, Hazel's sister, opened the door.

"May I help you?" she asked.

"I'm Janice Lookabaugh," Janice began, "I work with Hazel at the café."

"You're the one with the Marine boyfriend," Mildred said in confirmation that she knew who Janice was.

"Yes," Janice replied, "I have Hazel's kids in the back of my car."

Mildred's eyes narrowed as she squinted at the Chevrolet, "It's cold out here," she said, "let's bring them inside."

"Please," Janice interrupted, "we can bring them in in a moment. May I come in?"

Janice saw the concern as it appeared on Mildred's face as though surfacing from underwater. Mildred was similar in size and even appearance to Hazel without the other woman's spirit. Hazel always seemed to have some joke just about to bubble forth. Mildred had the look common among those whose poverty had led to surrender.

"What has happened?" she asked.

"May I come in," Janice repeated. She didn't want the children to see their aunt's reaction when she told her of the calamity on the Nutt farm.

"Of course," she answered, and held open the battered screen door.

The small front room of the Price home was clean, but the floor was littered with the toys of her three children. As Janice looked around, she imagined the impact of adding three more children to the tiny house. Almost on cue, one of the Price children, a boy slightly larger than Jimmy Nutt, stuck his head through the doorway that led to the front room.

"Go finish your homework,' Mildred said to him, "Miss Lookabaugh and I need to talk a moment."

"Yessum," the boy replied and disappeared.

"Would you like to sit down," Mildred asked. Janice shook her head.

"I don't want to leave the children sitting out there any longer than necessary," she answered. The other woman nodded her head and then indicated with a nod that she was ready for Janice to continue.

"I'm afraid I have some very bad news," Janice began.

"Oh my God," Mildred responded, "has that bastard put her back in the hospital?"

"I'm afraid it's much worse," Janice warned her. She could see the look of concern on Mildred's face turn to fear, "she's dead. They're both dead."

"Both?" Mildred's face was a kaleidoscope, first of fear, then surprise and shock. "Did someone break into their house?"

Janice told her what had happened. Her description was brief, but included Hazel's instructions to take the kids to her sister. As she described the events she had witnessed, Janice maintained her composure, but Mildred did not. Finally, Janice crossed to the older woman and put her arms around her shoulders.

"I'm so sorry," Janice began, "I loved Hazel, she was a wonderful . . ."

"Wonderful?" Mildred almost spat out the word, "wonderful?" she repeated, "how wonderful was it to bring those kids here? How wonderful was it for you to find them out there all cut to pieces. How damned wonderful was it for her to just give me three extra kids to raise? I told her! I told her he was dangerous. I told her . . . ," Mildred's voice failed and she stopped in the middle of her tirade and stood silently, her shoulders heaving as she cried. Another child, a girl this time, looked into the room. Mildred pointed to the back of the house.

"Momma's fine honey," she said in answer to the question in the girl's eyes, "now go on back to your room. I'll call you for supper in a minute." The child disappeared. Mildred stood silently for a moment. She looked at the floor, then at the remainder of the room.

"What in God's name am I going to do?" she finally continued, "we just barely make it from week to week around here as it is. How can I raise those kids?" She paused again. Then she looked at Janice. "I cain't," she finally acknowledged, "I just cain't do it."

"Mrs. Price," Janice said, stopping her before she could go too far, "you have three relatives in the back seat of my car. They are children, and only one of them knows they are orphans right now. They have nobody else. It may be true that eventually you'll have to get some help from the county, but right now they need your help. Somebody they know needs to comfort them and tell them what happened."

"I cain't do that," Mildred replied.

"Yes you can," Janice insisted, stridently continuing before Mildred could get up a head of steam, "you must. You're the only one who can do it."

"No I'm not," Mildred snapped back, "you could do it. You're the one who went out there. You're the one who stuck her nose in. You live in that big house over there on the east side of town. You could take them. . ."

"Mrs. Price," Janice interrupted her again impatiently, "I'm going out to the car to get your nieces and nephew. When I get back here you're going to tell them what happened. It's going to be dark pretty soon and those kids need a place to stay and somebody to love them. You may not like it, but you're elected. You're all they have, and that's just the way it is. I'll stay a few minutes, but I need to notify the sheriff and then I need to get home," Janice suddenly realized just how close she was to breaking down herself. As she continued her voice wavered slightly, "and tell my own mother that I'm OK and what happened."

Mildred Price reached out imploringly to Janice, "What am I going to do?" she begged her.

"You're going to do your best," Janice replied gently, "that's all anybody can do."

Janice turned and left the living room. She walked out to the car, helped the children out of the back seat and led them to the front door. Mildred was waiting. Janice returned to the car and retrieved the pillow case filled with the children's clothing and walked back to the porch. When she got there, Janice could see the children in a tight little bunch in the living room through the glass of the front door. They were facing their aunt who was on her knees in front of them. Janice opened the screen and placed the pillow case against the front door and allowed the screen to close until it pressed against the bag of clothes. She quietly left the porch and walked back to her car.

After she went to the sheriff's office and made her report she returned home. When she was finally back in the warmth and safety of her own house with her mother there to comfort her, Janice began to cry.

III

On the day of Hazel's funeral, Marge Lookabaugh signed Janice out of her classes and went with her daughter to the small Baptist Church where the memorial service was held. Seated on the front row of the small church, three small forms, Hazel's children, sat in a row to the left of their aunt. To Mildred Price's right sat her own three children. Stoically, Janice sat and watched them as they fidgeted their way through the service and eulogies to their mother. It was after two by the time the interment had finished, so Janice didn't return to school. Instead, she changed into her uniform, and at 3:30 reported to work her shift at the Wide-A-Wake.

Less than a half hour after Janice began her shift, Billy Morrison, her absent boyfriend's ten year old brother walked into the café carrying a floral arrangement behind which he was almost completely hidden.

"Look Janice," Billy called out proudly, "Tommy sent me money to get you these flowers." He handed them over then reached into his pocket and retrieved a small white envelope before he continued, "he also told me to give you this card."

Janice accepted the flowers and put them on the counter. She took the card from Billy and opened it. On it was written, **"I'm here, you're there. Otherwise I hope you had a perfect Valentines Day, Love, Tommy**."

"Well…" Billy asked expectantly, "what do you think, Janice?"

When she finished reading the card, Janice slowly returned it to the envelope, dropped down onto one knee and hugged the very surprised little boy. After she quit squeezing him, she held him at arm's length and looked into his face as tears coursed over her cheeks.

"Your timing was perfect," she answered.

It was Friday, February 14th, 1941.

Chapter Five

Cynthia

607 North Boulevard, Edmond, Ok.
Thursday: November 20, 1941
4:59 am

I

Cynthia Butler frequently dreamed in color. This time she wandered an Eden in pastels of blue, forest green, and daisy yellow. Suddenly, a wicked witch began demanding she leave her paradise. It wasn't a witch of course; it was her mother.

"Cynthia, get up honey, or you'll be late for work," Mrs. Butler coaxed.

It was five o'clock in the morning, pitch black, and cold. Even in the house it was cold. Winter hadn't officially arrived, but it was as cold as if it had, and getting up for her shift at the Wide-A-Wake was a horror.

"Leave me alone, Momma," Cynthia pled groggily as she tried to burrow back under the covers on her bed, "just five more minutes."

"If I did that you'd be late for work," her mother answered as she jerked the covers back. Cynthia squealed and snatched at the blankets that had just been pulled away.

"You need your job, so get up honey. Do it now," her mother insisted as she pulled the blankets even further from Cynthia's reach.

"Nghhhh" Cynthia groaned as she resigned herself to the inevitable and rolled over into a sitting position. Cynthia dreaded getting up and begged for a reprieve every morning. It was a fruitless effort. She never received one. Finally, she got out of bed grumbling under her breath, "I hate Jimmy Nutt."

The hallway, down which Cynthia padded on her way to the bathroom when she finally arose, traversed what was arguably Edmond's finest home. Two stories, fronted with columns of wood and granite, spacious and airy in the summertime, it was an icebox when winter came and there was no oil in the furnace. It had been her grandparent's home. Her father had inherited the place from his father, the much-revered "Doc" Butler who had accompanied the earliest settlers into the unassigned territory during the land rush in 1889.

As she walked, Cynthia carefully avoided a worn space in the ancient carpet runner. When she entered the bathroom, she punched the light switch button three times before the room was illuminated. The paint in the little room was cracked and the fixtures were old fashioned. Cynthia looked around her with resignation, shivered from the cold and began brushing her teeth. It hadn't always been like this.

On Cynthia Butler's ninth birthday, she and 35 other little girls in white party dresses, clutching their engraved invitations had descended on the Skirvin Hotel in Oklahoma City for a "real" tea party. The Skirvin was far and away the city's finest hotel, and no expense had been spared. Liveried footmen and waitresses in black and white uniforms scurried about to insure none of the little princesses-in-waiting wanted for anything. The society reporter from the "Daily Oklahoman" newspaper had even been there with a photographer in tow to record the day's excesses for Sunday's edition.

She'd been suitably impressed. In addition to using the term "soiree" to describe the event in her article, a first for Oklahoma City, the reporter, an ancient dowager with a hat as wide as the back seat of a taxi, linked each one of the guests to parents whose names included a title. There was no nobility in the crowd, and only two of the parental designations included "daughter of Dr. and Mrs. …" For the rest, the "titles" were those that mattered most in Oklahoma in the summer of 1929. "Penelope Carter, daughter of wealthy oilman and Mrs. Josh Carter, founder of Carter Oil." In the case of the hostess, the reporter wrote, "Cynthia Butler, daughter of successful attorney Thurman Butler of the Crane, Randall, and Wycliffe law firm here in the city, and his lovely wife Darlene, known to her friends as Dolly."

At Dolly's insistence, the entertainment had included Alberto Mann, the pianist, in town for a concert at the Oklahoma City Philharmonic. The children had applauded politely when the great musician had finished. At Thurman's insistence, a magician as well as a ventriloquist with a tuxedo clad dummy rounded out the afternoon to the squeals and delighted laughter of the guests. As Dolly had tucked her daughter into bed that night, Cynthia had reported that when she blew out the candles on her cake, she'd wished that the day would never end.

By the time of Cynthia's fourteenth birthday, in 1934, Crane, Randall, and Wycliffe no longer existed (neither did Carter Oil, for that matter) a victim of its debts and corporate extravagance exacerbated by the depression. Even before the law firm failed, Thurman Butler had been sacked. He'd had to declare bankruptcy when stock margin calls had wiped out his portfolio, his savings, and every dime he could get his hands on. Then the family lost their home in Nichols Hills, one of Oklahoma City's most posh neighborhoods, when they could no longer meet the mortgage payments.

With neither a job nor a place to live, Thurman returned with his family to Edmond where he'd grown up. They had lived with Cynthia's paternal grandmother until she passed away in 1937. Thurman had transplanted his law practice to try to eke out a living writing wills for farmers and handling the odd divorce, lawsuit, or other legal matter from a one-room office above the Citizen's Bank. The celebration of Cynthia's birthday that year had included only immediate family, a very small cake, and music from the radio. When Cynthia went to bed that night her mother asked her what she had wished for when she blew out her candles.

For a long moment, the girl had remained silent. Finally she looked at her mother and replied, "I wished that all of my memories were just dreams, Momma. Maybe then I wouldn't miss them so much."

When she'd been younger, Cynthia had believed the depression would just end; and afterwards her life of position and privilege would resume. Just as it had always been. But it didn't. The years went by as she was growing up, but nothing ever improved. It seemed like forever to her that they had just barely been getting by and the once proud house had always borne the brunt of the shortages and privations. Almost her whole life, Cynthia had watched in frustration as the furnishings, the carpets, even the house itself began to fray and wear out.

By 1941, as the rest of the country clawed its way out of the economic calamity of the past decade, Cynthia's father, Thurman Butler was still struggling to rebuild his practice and his livelihood. In fact, the only reason the family had not lost their home was because Thurman had inherited it free and clear from his mother. During the depression, payment for legal services had frequently taken the form of a few chickens or a quarter-side of beef and that sort of barter was still common. As a result, there was very rarely any real cash in the Butler household and even paying the taxes on the old home had always been the subject of much discussion and a series of last minute lucky breaks that, to Thurman at least, always resembled the hand of God.

Because the Butlers had never been forced into the street, the family had been able to maintain the genteel façade that was denied so many of their less fortunate neighbors. Although he walked a perpetual tightrope between security and catastrophe, most Edmondites believed that Thurman Butler and his family were doing much better financially than they really were. Maintaining those appearances had required a tremendous amount of energy and focus over the years and naturally extended to their daughter's education. The Butlers were determined their only child would attend college.

The Butler's determination would have to be matched with something of course, and that was money; money for tuition and books and the myriad other expenses associated with going to college. When she graduated from high school in 1938, Cynthia knew if she was to finish her education, it would be at Central State College, only a few blocks from their home so that room and board wouldn't comprise additional expenses. Also, for the first time in her life, Cynthia would have to go to work, because she'd have to pay her own way.

When Cynthia first arrived at the Wide-A-Wake Café looking for a job, it was to Cleo Noe that she actually applied. Because Cleo worked days, she did most of the hiring for the café. Without knowing it, Cynthia struck a chord with her prospective boss. Cleo was determined that her own children would someday go to college, and she could understand that other families would have that dream as well. Somehow, she saw in Cynthia somebody who, despite all of the outer trappings, really needed a break. She'd hired her despite the girl's lack of suitability for the job and overnight, the beautiful swan became an ugly duckling. Keeping her on the job had required a lot of forbearance on Cleo's part.

Theoretically, Cynthia appreciated the value of work, even her own. In the abstract she could even see that her character would be enhanced if she worked her way through college, and for that reason she wanted to be a good waitress. However, when Cynthia began working at the café, she had been fairly useless. Hazel Nutt's derisive nickname of "Crash Gordon" had been only one of the needling evaluations of her lack of capacity on the job. Cynthia did improve, of course. In time, she even became efficient and careful, but she never had the right attitude. The longer she worked in the café, the more her co-workers realized that she would never get the rhythm of the place. It was like she was attempting to live and work in a foreign country, one in which she knew neither the language nor the customs.

If she'd been confronted, Cynthia would have probably conceded it was an accurate assessment. Somehow, no matter how bad the economy or even her own situation, Cynthia couldn't shake the feeling she'd been born for better things. The combination of her attitude and her lack of commitment left her isolated from the others and largely alone on the job. She consoled herself with promises that this was only temporary. But for now, instead of cotillions and a debutante ball at the Oklahoma City Golf and Country Club, she poured coffee for cowboys who would leer into her face and try to pinch her bottom.

Following Hazel Nutt's murder the previous winter, the owners of the Wide-A-Wake Café, had experimented with waitress combinations before settling on Cynthia as part of a three-person rotation with Janice Lookabaugh and Edna Pryor for the early shift. In her heart, Cynthia knew it was a favor. She needed the wages as well as the nickels and dimes she received in tips from the truckers, farmers, and roughnecks on whom she waited every morning. She also needed to get to class. Finally, sometimes, she needed to sleep. This was the only shift that allowed her to do everything her schedule required. She still dreaded the assignment, and getting up before dawn drove her crazy.

"All I had to do," she frequently complained, "was give up sleeping so I could go to college."

II

Perhaps the most nettlesome of the burrs under Cynthia's saddle blanket, and she hated to admit this even to herself, was Janice Lookabaugh. Before Hazel Nutt's murder, Cynthia and Janice had very rarely worked together. Janice and Hazel had been friendly and Cleo had honored their desire to work together. Since the realignment following Hazel's death however, the two girls had worked together two or three days a week, and had for almost nine months. For Cynthia, at least, they had been nine long months.

It wasn't as though Janice wasn't nice to her, Cynthia acknowledged. She was. Although Janice could be sarcastic, she was generally polite and positive in the café. Cynthia also, God knows, recognized how awful it must have been for Janice to find Hazel and her husband after they'd killed each other. Those things were terrible, of course, but Janice always seemed so tough. She never talked about the incident, and it didn't seem to have affected her at all.

Anyway, Cynthia sniffed, with the exception of that one incident; Janice was one of those girls for whom everything always seemed to work out. Her daddy lost his farm. She was poor. Now her father was a shift supervisor at the brick plant and they were living in a nice two-story house only a few blocks from Cynthia's own. Janice Lookabaugh was never going to a cotillion, for heaven's sake, but her family was on its way up, and it looked to Cynthia like her own family was on its way down. Now here they were, she had to admit, meeting in the middle, waiting on tables at the Wide-A-Wake Café.

As the weeks of working together stretched into months, Cynthia came to understand why she was so uncomfortable with Janice. It amounted, she finally admitted to herself, to a question of relative focus. For example, even though Janice was almost three years younger, she seemed to have plans. Real plans. Not the nebulous, 'I'll get my degree and then see what happens' sort that Cynthia relied upon. Janice wore Tommy Morrison's high school ring on a chain around her neck. Essie Mae Noe, who was still on duty with the night shift when the girls reported for work was always asking her how Tommy was doing, and it was pretty rare when Janice didn't have a new letter or picture on which she could report. She was only eighteen, and it looked just like her life was all settled. Her own life, Cynthia had to admit, was chaotic and without direction. Other than being on schedule to get her degree in the spring of 1942, Cynthia didn't know what the hell would happen after that and it scared her a little - OK, a lot.

The class ring Janice wore on the chain around her neck had another more immediate advantage that Cynthia recognized. It always seemed to keep the roughnecks and truckers who ate at the café on their best behavior. Cynthia shuddered involuntarily as she was reminded of Henry, the truck driver from Dallas who had scared her so badly a year earlier. Henry's behavior when Janice reentered the café was fairly typical of their male customers. She always seemed to have their number. Even when they knew Tommy was serving on a battleship out in the Pacific somewhere, they still considered her to be off limits. In fact, when the customers knew Janice's boyfriend was a Marine they tended to be even friendlier AND leave better tips.

It was different with her. Cynthia always took care with her appearance; she was too egotistical about her looks to do otherwise. She wanted to appear ladylike at all times, despite the fact that in the summer they sweated like field hands in the inferno of the un-airconditioned café. Whatever the season, some of the men would flirt with her and drop broad hints that they would like to take her on a date. Cynthia never encouraged anyone, but that didn't seem to stop them. When it happened to Janice she always seemed to be able to deflect the man with a wisecrack or a joke about something. Practically every time, the lunch counter Romeos not only weren't offended, they seemed to like her even better, like a pal or a sister. Cynthia's own attempts at that sort of easy going patter never seemed to work. She would hem and haw and stumble as she tried to think of something appropriate to say. Then, when she would finally out and out refuse one of her would-be suitors, they sometimes got sore and would leave a one-cent tip or say something insulting or even downright gross.

Hell, Cynthia thought, *I should just get myself a class ring and wear it on a chain around my neck!* She knew she wouldn't do that. Despite the fact that she'd never met anyone special, that didn't mean she didn't think it was possible, nor was it something she didn't want. The job of men, Cynthia believed, was to take care of women, and after over three years of working her way through school, she was ready for it. One thing she didn't want was rumors that she had a beau to stop other boys from being interested. Unfortunately, men had become a largely theoretical issue. On those occasions when she took time to consider the opposite sex, Cynthia realized the entire issue was moot until after graduation. If Clark Gable had been interested in her she wouldn't have had time to date.

III

The café was empty. Janice was out back. Cynthia was seated on one of the stools staring absently out the windows. You rarely got a chance to just sit in a restaurant. There was always something to do, something that needed cleaning. Janice had swept the already spotless floor just prior to walking out back. The space behind the restaurant was where the employees went to smoke. Cynthia knew that Janice didn't touch cigarettes, but she always took her breaks out there, no matter how cold it became. Then she'd just sit and stare into nothingness. Her face would become wistful and even a little forlorn. Cynthia had seen her like that many times when she would go out to tell her a group of customers had arrived, or to take her own break. Occasionally, when Cynthia would speak, Janice would seem to come back from some faraway place or thought, wipe her eyes, then compose her face into cheery features and return to work as if nothing had been bothering her.

Janice wasn't moody - exactly. On the job, she was uniformly polite and upbeat. If she <u>was</u> moody, Cynthia thought gratefully, at least she didn't make everybody else live with it. Still, Cynthia admitted, she had no idea what the younger girl was thinking about, and with the exception of those few unguarded moments in the break area, her face gave nothing away. When she considered her, which truthfully wasn't that often, Cynthia couldn't suppress the thought that Janice might just be deep. It seemed unlikely, based on her background and education, Cynthia allowed, but it wasn't impossible.

"Janice," Cynthia said from the back door. Janice was seated on a box. Her knees were close together. Her spotless white sneakers were touching on the inside and flat on the pavement. She was hunched over with her chin in her hands. She seemed a little surprised to be addressed and she immediately used the balls of her hands to wipe her eyes.

"Whoops," she said, smiling through her tears, "you caught me." With that she stood, squared her shoulders, smiled bravely and walked to the door. For a reason she couldn't fathom, Cynthia didn't step out of the way.

"Are you OK?" she asked hesitantly.

"Sure," Janice responded, but she didn't look at Cynthia.

"Then why were you crying?" Cynthia asked. She wasn't demanding an answer, but after three quarters of a year working together, she was finally reaching out to the younger girl. "Are you thinking about Tommy?"

"Lands no," Janice almost laughed, "he's out there in Hawaii eyeing those Hula girls. Why should I feel badly about him?" The younger girl paused a moment before continuing, a faraway smile playing at the edges of her lips. "He wrote me the other day that he's saving his pay and plans to return here and attend Central State after his hitch."

"Hitch?" Cynthia asked.

"His enlistment. He still has two years to go, but he'll be back in the states next summer and he's coming home before he goes on to his next assignment. I'll actually see him in less time than he has been gone. I was . . .," Janice paused, then waved her hand around the little break area, "this place, especially out here always reminds me of Hazel. I miss her. I miss the way she was always

41

wisecracking and telling jokes. I miss her smile and the way she would go from laughing to all misty-eyed in ten seconds whenever she spoke about her kids. They're with her sister, and she already had three of her own. What's going to happen to them now? I hate Jimmy Nutt, may he rot in hell, and I will till the day I die."

That's funny," Cynthia mused, but when she saw Janice's shocked reaction she was quick to correct the impression. "I don't mean funny, ha ha, I mean funny like strange. I just told my mother today how much I hate him every morning when I have to get up at five a.m. I had been thinking about it only from my perspective. I never even considered it from the point of view of her kids, or you, or even how her death affected her sister's family. I feel kind of selfish."

"You shouldn't," Janice reassured her. "You scarcely even knew her. There are babies starving in China right now and you don't see me out here cryin' about them.

"I loved working with Hazel, but in a lot of ways she was almost a stranger to me. If you'd have asked either one of us, we'd have said we were friends, but what did we really know about each other? Until the day she died I'd never been to her house, never even met that rat Jimmy. I'd only seen her kids that one time - at the Christmas party last year."

Janice paused and stared at the back wall of the café for a long moment before she continued. "I probably knew her kids better than I knew her. I only really knew them through the things Hazel told me - their names, birthdays, what they liked, what they were afraid of. She talked about 'em all the time. When I was driving them back to town. . ." Janice stopped talking in mid sentence, she was no longer looking at Cynthia, instead she was staring at the box on which she'd been sitting a moment earlier.

"You know," Janice finally said in a voice that seemed far away, "I guess I really did know Hazel. I knew her here, in this place, and I miss her. I miss knowing that she's out there loving her kids and being a good mom. I knew her, and I knew her life was in danger. I tried to warn Hazel and she got mad. I tried to warn Chief Pynchon and he practically threw me out of his office. . . "

Talking about it proved too much for Janice and she turned away and covered her face. Like everyone else in Edmond, Cynthia knew the facts of what Janice had been through on the day Hazel died, but until that moment, she had thought Janice survived the incident unscathed. Cynthia was ashamed, and at a loss of what to do. Finally, she walked to the smaller girl and put her arms around her.

"Our poor Cassandra," she murmured.

"Who?" Janice asked in a small voice.

"Cassandra. She made a deal with the God's in mythology to be given the gift of being able to see the future. They agreed, but with those guys there is always a catch. Hers was that although she could see the future, no one would ever believe her," Cynthia explained.

Janice's moment of vulnerability was over and as the girls parted she smiled and remarked, "That's me all right." There was a brief pause before she continued, "Is that the stuff you learn in college?"

"That and stuff about as useful - or even less, I suppose. Are you going to college next year?"

"Actually in a few weeks," Janice replied. "After I finished high school last spring, I took this semester off to save some money and get help with trigonometry and physics. It turns out I get credit for those classes and Central is now going to accept me for second semester with six hours of credit."

"Good for you," Cynthia responded, as another pang of what she suddenly realized had always been her own insecurity hit her. Until now, Cynthia and Carlisle, one of the cooks, had been the only college students working at the café. Now, Cynthia thought, this little dynamo would add another laurel to her credentials. Somehow, though, seeing the younger girl in tears had softened her feelings towards Janice. Cynthia replaced her arm around Janice's shoulder and they reentered the café that way.

Cleo Noe was in the café during that shift and she smiled to see the two girls reentering the restaurant arm in arm. The term 'shift dynamics' would have mystified her, but she knew what was meant by it. Having the waitresses working well together made for a happy atmosphere and that was good for business.

"We're going to have ten turkeys delivered tomorrow," Cleo said. "Thanksgiving is always really slow, but Crawford wants to get us started with Turkey and fixings both Wednesday and Thursday. Anything left will go to the Christian Mission down in Oklahoma City."

Both girls groaned. In 1941, turkeys didn't arrive cleaned and frozen. They arrived alive. One of the owners would decapitate the birds and the help would then pluck and clean them while they were not touching food. Every shift would play a part, but the earliest shift had from 9 to 11 when business was slowest, and that time would be spent with the recently dead turkeys pulling out feathers and removing the guts of the big birds. To make matters worse, since they couldn't work with cooked food after touching the birds, there would be no tips during that time.

"Yuck," both girls said at once. They then looked at each other and laughed. Without consciously thinking about it, Cynthia wondered if Janice would be interested in pledging her sorority.

III

Thanksgiving came and went. November turned into December. The diner had been crowded earlier with Edmondites whose religious convictions didn't preclude Sunday dinner out. The radio in the diner was broadcasting a football game between the Giants and the Dodgers. It was almost 2:30 and the biggest part of the lunch crowd was gone, the afternoon almost at a standstill. Janice and Cynthia were relaxing as they discussed which of Central State's professors Janice should choose when she enrolled in a few days.

Cleo Noe looked at the two girls with satisfaction from her perch behind the cash register. *They're thick as thieves, all of a sudden,* she thought.

The blossoming friendship between the two young women with so much in common had surprised nobody except perhaps the girls themselves, and both had benefited. Cynthia was maturing as a worker, and Janice was learning a little about her own sense of style from the much more socially adept Cynthia. Cleo remembered smiling the first time she'd noticed Janice with a hint of lipstick and a touch of rouge on her cheeks. The all-business young girl was turning into a woman, almost in front of her eyes.

The radio announcer suddenly halted the football game's play by play coverage. "Ladies and gentlemen, we interrupt this broadcast to bring you an important bulletin from the United Press. Flash! Washington: Air raid on Pearl Harbor. The White House announces Forces from the Empire of Japan have attacked the U.S. Fleet located at Pearl Harbor in the Territory of Hawaii. U.S. forces have returned fire, but nothing more has been made available. Stay tuned for further developments to be broadcast as they are received."

In an instant, every eye in the restaurant was riveted on Janice. Her pride in her Marine boyfriend serving with the U.S. Fleet in Hawaii was well known to everyone there. At first, Janice's face bore an almost stupefied expression and Cynthia wondered if she had even understood the implications of what had been said. When the impact of the announcement finally penetrated her surprise, Janice's face became deathly white. Within moments she began shaking slightly, and Cynthia realized she might faint. She walked the few steps to Janice's side and placed her arms around the smaller girl's shoulder.

"I'll bet he's fine," Cynthia said soothingly, "I'll just bet anything he's fine." Her words sounded hollow even to her.

"Those bastards," Crawford Noe swore. The words were particularly harsh coming from him since none of the girls could remember ever hearing him curse before.

Cleo Noe sat at the counter with her hand over her mouth in stunned silence as she stared at a photo hanging on the wall of several soldiers in uniform. The caption read, "The food was better at the Wide-A-Wake, Love to all, Your boys in the 149th." The 149th Regiment was headquartered in Edmond as part of the 45th Infantry Division of the Oklahoma and Texas National Guard. After a year of federal service, the division had been extended on active duty only a few weeks earlier. Since they had opened the café, Cleo had watched an entire generation of Edmond's young people grow from toddlers to adults. So many were in uniform already, and whether they had worked for the café or just been its customers, they were like children to her, and now they were at war.

"How will I even know?" Janice asked nobody in particular. "How will I even know?"

"What ship was he on, honey?" Crawford asked. "Maybe Tommy's ship wasn't even in port."

"The U.S.S. Oklahoma," Janice answered absently, "they gave him his choice."

Chapter Six

Janice

29 Main Street, Edmond, Ok.
Sunday, December 7, 1941
3:40 p.m.

I

$\mathcal{F}$ollowing the radio broadcaster's announcement that the Japanese had attacked Pearl Harbor, Janice sat at the counter in the Wide-A-Wake Café in stunned silence. Finally, Cleo Noe walked up to her and hugged her before gently sending her home. She didn't go. Instead Janice walked around in the cold clear Sunday afternoon until she found herself standing in front of Tommy Morrison's house on Main Street, one block south of the Methodist church. She stood outside the stone home for fully ten minutes before she walked up the steps to the porch and rang the bell. It took a long time before the ring was answered. It was Tommy's dad.

"Hello, Janice," he said with a sad smile, "how are you holding up, sweetheart?"

"Pretty rocky right now," she admitted. "I came by to make sure that you knew, but I guess you heard the same as I did. I can't believe we don't know anything. For all we know, right now he could be safely at sea, or …"she paused perceptibly, then finished lamely, "or something else."

"Come in, my dear, please," Mr. Morrison beckoned as he extended his arm to hold open the storm door. "I was kind of thinking you might be Billy and his pals. They left here looking for Japanese infiltrators right after the radio announcement. I hope they don't stumble across Mr. Hong down at the laundry. They might not understand the distinction between Chinese and Japanese, and I was so flustered when they left I didn't even think that a bunch of 11 year olds with stick guns might get into mischief even with the most patriotic of motives."

"Thanks," she answered and proceeded under his arm into the large foyer, chuckling at the image of a squad of 6th grade commandos out protecting their town.

"Who is it, Dear," Janice heard from upstairs.

"It's Janice Lookabaugh, Gladys."

"Oh," Gladys Morrison answered audibly disappointed, then, "Dear, could you come up here."

"Yes, Dear," he answered, then to Janice, "please excuse me for a few moments."

Janice could only imagine what was getting ready to happen. To say Mrs. Morrison had made no attempt to conceal her reservations about her son's interest in a waitress was a vast understatement. Tommy had been quite a disappointment to his mother since his decision to matriculate in the Marines instead of the University of Oklahoma. Tommy had alluded to it once, then simply shrugged his shoulders when he told Janice why he had enlisted.

"With that bunch of maniacs in power in Europe and Japan, we're all going to be in the service before too long," he had observed. When the National Service Act had finally passed through the Congress, Tommy had quit waiting for the inevitable and enlisted, choosing the Marine Corps for no better reason than that his Dad and two of his uncles had been Marines in the Great War and served in France. When Tommy announced his enlistment to his family, his mother had feigned a nervous collapse and gone to bed for several days.

On one of Janice's earliest visits to the Morrison home, Gladys had been called to the phone. A few moments later, Janice overheard Gladys proclaiming sotto voce into the phone that "it was all well and good for a young man to have a little fun with a girl like that but she was hardly a suitable person for my son to be serious about."

That had hurt and Janice could feel the heat from the blood that rushed to her face in an injured blush. It was impossible for either Tommy or his father to pretend they hadn't heard her. Mr. Morrison had looked a little stricken and excused himself. He then walked to the nook where they kept their phone, removed it from Gladys' hands, said goodbye to whoever was on the other end, and hung up the instrument without fanfare. The shocked look on Mrs. Morrison's face was something Janice still remembered, as was her confusion when he gently took her elbow and after she was on her feet escorted her out of the room. Neither she nor Tommy ever knew what he said to her when they were finally out of earshot, because as soon as they were gone Tommy and Janice escaped into the night.

As they were walking down the street Tommy reached for Janice's hand. She allowed him to take it, but she didn't respond. After a moment, she removed her hand and then wrapped her arms around her chest.

"I am so angry at her," he began, "I don't even know where to start."

"It's OK," she answered without conviction.

"How could it be?" he asked plaintively.

"It just is," she replied.

"No it is not. I can't begin to explain it. She was such a great mom when I was little. She sacrificed to make sure I got piano lessons, she went to every one of my games, she was so proud of me. I know it is tough for her to see me growing up, leaving home, and all that, but that was weird. Why she would say something like that is utterly bizarre, and you and I both know it just wasn't acceptable

"One of the weirdest parts is the pretentiousness of it. Don't get me wrong, Janice. I'm proud of what we are. But we're a bunch of Okies, for goodness sake. Is there someplace socially <u>under</u> where we are? Why in the hell would she suddenly feel like we can start putting on airs?" He paused for several steps before he finally continued, "Oh bahhh," he expelled in exasperation before turning his face to look at her again, "Janice, I don't want to get in a position of either attacking her or defending her other virtues. I just want you to know that I've never thought about you that way for one second."

She looked sideways at him, "You haven't?" she asked.

"Of course not," he answered sincerely.

"Well, that's too bad," she replied, "because I was only using you to have a good time, myself."

A brief flash of shock washed over Tommy's face before he realized his leg was being thoroughly pulled. He chuckled. "You're tougher than my drill instructor," he said with admiration.

"Don't you forget it," she replied and retrieved his hand.

After their first date, Tommy began meeting Janice at the end of her shift each day in order to walk her home. At first this had bothered Janice since eight hours of serving diners in the sometimes almost broiling heat of the café left her feeling enervated and smelly. If Tommy even noticed, his natural good manners made it impossible for her to tell.

Before long Janice was really looking forward to seeing Tommy at the end of her shifts, and for the first time in her life became a committed clock-watcher. Hazel Nutt took note immediately and wasted no time making Janice the butt of any number of workplace jokes. Janice accepted the gibes with grace and even contributed to the humor by showing up for work one day with a huge strap from a piece of farm harness which she professed was a watchband for the large six-sided clock that was fixed to the front of the café. Janice proclaimed she was going to turn it into a wristwatch so she'd know the exact moment her shift ended.

The incident in the Morrison's living room occurred during the second and last week of Tommy's leave. When the couple arrived at the Lookabaugh's home Tommy was visibly uncomfortable. Finally Janice could ignore it no longer.

"What bee is in your bonnet, Marine?" she asked.

"My time home is almost up," he answered.

"Don't I know it," she agreed.

"I feel like such a kid right now. I want to tell you something, and I scarcely know how to begin. That whole business with my mother makes it even tougher because I am afraid that you will think the two are related somehow, and I promise you, they are not."

"What are you getting at?" Janice asked. Because Tommy was leaving in a few days, Janice was expecting the brush-off. They'd had a lot of fun together, going out, playing tennis, swimming in the red waters of the Kiwanis pool, going to the two movies a week that had shown at the Broncho Theater during his stay, and walking together almost every day. But Janice also knew it had only been temporary fun. Tommy's stay was almost over. Janice had loved seeing the surprised and somewhat envious looks on the faces of the other girls in town when they saw them together. It was too good to be true, she acknowledged, and pretty soon it wouldn't be any longer.

"I want you to know that this has been really special for me," Tommy began. "From the moment my brother Bill and I went into the café for a Coke and I saw you the first time, I was a goner. I could hardly sleep that night thinking, heck hoping that you would be there again the next day. When you waited on my table, and that whole business with the coffee; going to the movies that night; getting to know you better, I just cannot think of any day so perfect in my whole life."

"Including almost knocking me unconscious?" Janice interrupted.

Tommy chuckled at the memory of their heads colliding the morning she had waited on him at the café when he'd tried to stand at the same moment she had been bending over to stop the flow of hot coffee from a spill. "That was just part of my cave man charm," Tommy continued, "I have found that unconscious girls don't resist so much."

"Ha," she rejoined, "I would."

By this time they had arrived at the Lookabaugh home. They climbed the first three steps to the porch, and then Janice mounted the fourth step so that when she faced him they would be closer to eye to eye.

"I've had a good time too," she said quietly.

"I'm glad," Tommy replied softly, "but it's a little more than that for me."

"It is?" she asked. Janice had a moment of panic when she thought her heart was beating so loudly that Tommy must be able to hear it.

"I'm not trying to tie you down, OK," Tommy began, "and I know that two weeks is hardly the sort of time frame in which to make important decisions. . . and that isn't what I want," he hastily added. "What I want is to ask you to write to me. Nothing too personal, just notes about school, your friends, work, and so forth. I found in boot camp that I was more homesick for the every day stuff around here than I was for anything."

"Anything?" she intoned archly.

"Fat lot I know about that," Tommy answered, playing along with the entendre'.

Janice reached forward and took his face in her hands. She looked into his eyes and replied. "I will write to you. Even if you hadn't asked me to I would have done that, but since you did ask me, I want to tell you something else."

"What?" he asked.

"They aren't going to be completely impersonal," with that she leaned forward and kissed his lips before she concluded, "my letters I mean."

Even before Janice could finish speaking, the damage was done. Tommy had been thinking about this first kiss for two weeks. He had imagined every sort of strategy to initiate it, but when it finally occurred, he was almost too surprised to react. When he finally did, he began leaning forward at the same moment in which Janice, her kiss completed began to lean back to finish her sentence. When she did he lost his balance as well as his precarious perch on the edge of the step and for a horrifying moment realized he was falling before toppling off the riser into the holly bush that was planted next to it.

"Holy shit," Tommy exploded in surprise, "this thing is covered with stickers."

It took a moment before Janice could even register what had occurred right before her eyes. Suddenly she saw Tommy basically seated in the holly bush, his Marine Corps brogans waving frantically at about the same level as his eyes, and she began a laugh, which almost instantly became hysterical.

"Well," she gasped when she finally got her breath, "of course it's covered with stickers, Tommy, it's a holly bush for heaven's sake. Now get out of there," she added uselessly, "you're tearing up the bush." She then laughed anew at her own wit.

As they struggled to free him, the front door opened showing the light from the living room, and Janice's mother appeared in the doorway behind the screen.

"Are you two all right?" she wanted to know.

"Tommy's fallen into the holly, Momma," Janice replied still laughing.

"What?" Marge Lookabaugh responded uncomprehendingly.

"The holly, Momma, Tommy slipped off the side of the porch step here and has fallen into the holly bush."

"Oh my gosh," Janice's mother replied as she craned her neck to look, "so he has. Wait right there Tommy, and I'll get John."

Tommy had no choice but to wait right there. Every struggle to free himself had only resulted in him slipping further into the spiked leaves of the bush. In a moment John Lookabaugh came onto the porch, assessed the situation, pulled Tommy's legs so his feet made contact with the edge of the step below the one from which he'd fallen and then grabbed his hand and pulled him upright onto the step.

"Are you all right, son?" John Lookabaugh asked.

"Yes sir, I - I guess I am, thanks Mr. Lookabaugh," Tommy answered sheepishly.

With that Tommy could almost see the workings in John's mind as he looked from his daughter who was struggling to control her mirth, to Tommy, then down to the step and finally into the holly. When he had worked out the scenario to his own satisfaction he shook his head and chuckled for a moment before concluding, "Well," he said, "that was some kiss wasn't it?" He then looked expectantly at Janice

"John Lookabaugh," his wife gasped in shock, "how dare you?"

With that John clapped the hapless Marine on his shoulder, looked at his daughter, shook his head yet again, and started up the stairs. When he was about to reenter the house he turned back to the young people. "It's a nice night, not too hot, will you be coming in soon Janice?"

"In a minute, Daddy," she replied.

"Don't stay out too long."

"OK," she agreed.

"Good night sweetheart, good night Tommy," he finished and reentered the house, closed the door and turned on the porch light.

As soon as the door was closed, Janice resumed her laughter. Tommy was occupied with a fruitless attempt to straighten his uniform and relieve the itching from the minute amounts of poison he had received from the holly's thorns. When he was more or less settled, Janice took his elbow and directed him onto the exact center of the last step before the porch, then centered herself on him on the porch itself. She put her arms around his neck and pulled him towards her. Her laughter was now gone. She gently kissed him, then looking directly into his eyes said, "Tommy, I genuinely hope it works out between us, because I want to be able to tell my grandchildren about their granddaddy falling into the holly bush the first time we kissed." With that her suppressed laughter resumed until Tommy picked her up and acted as though he was going to toss her into the holly.

"Stop, Tommy," Janice hissed, quietly insistent, while at the same time trying fruitlessly to cover her bottom with the hiked up hem of her skirt, "my parents are right on the other side of that wall."

Tommy gently put her down, but he left his arms around her. "I hope so too," he said.

"What?" she asked.

"I hope you can tell your grandkids that story as well." With that an agreement was sealed with a kiss that neither of them mentioned to another soul.

II

The next four days were quicksilver. They were the final ones of Tommy's leave and the couple contrived to spend every moment together they possibly could. Tommy and Janice had been consciously building memories, and they had, too. But that had been sixteen months earlier. In all the time that had passed, Janice's only contact with Tommy had been letters, a telegram on her birthday, and the visit from Billy Morrison on Valentine's Day bearing flowers his brother had gotten him to buy her from almost half a world away. On that day, already emotional about Hazel's funeral earlier in the afternoon, Janice had cried openly when 10 year old Billy arrived at the café bearing the huge bouquet.

Now as the cold crisp air lay quietly outside the Morrison's home, Janice waited for Tommy's dad to return from upstairs. The house was quiet, she was surrounded by a remarkable calmness, but her mind just wouldn't cooperate. Her thoughts flitted dramatically from her memories of Tommy to the devastation she imagined had occurred at Pearl Harbor earlier in the day. A tear worked its way down her cheek, followed by another, then others as she sat quietly wringing her hands in the large front room.

"I wish I could promise you that everything is going to be OK," George Morrison said softly, breaking her reverie as he reentered the room. He crossed to her and handed her a spotless handkerchief from his pocket. Janice accepted it gratefully and dabbed at her eyes, then blew her nose.

They sat quietly for a moment before the girl spoke.

"Do you know what occurred to me this afternoon?" Janice asked.

"Tell me," George responded.

"We're at war." Janice raised her face towards George who looked back with a quizzical expression. "I know that doesn't sound very profound, but nobody ever went to war in history without thinking it would be over in a really short period of time."

George nodded his head in agreement.

"But, what if it's not, Mr. Morrison? It is an awfully big world out there and as nearly as I can tell; most of it was already at war when we got in it this afternoon. For over a year I have been counting down the months until Tommy was going to be home again. Even assuming the best, he is a Marine in a world at war. Now what, Mr. Morrison, now what?"

Physically, George Morrison was an older version of his son. At just under six feet, he was taller than many men his age, of average build, thinning hair, and dependent upon his wire rimmed glasses in order to see and read. He was wearing the charcoal gray trousers and vest from the suit he'd worn to church earlier in the day, over a white shirt. At that moment, he looked every inch just what he was, a middle aged man with an awful lot on his mind. George walked to the fireplace and placed his right hand on the mantle. He was staring at nothing in particular when he began to speak.

"I've been thinking along those same lines all afternoon," he began. "I'm afraid that those who seem to have been trying to get us into this war for the past year may have overlooked your concern. War isn't like poker. You can't play a few hands, assess your winnings and then excuse yourself and go back home. Once you're in, you're in and you stay in until one side or the other just can't take it any more. One of the most horrible things about war is just how much hell men can create when they really set their minds to it. Even worse, Janice, is how much hell people can be made to take when they have no choice.

"In the last war, the nations of Europe slaughtered most of an entire generation of young men in one senseless catastrophe after another. It was touch and go right up to the end. When America joined in, the reserves of men suddenly available to the allies tipped the balance and finally ended the war.

"The allies may have chosen to call the Armistice a victory, Janice, but let me promise you, after the war was over, it was pretty tough to tell who had won. Of course France was in shambles; but the economies of every combatant were destroyed. For two years we had to ship food to Europe to prevent wholesale starvation. The biggest calamity, though, was a human one. Literally millions of men killed in every way imaginable, governments toppled, kings deposed." Morrison stopped and shook his head at the image then turned to face Janice before continuing.

"I wish I could tell you that this war will soon be over. But if I did, you'd know that I was lying. Even if Tommy is OK, he's in it. He's in the toughest outfit America has to offer and I doubt he will be spending the war in some soft billet somewhere. He's just a junior enlisted rifleman. Even if he could get out of combat, you and I both know he wouldn't want that. He's just not set up that way.

"He comes by it honest, I suppose. Both of my brothers and I were in France in the last war, Janice. Whenever the three of us would get together, we'd wind up telling stories about the Corps. Tommy was always so fascinated, and I never even tried to tell him how horrible the war really was. Instead we talked with gusto about what we'd done. God help me, when he joined the Marine Corps I was — proud of him. You know, a chip off the old block and all of that. Now I feel like such a fool. What was the big damn hurry, anyway? We weren't at war. If he hadn't joined the Marines he'd be here right now, or down in Norman at school, and I'd be worried about what might happen to him in the future, instead of what might already have occurred. All of his life I've wanted to protect him, advise him, keep him from harm. Now, on the most pivotal day of his life so far, I realize I can't do a single thing to help him. Instead, everything I've ever done just served to put him in harm's way.

"While I was punishing myself about all of that, it occurred to me that one of the differences between war today and the one I was in is that the machines of war are more powerful now, more deadly, even more inhumane. Not only do I not have any idea how long all of this will take, I can't even imagine what kind of world we'll be living in when it's over. All you and I can do Janice, is pray. I plan to do a lot of it. I've been doing a lot of it."

By the time George Morrison was finished Janice was crying into the handkerchief he had loaned her. The father of sons, he had little experience with crying girls and her tears were a phenomenon with which he was ill equipped to be of much help. Awkwardly George pulled a leather ottoman up to the chair in which Janice was sitting, seated himself on it and took her hand in his. "There, there," he said uselessly, "there, there."

Since Tommy had been gone, Janice had made a real effort to improve her relationship with Gladys Morrison. She used any excuse to drop by the house to share news of Tommy or bring by the photos he sent her. George would have had to be deaf and dumb not to have realized that there was more going on here than just a boy meeting a girl for a couple of movies during a brief home leave. Although her efforts hadn't worked too well on Gladys, George had formed a real affection for the girl his son had apparently chosen for himself. Now, as he looked at the tearful young woman seated in front of him his heart melted again.

"Janice," he said softly, "I'm so sorry. My mind is just running away with me. I had no business burdening you that way."

"Please, don't apologize, Mr. Morrison," Janice tried to force control into her voice, "it can't have been easy for you to tell me all of that. I'm happy it was me you shared it with."

"You're a remarkable girl, Janice," he replied, "and I feel both better and worse for telling you what was on my heart. First, I needed to get that off my chest, but I also feel like such an ass for painting that gruesome picture of war for you a moment ago. You didn't need that. We weren't talking about war; we were talking about Tommy, and all I did was load you up with a bunch of emotional claptrap that had nothing to do with him.

"I'm scared, all right, but until we know something for certain, I choose to believe Tommy is OK. He is my son and I love him as much as I could love anyone or anything. I don't know what happened at Pearl Harbor today, but I can tell you this, Tommy has a heck of a lot to live for and I think both you and he know it. If he can, I believe he'll move heaven and earth to get back here to you – to all of us. Don't worry about the stuff you can't control, Janice. Pray him home if you can, that's what I plan to do. Maybe between the two of us we'll pull it off."

Janice looked at George and tried gamely to smile. "Thanks Mr. Morrison. I'll try."

"What's going on here?" Gladys Morrison demanded from behind them. "Why is she still here? I asked you to send her home!"

Janice was dumbstruck by the apparition that had suddenly appeared in the arched doorway to the living room. Mrs. Morrison was wearing her slip, the massive foundation garments worn by women of her age and time, and little else. One of her hose had collected at her ankle, her other leg was bare. Her hair was completely awry, sticking out in weird angles from her head and she appeared dazed, almost like she was drunk, except there was no smell of alcohol.

"Dear," George Morrison said gently as he rose to his feet, "Janice and I were talking about Tommy and the events of today. You need to go back to bed. You're not yourself." As he spoke, George walked to his wife's side and attempted to escort her out of the room. She shrugged her husband's hand from her arm and straightened with visible effort.

"This is my home," she said forcing firmness past the slur in her voice, "and I want her out of it."

"This is my home as well, Gladys," George said quietly, "and she is as welcome here as Tommy would be."

"As Tommy would be," she demanded, "as Tommy would be! Are you mad? Tommy is my son, and this girl is a nobody. How dare you tell me she is as welcome here as Tommy would be? He is my son...he...he...he was my baby," her voice suddenly cracked, but she continued, "my little baby, and now suddenly he cares about her and the Marines, and those horrible Japanese are trying to take him away from me. I can't stop them; I can't stop anything. Oh, Lord, what am I going to do!" With that Gladys erupted in tears, sliding down the frame of the doorway into the living room until she collapsed in an undignified heap in the entry to the room. Great wracking sobs emanated from her as her shoulders heaved from her crying.

George went to his wife. In a moment, Janice was with him. "Let's get her up to her bed," Janice recommended.

"Thank you," George responded. "I think I'll need the help."

Between them they got Gladys to her feet then with one of her arms around each of their necks, gently moved her to the stairs and then up to her room. Once they arrived, Janice pulled back the chenille spread and then turned back the blankets and sheet from the already rumpled bed. George sat her on the bed, then put her feet up while Janice pulled the blankets over her.

Janice had never been upstairs in the Morrison's home. As she looked around, she realized that this was clearly the master bedroom. Windows lined two of the walls. The curtains were flowered chintz, the accent pieces, pictures, and pillows all feminine. One of the doors led to a large closet filled with women's clothing, through the other, Janice could see the fixtures of a small bathroom. If George also lived in this room, Janice realized, there was no evidence of it.

"Janice," he said quietly to her, "I want you to know that my wife really is a wonderful woman, but she hasn't been herself for some time, maybe since Tommy went away, or even before. From the first time I met you, I thought how much you reminded me of her when she was young and tough and smart, just like you. Considering the sum of your experiences with her, that must seem difficult to believe, but it is true.

"I've discovered I don't understand nearly as many things as someone my age should. In fact, as I get even older, sometimes I wonder if I understand anything at all. We're heading into tough times Janice, and it looks like, for whatever reason, Gladys isn't going to make them easier for any of us. I don't expect you will find it easy to forgive her, but I hope you'll try."

George then pulled the chair from the dressing table up to the side of Gladys' bed. He seated himself and then turned and looked at the young woman. "Now, I hope you'll forgive me Janice and see yourself out. My wife needs me right now." With that, George took his wife's hand gently in his own and focused his attentions on her, speaking quietly to Gladys while she stared absently at the ceiling.

At the door, Janice stopped for a moment and observed the commitment of George for Gladys. She didn't say goodbye. She just walked silently down the stairs and let herself out into the cold twilight of one of history's most infamous days.

Chapter Seven

Ace

Central State College
Wednesday, April 22, 1942
11:35 a.m.

I

*J*anice Lookabaugh was seated on the grass along the East side of Central State College's "Old North" the college's administration building, reading Gilgamesh.

"Hi," the boyish voice announced.

Janice raised her eyes. The boy was wearing an Army uniform. He had several books under his arm.

"Hello," she responded coolly. Janice didn't want to be mean to this soldier who was probably a long way from home and almost certainly lonely, but she didn't want to encourage him either.

"I see you here pretty often," he began.

"It's a good place to study," Janice answered, emphasizing the final word.

"Yes, I gathered," the boy continued unfazed. "I'm new here. I'm scheduled for flight training in a few weeks … or months. The Air Corps is parking me here until they can find a slot."

"Central has been home to a lot of future aviators in the past few months," Janice confirmed.

"None like me," the boy interjected.

"Oh," Janice replied, "I'm sure you're right about that."

"No, really. I'm already a pilot. I started flying on my 16th birthday."

"As long ago as that," Janice answered drolly. The boy looked like his 16th birthday couldn't have been more than 6 months earlier.

"Seriously," he continued, "I have over 200 hours. Much of it spent crop dusting. I aced the written exams. I can't wait to get started, but so far, nothing, except typing classes, weather classes, and junk like that."

Finally, Janice closed her book and got to her feet.

"Well," she said, dismissing him, "I have to be going."

"Swell, me too. Where can I walk you?"

"Nowhere, please. I'm just on my way home."

"Let me walk you. I know by now you probably think I'm weird, or Jack the Ripper or something, but really, I've noticed you here on sunny days and I've been trying to work up my nerve to talk to you since the first time I saw you. I haven't talked to a girl since I got here. I promise I mean no harm."

"I'm sure you're very nice," Janice responded, "but I don't live on campus, I'm on my way home . . . and besides," she finished, thinking of Tommy, "maybe you'd be happier talking to another girl."

"Fella in the service, huh? Well, that's OK. I wasn't looking to officially announce our engagement today anyhow. My name is Jerry Harper, everybody calls me 'Ace.' Let me get your books." With that he gathered Janice's books and made a gesture indicating that she should lead the way.

Janice looked at the boy who seemed about as threatening as an unweaned kitten. *How bad could it get,* she thought to herself, *I could probably take him two falls out of three.*

"OK," she responded, "but only as far as the edge of campus. No offense, but I don't want my nosy neighbors to assume I'm entertaining soldiers. Everybody in this town minds everybody else's business."

"Don't I know it," Ace responded, "I'm from Weatherford. It's even smaller than this burg. You couldn't throw out the trash without everybody knowing what you had for supper the night before."

"Weatherford!" Janice said, "Weatherford is only about 60 miles from here. I just assumed you were some lonely guy far from home."

"I am," Ace responded immediately, "just try to get to Weatherford from here. It can't be done in the amount of time I ever have available. The bus runs during times I can't catch it. If I did get there, I couldn't be back in time for reveille on Monday morning. It's awful."

"I guess you're right," Janice allowed.

After walking silently for a few minutes, Janice's resolve melted and she finally initiated a comment.

"Isn't an Ace somebody who has shot down five enemy aircraft?" she asked.

"Yep. I know what you're thinking. How presumptuous can you get, right?"

"Actually, that is exactly what I was thinking," she answered.

"I got into this program for one reason only. I want to fly fighters. P-38s, P-47s, whatever, I'll only be happy if I wind up in fighters. At first, I know the fellas were just riding me, jealous because I'd already done so much flying. But I don't care. If they want to call me Ace, I accept. Eventually, I'm going to earn their respect. If the instructors down in Texas, or wherever I wind up decide to make me a fighter pilot then it will all be worth it. If the Air Corps gives me the chance to go up against ME-109s or Zeros, I'll earn the name and the kidding will be history."

By disposition and wit, Janice Lookabaugh was one not prone to suffer fools and braggarts, but Jerry's face was so sincere and without guile that the sarcastic quip that leapt to her lips died there. Instead she walked along in silence as the boy prattled along about flying, the war, Edmond, Central State, and any number of subjects Janice was sure he knew nothing about. Despite all of that, his enthusiasm was infectious. She settled into a comfortable rhythm, walking with her perfect posture; head upright with his high pitched voice as accompaniment. When they reached the edge of the campus Janice turned to him and retrieved her books.

"It was nice to meet you," she said.

"It was nice to meet you too, Janice," he answered.

Janice stopped short, surprised. "How did you know my name?" she asked.

"It's written on the inside cover of your books," he answered. "There are several names in there, but Janice Lookabaugh is the only name that's repeated in all three of them."

"Aren't you the little Sherlock Holmes," Janice said in exasperation, then paused before adding, "how old are you anyway?"

"Almost 20," Jerry responded, but Janice's expression showed how little she believed him.

"OK, almost 19." Her further incredulity finally sparked the confession, "OK, OK, eighteen three months ago. But it takes over a year to prepare a pilot for combat. I'll be old enough."

"Old enough for what?" Janice interrupted sarcastically.

"Old enough to help win this war, that's what. Let me tell you something, Janice. Wars aren't won by guys the age of Abbot and Costello or Bob Hope, no matter what Hollywood wants you to believe. They are won by guys my age. They always have been. If I can't hold up my end of the bargain in this thing it won't be because I'm too young. It'll be because I just wasn't good enough. But, I'll tell you something else, I'm gonna' be good enough. I'd die before I'd fail."

"Don't say that," Janice snapped. "There's going to be enough dying to satisfy everybody before this war is over. If it gets to be your turn then so be it. It may be because you weren't good enough, or it may be because your airplane breaks, or because you're just unlucky and a bomb falls on you. If you die, you won't be the best one it happens to or the worst. My boyfriend was on the U.S.S. Oklahoma when it was sunk at Pearl Harbor. Over 400 men died without proving whether they were better or worse than the Japanese who murdered them. Save your bravado, Jerry, it only reminds me of how innocent you are. So far this horror has done enough to me that at this point, I may know more about war than you do."

With that she turned and stomped across Second Street on her way home, leaving the open mouthed Jerry to watch and wonder. When she finally turned the corner onto Third Street a block away Ace turned back towards the campus.

"Man," Ace said to no one in particular, "that girl has the finest ass I've ever seen."

II

Jerry Harper made sure he gave Janice Lookabaugh every opportunity he could to get to know him better. He spoke to her when he saw her on campus, sometimes sitting down at her table if she was in the cafeteria. He also joined her Sunday School class at the First United Methodist Church. He always attended class events including an ice cream social at Janice's own home. After he discovered that she was a waitress at the Wide-A-Wake, Jerry made a point of stopping in for a Coke during some of her shifts.

If their relationship didn't work out exactly as Jerry had planned; Janice never responded to him romantically, they did become friends. Following the ice cream social, Janice's mother received a thank-you note from Jerry that cemented his welcome in their home. From that day forward, he was frequently present for meals and snacks and was generally treated by Janice's whole family like a nephew on his way to war. Even Janice came to think of him like a kid brother, and when Private Jerry Harper left Central State College to become Aviation Cadet Jerry Harper, Janice promised to return any letters he wrote. Never, though, neither in person nor in any of her letters, did Janice ever give him the satisfaction of calling him Ace.

III

12 October 1942

Dear Janice,

There is no joy in Mudville.

It seems my skill as an aviator must have escaped the Air Corps' notice. We received our orders and I am being assigned to B-17s. Everyone in our entire class has been assigned to B-17s. It wouldn't have mattered if Lucky Lindberg himself had been in this group. You know what that means? Some other class is all going to go to P-47s, or those new P-51s I've heard about. Someday I'll be flying my big old bus over France and some yahoo that doesn't know his stick from his rudder will be flying cover for me even though I could fly rings around him.

What can I tell ya', the old Air Corps needs bomber pilots. I'm not sure I can ever drink this one off, but tonight I'm gonna try.

Keep 'em flying, kid,

Jerry

March 22, 1943

Dear Janice,

OK, I was wrong.

The B-17 is a marvelous aircraft. I wish you could stand on the end of the field and watch one take off. They seem to lumber down the runway and as they commence their taxi you'd swear there is no way something that huge could ever get airborne. By the end of the take off run, the engines are screaming and the very earth is trembling beneath the aircraft. Then suddenly they're in the air and from that moment you know that big beautiful SOB was made for nothing else! They just soar.

Our crew has been together for three months but now one of the pilots in the group has pneumonia and won't be going to Europe with us. I'm going to shift to the left seat in his plane so I have the satisfaction of being first in my class to command his own bomber. I'm still a second lieutenant, but that won't be true much longer! My new plane already has a name, "Homewrecker" which I think is pretty good, but if I'd gotten to choose I'd have probably gone with "Oklahoma Girl" or something like that.

The new crew is pretty good. I guess they'd need to improve some to come up to the standards of my old airplane, but they seem like a great bunch of guys to be going into combat with. There are ten of us on the Homewrecker, one Okie (guess who), two from Texas, one each from Mississippi, Wyoming, Kansas, Louisiana (Cajun co-pilot), and three from California. The Yankees must all train somewhere else!

We're ready to go I think, but I'm glad to have a few more training and navigation flights before we do. We had hoped for a leave prior to going overseas, but it ain't gonna' happen.

Wish me luck,

Jerry

July 15, 1943

Dear Janice,

I flew my first combat mission today.

It was different from anything I'd imagined, and I imagined this day a lot.

I wasn't with my own crew. They always send up the new pilots in the co-pilot's seat with a seasoned crew for their first mission. That way, at least one of us will have a little experience on our first mission together. It's a good idea and I was pretty impressed with how good those guys were.

I'm more convinced than ever that we're flying in the finest aircraft that has ever been made and our training was good, but also that we all have a lot to learn.

After I joined the Air Corps I kept on crop dusting for a few months while I waited for my orders to arrive. One day when I was flying a furrow just a few feet off the ground, a whole cloud of grasshoppers took flight right as I got there. They were everywhere, banging into the wings and guy wires, the engine and mostly my head. They beat the crap out of me. It's a miracle they didn't bring the plane down. It was the scariest thing that had ever happened to me in an aircraft. I remember thinking at the time 'this must be what flak is like.' I've been through anti-aircraft fire now Janice. It was nothing like those grasshoppers. Nothing is like I thought it would be.

Pray for the "Homewrecker" Janice, pray for me, too.

Jerry

November 15, 1943

Dear Miss Lookabaugh,

Today we received Jerry's possessions from the War Department. A footlocker, one suitcase I'm told is known as a Val Pack for some reason, his uniforms, toiletries, medals, and letters including a few very ladylike ones from you. I suppose there is no way you would know otherwise, but Jerry's bomber was shot down over Germany and according to others in his squadron, there wasn't time for anyone to parachute from the plane before it exploded. Even though he was listed as missing, there seems little likelihood that he'll show up after the war.

You'll never know how much I appreciate how nice you and your family were to him during his stay in Edmond. I know from his letters that you were just friends, Miss Lookabaugh, but he always wrote of you in an almost forlorn way. Although you seem to have resisted his charms, he had an awful crush on you.

One footlocker, a suitcase, some uniforms and a few medals signifying service in Europe and the completion of a few missions. It doesn't seem like much compensation for the years of love and company we'll be denied, grandchildren, a life lived well, and whatever other accomplishments he might have had. I can scarcely think of him for a moment without tears. He was our only son. I wanted to petition to keep him at home but he wouldn't hear of it.

I hope you won't think I'm imposing on you, but I like to think that you'll remember him somehow. That years from now you'll recall the boy from Weatherford you met during the war. In that way, maybe he will go on even after his father and I are gone. I hope you'll try. I am enclosing a photo of him in his plane. They call the painting "nose art" and he swore she was the spitting image of you.

I would love to hear from you.

Sincerely,

Mrs. Henry (Wilma) Harper

The photo showed Jerry at the controls of his B-17 smiling from the window. His hat sported the 50 mission crush pilots affected and his thumb rose upward from his fist in the approved fashion. On the nose of the airplane was a fanciful and pneumatic blonde in a sexy negligee' looking languorously over her shoulder. Janice quickly determined that the siren painted on the nose of the bomber looked nothing like her at all.

Janice stared at the photo for several moments before she realized that the name of the plane had been changed after Jerry took command. In two obviously different print types the name "Oklahoma Homewrecker" was painted next to the blonde's rear end.

Janice waited for some sort of emotion to affect her. She recalled how steadfastly she had kept the now dead boy at arm's length. She hadn't wanted to become too close and as she stared at the photo she determined that she must have been successful. Boys like Jerry were dying every day. Even though she knew this one, and now she also knew his mother in a way, Janice was almost surprised that she didn't feel the anguish a dead boy should have engendered.

Idly determining to answer Wilma Harper's letter, Janice opened her portfolio and removed a sheet of paper. She set Jerry's photo aside and began composing her response. Janice wanted to share with Jerry's mother some of the stories she recalled from her son's time in Edmond. After a few moments though, she was shocked to realize she couldn't recall what Jerry looked like, or even a single event from his life in Edmond. She retrieved the photograph and studied it again, but it didn't help. Instead, as she looked at the childish face sitting at the huge plane's controls, all she could think about was an aircraft flying straight and level over a heavily defended German city with ten scared men aboard while flak and fighters attempted to tear out its vitals. As she stared at the photo her vision blurred and her breathing became ragged, and the only things that came to her were tears.

"Oh Ace," she gasped, and buried her face in her hands.

Chapter Eight

Christmas 1942

410 E. Third Street, Edmond, Ok.
Sunday, December 21, 1942
4:15 p.m.

I

$\mathcal{J}$anice Lookabaugh sat glumly at the small table in the kitchen of her family's home, chin in her hands, staring absently out the window at the barren trees in the back yard. It was the approach of Christmas 1942 that had gotten her out of sorts, and it began when she realized she could scarcely even recall the previous year's celebration. The shock of Pearl Harbor had scarcely begun to wear off by late December 1941. The whole country seemed to feel that with the nation at war, indulgences like holidays needed to be set aside for the duration. Almost as one, Americans seemed to be asking, "Should we be celebrating when our men are fighting overseas?" Many towns had failed to even decorate for the season, and although most families recognized that they didn't want to deny Christmas trees and gifts to their small children, little else had been done. Christmas 1941 had been dark and dreary - a time for prayer and contemplation, but not for celebration.

The intervening year of grim and difficult news had shown Americans something of what war meant. The invasion of Northern Africa had occurred in August and although the only military actions against the Germans had been a few tentative bomber missions flown from England; our fighting men were already heavily engaged in the Pacific, with major battles at Midway and Guadalcanal. People from every walk of life were beginning to realize just how long the war was going to be. At home, the entire country was mobilizing to support the invasions and battles to come. Shortages and rationing had already started as of the previous summer, and as the year progressed, a perception that there would be plenty of sacrifice began to evolve. There would be no need to relinquish much loved traditions like Christmas on the altar of the country just so people would feel they were doing enough for the war effort. As the holiday season approached again, Americans wanted some level of normality back in their lives.

Even in Edmond, life seemed to be drifting on a vast sea of decisions and events over which nobody could exercise any sort of control. Janice felt the shocks and alarums she'd experienced during the previous year almost like a punch drunk fighter who continued to hook and jab, but only out of habit and form. Now as Christmas came again, Janice felt like she was coming out of a coma. More than anything, she wanted to be reminded of the way her life had been.

Recapturing the feeling of a traditional Christmas, Janice realized, would be the perfect tonic to bring her out of her funk. Janice loved Christmas. The Lookabaughs had always kept the holiday close to its Christian fundamentals but they embraced the traditional family aspects as well. Intuitively, Janice developed a philosophy of Christmas that was at once religious, cultural, and mystical. The holiday was about the gathering together of family and friends, the thrill visible on the face of a child, the cohesion and continuity that grew from neighbors wishing one another the happiest of holiday seasons. Janice missed it, she missed it all and she wanted Christmas back.

On the table in front of her was a start. It was an invitation to the annual Christmas party at the Wide-A-Wake Café. Every year the Noes encouraged all of their employees to come to the café with their families for a few hours on Christmas Eve. Nobody was under any obligation to attend, and despite the fact that there were almost no customers; the café was open for business. Nevertheless, almost everyone who worked in the café, and a good many people who had worked there in the past, made it a habit to attend the annual Christmas party. Janice always enjoyed it. The other waitresses were usually there, and it gave her a chance to visit with the women from shifts other than her own that she saw only rarely during the year.

The party was a drop-in affair that extended from shortly after noon until about nine o'clock. By unspoken agreement, most people came by during the early evening hours. Janice planned to arrive about five. At seven, she would leave and walk to the First Methodist Church over on Jackson Street in order to attend Christmas Eve services with her family.

The invitation on the table in front of her was a double edged sword. In addition to making her think of Christmas, it had also reminded Janice of Hazel Nutt, dead almost two years now. Her husband would never have allowed her to attend a party, so Hazel simply arranged to work the Christmas Eve shift, bringing her children with her on that one day. The kids had loved the party, sneaking cookies and punch and playing board games with the children of the other waitresses who were there. During the 1940 party, Janice had spent the evening happily entertaining Haley, Hazel's youngest and although in kindergarten, really little more than a baby that year. She had led or carried the youngster around the room as she visited with the other guests and customers and they'd both had a wonderful time. As she sat in the kitchen of her home and thought of the 1942 party yet to come, Janice made a decision and reached for the phone book.

"Number 216," she said to the operator when she had her on the line. A moment later she heard the voice of Mildred Price.

"Mrs. Price," she began, "this is Janice Lookabaugh, do you remember me? I'm . . . I was Hazel's friend."

"Good afternoon, Miss Lookabaugh," Mildred replied, "I remember you."

"Merry Christmas," Janice offered.

"The same," Mildred replied then continued, "what can I do for you, Miss."

"I was just thinking about the Christmas party at the Café," Janice replied, "and how much Jimmy, Haley, and Ruth enjoyed it before," Janice hesitated again, then continued, "before the war. I was hoping it would be OK if I took them with me this year. There are usually a few small gifts for the children. Nothing much, just a game or something, but I would love for them to go so the others could see how they have grown."

There was silence on the other end of the line. Uncertain of the cause, and in an effort to clinch the deal, Janice added hopefully, "If you'd like, I'd be happy to take your children as well."

"That won't be necessary," Mildred replied, "I'd be happy for you to take them for an evening. It will give me a chance to be with just my own children for a change, and if there are going to be gifts for the kids, we'll have our tree while they're gone." A feeling of just how difficult a time Mildred Price was having washed over Janice in a guilty wave. She resolved to try to find an opportunity to take Hazel's kids to the movies or on a picnic in the months ahead. Her class work and job had occupied so much of Janice's time that she had almost forgotten the children of her friend.

"Oh thank you," Janice said, then after a moment's pause she continued, "I usually attend the Christmas Eve services with my family after the party. If it's OK, I'll take them with me this year and then bring them home a little after eight."

"That would be fine," Mildred replied and Janice could hear the lifting of the burden, however slightly from Mildred's voice.

II

The party was a wonderful success. Janice had told Cleo Noe that she was bringing Hazel's kids and when they arrived the sisters-in-law, Cleo and Essie Mae made an enormous fuss over the three children she had in tow. There were

71

introductions to everyone who was there, mostly lost on the youngsters, and then a meal of turkey and dressing with all the fixings. The children ate heartily, and after they were done, Janice took Jimmy Nutt's plate and filled it again. All evening, the assembled women took turns visiting with the orphans, playing games with them or just generally making a fuss over them.

When it was almost time to go, Janice saw Bertha Potts, one of the morning shift waitresses, laughing as she played a board game with Ruth and Haley. Bertha always seemed so stiff and stern to Janice that she was surprised to see her so thoroughly enjoying herself. The magic of Christmas seemed to be affecting everyone, Janice realized, and a happy smile creased her face.

Just before seven, as Janice was pulling coats and gloves onto the children, Cleo Noe approached with three gaily wrapped packages.

"Everyone chipped in," she began, "and got you kids a little something. I don't know if you should open them now or wait until tomorrow. . ."

"Now, now!" Ruth Nutt called out. Cleo laughed and relinquished the packages to the children who quickly tore the paper from them. There was a baseball glove for Jimmy and dolls for the girls who cried gleefully at the sight of the unexpected bounty. Faces aglow, the children started with Cleo and Essie Mae and hugged everybody in sight. It was just the sort of exuberant display Hazel would have loved seeing, Janice realized, and it brought tears to her eyes. When the children finally worked their hugging way to Janice she dropped to her knees and hugged them in return.

"OK, you guys," she said firmly, "we gotta' go or we're gonna' be late for church." With her charges in tow and Haley's small hand in her own, they walked into the frigid night to cover the few blocks to the Methodist Church.

III

Other than standing when the others around her did so, Janice paid almost no attention during the service. She was completely captured by the sight of the two little girls as they hugged and cradled their new dolls on the pew beside her, and she couldn't keep a smile from her face.

Everyone was silent in the car on the way to the Price home after church. John and Marge Lookabaugh and Janice's little brother, John Junior occupied the front seat while Janice and the Nutt children were in the back. Jimmy sat quietly looking out the window pounding his fist into the pocket of his new glove. Janice had her arms wrapped protectively around little Haley who was sitting on her lap petting and rocking her new doll. In the middle of the seat, Ruth Nutt sat crooning quietly to the doll in her own lap.

"Janice," Ruth began, interrupting her song, "thank you for bringing us. This is a wonderful Christmas."

Janice looked out the window of the car at the mean little houses along the deserted street. It was cold. Frost had already begun to form on the windshields of the cars along the side of the unpaved road. There were halos around the street lights from a frigid mist that Janice knew had no chance of turning into snow for a white Christmas. America was at war. Pearl Harbor had smashed the world she knew, but Janice nodded her head in agreement.

"You're right, Ruthie," she said as she reached over and gently patted the child's head, "it is a wonderful Christmas."

Chapter Nine

Edna

The Wide-A-Wake Café
Wednesday, April 14, 1943
5:55 a.m.

I

"*H*appy birthday, Edna," Tina Clark called out loudly as Edna Pryor entered the Wide-A-Wake Café for her shift.

It was Edna Pryor's 41st birthday and absolutely the last thing she wanted was a general announcement. Instead of the anonymity she normally craved, every patron in the café sounded off with birthday greetings. Edna fled into the kitchen where Tina found her a few moments later industriously stirring pancake batter in a bowl.

"What are you doing hiding in here?" Tina demanded.

"What does it look like," she retorted, "we need pancake batter and I'm making some."

"We do not," Tina replied holding up the almost full metal bowl in which pancake batter was always kept, "there's a gallon of it right here, and if we get where we need more, Sam can make it. He's the cook, and that's his job, you're hiding out, admit it. Now march your little butt out there and let those people sing "Happy Birthday" to you "

"How could you do this to me?" Edna hissed at Tina.

"Because I love you and so do the customers you wait on around here every morning. Let us tell you you're special to us," Tina responded as though lecturing a child.

"My 41st birthday," Edna pointed out, "is scarcely a reason to celebrate."

"Oh but it is," Tina insisted, "just consider the alternative."

Edna smiled ruefully. "OK, maybe there is something that's worse. I just don't know how much worse."

"See," Tina said, "you feel better already. Now, get out there and let those people show you they love you as much as I do."

Walking as though on her way to the gallows, Edna passed through the doorway and smiled gamely while the early morning crowd began singing "Happy Birthday" to her. When they were done she executed a passable curtsy, grabbed the Pyrex coffeepot and began working the room.

Throughout their shift, Tina would periodically begin banging on a glass, announce Edna's birthday again, and the entire process would be repeated. Edna responded to the attention better with every passing hour. Just before their shift ended, Edna called Tina to her side.

"Look at this," she said, holding her apron pocket open for Tina to look inside. It was full of change and even a couple of bills.

"Are those your tips?" Tina asked incredulously.

"There's almost nine dollars in there."

"What!" Tina demanded incredulously. "I think I collected like fifty cents during this shift."

"It was all of that birthday business. About half of my tickets had a note on them saying something like 'happy birthday,' or 'go to the movies on us' and then a quarter or fifty cents, even two with a dollar bill attached."

"Holy mackerel," Tina exploded, "this is a gold mine! Let's do it every day and split the take. In three months we'll have our own restaurant."

"No thanks," Edna answered, "one birthday a year is plenty. But," Edna reached into her apron pocket and counted out four dollars, "I will share this one with you."

"No way," Tina replied, hiding her hands under her apron. "This is your birthday, not mine. Besides, if I took half you wouldn't have the record anymore. I heard that Clara got five dollars one Saturday night when the place was full of drunks. I don't think anybody ever got eight bucks before. Just promise to tell everybody all day when my birthday comes along."

"It's a deal," Edna promised, then smiled with a sudden realization. "Hey, tomorrow is Thursday, we're off."

"I know," Tina replied with a happy smile, "I have a date tonight."

The darkness of concern drifted through Edna's eyes before she asked hopefully, "Anybody I'd know?"

Tina shook her head. "He's a flight engineer I met out at Wiley Post last week," Tina admitted. She saw the look on Edna's face. "Would you quit worrying about me, I know what I'm doing."

"It must be great to be young," Edna replied with a mixture of motherly concern and a tinge of something almost approaching envy. "You'll be careful, won't you Tina, it's a hard old world out there, OK?"

Tina responded with a patronizing smile and hugged her friend. "I'll be careful," she promised.

As they parted, Edna finished with, "I'll see you on Friday morning."

"Happy birthday, Edna," Tina concluded with a wave.

II

Normally, when her shift ended, Edna walked straight home to a decrepit boarding house three blocks east of the café along Second Street. In it, she occupied the same room she'd lived in since 1908 when she was 6 years old. That was the year her father, a hard drinking, itinerant railroad worker had left to purchase a bucket of beer and disappeared into the night. When the shock passed, Edna's mother, Lucerne, had accepted the job as cook in the boarding house in which they'd been living when he left. They had lived in the house for two years when the previous owner failed to come to breakfast one morning. Edna had been sent to the landlady's room to awaken her but instead discovered she'd died in the night.

After the old woman's body had been removed from the house, Lucerne Pryor had looked about her, shrugged her shoulders and begun preparations for lunch. This was Oklahoma, only one year after statehood, and legal niceties paled before the harsher judge of practicality. Lucerne simply continued to operate the house. If there were legitimate heirs, they either never found out about their legacy or chose to ignore it. With each passing year, Lucerne paid the taxes, eventually "proving out her claim," and had owned the old house ever since.

The night after the old woman died, long before she knew she would be able to stay, Lucerne moved her possessions into the former landlady's room, leaving Edna in the tiny, windswept, third floor garret they had shared earlier. Edna occupied this room even yet. The Pryor Place, as the boarding house became known, had been one of the last structures in Edmond to be electrified or fitted with a hot water heater. It had yet to be equipped with a telephone. The floors creaked and the windows fit unconvincingly, but the roof didn't leak, and the old house had provided Lucerne with a perilous livelihood for thirty-five years.

The decrepit boarding house also provided Lucerne Pryor with a domain. The longer that was true, the more imperious she became, eventually even hiring a cook, the black woman Clarisse, to replace the labor the passing years would no longer allow her to perform. In truth, she had a staff of two. Clarisse, paid 75 cents a day to cook and keep the kitchen, and Edna who was paid nothing, to service the furnace, clean the rooms, scrub the toilets, and do anything else her mother demanded.

After being deserted by her husband, Lucerne formed an abiding hostility towards all men. The sentiment was given expression among her tenancy comprised mostly of railroad workers, roughnecks, and more recently, college boys whose aplomb while outlasting Lucerne's frequent tirades only aggravated her more. Her hatred of men was given purpose as Edna blossomed into an attractive young woman.

In 1919, two days after she graduated from high school, and less than a month after her 17th birthday, Edna attempted for the only time in her life to leave home. She departed Edmond on the Santa Fe Rail Road train bound for Dallas with a boy who had lived in their home for three years. Edna left a note so her mother would know there had been no foul play, that the young couple loved each other, and would marry as soon as they arrived at the boy's home in Texas.

When Lucerne read the note she didn't cry or wonder what she'd done wrong or any other reaction that might have been expected. Instead, she went immediately to the Western Union office at the train station. She sent a telegram to the Dallas Police, the Dallas County Sheriff, and the sheriff of every county seat between Edmond and the Texas border reporting that her minor daughter had been kidnapped, would lie about it because she was retarded, and that the young man with her was a dangerous lunatic who was probably armed. The young couple only made it to Payne, Oklahoma before they were dragged from the train. In the confusion, Edna's fiancée was beaten with a pistol, and Edna was placed in a cell until her mother could arrive. Lucerne reached Payne on the earliest train the next day, gathered up her only child and returned with her to the old boarding house.

When she arrived home, Edna, shy and lacking self-confidence under the most benign circumstances, took to her room and stayed there for over a year. Even now, twenty-four years later, her only real freedom came in the form of the voracious reading of romance novels the likes of which she knew her mother would heartily disapprove.

Other than reading, when Edna considered rebellion, it was in the quiet of the night and the privacy of her tiny bedroom. Because she never heard from the young man again, she had no idea what happened to him. His kisses, and that was all there had ever been, were the only romantic memories she had. Like leaves pressed between the pages of an old book, Edna would remove those memories and lovingly examine them from every possible angle to insure the details stayed sharp in her mind and that she never forgot. Edna never did forget, and within the quiet recesses where there was no real expression, she never forgave.

The only other measure of independence Edna ever achieved occurred when she went to work at age twenty-five. Over the years, she held jobs as a cook, washerwoman, maid, and for the past eight years, as a waitress. Working outside the home had given Edna not so much a level of freedom, as respite. It surprised Edna when Lucerne didn't put up a fight over her getting a job until she realized her mother was assuming she would simply turn over her pay envelope every week. To keep the peace, such as it was, and more interested in having a job than money, Edna didn't say no, and for eight years she turned over every penny she earned to her mother in exchange for the privilege of being a maid in her own home. Lucerne needed the money, especially since the old boarding house was in almost constant need of repair and Edna's meager earnings were especially vital during the depression.

When Edna accepted a job as waitress at the Wide-A-Wake, however, a new era began. Edna insisted on the right to keep her tips. Her mother had cried and carried on in the beginning, calling Edna ungrateful, a Jezebel, and hateful, but eventually the old woman agreed. Today, in accordance with her extremely modest expectations, Edna was rich, and she knew just what she wanted to do with the money.

III

As it had been for several days, it was unseasonably warm when Edna left the Wide-A-Wake at the end of her shift. Instead of heading east towards home after leaving the café, as she had done essentially every other work day for the past eight years, Edna crossed Second Street going north. North of the café was Edmond's tiny downtown business district. After crossing the street, Edna turned east and crossed Broadway. Everywhere else in Oklahoma, those two roads are known as Highway 77 and U.S. Route 66, famous as America's first national highway. The intersection of the roads at that location was the very reason the Wide-A-Wake had been built where it was. Edna turned left and walked past the Conoco station. Fred Weibel, the garage's proprietor, and a Wide-A-Wake regular, looked up from the open hood of a Studebaker and returned Edna's wave.

Just as she was passing in front of the window of Van's Bakery, next door to the garage, one of the workers placed a sign in the window that read, "Fresh Sugar Buns." On a whim, Edna walked into the bakery and exchanged one of her nickels for one of the still warm rolls. She then walked on down the street, taking small nibbling bites of the bun and anticipating what she would see when she passed in front of the window of Baker's Dry Goods Store.

Suddenly, there it was. Edna smiled. Adorning the mannequin in the dry goods store window was the dress. She was standing in front of Snyder's Hardware, across the street from Baker's, the better to give the dress perspective. Slowly she recrossed the street and studied the dress as she approached it. Made of "butcher spun linen," a nubby linen-like spun rayon that was available despite wartime restrictions, the dress was a flower patterned knee length affair closed by pearl buttons up the front. It was topped with a short solid colored jacket that picked up the blue in some of the flowers. To Edna, it represented everything dressmaking was all about: The ability of a garment to transcend the hum-drum of everyday life and provide the wearer, no matter how humble, with a vision of glamour that included even her. She loved it.

Edna had first seen the dress the previous Friday night when she and her mother had walked towards the movie theater for the one and only weekly outing they never missed. When she slowed down to study the dress, her mother had jerked her elbow.

"What are you dawdling about," Lucerne Pryor had demanded, "we're going to miss the newsreel if we don't step out."

"We have plenty of time, Mama," Edna replied in a well practiced tone that combined being firm with being non-confrontational; "I'm just looking at the dress in the window."

"Of all the foolishness," Lucerne retorted, dismissing the dress with a quick glance. "You don't need a new dress. Anyway, where in the world would you even wear it?"

"No where, I suppose," Edna allowed, "but it's free to look."

"It's free to waste your time," her mother snapped as she jerked on Edna's elbow again, "let's go."

Today, she dawdled. Beneath the dress mannequin was a small placard quoting the price of the dress as $10.98. As she stood there, Edna realized she had finished the sugar bun. There was a wastebasket next to the door of the store, and as Edna walked to it to throw away the paper napkin she had used to hold the bun, she just continued to walk and entered the store.

"May I help you, Edna," Pauline Baker asked as soon as she was inside.

"Hello Pauline," Edna responded. The two women had attended school together and had quite literally known one another almost all their lives. "Well, maybe," Edna continued, "that dress in the window, do you have it in size 4?"

Pauline drew in her breath, and grimaced. "I don't know," she replied. Size four was very unusual in the 40's especially among mature women.

"Well," Edna conceded, "that's all right," and she began to walk towards the door.

"Now wait a minute," Pauline Baker said holding up her hand. "Let's take a look first. We only bought four of those. They may sell dresses over $20.00 in the city all the time, but almost eleven dollars is a tad pricey up here. Let me just see." With that she walked to the few racks of women's dresses the store carried. The proprietress ran her practiced fingers along the top of a circular rack until she whipped out the very dress Edna had seen in the window.

"Would you look at this," she announced with a flourish, "we do have it. Size four, just what the doctor ordered. Would you like to try this on Edna?"

"Oh, I don't know. My fingers are a bit sticky, and I'm afraid to touch it. It's so lovely, I'd hate to get something on it."

"Well of course you would," Pauline agreed. "Why don't you just head on back to the restroom and wash your hands if that would make you more comfortable. I'll just set this aside for you."

As Edna entered the tiny toilet, she noticed her reflection in the cracked and coppered mirror above the sink. She recognized the tired circles and crow's feet near her eyes, but the excitement she saw was new. She placed both hands on the sink and looked at herself for a moment before she announced, "I'm going to do it!"

Edna dried her hands and then marched back out to the counter and retrieved the dress. She entered the small dressing room and after slipping out of her uniform, pulled the new dress on, buttoned it all the way up, and donned the jacket. She was almost afraid to walk out to where the three-sided mirror was located, fearful that she would look foolish. When she finally looked at her dressed reflection she was unable to suppress a smile. After a moment, she twirled slightly in order to see the back and in one of the only purely sensual acts of her life, to just watch as the skirt swirled around her calves.

"Oh Edna," the heavy set Pauline remarked with undisguised admiration, "I just hate you. Here we are, the same age, and you're a perfect size four, and that dress," she finished with emphasis, "was just made for you. Please, tell me you're going to buy it."

"Well," Edna seemed to be hedging, "if I do, I'll have to put it on layaway."

"That's just fine," Pauline responded, "I'd be happy to hold that for you."

First, Edna returned to the dressing room and reemerged a minute later wearing her uniform and carrying the dress. It took a few minutes, but when they were almost finished with the paperwork, Pauline asked Edna how much she wanted to put down to hold the dress.

"Eight dollars," Edna responded, then a surprised look came onto her face as she recalled she had a dollar in her purse when she went to work that morning, "no wait, nine dollars, in fact, nine dollars and thirty-eight cents."

"Nine dollars and thirty-eight cents," Pauline replied with confusion, "but Edna, that only leaves one dollar and ninety seven cents due even after we add the tax."

"If it was another twenty-five cents I'd still need to put it on layaway. I wasn't planning to shop when I left the house this morning. I'll bring the rest in after my next shift."

"Edna," Pauline countered, "I've known you since first grade. I'm not about to hold onto a dress for which you owe less than two dollars for two days or two hours. You take this with you. Then come pay me next time you're in."

"Pauline, I don't want that, it would be like you extending credit to me," Edna answered.

"That's not it at all. I just want you to wear that dress. Consider it advertising. Anyone who sees you in it will want to come here and see if we have something that could make them look as pretty as you did when you were wearing it just now. We won't be able to keep anything in the store. Plus," Pauline finished, "I want you to take this with it."

"What?" Edna asked.

"It's lipstick that I swear is exactly the same color as the red in the periwinkles in the print. I noticed it when we got those dresses in. It would normally cost seventy eight cents, but I want you to take it."

"I couldn't do that."

"Oh yes you can," Pauline responded as she carefully laid out tissue paper in a dress box and folded the dress into it and closed the top. She tucked the lipstick into Edna's apron pocket.

Less than a minute later, Edna was walking down the street with the disquieting bump of the box against her leg. Each movement seemed a cadence of ridicule, "What the hell," it seemed to say, "have you done," it finished.

"Now comes the hard part," she said to herself as she turned east on Second Street and headed home.

IV

"Where have you been?" Lucerne Pryor snapped from the dining room as soon as Edna entered the boarding house's front door. She didn't even turn around to see. "You've been off work for an hour. Dinner's almost ready and the table's not even set. Do Clarisse and I have to do everything around this place?"

"Well, I'm home now, Momma. No harm's been done," Edna answered as she slipped the box into the hall closet. She immediately went to the kitchen. The instant she opened the door, Clarisse handed her the stainless flat ware and napkins they used every day. Edna re-emerged an instant later and began setting the places.

Dinner was served every night at exactly 5:45 p.m. Anyone arriving after Lucerne took her place would not be fed. It was an ironclad rule of the house, enforced with typical Lucerne efficiency, since she could almost always tell if leftovers had been pilfered. The instant the kitchen was clean following the evening meal, Lucerne locked the room.

The meals at Pryor House were not cheerful affairs, but the food was good. Because Lucerne Pryor considered it her primary function in life to suppress the natural ebullience of her tenants, they rarely stayed more than a year. Those who did usually confessed that it was the food, and not the ambiance, that kept them there. When the students were behaving, Lucerne turned her attention to the humiliation of her daughter. Tonight the boys were quiet.

"What's in the box?" Lucerne demanded when the food had been served.

Edna started in surprise and kept her eyes on her plate. She should have known she couldn't put the dress into the closet without her mother seeing it.

"A dress," Edna replied as calmly as she could.

"A dress," Lucerne mocked her. "Why would you need a dress? You have a dress for church. What dress?"

"The one in the . . .," Edna began.

". . . window at Baker's," Lucerne finished in a sarcastic tone. "Oh you stupid girl. You'll look like a whore in that dress."

The young men at the table made no pretense of ignoring the exchange as their heads swiveled between the women as though they were watching a tennis match.

"Don't Momma," Edna requested.

"Don't Momma," Lucerne parroted snidely, "don't Momma, don't Momma, don't you 'don't Momma' me. You had no right to spend that kind of money on a dress you don't need and can't wear."

"I can wear it, Momma. I will wear it," Edna replied calmly.

"No," Lucerne demanded sharply, "you cannot wear it. Not in this town you won't. You'll look like a whore, and I won't have it!"

Edna stood; leaving her almost untouched dinner on the plate, she walked to the closet, retrieved the box holding her dress and then began climbing the stairs.

"Whore!" Lucerne shouted after her, "whore, whore."

Edna climbed slowly up the stairs, struggling to maintain her dignity under the onslaught of her mother's imprecations. When she arrived at her room on the third floor, she changed into her robe and walked back down one flight to the bathroom. She bathed and then returned to her room where she dressed in a clean bra, panties, and slip. She then positioned herself in front of the mirror on the old fashioned dressing table and slipped on the dress, carefully fastening each of the tiny pearl-like buttons. When she was finished, she brushed her hair, pulled on the light blue jacket and headed for the door. Just before she walked out, she returned to the closet and removed the lipstick from the pocket of her apron, grabbed five dollars from the coffee can that served as her bank jammed them into her purse, and walked out.

At the exact moment Edna was leaving her room, one of the student tenants was entering his. He smiled and said, "You look very nice tonight, Miss P."

"Thank you, Leon," she replied.

"Where are you going?" he asked.

"To the movies," she replied.

"On Wednesday?" Leon asked. "The theater's not open tonight."

"I'm going into the city," Edna replied at the exact moment in which she thought of it. Then as if explaining it to herself, she continued, "What the heck, I'm not working tomorrow."

"Well, have a good time then," Leon advised her. Edna started down the stairs.

As soon as Lucerne finished her dinner each night she retired to her first floor bedroom. Thereafter, for two hours, the old woman always listened to the radio, usually set with sufficient volume to awaken the dead. Right then it was blaring out war news Edna suspected would be audible in Germany, but certainly by every tenant in the house.

Edna walked out the front door and began retracing her steps from earlier towards Edmond's business district. At the corner of First and Broadway, the Interurban streetcar picked up passengers every 15 minutes all day and night. The streetcars ran from the turnaround in Edmond, all the way to Norman almost fifty miles away. In the middle, lay Oklahoma City, and Edna's knees were shaking a little as she realized that in all her life she had never been there after dark or for that matter alone.

V

When the streetcar arrived, Edna paid her fare and sat primly with her back straight and her purse on her lap as the old car rattled and wheezed its way towards Oklahoma City. As was usually the case, there was a Daily Oklahoman newspaper on the car left by an earlier rider. Edna picked it up and began studying the movie ads to determine where she was going to go. "Hello Frisco, Hello" with John Payne and Alice Faye was playing at the Tower Theater which had the added attraction of being the venue closest to Edmond. Once the decision of which theater to attend was settled, she spent the rest of the ride reading the paper she had found.

Edna's favorite part of the paper was the want ad section. Because she frequently fantasized about taking a new and more interesting job, she always read them with care. Since the start of the war, the paper always contained lots of ads for companies needing help. Tonight, there was a large ad from the United States Employment Service. It called for men from 18 to 60 and women aged 21 to 45 as either journeymen, apprentices or trainees in almost all of the building trades as well as guards, to apply now for immediate placement. At the bottom of the ad was the mysterious promise that qualified applicants would receive travel, housing and food allowances. Edna read the ad several times without discovering where the workers would be traveling. As she often did, Edna tore out the ad, folded it, and put it in her purse even though she knew she lacked the nerve to ever even apply.

While her purse was open, she noticed the lipstick. As carefully as the lurching streetcar allowed, Edna used her compact mirror to apply the beautiful red shade Pauline Baker had promised would bring the red in the dress' periwinkles to her lips.

Edna dismounted from the streetcar on Classen near 23rd Street and began walking the few blocks to the Tower Theater. When she was still 20 yards or more from the box office, Edna noticed a man studying the marquee above the cashier's head and then returning his wallet to his pocket. When she herself arrived she saw the problem. The movie began at 7:10 p.m. and it was now 7:45. The next showing wouldn't be until 9:20.

"Oh dear," Edna exclaimed to herself.

"That's precisely what I said," the man offered.

"What," Edna replied, somewhat shocked to be addressed by a man she didn't know.

"Oh dear," the man explained in a friendly voice. "That's just what I said. It is over an hour and a half until the next showing and I was just lucky enough to find a place to park. I'm totally at loose ends."

Edna looked down to avoid eye contact. She was mortified to realize she had no idea what to say to the man. *He doesn't look like a wolf. In fact, quite the opposite,* Edna thought. He was about her age, wearing a very nice, probably prewar three piece suit, that still hadn't seen too much wear, an expensive hat, glasses, and across his middle was a very thick and expensive looking watch chain. He was slightly less than average in height, with a build that was neither thin nor stocky, *purely average,* Edna thought.

After a moment's silence, the man tipped his hat to Edna and began walking down the street. Edna watched him as he departed. Suddenly she realized that she was standing alone at the box office. It would have been easy to go ahead and buy a ticket and enter the theater. The movies ran continuously, and she could have simply departed when the film returned to the point in which she had entered the theater, but Edna hated to see the end of a movie before the beginning. Suddenly, the image of her untouched dinner came into her mind and she realized she was hungry. She recalled that the Oklahoma City Borden's ice cream plant maintained a retail outlet only a few blocks away on Walker Avenue. She determined that to go there and eat an ice cream sundae was the most pleasant option she had to use the hour and a half before the movie began again.

The walk was longer than she thought, and several times Edna considered just going back to the Interurban stop and returning to Edmond. With each step, that option became less attractive, until finally she saw the welcoming lights of the Borden store.

The dairy bar was filled with customers, and after Edna finally got her sundae, all of the tables were occupied. Suddenly, a man's voice said, "There's an empty chair here, Ma'am."

Edna looked up into the face of the very same man who had been at the Tower Theater's box office fifteen minutes earlier. He had half-risen to his feet in a gesture of civility, but Edna stood frozen for so long that he finally slumped back into his chair. Immediately, he rose fully to his feet and gestured at the chair opposite his with an outstretched arm.

The prospect of sitting down with a total stranger in an unfamiliar place had quite literally never occurred in Edna's life before. She was hesitant of course, but her only realistic options were to put down her sundae and walk out, or eat standing up. Finally, after an interminable period in which she was certain that every eye in the store was riveted on her, she sat down at the man's table. Once she was settled, Edna took a small bite of her sundae, and then placed her hands in her lap.

"Chocolate," the man said after a few moments.

"What?" Edna asked as though awakened from a dream.

"Chocolate," he repeated. "I was just noticing what a coincidence it was that we both ordered chocolate sundaes."

Edna said nothing.

A moment later the man continued, "I guess it's not that much of a coincidence after all. It looks like over half the people in here are eating chocolate sundaes."

Edna risked a look around the crowded restaurant as though verifying the truth of what he said, but she still didn't reply.

"I'm Nate Daniels," the man informed her.

"Hello, Nate," Edna replied, but neither looked directly at him nor gave her own name.

The man sat quietly for a moment before he continued. "Can I ask you something?"

"O.K.," Edna replied.

"Do you always talk this much?"

Edna smiled politely at his poor attempt at humor. "Usually," she replied.

"You know," he continued, "for some men that would be a problem. In my case, I sort of talk for a living. I'm a drummer."

Edna wore a look of confusion for a moment. "Drummers talk for a living?" she asked in the longest exchange since she had sat down.

"Holy mackerel," the man replied, "you can speak in entire sentences."

Edna looked at her hands but a small smile touched the edges of her lips.

"The kind of drummer I am is a salesman, not a musician. It's an old fashioned term, but it's one I like."

"What do you sell?" Edna asked.

"Machine tools and aviation parts," Nate replied. "There is a world of aviation along the arc between Tulsa and Dallas with Oklahoma City right in the middle. Right here we have the Naval Aviation facilities down in Norman, Tinker Field here as well as the Will Rogers field out west of town. We make parts for several Air Corps models, but we are becoming much more involved in Navy planes as well."

"We?" Edna asked.

"Well, our firm. I am in business with my brother. He's the brains of the outfit. He graduated with an engineering degree from Oklahoma A&M right up there in Stillwater. We started in the oil business, but the war has made what we do much more specialized to aviation.

"He actually started the business. I was working for an office supplies firm doing for them the same as I'm now doing for him. Selling is selling. Anyway, when the firm started growing he asked me to come in with him and I jumped at the chance. I'm too old for the military, and this is probably the only thing I can do to help win the war. I like that."

Edna looked at him. Nate seemed very nice and she admired his comment about helping in his small way to win the war. It was so easy to sit here with him. The non-stop manner in which he talked made no demands on her at all. She decided to start counting off seconds of silence to see how long it would take for him to start up again.

One Mississippi, two Mississippi. . .

"I should probably move to Oklahoma City since it's in the middle of my territory," Nate began, "although I guess it doesn't make any difference where I hang my hat. My children are grown, both boys are in the service, and my daughter has a family of her own."

I should have realized, Edna thought to herself, *he was bound to be married.*

"Can I ask you something?" Nate began after a pause too short to measure.

"OK," Edna replied.

"When I first saw you at the theater, I just assumed you were waiting for your husband. Now I notice you're not wearing a ring."

Edna dropped her hands into her lap, a crimson blush began creeping up her neck. Edna was so stupefied by this development she didn't know what to do. She simply stared back down at her hands.

"I'm sorry," Nate began, "I didn't mean to make you self-conscious."

"You didn't," Edna lied.

"Then eat your sundae. The ice cream is melting."

"I was almost finished anyway," Edna replied, raising neither her hands nor her eyes.

The silence became deafening, and finally the man resumed speaking with, "I'm sorry. I've made you uncomfortable, the very last thing I wanted to do. Please excuse me," Nate said, standing to leave.

"Don't - go," Edna requested haltingly, "it - it - it's me that should apologize."

Nate slid back into his seat.

"I'm afraid I'm not at my best in unfamiliar circumstances. I didn't mean to act as though you were Jack the Ripper."

"I can understand that perfectly," Nate responded.

"I shouldn't even be here," Edna explained.

"But why?" Nate asked.

"I am so out of my element," Edna continued.

"Now that, I cannot understand," Nate replied in counterpoint. "You look like you'd be perfectly at home in any circumstances."

Edna smiled at her hands before she replied even while still looking down, "You're a most generous liar."

Nate laughed. She liked it. It was a genuine and friendly laugh and Edna could tell it was directed at himself and not her.

"Well, OK," he confessed, "you're probably right. I must admit it's rare for me to see an unaccompanied woman of my own generation, although you're clearly a good deal younger than me," he added graciously. "I so rarely have someone to talk to on these trips and I have enjoyed our visit tremendously."

"Where do you live?" Edna asked.

"Dallas, but I come to the city and go from here to Tulsa several times a quarter. I don't like to drink alone in bars, yet I hate to just sit around my hotel room at night. That's why the movies have become so important to me."

"Do you go to the movies a lot?" Edna asked.

"Oh I love the movies," he replied instantly.

"Me too," she agreed.

"What's been your favorite?" he asked.

"I used to think it was 'Gone with the Wind,' " Edna began, "although I really loved 'Mrs. Minever,' "

"Used to think," Nate prodded.

"I saw "Here Comes Mr. Jordan" about the prize fighter that gets taken to heaven too early and comes back as a millionaire. That has become my favorite film of all time." Edna's face was lit up with excitement for the first time in the conversation. It took years from her face.

"You want to be a prize fighter?" Nate asked, seeming incredulous at the thought.

"No," she began as though explaining and then saw the glint in his eye, "oh you silly," Edna interjected then was silent a moment before she continued, "but wouldn't you like a chance to start over as someone else sometimes."

"I was only teasing you," Nate confessed. "I guess most of us would like to wipe the slate clean occasionally."

"I would," Edna agreed.

"But why," Nate asked, "when you seem to have so much going for you."

"I'll spare you the details since I need to be going if I'm going to get back to the theater before I'm late for the 9:20 showing." She stood and Nate reached out to her.

"Please," he asked, "let me take you in my car. It is quite a long walk, and we can be there in plenty of time."

"Oh, I couldn't," Edna began, but then thought better of it, "OK, my feet are killing me from the walk over here. I'd love a ride."

"OK," he said, "but I have a condition."

"A condition?" she asked.

"What's your name?"

VI

When they arrived at the theater, Nate bought their tickets, offered Edna popcorn or a drink which she refused, and they sat together without speaking in the middle of the crowded show. When it was over, Edna offered her hand to Nate.

"Thank you so much," she said, "I hate to go to the movies alone."

"I've had a wonderful time," he acknowledged. "I know I scarcely know you, and it seems like the greatest collection of circumstances that we ever got started talking at all, but I'd like to know you better. May I call you the next time I am in the city?"

"I don't think that would be a good idea," Edna said.

Nate seemed to ignore her answer. "Look let's go somewhere and get a cup of coffee."

Edna began to demur, but at that moment they saw the lights of a small café and made their way inside. Edna smiled at the similarity to the Wide-A-Wake. They took a booth. The waitress approached with a Pyrex pot and Nate nodded.

"None for me," Edna announced.

"What about it?" Nate asked. "Let me call you next time I'm here."

"I almost never come into the city," Edna began.

"I know where Edmond is," Nate countered.

"No, no," Edna replied immediately, "that wouldn't do." After a moment she continued, "Actually, I was thinking about your family."

"I'm a widower if that is what you're worried about. It is the reason I said it doesn't really matter where I live.

"I'm sorry for your loss," Edna replied.

"It was many years ago," Nate replied. "I still miss her at times. I often wonder what might have happened to all of us had she lived. The boys were seven and nine, my daughter was thirteen, the very age when a mother would have been so important."

"That's so sad," Edna acknowledged.

Nate shook his head. "Let's speak of something else. Would that be all right?"

"Of course," Edna replied, but there was little else to speak of now.

"I tell you what," Nate interjected before the lapse of his customary two-second pause, "let's go dancing."

"Dancing?" Edna responded. "I'm afraid I wouldn't have a clue about how to do that."

"It doesn't matter," Nate responded, "I'll show you what to do." Nate stood and took Edna's hand. "I'm staying at the Black Hotel. Guy Sanderson and his Orchestra play every night in the Silver Lounge. They play 'til midnight," he looked at his watch, "that's almost an hour. Let's go."

Edna allowed herself to be led out of the café. In a few minutes they were back in Nate's car driving south. When they arrived at the hotel, they took the elevator to the Silver Lounge and Nate paid the Maitre d' a dollar for a table. They ordered drinks and within moments, Nate was leading Edna onto the dance floor.

As Nate confidently pulled Edna towards the dance floor of the seedy nightclub, she smiled to think how far she'd come since her visit to Baker's Dry Goods a few hours earlier. The ceiling of the lounge was impregnated with small bits of mirror. The twinkling reflection caused by the lights on the bandstand distracted her as she came gracelessly into Nate's arms while looking up at the ceiling. She stepped on his foot.

Instead of asking his pardon, she said, "It looks like we're dancing under the stars." The only other nightclubs Edna had ever seen were movie sets from the musicals she attended with her mother. To her, the cheesy little room was beautiful, Nate smiled at her enjoyment.

True to her promise, Edna had no clue what she was doing on a dance floor.

"Excuse me," she said again after stepping on his foot for the tenth time.

"Hey, it's all right," he responded, "I've been walking on the bottoms of them all day. The tops could use some work. Look, let's try this. Take off your shoes and stand on my feet for the next number. You're light enough that I think I could dance for both of us. That will give you an idea of the steps. In no time you'll be able to do it on your own."

Obligingly, Edna removed her shoes and came back into his arms. For a few bars she allowed Nate to hold her until she realized with a shock just how close they were. She could feel him - down there. She broke from his arms and walked back to their table and sat down to replace her shoes.

"I'm sorry," Nate began after he caught back up with her.

"Don't be," Edna replied, "I'm afraid I don't know much about that sort of thing . . ."

"Would you like for me to take you home?" Nate asked her.

"As I was saying," she began again with a small smile and a look that avoided contact with his eyes, "I'm afraid I don't know too much about that sort of thing, but I do believe it is more or less a sign of desire. If I have fostered any of that in anybody during the past twenty years I'm unaware of it. I was just surprised, I suppose. I had a chance to put it into perspective just now on my way back over here." Edna paused for a moment before she continued, finally looking directly into Nate's eyes, "I thought about it and I've decided I liked it. You said you were staying in this hotel. I want to see your room."

"Check," Nate said to the waiter. He was already standing, and an instant later, he had his hat in his hand.

VII

The next morning, Edna awakened Nate long before daylight and they made love slowly, as though they had no place to go. When they were finished, Edna got up and took a shower, luxuriating in the heat and steam of water that didn't turn ice cold within moments of becoming warm in the first place. She both washed her body and examined it. She knew it didn't look different, but she felt different in it.

When she emerged from the shower, Edna wrapped one towel around herself and another over her hair. She then sat down in front of the mirror over the sink and studied herself in the glass. She knew she had some decisions to make, and she wanted to make them now, here in this unfamiliar place. She realized if she waited until she got home, the habits of her life would reclaim her. When she walked out of the bathroom, she was fully dressed. She could see Nate's disappointment and it caused her to smile.

"I come to Oklahoma City pretty often," Nate began, "and I want to see you again."

"I don't think so, Nate," Edna replied.

"But why?" he responded. "Last night was wonderful, and unless I'm crazy, I think it was wonderful for you too."

"It _was_ wonderful," Edna laid her hand on Nate's cheek. "But I won't begin a relationship with a married man."

"But I told you, I - I'm a widower." Edna could see the red creep up his neck. It spoke as eloquently as a confession. She had a quick mental image of his wife at home waiting for him. A tremendous pang attacked Edna's heart now that she knew for sure. A day earlier, she might have taken comfort in knowing that she really wasn't that sort of woman, but right now she didn't know what sort she was.

"I know you did," Edna responded without emotion, "but I didn't believe you."

"Then why," he gestured in a way that took in the bed and the rest of the room.

"Because I wanted to," Edna explained, and with the words still coming out of her mouth, realized she was telling the truth. "Now get up and get dressed, Nate, I need a ride," she finished.

"Sure, anywhere, do you want me to drive you home?" Nate asked.

"No," Edna said and shook her head, "I'll take the street car later. Right now I need a ride to the U.S. Employment Service." In response to the quizzical look on his face, she pulled the want ad from the previous night's newspaper from her purse and showed it to him. Her face was lit with excitement when she said, "They are doing something really big, Nate and it's someplace else. I don't even know what it is; I only know I want to be part of it."

"But how do you know they'll hire you?" he countered. "What if it's something you don't want to do? How can you just take off like this?"

"That's a lot of questions Nate. Right now I don't know the answers to any of them, but I never will know if I just go home. I wish I didn't even have to go back to Edmond, but I owe somebody a dollar and ninety-seven cents and I want to pay it. After that, I need to go to my house and collect my things." She smiled ruefully before she continued with a small laugh and a shake of her head, "I can only imagine the reception I'll get after staying out all night, but you know, it will have no impact on me now. It's time for a change in my life. Thank God it's not too late, but it's sure as hell not too early either. You helped me, Nate, believe it or not, and I appreciate it. Now it's time for me to get started with whatever comes next.

"Now get dressed, I need to get going."

Chapter Ten

Clara

I

"*O*h please, Janice, please, please, please," Clara begged for the tenth time. Clara Beech had been working on Janice since receiving a long distance call from Tinker Field on the café's phone an hour earlier. Janice looked heavenward. In fifteen minutes their shift would end and she could put a stop to this by making a break for home.

Even now, Clara Beech could scarcely believe how close she was to seeing her boyfriend, Bill Otis. All she needed was for Janice to take her.

"Clara, does the term 3 gallons a week mean anything to you at all?" Janice asked referring to the A sticker that was glued to the windshield of the Lookabaugh's Chevrolet.

"The problem is gasoline?" Clara countered.

Suddenly cautious, Janice responded, "At least one of them is. It's over 20 miles to Tinker Field from here. That's almost a gallon going and another coming back. What if somebody had an emergency? When my sister had her baby, she and her husband saved coupons for weeks to make sure they had enough to get to the doctor's office and the hospital when the time came. Wasting our gas ration just doesn't make sense."

"What if I got you some gasoline?" Clara demanded. "Would you take me then."

"Where would you get gasoline?"

"Answer the question," Clara insisted.

"Legal gasoline?"

"Legal, schmeegal," Clara said, "answer the question."

"It's not my car," Janice countered.

"But you have it right now," Clara whined. "Your parents don't need it tonight. I need it desperately. Do you want me to be an old maid?"

"Clara, you're not going to be an old maid."

"Janice, Bill is going to be here one night; one night, TOnight. I have no other way to get there. My family doesn't even own a car or I'd steal it at gunpoint. I'll get you some gas."

"How?"

"A service station silly. There are always ways to get stuff."

"You mean black market."

"Oh no," Clara responded sarcastically, "Miss Goody-Two-Shoes is being introduced to the world of sin."

"I'm not a goody-two-shoes," Janice countered.

"You are too."

"I am not."

"Are."

"Am not." By now Janice had crossed her arms over her chest and her lower lip was sticking out. Suddenly realizing how ridiculous the conversation had become the two girls were staring at each other and simultaneously burst out laughing.

"OK," Janice yielded, "I tell you what. You provide the gas and I'll ask my parents if it's OK."

"Ask your parents?" Clara exploded. "Are you crazy? They'll never say yes. Besides, you're 20 years old for cryin' out loud. What are you asking your parents for?"

"As I told you a moment ago, Clara, it's not my car. Besides, you might be surprised at what my parents would say."

"Well if they say yes, I'll sure be surprised."

Janice picked up the phone behind the cash register. Her father picked it up on the third ring.

"Daddy," Janice began, "Clara's boyfriend is an Army pilot whose plane is remaining over night at Tinker Field. She wants to go see him but cannot get there without a ride. She claims she can get gasoline for the trip. May I drive her down there and bring her home?"

"Legal gasoline?" John asked.

"Honestly, I don't know. But if I had to guess I'd say no."

Clara had put her head next to the phone so she could hear. "Are you trying to mess this up?" she hissed.

"Is that Clara?" John Lookabaugh asked.

"Yes, Daddy."

"Put her on."

"Oh my gosh," Clara gasped, almost falling over one of the stools as she backed away from the phone as though it had grown fangs.

"Oh quit being such a baby," Janice replied with her hand over the mouthpiece, "he can't bite you through the phone lines."

"Hello Mr. Lookabaugh," Clara squeaked hesitantly.

For the next two minutes John Lookabaugh put Clara through the 3rd degree. He wanted to know where they were going, when they would return, the name of Clara's boyfriend, his unit, and hometown. To each question, Clara looked skyward and surrendered the information. He then asked to speak to Janice.

"OK," he said.

Janice tried to say thanks, but her reply was drowned out by the joyous squeal released by Clara. When Clara was finished, Janice said, "Thanks, I think."

When they had broken the connection, Marge Lookabaugh asked her husband what that had all been about. He told her in a few words, and finished with, "I told her 'OK.'"

"Good," Marge agreed, "she needs to go out. She's been a nun for three years."

"That's what I thought," he answered.

Clara was on the phone ten seconds after Janice relinquished the handset. It took several minutes for 2d Lt. Bill Otis to be found and then to get to the phone.

"Billy, I'm coming. We'll be there as soon as we can after work."

"How long is that?" Bill asked.

"Bathe, change, drive - at least an hour and a half. Let's say you meet us at the gate at 5:30," Clara responded.

"OK," he answered.

"I love you, Billy. Oh, and by the way," then too quickly for Janice to stop her, she rushed to a finish with, "Janice is bringing me, so bring a friend for her, OK? I'll see ya'." And she hung up the phone.

"No!" Janice demanded.

"Don't be silly. There are about 10,000 beautiful boys down there. Why should we waste all of them?"

"Clara, this is exactly what I didn't want."

"So you say," Clara responded, "look, what were you going to do, sit there all night with your hands in your lap? You won't have to marry him. We'll have dinner, then go dancing at the officer's club, then back home before our chariot turns into a pumpkin, OK?"

"You rat," Janice said, but she was smiling.

II

Less than two hours into her first shift at the Wide-A-Wake Café; Clara Beech had discovered an amazingly powerful weapon. Men thought waitresses were sexy. She had so rarely been a customer in a café or restaurant in her life that she'd never noticed this phenomenon before. Right after she started to work, she was winked at, pinched, ogled, leered at, and even approached. With the exception of the pinching, she loved every bit of it.

For her first 17 years, far longer than it had been true, Clara had been the perpetual ugly duckling in her classes at school. Held back in the third grade, she'd had one of her many growth spurts during her reprise year. Suddenly, she was head and shoulders taller than every other child in the class. In addition, she was heavy, a fact that made her a target to the most vicious humans alive, children who aren't different from their peers. Once when she'd tried to join some of her classmates at play, one of the girls had rebuffed her by saying, "What sort of name is Clara anyhow? My grandfather's cow is named Clara. Why don't you moo for us?" And her fate was sealed. She was 'Moo Cow Beech' for the rest of her school years.

Between the 8th and 9th grade, a miracle occurred. Clara Beech shot from 5'4" to 5'10" and from pudgy to slinky. Suddenly tall and slender, her self-image didn't change an iota. When Clara registered for her classes at Edmond High School, she came to the attention of Sarah Wiedekehr, the coach of every one of Edmond's distaff athletic programs, including the perennial also-ran Edmond High School girl's basketball team. To Sarah, once she looked past the gawkiness, Clara looked like an angel from God.

Clara wasn't inclined towards sports, so Coach Wiedekehr had the dual challenges of first getting her interested, and second, training the uncoordinated and poorly conditioned giant that had been suddenly put into her hands. When the coach initially approached Clara about joining the team, the girl had stared at her in shock, speechless to be wanted for anything. After a few moments of silence, Clara found her voice and refused to consider the offer to try out. As Clara ambled gracelessly away, Sarah thought she'd never seen a girl so in need of developing her athletic potential. Before Clara was out of sight, Coach Wiedekehr considered the girls who had tried out for the team, and realized she'd never needed a 5'10" center more in her life. Moo Cow Beech was just the sort of challenge she lived for.

It wasn't that Clara wasn't interested in sports. She loved sports. In her mind, she could see herself playing on the team the instant Coach Wiedekehr brought it up. The problem was that actually trying out for the team would occur on the wrong side of the reality line. Getting Clara interested in anything real was a bigger challenge than Coach Wiedekehr could have known. Clara was a girl whose fantasy life served almost all of her needs. In that world, she wasn't "Moo Cow Beech" she was simply Clara, or Princess Clara, or Nurse Clara, or Miss Beech, the much loved teacher, or movie star, or brave missionary sailing into Africa's jungles. Real life held so few attractions for Clara she spent as little time there as possible.

To her credit, Coach Wiedekehr never gave up, and on the last day of tryouts Clara walked nervously into the gym. In her fantasy lives, it usually took Clara about two minutes to fall in love. Well within the requisite time, she did it again, but this time it wasn't with an unattainable boy, it was with basketball. Clara loved the patterns, the symmetry, the tactics, the inexorable demands of the clock, even the squeak of sneakers on the hard wood floors. It was a passion she would retain her whole life.

Unfortunately, a life spent avoiding her peers at school and trying to remain invisible in a home with seven brothers and sisters, left Clara with few of the physical skills she needed to be a good athlete. Uncharacteristically, she refused to allow that to stop her. With a single-mindedness of purpose unlike anything before in her life, Clara set out to develop what she needed, and Sarah Wiedekehr never saw a girl more dedicated.

In a perfect world, Clara would have become an All-State Center as a reward for all of her hard work. In the life she actually lived, however, she never became the star athlete who crowded out so many of her other alter egos. Edmond didn't go to the State Championship game. But, Clara was still an important part of the team. She also learned how to interact with her teammates. Finally, somewhere in there the exercise combined with her natural body processes to turn 'Moo Cow Beech' into a tall, fit, tousle haired, blue-eyed blonde. This was the girl who met the patrons of the Wide-A-Wake Café when she'd come to work there two years earlier. Although no amount of attention would ever give her all the reassurance she needed, the lunch counter Romeo's served to temporarily salve some of her feelings of inadequacy. She never quit trying though, and after numerous attempts mostly focused on soldiers, Clara finally met Bill Otis, a boy on his way to flight school.

III

At 6:30, Janice drove up to Gate Number Two at Tinker Field. They were an hour late. The girls had spent much less time getting black market gasoline than Janice had thought possible, and much more time getting to the Army Air Corps Base, than either girl had expected. This had included about 20 minutes totally lost as they drove through Midwest City, the town built on Tinker Field's Western perimeter to support the base. Second Lieutenant Bill Otis, a tall, almost handsome young man from Redwood, California, was standing at the guard shack with another boy wearing the "pinks and greens" uniform of a first lieutenant in the Air Corps. Unlike Bill, who was wearing the popular frame cap, the other officer was wearing the "fore and aft" overseas cap.

Clara leapt from the car and ran to Bill. They kissed somewhat chastely in deference to the MP on duty, then all three of them walked to the car.

"We'd almost given up on you," Bill said.

"I was getting pretty frantic myself," Clara replied. "Neither of us had ever driven down here on our own before. I'm just glad we aren't passing a 'Welcome to Texas' sign about now."

Bill smiled as they approached the window of the Lookabaugh's Chevrolet.

"Janice," Clara gushed, "this is Bill Otis, Bill this is Janice Lookabaugh, and this is Bill's friend," she finished gesturing to the other young man.

"Charlie Morgan," Bill filled in. Then he added, "It's a pleasure to meet you Janice. You have no idea how much."

"My pleasure, Bill," Janice said as she leaned towards the passenger side window, "Clara has told me all about you."

"I can only imagine what that involved, since I don't know how she could have told you anything good about me," Bill said with a smile as he pulled Clara to his side.

"Charlie is Bill's pilot, Janice," Clara explained. "He commands the aircraft. I know that from Bill's letters, I just didn't know what he looked like. Bill, he's beautiful."

"In that case," Bill responded with a laugh as he pulled Clara closer to him, "keep your baby blues off of him."

"Bill and I are going to sit in back, Charlie, so you get up front with Janice and direct her to where we're going."

It took a while to get the girls checked onto the base. Finally they drove the car onto a small parking lot about a quarter mile from the gate and got out. They would ride a bus to the O'Club, which arrived within minutes, since several of them circled the base constantly all day and all night to service the various work schedules on Tinker Field. Once they arrived at the club, the foursome ate dinner, then repaired to the ballroom that was jammed with young men in uniform and girls in dresses of as many colors as the rainbow allowed. After they found a table and ordered drinks, gin and tonics for the men, a Rob Roy for Clara, and a Coke for Janice, Clara and Bill departed for the dance floor.

"Well," Charlie began after they were alone, "enough about me. Tell me about you now."

Janice smiled. In all the time they'd been together, Clara had done about 90 percent of the talking and Bill almost all of the remainder.

"Would you like to dance?' Charlie asked.

"Let me sit this one out. I'm afraid most of my dancing was prewar," Janice explained. "I better start with a slow number; we'll probably have fewer casualties."

"That suits me," Charlie responded. Their drinks arrived, and Charlie wisely ordered another round since it was clear the wait staff was inadequate to the crowd. The drinks arrived in paper cups.

"Can I tell you something without you deciding it's a judgment?" Janice asked.

"Sure," Charlie responded.

"This isn't exactly what I thought an evening at the Officer's Club would be like. Not that I don't like it, it's just different."

"No cut glass chandeliers, crystal stemware, and sterling service?"

"Yeah, I guess."

"I don't know what it was like before the war," Charlie began. "I've only been an officer for a year, but I suspect all those things are in storage somewhere. The war creates a wholesale atmosphere for everything. The service has gone from years of doing without, sort of all tradition and no progress, to all progress and no traditions. There is too much of everything all of a sudden, and it's tough for the service to digest it all. I can only imagine how chagrined some of the long service types are to watch their cherished standards being diluted by guys like me who make First Lieutenant in 6 months instead of six years."

"That's a pretty big answer to a comment about crystal stemware," Janice chided him.

"That's me," Charlie responded with a wry smile, "why use 10 words when 150 will do the same thing."

Janice chuckled. Almost despite herself she began to relax as she discovered she liked Charlie. At that moment the band began playing "I'll Be Seeing You" and Charlie held up his arms in pantomime of dance. Janice stood and they worked their way into the swirling hubbub of dancers already on the floor.

"Have you lived in Oklahoma City a long time?" Charlie asked.

"I don't live in Oklahoma City at all. I live in Edmond. It's a small town about 20 miles north of here, and I've lived there or right outside of it all my life."

Charlie smiled at that, and as they danced told Janice he was from Casper, Wyoming where he'd been raised on a ranch that was lost to the bank the year he turned 13. His parents had then moved to Oregon, then finally to Washington State where they both now worked in a defense plant. Before the war, Charlie had attended Washington State University for two years, where he played baseball and majored in journalism. Janice commented on the number of things they had in common in their backgrounds. Janice didn't mention Tommy.

For two hours their conversation was interrupted only when they walked onto the dance floor themselves, or when Clara and Bill returned to bolt down their drinks, order another round and then return to the dancing themselves. Janice couldn't remember when she'd been such a chatterbox and the hours flew by. Suddenly, as Janice was beginning to worry about the time, Bill and Clara seemed to materialize at Charlie's side.

"Come on," Bill said, "we're blowing this pop stand." With that he grabbed Charlie's elbow as Clara was hauling on Bill's other hand. Almost as he was pulled out of reach, Charlie reached out and grabbed Janice's hand and the small chain of humans began working its way through the multicolored mob towards the large double doors that led to the street.

When they were finally outside waiting for the bus that would return them to the automobile, Clara began nudging Bill's arm in the classic "tell them" gesture. Finally he relented.

"Charlie, old buddy, Janice, you two are the first to know. Clara and I are going to get hitched."

"What?" Janice gasped.

"When?" Charlie finished.

"Soon. Right away. As soon as we can set it up. We'll get our blood tests, she'll come down to Kelly Field and we'll tie the knot."

"No," Janice said before she realized she was speaking instead of just thinking her reaction to the news.

"What do you mean 'No' Janice?" Clara demanded.

"Clara, you're barely 19 years old. Bill is going overseas soon; you said so yourself. Why not wait until he gets back?"

"What are you my mother all of a sudden?" Clara snapped.

"No, I - I - I'm sorry, Clara. Congratulations, really. I guess I was just being a drudge."

"Me too," Charlie said, "Congratulations." He looked at Janice, then looked heavenwards as if to say, "Whoo boy!"

By this time the bus arrived and the two couples were quiet until they were deposited at the parking lot that held the car. Clara and Bill fell into the back seat with Clara pushing the uncomplaining aviator down onto the cushions.

Janice started the car and began driving, but soon realized that no amount of engine noise was going to drown out the sound of Clara and Bill's kisses, fumblings, and whispers, or the snaps, zippers, and buttons that were being released in the back. Almost frantic to get out of the car, Janice parked at the first convenient spot and fled. Charlie climbed out on his side as well.

"Let's give 'em a few minutes, what do you say?" Charlie suggested.

"How long will they need?" Janice asked with an embarrassed chuckle.

"Probably not as long as Bill would tell you."

A smile played invisibly on Janice's lips in the dark. There was something about Charlie that reminded her she didn't need to be so serious all of the time. This was Clara's night, not hers and she was Clara's friend, not her mother. She began to relax.

They walked along in silence for a moment before Janice remarked, "I'm really not that big of a prude, I swear, but does this marriage thing sound like a good idea to you?"

"It wouldn't be a good idea for me, but then I'm not the one doing it. Bill and Clara are. They're the only ones who can ever know if it's a really good idea, but since you asked, I'd say the odds are stacked against it. At least they have known each other for several months. I've known guys to get married to girls they've known for a few days. The whole world's gone nuts, Janice, why should 20 year olds be exempt?"

Just ahead of them, one of the base's many bus stops beckoned them. For several minutes they sat silently side by side on the bench. Finally, for reasons she couldn't begin to understand, Janice began to tell Charlie about Tommy and Pearl Harbor.

"One of the problems with wars," Charlie said when she was finished, "is that they produce more history than we can consume while they are going on. Pearl Harbor, Wake Island, Doolittle's raid on Tokyo, Midway, those events are the stuff of legends. Yet each of them is overshadowed by whatever comes next. I don't know what I think about heroes right now, but if they exist, then guys meeting the enemy when they had no reason to expect him and fighting back with whatever they could get their hands on seems heroic to me."

Janice didn't respond. The serendipitous bench they'd found faced the runway and suddenly, the thunderous roar and then the sight of a B-17 taking off on a night training flight surprised Janice. She watched as the aircraft's lights faded and then disappeared. She recalled Jerry Harper's most recent letter letter wishing she could watch a B-17 take off. It was, indeed, an awesome spectacle.

"It seems like an amazing feat," Janice observed.

"What's that?" Charlie asked as he absently critiqued the efforts of the pilots.

"To make something that large do just what you want."

"It doesn't all of the time. Sometimes it does just what it wants. The trick is to stay ahead of it and smooth the way."

"I don't believe that. You're just being modest," Janice responded.

"Modest? Young lady I'll have you know I am a United States Army Air Corps aviator, qualified in multiengine and instrument flight. There isn't a modest bone in my body. It's against regulations."

"That part I believe - especially the bit about regulations. I don't know, maybe it was that little speech about history and legends, but you seem different to me somehow."

"No way. I'm just another girl crazy on his way to Europe." He paused for a moment as he looked at his hands, clasped between his knees, then looked sideways at her and continued. "It's you that's different. If you were more like Clara, I'd have already told you the story about how scared I was and how I'd never been with a woman, and that I was afraid of dying without being a "real" man. Heck, by now I might even have proposed to you."

A cold grip seized Janice. "Is that what Bill has done to Clara?" she asked instantly.

"No, no way. I'm sorry," Charlie replied a little flustered at his own maladroit comment, "I guess that hits pretty close to home doesn't it? I shouldn't have planted that thought in your mind; I didn't think how it would sound. I really believe he's serious. That doesn't mean it's a good idea, but I do believe he's planning to marry her."

Janice looked as closely into Charlie's face as the darkness permitted. *The problem with these Air Corps types,* Janice thought, *is that they are all so blasted smooth. Fear of death lubricates them over all the social conventions.* All of her good feelings from a few minutes earlier had now evaporated, and Janice now added Clara to the list of those she had to worry about.

The ignition of a cigarette in the Chevrolet made Janice realize Clara and Bill had completed whatever it was they'd set out to do in the back seat.

"We'd better be going," Janice announced a trifle stiffly.

"OK," Charlie replied, "but let's make some noise so they know we're returning to the car."

At the gate, Janice waited five more minutes while Clara and Bill said goodbye. Finally they were on their way home. Clara was bundled in the corner formed by the front seat and the door.

"Mrs. William Otis," Clara recited, "doesn't that sound wonderful?"

"Wonderful," Janice agreed without enthusiasm. Clara didn't even notice.

Janice didn't suffer from the delusion that Clara was perfectly innocent. There had been too many soldiers, too many asides and veiled comments. The glow on Clara's face could mean anything, Janice determined, from true love to having gotten what she wanted as much as Bill had. Somehow, though, Janice just couldn't leave it alone.

"Clara, how sure are you?"

"How sure of what?"

"That this is it."

Clara snorted, "I'm not."

"Then why did you say yes?" Janice wanted to know.

"Janice," Clara responded as though speaking with a child, "I have seven brothers and sisters. I am stuck in the middle of all that. I've never had my own room, never even had my own bed. When Cleo Noe gave me my uniform to wear to work, it was the first garment I ever had that one of my sisters hadn't worn before me. How sure do you think I need to be for my life with Bill to be better than the one I have now?"

"The war won't last forever. Bill won't be an officer after the war. What happens then?"

"Janice, you are such an old grandma. Bill has two years of college. He's young, good looking, and he told me he loves me about 25 times tonight. Believe me, I haven't been told by somebody - anybody, that they love me 25 times in my whole life. This may not be perfect love, but its close enough for me."

Janice drove in silence for several minutes. Finally she couldn't stand it any longer.

"Can I ask one more thing without making you crazy?" Janice asked.

"Shoot."

"What if Bill is as matter-of-fact about all of this as you are?"

"So?"

"OK, what if he doesn't really plan to come back and marry you."

"Then you and I had a really fun night," Clara said with finality.

"Are you serious?"

"Look, I am planning to marry Bill. If I'm wrong about his intentions, you're gonna' see some pretty serious heartache. Maybe not like you right after Pearl Harbor, but plenty nonetheless. I have been looking for a miracle since I was about 7 years old. I'm not going to college. I got held back in 3rd grade for crying out loud, and I just barely graduated last spring. It's either Bill or somebody about like him. I don't want to be a waitress all my life like Edna and Bertha, and I sure as hell don't want to be my mother 20 years from now. How many choices do you think I have?"

Janice had been raised on stories of how her parents and grandparents had met, fallen in love and stayed together through thick and thin. Clara's was a story of romance as a commodity. When she didn't respond, Clara filled in the silence.

"Janice, you must think I'm awful. You fell in love in peacetime with a boy from your own hometown. Then you got to let that love grow in a calmer and less hurried time than this one. Let me ask you something? If you could go back and have some inkling of what was going to happen, would you marry Tommy before he went out to Hawaii?"

"I was only seventeen," Janice answered.

"Do you wish you could have?"

Janice didn't respond.

"OK, let me ask you in a different way. How many weddings are there in the Edmond Sun newspaper every week? Now, multiply that by the number of towns in Oklahoma and that by the whole 48 states. Do you think every one of those couples thought it all the way through? Don't be silly. Lots of those folks don't know one another any better than Bill and I do. Yet, I'll bet many of them will stay happily married - or at least married, for the rest of their lives. Times are different. You may have heard that there's a war on. How many boys do you and I know who have already been killed? How many more will be? We have to snatch whatever happiness we can, Janice. It may be all we ever get."

Janice looked at Clara for a moment before she spoke.

"You know," she began, "for a girl who was drunk an hour ago you certainly got profound all of a sudden."

"Just because I didn't do well in school doesn't mean I'm dumb. I'm just smart about stuff schools don't care about."

"Right now, I'd say you're pretty amazing," Janice confessed.

"I've always thought that about you," Clara replied.

Nothing was resolved in Janice's mind, and every question she'd asked had only made her more certain that Clara had no business getting married. Despite her misgivings, she couldn't help but be impressed, even if only sadly, at Clara's logic. Janice reached over and squeezed the other girl's hand. "For his sake, I hope Bill remembers his promise. I don't see how he'd get a nicer girl," Janice lied.

"Oh, he's gonna' remember me all right," Clara said with confidence.

"How's that?" Janice asked.

"Well, for one thing," Clara explained, "he's got my panties in his pocket."

Chapter Eleven

Tina

The Wide-A-Wake Café
Monday, April 26, 1943
2:55 p.m.

I

"*I*'m late," Tina Clark said quietly to Janice after she entered the empty café and sat down at one of the counter stools next to the other girl.

Janice Lookabaugh was reading her chemistry book as Tina spoke, and absently looked at the clock on the wall of the restaurant before the import of Tina's words suddenly sunk in.

"Oh no," Janice responded, swiveling her head to look at her co-worker, "are you certain?"

"You could set your clock by me," Tina replied with a worried look and a whisper designed to keep the conversation just between the two of them.

"I don't even know what to say, Tina. What will you do?" Janice asked.

"Honestly, I don't know."

"Tina, we've been friends a long time. I've known you since my family moved to town. I don't want to say anything too stupid, but how did this happen? I didn't even know you were seeing somebody that seriously. Who is the father?"

The question caused the blood to rush to Tina's face as her downcast eyes and expression told the other girl what she was too embarrassed to admit. Janice reached out and placed her hand on Tina's.

"Oh God," Janice said.

Although she fought it, and almost always denied it, Janice tended towards the judgmental. Reticent by nature, she rarely rushed headlong into any situation. When she was impatient with others, it usually reflected what she considered to be a lack of maturity or reason. As she studied the top of Tina's head, Janice shook her own and stifled the impulse to sound like a parent. At this point, it would do no good whatsoever, but she couldn't help wondering how this popular former high school cheerleader could be pregnant without even knowing who the father might be. "Oh God," she repeated.

"What am I gonna' do?" Tina asked, looking up with tear filled eyes.

"Who else have you told?" Janice asked.

"Nobody," Tina replied, "for a month I kept hoping I was wrong. Then when I missed again, I knew it was true. I'm just sick about this, but I can't go on ignoring it any further. I am going to have to face up to it and move on, but I'm so scared, I just don't know how."

"Well," Janice replied, "first you need to know for sure. Go see a doctor and find out. He should be able to tell you how far along you are. At that point you have to decide if you are going to tell the father. Surely you can do the math and figure out who you were with if you know about when you got pregnant."

"I've already done the math, Janice," Tina replied softly without looking at the other girl, "I'm not going to know,"

"Good Lord Tina, what have you been doing?"

Tina's reply was stifled as a couple of roughnecks entered the café and ordered a late lunch. Before they left a trucker on his way to Tulsa stopped at the café to have his thermos filled with coffee. When the restaurant emptied, Charlie, the short order cook came out and sat with the girls for a few minutes. Finally, to Charlie's great surprise, Tina interrupted him in the middle of a story to which neither of the girls were actually listening, by grabbing Janice's hand and half leading her and half dragging her to the break area out back.

"I've been an idiot," Tina began when they were out of earshot. "Last winter I met a boy at a dance out at Wiley Post field and we just clicked. When he asked me for my phone number I gave it to him. He was handsome, in uniform, on his way to the war, you name it, Janice. Anyhow, one thing just sort of led to another. Janice, I swear, I hadn't been that kind of girl before. When we first did it, I could scarcely believe it was me. He left for Kelly Field in Texas back in March telling me how much he loved me and how he was gonna' write and all that, but he didn't. I was feeling pretty low, and I was more susceptible to the next guy. I kinda felt bad about that one and in a way that made me more susceptible to the next one, and then, the one after that."

Tina paused for a moment before she continued in a quieter, more subdued tone. "I - I also discovered something about me. Janice, I liked it. I liked it as much as they did. I don't know where some women get the idea that we're not supposed to like sex, but it sure isn't true in my case. Plus, I," another short pause followed, "kinda' got the idea that I was doing something for the war effort. The boys are all so lonely, and most of them are so young they haven't ever even been with a girl back in their own hometowns or anything. I know this sounds crazy, but I loved the look on their faces when they knew we were actually going to do it. I loved how excited they were. It made me feel . . .grown up," Janice arched her eyebrows at that, Tina continued, "I know, I know, it's just stupid, but that's how I felt. Now I'm pregnant, and I am scared, and I don't know who the father is.

"What am I gonna' tell my parents, Janice, what am I gonna' do?"

Janice led Tina back inside the café and to the bar that held the cash register. She reached behind the counter and picked up the Oklahoma City phone book. She rifled through the pages for a few moments and then picked up the telephone handset. "Central," she said to the operator, "please connect me with the Oklahoma City operator." Once she was connected, she announced the number and less than a minute later was connected.

"Hi," she said, "my name is Mrs. Tina Clark and I need to set an appointment for an examination." She waited a few minutes as she examined the calendar behind the cash register on which all of the work schedules were written. "Yes, thank you, Tuesday at 1 p.m. will be fine. Thank you."

"Janice," Tina's face was stricken, "what if someone from here sees me in that doctor's office. Everyone in this town has known me all of my life. If someone from here sees me go in there, the word will get back to my parents in about ten seconds."

"Well," Janice replied, "then you have until Tuesday at one to tell them. Tina, everybody in this town is going to know in a couple of months. It isn't fair to your baby to simply go along without acknowledging that this has happened. You need special vitamins, more calcium, stuff like that. The first three months of pregnancy are really important. Go see the doctor, and then let's talk again."

"I'm afraid, Janice. Can you go with me?" Tina requested.

"I can't, Tina, I am either in class or here during every daylight hour from now until the semester ends. Cleo hasn't been able to find a replacement since Edna left and you know how understaffed we are. Maybe you could tell your Mom and have her go with you," Janice suggested.

"No," Tina replied emphatically, "what if I'm not really pregnant? Then I'd have to go through the hell of hearing my mother tell me what a tramp I am for the rest of my life for nothing." Tina paused for a minute. "I know what I'll do," she continued, "I'll ask Clara. She's the one girl I know that can identify with my predicament. The only difference between me and her is her luck."

Janice smiled but said nothing.

II

On Tuesday, May 4th, Clara and Tina took the Interurban streetcar into Oklahoma City. The doctor took blood and killed a rabbit. The news was just as bad as Tina had feared. On the way back to Edmond the girls sat quietly on the trolley as Tina stared absently out the window.

"I've got it." Clara cried out and grabbed Tina's arm.

"What?" Tina replied.

"You're going to write to the father and tell him he's going to be a daddy," Clara said.

"Way to go Einstein, I already told you, I don't know who the father was. I was with three guys during that time. . . no wait, four guys during that time."

"Four guys," Clara responded shocked, "and everybody calls me a tramp."

"Thank you for your support," Tina replied dryly, "calling me names doesn't change anything, Clara, I still don't know which one it was. How do I write the father?"

"Write them all," Clara replied firmly.

"What?"

"Write them all, Tina, write every damned one of them and tell him he is the only guy you have ever been with and that you're gonna' have his baby. Tell him he is going to have an heir right here in Oklahoma, no matter what happens to him in the war. Finally, make it real sad and tell him that you almost didn't tell him, but that you want your baby's father to at least know he had a child. Then, when you have him all softened up, tell him you can't really support his child, and that you hope he will do the right thing."

"But what if none of them respond?" Tina wanted to know.

"Then how are you worse off than you are now?"

"O.K., then what if all of them respond?"

"You really don't know much about men do you," Clara replied.

"Look," Clara continued in a tone she might have used with a particularly dim student, "at least half the guys out there would respond to a letter telling them they are going to be a father by going to their commander and requesting immediate transfer to the combat zone. At least in your case, you have four chances to get one to write back and tell you he will marry you."

Tina looked back out the window of the trolley, and considered the plan. Finally, without turning back to Clara she said firmly, "I'm going to do it."

III

When Tina and Clara told Janice about the plan she was appalled.

"See," Clara announced triumphantly, "she hates it, that means we have to do it."

"Because I hate it means you have to do it?" Janice replied to Clara.

"Sure," Clara said, "you're like that paper that turned pink in Science class."

"I'm litmus paper?"

"Of course," Clara replied without a hint of reticence, "I knew that if you thought it was awful, it would be because you knew it might work."

"That's the problem exactly, Clara," Janice shot back, "it might work." She then turned towards the other girl. "Do you really want to trick somebody into marrying you Tina? What if he's not the right one? What if it turns out that you hate each other? What if the one who says he'll marry you is short and dark like you and the baby turns out tall and blond? Damn, Tina, can't you see that your whole life would be a lie?"

Tina was silent for a moment before she replied quietly, "but my baby wouldn't be a bastard, Janice, and someday, someplace else, I might not be a whore to the town I live in."

The three girls looked at each other for a few moments before Janice finally broke the silence,

"Make sure it's a good letter, Tina," Janice admonished them.

> 123 West Second St.
> Edmond, Oklahoma
> May 7, 1943

Dear George,

I know you're probably surprised to hear from me. I hope this letter finds you in good health and doing well in your training.

I am still working at the café and doing volunteer work at the Red Cross. I'll be stopping that pretty soon, and that is the reason I am writing to you. I don't know any easy way to bring this up, but I'm pregnant with your baby. I was tempted not to tell you, but I realized that if I was a man about to go to war, I would want to know that I would have an heir if the worst happened to me. You will, George.

Darling, what we had together was the most beautiful experience in my life, but it had consequences, and I am afraid to deal with them alone. This may be an unusual proposal, but I hope you will make arrangements to come back here and marry me. I think I know how much of a shock this is for you, because I had the same one. I hope you won't use that shock as an excuse to leave me alone. I know that what we had together was very special, and that we can make a life together for our baby after the war. Please write me or send me a telegram telling me you will marry me.

> **Until I hear from you.**
> **Love,**
> **Tina**

Tina and Clara worked on the letter for two days. After a good deal of begging, they got Janice to proofread it for errors and word choices. When they finally had it the way they wanted it, the girls mailed four copies, and then they waited.

It took almost two weeks. By then, Tina was three and a half months along. She had been to see the doctor a second time and her pregnancy was advancing normally. When the letter finally arrived, she was afraid it would be a rejection; that somehow the boy knew about the others, anything but what she wanted to hear. She carried the letter unopened to the café and showed it to Janice.

"I can't open it, Janice," she explained. "Read it for me."

"Beans," Janice replied, "don't try to make this into some melodramatic Hollywood scene." But she took the letter and tore open the flap. The reply was on a single sheet of paper. Janice read it at a glance, shook her head no at Tina, and handed her the page.

"You're not going to like it," Janice warned.

Naval Air Station, Coronado
San Diego, California

May 18, 1943

Dear Tina,
I was very happey to hear from you. I think about you a lot. I am proud to be the father of your baby that you have comeing. Please know that I wuld marry you in a minute if it was up to me, but I am about to finish my training and will be going to sea reelly soon. I can't get no leave between now and when we go.

I wish you good luck. If I am still living after the war, maybe I'll come to Oklahoma and see you and the baby.

Good luck,
Steven Moore
Seaman Apprentice, US Navy

Tina read the short letter, folded it and put it in the pocket of her apron.

"It's not going to work is it?" she asked.

"Maybe not," Janice replied. "But if it doesn't, is that really the worst thing?"

"Yes it is," Tina answered.

It was two more days before they heard again. Tina entered the café when Janice and Clara were working a shift together. This time the letter was from an army air base in North Dakota.

"Well," Clara said when she saw the letter. At least there wasn't any inter-service rivalry. Is there a Marine in our future?"

"Shut up, Clara," Tina snapped, "read the damned letter."

May 20, 1943

Dear Tina,

I am writing because I got your letter telling me you were pregnant with my baby. Needless to say, since we don't really know each other all that well, I was surprised to hear from you. Despite that, I will marry you. Our crew is now training in Minot and will be here for at least another two or three months. See if you can get a train ticket and come on up. I have no idea what sort of a place to stay in we'll be able to find, but I'll go door to door in town until I find somebody who will rent us a room.

Tina, it is only fair to tell you that the Air Corps sends flight crews back home after 25 missions because if they didn't make that promise, nobody would go up after about the fifth one. Not too many crews actually make it. I don't want to die with not marrying you on my conscience, so I'll do it.

Let me know by return mail when you'll be here and I'll either pick you up, or make sure somebody else does.

Sincerely,

Peter

When Janice saw the letter, her eyes dilated involuntarily before she looked up at Tina's expectant face.

"Oh for God's sake," she exploded, "surely you're not going to do this."

"Of course I am," Tina countered, "I have to. For my baby if nothing else."

"For the baby?" Janice said in mock confusion. "According to this jasper, he won't even be alive when the baby is born. Tina, he has agreed to marry you without consideration of the fact that he doesn't love you. He is simply afraid God will punish him if he leaves you in the lurch."

"So what," Clara interjected. "Let the bastard do the right thing. If he dies, Tina won't have to live with him."

"What the hell are you talking about," Janice spat. "This letter is terrible. Surely just having her baby and pretending she married the father would be better than actually doing it with this jerk."

"He wasn't a jerk," Tina interrupted.

Janice had been speaking to Clara. Suddenly she realized that neither she nor Clara knew a thing about this boy. She took Tina's hand in hers.

111

"I'm sorry, Tina," she began, "you're right. I don't know if he's a jerk. But you can't read this letter and think he will be the right guy for you."

"Why not? He is the only one who said 'yes'. Maybe he is the only one I could have been happy with. Maybe God put me through this whole thing so that Peter and I could be together," Tina replied.

Janice looked at Tina's face. The retort that jumped to her lips died there when Clara touched her hand.

"Don't," Clara begged, "she's doing the right thing. You'll haunt her with what you're thinking."

Janice looked down at the counter and kept her counsel.

"When are you going?" Clara asked.

"As soon as I can get a ticket. I don't want to give him a chance to change his mind," Tina replied resolutely.

When Janice reported for her shift following her last class the next day, Tina was still there, finished with her shift, but waiting for Janice and Clara.

"I got a telegram last night," Tina told her.

"From Peter?" Janice asked.

"No, from Steven."

"The sailor?" Janice asked uncertainly.

"Yes, the sailor." Tina confirmed.

"What did the telegram say?"

"He's coming."

"Oh shit," Janice said, "I mean, oh no."

"Yeah, whatever," Tina was crestfallen.

"So, what is God's plan looking like now?"

"Don't pick on me, Janice, I don't know what to do now."

Clara arrived at that moment and the girls brought her up to date.

"When I have a problem," Clara observed, "I like to see what parts I can do something about, and what parts I can't. It seems to me, the sailor is coming whether you do anything or not. When will he be here?"

"Saturday," Tina replied.

"When were you leaving?"

"Tomorrow," Tina said.

"Can you change your ticket?" Clara asked.

"Do you know how much trouble I went to just to get that one seat?"

"No," Clara admitted. "Tell me about Steven."

"I met him at a dance at the South Base down in Norman. He was learning to be a radio operator. He's from Muleshoe, down in Texas. He was sweet."

"I thought they were all sweet," Janice prompted.

Tina smiled. "OK, they were all sweet."

"Even the Air Corps guy?" Clara asked.

112

"Let's just say they are all sweet until they get what they want. Steven was always sweet," Tina acknowledged.

"So maybe you wait 'til Saturday," Clara suggested.

"I spent two hours standing at the window in the Santa Fe station trying to work out the details of that one ticket, but OK, I'll wait."

Tina left the café and headed to the Santa Fe train station. When Janice and Clara arrived for their shifts the next afternoon, Tina was there waiting for them.

"How did it go with the train ticket?" Clara asked.

"I was in and out of there in about five minutes," Tina chuckled, "they are darned supportive if you want to cancel a trip. It's only when you want to GO somewhere that the obstacles appear."

"Well," Clara observed, "you know what they say, 'is this trip really necessary?' maybe it won't be. What time will Steven arrive?"

"He should be here Saturday night on the 7:14. My mother is going to go with me to pick him up. I finally had to tell her so she'd know what was going on. She cried for a couple of hours. I wasn't buying it too much, and sure enough, my dad walked in and she was cleared up before he could get from the front door to the kitchen.

"Poor daddy just thinks some boy who wants to marry me is coming. We have had to kinda invent a whole dating history for Steven and me, so mom and I are going to go get him and fill him in. We don't want him to accidentally spill the beans in front of my dad and wind up getting both or maybe even all three of us killed."

"You mean you, Steven and the baby?" Janice asked.

"Oh hell, I forgot about the baby, all four of us, I guess, I was actually thinking of my mother," Tina replied.

"Bringing your mom in on this was a master stroke," Clara observed, "she's now as guilty as you are. . . "

"As guilty as she is?" Janice interrupted archly.

"OK, Miss Priss," Clara replied, then corrected herself as she looked back at Tina, "almost as guilty as you are. Now if the 'you-know-what' hits the fan, your daddy will be more mad at your mother than he'll be at you."

"Well," Janice observed sarcastically, "that'll help. Look, I don't know Mr. Clark all that well, but I'd bet he can do math down from nine months as well as most people. I'd say he is gonna' figure this out eventually."

"By then," Clara filled in, "Tina might be married to Steven, or Peter. Anyway, Daddies get pretty forgiving when they see a grandbaby the first time. Just you wait. I've got two sisters, a brother, and a cousin with kids, and only one of them had their first one born long enough into the marriage to have gotten its start on a marriage bed. My daddy and my uncle are more ga-ga over their grandchildren than they ever were over their own kids."

"That's because grandchildren go home when you're tired of them," Tina observed, "if I don't get this worked out, mine will be living in the same house."

"It's gonna' work out great, Tina, don't you worry about a thing," Clara reassured her.

Tina smiled slightly, and Clara hugged her shoulder, but to Janice the pregnant girl's smile looked like that of somebody about to go to the gallows.

IV

Janice's shift at the café on Saturday ended at 3 p.m. When she arrived home her mother told her that Tina Clark had called and asked her to call back.

"Oh, thank God," Tina said when Janice had her on the phone.

"What's wrong?" Janice asked, concerned, "aren't you going to get Steven tonight?"

"That's just it. Momma was going to go with me, and my gramma got sick so she had to go to Crescent and be with her. Janice, I was going to just sit there and listen while Momma told him how the cow ate the cabbage. Now she's not coming, and I don't want to be alone with him. Janice, I know you don't approve, but Clara is down at the Navy Base in Norman tonight. Please, please, go with me. I'm scared to death to be alone with him."

"Tina, he's coming here to marry you. Don't you think you might wind up spending a few days alone with him during the rest of your life?"

"That's not what I mean. He's gonna' be here in a few hours and I don't know what I am going to say to him. Please," Tina pleaded.

"Don't beg, Tina," Janice replied, "I'll go."

"Oh thank you," the other girl replied.

"Tell you what," Janice continued, "he'll probably have a bag of some sort with him and it's a long way to your house. Mom and Dad are home tonight, what the heck, they're in their forties, they're home every night. Anyway, I'll get the car and we can pick him up. Then we'll take him to the Wide-A-Wake and park while we tell him about your Dad. OK?"

"I love you, Janice," Tina said with excitement. "that's just perfect. Thank you so much."

"I'll be at your house at 6:30, be outside, I don't want to have to face your Dad any more than poor Steven would if he knew what he was getting into."

When Janice arrived at the Clark's home, Tina wasn't waiting at the curb. Janice got out of the car and knocked on the front door. Troy Clark, Tina's dad, answered the door immediately.

"Hello, Janice, I'm sorry you had to come out tonight. I told that gal I would go with her, course her momma's got the car but hell we coulda' walked."

"I'm happy to do it," Janice answered.

"Well, Tina's been dressing and all, for the past two hours solid, and she ain't ready yet. Sit down, Janice, I bet she'll be along directly."

"Maybe I should go on back there and help her," Janice answered hopefully.

"It won't help," Troy said, "I been yelling at her for twenty minutes that you was 'bout to arrive, an' that didn't help."

"Can you imagine that," Janice replied unctuously.

"Tell you the truth, Janice," Troy continued earnestly, "I'd appreciate it if you would sit here an' talk with me a minute. Nobody I'm kin to will tell me jack about this business. Hell, I don't even remember this boy. How could he be in love with Tina an' I ain't even laid eyes on him in my whole damn life?

"Now, here this jasper is comin' all the way from California," Troy pronounced it Cal If For Nigh Aaa, Janice shook her head and widened her eyes, "planning to marry my little gal and instead of bein' sentimental or something, her momma cries ever' damned time somebody, well, hell, ever' time I mention it. I guess what I want to know is what the hell is going on, Janice?"

Janice didn't say anything for a moment. Then she turned to Tina's father and smiled, "Well, Mr. Clark, you know women are supposed to be impossible to understand. It only gets worse when we're mothers I guess."

"Well, God knows ever' woman in this house has been impossible to understand since all of this come up," Troy conceded.

Janice smiled briefly and without conviction and then found something on her shoe that anyone observing her would have believed she was finding utterly fascinating.

Troy Clark watched Janice for a moment in hopes that she would share some insight into the impending betrothal of his daughter but she said nothing. Finally, he stood and walked to the hallway that led to the back of the house.

"Tina," he shouted, "dammit, that boy is going to be standing on the platform wondering where in the hell you are. Are you ever comin' out?"

In answer, Tina finally appeared. She was dressed as if going to church, right down to the handbag and matching shoes. Janice pulled her head back as she visually took in the appearance of her friend.

"Fancy," she said with a hint of sarcasm.

"Oh shut up," Tina replied with a chuckle, "I've tried on everything I own since I called you. This is just what I was wearing when I ran out of time. Let's go."

"Well," Janice said as an aside when they were out the door, "at least Steven will think your family is accepting of him. Of course, the way you're dressed, he'll probably think your mother came to get him and you're the one up in Crescent."

Tina laughed and pinched Janice's arm, "Thanks for bolstering my confidence, pal."

"That's what friends are for," Janice assured her with a grin and then took her hand and tucked it into her arm as they walked down the uneven sidewalk in front of the Clark's home.

V

The Santa Fe station was baking in the heated air of the early summer twilight. Janice and Tina waited for the engine to arrive, heralding as it did the passenger and cargo cars behind it. Tina fidgeted endlessly, brushing imaginary dust or lint from her jacket, or walking a few yards down the platform in an effort to see farther into the approaching darkness.

"For the love of God, Tina," Janice snapped at her, "that train isn't going to arrive one instant earlier no matter how much hopping around here you do."

"And it won't be any later, either," Tina snapped right back.

"Suit yourself," Janice replied, "but you're starting to sweat."

"Oh, shit," Tina replied, and raised her arms to see if she could see sweat stains on the garment. When she didn't, she looked at Janice for more information.

"Well, maybe, you're almost starting to sweat then."

"Janice, for the love of Mike, would you quit giving me a hard time, I'm about to jump out of my skin as it is."

"Has it occurred to you yet what a poor choice I was for this job?" Janice asked in a smarmy voice.

"About three seconds after I walked out of my bedroom," Tina replied.

"Then live with it, Tina," Janice insisted, "I'm only trying to help you relax. You seem a trifle tense to me."

"You think?" Tina agreed sarcastically.

At that point they heard the whistle as the engine pulled through the intersection at 33rd Street, about two miles away.

"It won't be long now," Tina said softly, looking towards the sound.

"You're going to be fine," Janice reassured her.

It took another few minutes for the train to travel the final distance to the station. When it finally arrived, Janice remained seated while Tina looked through the windows of the passenger cars as they rolled by.

"I think I just saw him," Tina said to nobody in particular.

Within moments, the conductors had placed the small blue wooden steps on the platform used by travelers to get safely from the bottom step of the train's ladder to the platform itself. Tina took a deep breath and exhaled loudly.

Steven Moore was the first person off the train. He was wearing the U.S. Navy blues Janice thought of as the "cracker jack" uniform and dixie cup hat of an enlisted sailor, much the worse for his three day trip half way across the

116

country. Seaman Apprentice Moore was slightly below average in height, nicely set up, however, Janice noticed, with the wiry build of a high school wrestler. When he looked towards the girls Janice could see that while not handsome, perhaps, his features were regular and he looked nice. He also looked to Janice like he was about twelve years old. He waved at Tina as he put his small AWOL bag on the platform and then turned back into the doorway and assisted a woman, well past middle age, safely onto the platform's surface.

Oh my gosh, Janice thought to herself, *he's brought his mother to meet his pregnant girlfriend!*

But he hadn't. He was just helping a fellow traveler. The elderly woman thanked him and went on her way. Steven then picked up his bag and half ran to Tina. He dropped the bag just as he reached her and took the surprised girl into his arms. Instead of melting into him, Tina hugged him stiffly and looked at Janice with a slight grimace on her pretty face.

"Steven," she said when they parted, "this is my friend Janice Lookabaugh. Janice, this is my . . . friend, Steven Moore.

"Hello, Miss Lookabaugh," Steven said. His voice was high pitched, in keeping with his unbelievably youthful appearance.

"Janice, please," she requested of him, "I'm pleased to meet you."

"The pleasure is all mine," Steven replied. In a part of the country known for its strong regional accents, Janice had rarely heard one that sounded so much like a cowboy in a Saturday morning western serial as Steven's. They shook hands.

"Janice is giving us a ride," Tina explained.

"That's really nice of you, ma'am," Steven added.

"Steven," Janice interrupted, "if you don't figure out how to say Janice pretty soon, you may make me think I look like an old lady. Even my mom feels old when someone calls her 'ma'am.'"

"No offense, ma...I mean Janice," Steven stammered, "I guess I been siring and ma'aming danged near ever'body I seen in the past four or five months. Give me a bit and I 'spect I'll get squared away directly."

"Sure Steven," Janice said with a friendly smile, "welcome back to Oklahoma."

"Thank you," he paused a moment before he continued, "Janice. Now, if you'll excuse us, Tina and me got some binness to take care of." Steven then turned his attentions back to Tina. The boy took her hand in his and looked into her eyes. Janice began walking away in order to give them privacy, but she still heard him speaking.

"Tina, I've done nothing but think about you ever' since I got your letter. I'd sit above my telegraph key and tap in your name so often my Chief thinks he knows you better'n I do. Leavin' here thinkin' I wan't ever gonna' see you agin was 'bout the toughest thing I ever done. When I got your letter, my heart just sang, but my chief told me there wan't no damn way I wuz getting leave to come here so I sent that letter. Then a buddy told me about seeing the Chaplain and he got me out of there an' here I am.

"Tina, will you marry me?"

Tina leaned into the boy and kissed his lips. "That's what you're here for isn't it?"

"Wahoo," Steven let out a yell, and picked Tina up and swung her around. Suddenly realizing what he was doing, the boy stopped and gently lowered Tina to the platform.

"Jiminy," he said, "what was I thinkin' about. I gotta' be gentle with you. Hell, you're carrying our baby. Forgive me honey, I was just so happy I couldn't keep it quiet. Thank you, thank you, thank you, Tina, you've made me so happy."

The look on Tina's face was one of stunned surprise, whatever she'd been expecting when Steven arrived, this enthusiasm wasn't it. After watching her friend for a moment, Janice turned her face away and began walking to the car.

"I'll meet you in the parking lot," she told them over her shoulder, "take your time."

When they arrived at the café, Janice got out of the car to go get coffee for Steven and a soft drink for Tina. After she returned, Steven sat quietly sipping his beverage as the girls explained that Mr. Clark didn't know about Tina's condition and that they wanted it to stay that way as long as possible, but certainly until after the wedding. Tina sketched out the imaginative romance they had supposedly had so that their stories would be the same, with Steven nodding occasionally and asking the odd question from time to time.

"It's just that I want Daddy to be in favor of this wedding," Tina explained, "and I don't want him to think badly of me, or you."

"Honey," Steven interrupted, "just tell me what you want. From this day on, you don't have nothing whatever to worry about."

Tina looked at Janice, "Take us home, OK."

"OK," Janice said.

On Monday morning, Tina planned to take Steven to the county courthouse and apply for a marriage certificate. During the next few days Janice saw the couple twice. Both times Tina was smiling and Steven was enraptured. Curiosity for details was about to kill Janice, but she didn't want to call since she knew she would be seeing Tina when they changed over shifts on Tuesday afternoon. When Janice was ready to go home, Tina didn't arrive. Instead Ellen walked into the café to work with Bertha.

"What's going on?" Janice asked.

"I don't know," Ellen replied, "Cleo called me and asked me to take Tina's shift. Maybe she's quit since she's getting married."

"I guess that could be," Janice agreed.

Instead of going home after she left the Wide-A-Wake, Janice walked to the Clark's home. Tina's mother, Evelyn, met her at the door. It was obvious she'd been crying.

"Hello, Mrs. Clark," Janice said, "I came to see Tina and Steven, but it looks like I have arrived at a bad time."

"Don't mind me, Janice, there're here. Tina is in her room and Steven and Troy are out back," Evelyn informed her. "Janice, speak with her for God's sake before she does something stupid or awful, or both."

"You don't want her to get married?" Janice asked.

"What," Evelyn asked, surprised, "what are you talking about. Of course I want her to marry him. He's wonderful. Look at him and Troy out there. They are like two peas in a pod. They hit it off in about ten seconds. It's Tina that suddenly doesn't want to marry him."

"She doesn't?" Janice asked surprised.

"She's pregnant for God's sake," Evelyn shot at Janice in an exaggerated whisper as though the door jam might be offended, "she'll be shamed in this town forever, and the baby will be a bastard. I don't know what she's thinking, but this business is about to kill me, Janice."

"Can I go see her?" Janice asked.

"Yes of course, please help her see what she needs to do."

Janice walked back to Tina's room. The other girl was packing.

"What are you doing?" Janice asked her.

"Surely you're not that dumb," Tina replied with exaggerated patience, "I'm putting clothes in a bag — it's called packing, people do it before they go somewhere."

"But, your mom just told me that you weren't marrying Steven," Janice explained.

"I'm not."

"Then why are you packing?"

"Janice," Tina began, "I made a real mistake letting Steven come here."

"But he seems so taken with you."

"Hell, he is," Tina agreed, "if I had gone up to Minot and been met by that bastard Peter I probably could have gone through with this, but not with Steven."

"You want to marry a bastard?" Janice asked, confused.

"No, of course not. I want to marry somebody I love, not just somebody who thinks he loves me because I'm the only girl he's ever been with. But, if I'm going to trick somebody into marrying me, then I'd just as soon it was somebody awful like that Peter guy in North Dakota. At least then I wouldn't hate myself quite so much."

"Tina," Janice began exasperatedly, "what are you talking about?"

Tina put down the slip she was folding. "Janice, he's wonderful. He told me all he went through to get this leave. Just getting here was awful. He didn't have a Pullman. He sat upright on that train for almost three days. Look at them out there," Tina said pointing at her father and Steven through the window that faced the back yard. "He and my daddy have been like old friends since he walked through the door. You're not going to believe this, Janice, but Steven is a Texas Junior Champion bull rider. The instant Daddy learned that he was won completely over. They've been out there talking rodeo for two hours. Even Momma, who knows what happened, likes him - heck why wouldn't she? He's just like Daddy."

"Then what's the problem?" Janice wanted to know.

"It's me. I can't go through with it. He doesn't deserve this. He is a good and decent boy who deserves to know what he's getting. You were right, Janice. I can't pull this awful trick on him," Tina's voice was about to crack, she sat down on the bed and turned her face to the wall.

"I guess better now than a few weeks from now," Janice agreed, "so if you're not getting married, where are you going?"

"I got another letter in Monday's mail."

"Three out of four?" Janice asked surprised. "Well there goes Clara's theory about the lack of honor among American men."

Tina smiled, "This one wasn't from one of my former lovers, Janice, it was from Edna."

"Edna Pryor," Janice exclaimed, surprised, "why did she write?"

"We've stayed in touch since she left. She's in Oak Ridge, Tennessee working on some big government contract. She's learning to be an electrician and the pay is great. When I told her what we were doing, she agreed with you. She thinks what I'm doing is wrong. She also told me I could go out there and hire on immediately. They will let me work as long as I feel like it. Office work probably, since I can type and know the alphabet well enough to do some filing and stuff. But who knows, maybe I'll be an electrician too. I only know I can't do this to Steven. I wish," Tina stopped as her eyes grew misty as she seemed to be looking far away, "you know, when I saw him get off that train on Saturday I thought 'good grief, what am I going to do with this goofy little infant.' But now I know him and I wish," she paused again and wiped her eyes with a tissue before she continued, "I guess that I'd been more deserving of him.

"That sounds funny doesn't it," Tina remarked looking up at Janice, "if he was a jerk, I'd marry him in a heartbeat and then send his little butt off to war. As it is, I only know that I can't start on a lifetime of lying about something this big. In Tennessee, I'll just be another person with no past that anybody knows about. Maybe folks'll think I lost my husband in the war. If they do, fine, but I'm all through lying about it."

"Have you thought about how tough this is going to be?" Janice asked gently, "Raising a baby without a father is going to be hard Tina. You may even be alone forever. Lots of men might not be as good about it as Steven has been."

"He thinks it's his," Tina reminded her.

"It could be," Janice said softly.

"I hope it is." Tina responded, "I'd like to have a baby who might grow up to have a spirit that gentle and loving."

"Tina," Janice began, "when you and Clara cooked this up I was more worried about you than I was about one of the boys you might attract. Right now, though, I am inclined to wonder if maybe you shouldn't go through with this. He seems crazy about you, and it seems to me that in this short time you've grown pretty fond of him too. Maybe marrying him isn't the worst thing that could happen to either of you."

"He'd never marry me after he knew," Tina replied, "and I'd never marry him until he did."

"So tell him," Janice replied, "see what happens."

Tina sat quietly on her bed for a long time before she finally nodded and looked up at Janice.

"OK," Tina replied, "I won't be any worse off if he calls me names and stomps out. But stay here for me, OK. I'm gonna' need some moral support after this is done." Tina then stood and walked out of the little bedroom. In a few moments, Janice saw her through the window, walking across the back yard. As she approached, Steven rose to his feet, a smile creasing his face. Janice could see Tina speaking to her father, and then watched as the older man stood and walked casually towards the house.

Steven then made room for Tina on the old glider the men had been sharing. Tina took his hand and looked at his face as she began to speak. It didn't take long. Even from this far away, Janice could see from the look on his face when she must have been telling him about the fraud.

When she appeared to have finished, Tina stood and began walking back to the house with her chin almost on her chest and her shoulders drooping. Before she had taken three steps, the boy was on his feet and Tina stopped and turned as if he'd called her name. He walked slowly to her, put his hands on her arms and began what looked like an earnest speech. After a moment Tina came into his arms and they kissed. Janice had no idea exactly what they had said, but it looked like Tina wouldn't need moral support, and might not be moving to Tennessee.

VI

On Thursday, June 3rd, 1943, Miss Tina Clark and Seaman Apprentice Steven Moore were married at the First Christian Church of Edmond, Oklahoma, the Reverend William Tracy presiding. Miss Clara Beech served as Maid of Honor. Janice sat smiling on the third row of the church between her mother and younger brother. About half-way through the ceremony, Janice noticed as Marge Lookabaugh took her husband's hand. Janice had attended many weddings in the past, but this was the first time she'd ever had tears come to her eyes.

Steven Moore returned to San Diego, California three days later, proud of his new wife and child to be.

The day after he was gone, Tina was waiting for Janice to relieve her from her shift at the café. When she tried to leave, Janice gripped her arm and wouldn't release it until Tina agreed to stay and tell her what had happened.

"You know, Janice, when I told him, he wasn't the least bit surprised. He said he already knew," Tina reported.

"How?" Janice wanted to know.

"He was told by his Chief Petty Officer," Tina explained, "that this was an old trick that girls had been using to get sailors to marry them since the days of wooden ships and sails. But he didn't care, Janice. He told me that the only thing he'd ever been worried about was that I'd change my mind."

"It's funny the way things work out, isn't it?" Janice asked.

"Yeah, for instance, if you'd have told me when he got off that train that I'd be married to him less than a week later and consider myself the luckiest girl in the world, I'd have figured you must have been dropped on your head.

"There is just one more thing that I'd like to figure out," Tina continued.

"What's that?" Janice asked.

"When we were hatching this plot, you were dead set against it, and Clara was obviously in favor of it since she thought it up. Which one of you was right?"

"How could you even ask?" Janice replied with a smile. "Obviously, we both were."

Chapter Twelve

Betrothed

The Wide-A-Wake Café
June 8, 1943
5:59 a.m.

I

Clara Beech yawned as she walked into the Wide-A-Wake just moments before her shift began. She was not happy to be awake at this hour. The departure, without notice, of Edna Pryor to take a war-related job in Oak Ridge, Tennessee had left a gap in the early morning waitress rotation that Edna had filled without complaint for over eight years. There had been a good deal of speculation about Edna's departure, fueled in part when one of the boarding house tenants told Tina Clark about the gigantic fight Edna and her mother had the day she packed her bags and left. The boy's story had been so lurid, that when Janice heard it second or third hand, she didn't even believe it. The only thing she did believe was that Edna really was gone.

To fill the gap in the waitress rotation, Cleo Noe moved Clara from weeknights and afternoons on the weekend, to the morning shift. Today, she was working with Janice. They nodded when Clara walked in, but there was no time for chitchat. Instead of the normal smattering of early morning customers, the café was a full of customers eating, drinking coffee, or waiting for their food. Bertha and Ellen stayed on to help Janice and Clara keep pace with the demands of the crowd.

"What did they do," Clara wanted to know, "bomb Royce's Café last night?"

"This is nuts," Janice agreed, "is there such a thing as a fried egg frenzy? If there is, everybody in town seems to be having it at once."

"It's been like this since 5 a.m.," Ellen confirmed, "everybody's here to catch the buses to work. Mr. Weibel just added a third bus and nobody else has any gas." Before the war, Fred Weibel had run the Conoco station on the corner opposite the Wide-A-Wake. He now used the location as a bus stop for Edmondites commuting to Tinker Field and the Douglas Aircraft Plant in Midwest City. "It could be like this every morning from now on," Ellen concluded.

"Oh brother," Clara exclaimed.

By seven o'clock the rush had subsided as the last of the buses departed for the Air Depot's morning shifts. Hiring at the Douglas Aircraft Plant adjacent to Tinker Air Field, was at a fever pitch as demand for the C-47 aircraft made there far exceeded the ability of the plant to produce the two engine transport airplanes. A good many people from Edmond applied for and got some of the high paying jobs at the plant.

"Your husband works out there now, Bertha, are they that busy?" Clara asked.

"Ever' bit," Bertha confirmed. "The aircraft roll off the assembly lines and they fly 'em off immediately to be fitted with radios and then off to somewhere's else. They put Phil on swing shift out there since they're going 24 hours a day. They cain't make 'em fast enough."

"Girls," Janice interrupted, "maybe we shouldn't be talking about this."

"What?" Clara asked.

"Maybe we're talking about stuff that's none of our business," Janice suggested.

"What are you talking about?" Clara exploded sarcastically, "Geez Louise, Janice, you've seen too many of those 'Loose Lips Sink Ships' posters. Do you really think we've got German spies right here at the Wide-A-Wake? "

"I - no . . . well, I don't know. I doubt old Charlie over there, or Cliff is a spy," Janice conceded, referring to an elderly farmer and one of Edmond's police officers. "But we're talking about production at a strategically placed plant. Those airplanes are used to carry supplies and paratroopers. I don't know. Why gossip about that? It just seems dangerous to me."

Clara put her hand on Janice's forehead. "Well, you don't feel sick, but then I'm not sure 'weird' causes a fever anyhow. Janice, you're going Asiatic or something."

"I agree with Janice," Ellen said, "my brother is overseas. I don't want to be careless with his life."

"His life? By golly, you're both nuts." Clara remarked and shrugged her shoulders. She was ready to change the topic since the war bored her anyway. "OK, let's talk about something that's not classified. What about me getting married to Bill Otis?"

"Oh brother," Janice said with a shake of her head, "well let's see, we've talked about that about 348 times in the last three weeks, why not one more time?"

"We haven't talked about a date yet," Clara said, "but now I have one."

Now it was Janice's turn to be surprised, "What?" she asked, surprised.

"That's right. It's going to be one week from next Saturday. Bill is flying up here with his whole crew. We're gonna' get married and he and I are going to take the Pullman cars back to Kelly Field. They are bringing an extra co-pilot up so Bill can return with me. Can you believe it?"

"That's nuts," Janice allowed, "why is the Air Corps going to allow them to fly a whole bomber up here for your wedding?"

"They have to fly somewhere to practice long distance navigation. It's just my luck," Clara pointed out.

"OHMIGOSH," Ellen cried excitedly, "you're really getting married." Ellen was 17 and thought everything was romantic. A wedding, even someone else's, was a magical event to her.

Clara was the star of the moment. It was one of her favorite fantasies. Now it was really going to happen. She was going to get married, and every eye would be on her. Clara thought it was just too delicious to describe.

II

After Ellen and Bertha left and the breakfast customers had gone, Clara popped her own most important question.

"Janice, will you be my Maid of Honor?" Clara asked.

Janice wasn't exactly stunned. Ever since the announcement, she had been dreading this. She questioned everything about the wedding. Why were they getting married? Did they even love each other? Would they ever? How successful could a marriage like this one be? Janice didn't want to be Clara's Maid of Honor because it would bespeak a belief in the marriage to come she just plain didn't feel. She had even practiced a little speech she would give when Clara offered her the job. She looked into Clara's joyful and expectant face and lost her nerve immediately. She tried anyway.

"Thanks Clara," she began, "but this is a time for family. How are your sisters going to feel if I'm the Maid of Honor?"

"Are you nuts? I don't want one of those cows in my wedding. They'll make my wedding pictures look ridiculous. Hell, I even tried to talk Bill into letting me come down to Kelly Field, but for some reason, he wants to get married up here. I wasn't about to argue with him. When all is said and done, its getting married that really matters to me and I wasn't about to risk gettin 'into a row with him about where it was gonna take place.

"Besides, you were there the night Bill proposed," Clara explained, "he knows you. So does Charlie Morgan who is going to be the best man. Please Janice," Clara begged.

Janice looked into Clara's eager face; she knew when she was whipped, "I'd be honored, Clara," she said before the delay became uncomfortable. "What arrangements still need to be made?"

Clara squealed and hugged Janice's neck. "Oh thank you, thank you, thank you, you've made Bill and me so happy. Well, let's see," Clara turned her thoughts to the arrangements. "We're going to get married at the Baptist Church," she began. "My mom has that all taken care of. There won't be much in the way of flowers, except stuff out of our garden, and my bouquet. I'm going to wear my suit since there isn't enough satin or other suitable material in this county, or this state for that matter, to make a real wedding dress. We are going to put up Bill and Charlie at my house to make sure there isn't a transportation snafu at the last minute. I hope that doesn't create more problems than it solves. I have no idea where they will sleep." Clara hesitated for a moment before she asked, "Janice could you help me out there. Ask your Mom if they can stay at your house."

Janice's eyes widened for a moment recalling that the last few minutes of her blind date with Charlie had been less than perfect. Then she shrugged her shoulders and nodded her head. "I don't need to ask. My sister has moved to California to be with her husband until he goes overseas. They could sleep in her old room, and we'll just move my little brother on down to the couch in the living room."

"Ohmigosh," Clara said, "that would be so great. Are you sure it will be OK?"

"I'll call Mom in a few minutes and let her know, but I'm sure it will be OK. Of course, they may not get much sleep at my place either. When my brother finds out we're going to have two B-17 pilots in our house he may screw himself into the ceiling in his excitement."

"Tell him I feel the same way," Clara said with a laugh. "Janice, you are such an angel. The less of my family Bill sees before it's too late the better. Somehow, the idea of all of us trying to get dressed in a house with one bathroom, five women, four men, AND Bill and Charlie, seems like a nightmare in the making. You might imagine I don't want to set that kind of mood for Bill just hours before we are joined, whoops, I was gonna' say 'joined at the hip' but then I realized that might sound like something else," she finished with a smirk.

Janice shook her head and covered her eyes as she wondered for the fiftieth time why this girl was marrying.

III

Even for a simple wartime wedding, the week before was filled with last minute arrangements. There was a bridal shower attended by Clara's family and most of the waitresses who weren't on duty, as well as several girls from Clara's old basketball team. Janice was hostess, and she and her mother were up until almost one the night before baking, cooking, and preparing the house. The rationing of sugar and other foodstuffs required a certain imagination. They baked bread, made as many cookies as they could, and planned on cucumber and tomato sandwiches using vegetables right from their garden. It would be the sort of simple fare that was common during the war.

On Thursday, two days before the wedding, Janice left her home to walk to Clara's. The distance totaled less than ten blocks and Janice would have no more considered driving than flying. As she crossed the intersection at Main Street and Fretz, Clara's house came into view. Janice could see a man in uniform standing with Clara on the front steps of their tiny home. As she approached, the man, whose uniform was that of a Lieutenant (jg) in the Navy was walking the other way and they passed one another. He said hello and continued walking. When Janice arrived at the Beech's home, Clara was standing on the porch with her arms crossed and her head down, waiting for her.

"Who was that?" Janice asked.

"A boy," Clara responded as she caught a basketball that had been sitting on the porch with her toe and started it rolling towards her then kicked it up into her hands.

"Thank you," Janice responded dryly, "I almost had that figured out, but now I can quit taxing my brain. What boy, Archimedes?"

"Who?" Clara asked as she stepped off the porch and dribbled the ball towards the net nailed to a tree in the yard..

"Never mind." Janice said with exasperation as she followed the other girl, "now give me a straight answer."

"His name is John Lewis," Clara answered, "I met him at the Officers Club at the Navy Base down in Norman."

"What's he doing up here?"

"He just asked me to marry him."

"Oh shit, Clara, tell me you're kidding," Janice demanded.

"I didn't say 'yes' for crying out loud," Clara whined, hunching her shoulders inward.

"What did you say?" Janice asked with foreboding.

Clara stood silently for too long before she finally answered, "That I would think about it," she acknowledged in a tiny voice.

Janice literally looked at her hands in the hopes that a weapon had suddenly appeared in one of them so she could beat Clara senseless. Finally, the fight or flight adrenaline rush dissipated, Janice lowered her hands to her side and her chin to her chest.

"I could just slap you," Janice finally said. "Everyone you know has been working their fannies off getting ready for this wedding, and you're still entertaining offers. Clara, I can't take this any more." Janice turned and began walking back towards the street.

"Wait," Clara demanded. Janice neither sped up nor slowed down. She just kept walking. It only took a moment for Clara to reach Janice and grab her arm. "I know what you're thinking, but you're wrong."

"I don't care," Janice replied in a weary voice.

"It wasn't like that," Clara said in a pleading voice. "I went out with him a few times and he came up here to tell me he has orders to the Pacific. He rode the Interurban streetcar all the way from Norman, Janice, my gosh, that's over fifty miles on that jolting old bucket of bolts. When he was standing there he just had the sweetest and most hopeful look on his face. What can I say, when he asked me I just got swept away. I don't want to marry him, but he's scared Janice, he's going to war and I just didn't want to hurt his feelings."

Janice finally looked at Clara. "That is the dumbest speech I have ever heard. 'Hurt his feelings?' How do you think he's going to feel when he discovers you're married in two days? Hell, what if he shows up here on Saturday wanting to take you to the movies? Will you invite him to the wedding? Jiminy Christmas, Clara, that's a real guy there with real feelings. You gave him some reason to think he could come up here and propose to you. What about Bill's feelings? He's going to war too!"

"Janice," Clara began, "I know what you're sayin' is right. But, I'm not like you. I'm not deep and I'm not going through life with my emotions in a safety deposit box. Pretty much what you see with me is all there is. You can't imagine what it was like to be me growing up. I was fat old 'Moo Cow' Clara Beech. Unless they was pokin' fun at me, nobody paid any attention to me at all. Now, when a man smiles at me, I cain't help it, I smile back. When they talk to me, I answer. That don't mean I 'm suddenly in love with all of 'em, even though they think it sometimes. When they do, I have a real problem bein' as mean to them as folks always was to me."

Tears were flowing down Clara's face. Janice gently took her arm and led her up onto the sagging front porch of the Beech's home until they were standing in front of the window to the front room of the house. With the darker background of the home's interior, the window made a passable mirror.

"Look at yourself," Janice commanded. "Clara, I don't remember you before you started playing basketball, cause I didn't even come to town 'til I started high school. But that fat little girl is gone, Clara, what everybody sees today is that girl right there in the glass, not the one that's in your head.

"You can't go through life thinking that anyone who'd have you might just be the one. Look at yourself. If somebody had to come up with one word to describe you, it would either be "built" or "babe." You can afford to be choosy. You can afford to get what you want. It's not too late to call this wedding off. You can still do it."

"That's not what I want," Clara shot back immediately, a touch of panic in her voice. "I just wish for one minute you could know what it's been like to be me. Seeing John doesn't mean I love Bill any less. Everybody's not like you, Janice."

"I don't expect you or anybody else to be like me," Janice countered. "Anyway, what you said earlier is not fair."

"What?" Clara asked.

"About me keeping my feelings in a safety deposit box. I'm not like that," Janice insisted.

Clara snorted, "The heck you're not. Janice you're the conscience for the whole world. You cain't be any way different than you are; you're like the Canadian Mounties for God's sake. Everyone who knows you knows you're gonna' come down on the side of what is right and true come what may. It's one of the things we all love about you. I just wish you could relax some and love me for the way I am."

Janice waited for a moment before she responded. "I do love you," she said, but then she insisted, "and I am <u>not</u> like that."

Clara laughed out loud. "You know what?" she asked, "you're as easy to pick on as I am." Clara put her arm around Janice's slim shoulder and hugged her. After a moment, Janice relaxed and laughed.

"O.K.," Janice finally acknowledged, "maybe I am a little like that."

Clara laughed again. "Yeah," she agreed, "maybe just a little."

Janice laughed sheepishly. "All right, Clara," Janice relented, "but you have to promise me you'll call that poor sailor and tell him something approximating the truth."

"I will," Clara agreed, "I swear."

Chapter Thirteen

War Bride

Entry Gate #2, Tinker Field Air Base
Oklahoma City, Oklahoma
June 18, 1943
5:38 p.m.

I

*O*n Friday afternoon, Janice and Clara returned to Tinker Field in the Lookabaugh's Chevrolet. They were met at the gate by Bill and Charlie, as well as the entire crew, including the spare co-pilot, of "The Scarlet Woman," Bill's aircraft. They were there to kiss the bride. Clara gleefully submitted to the kisses of the airmen, squealing happily as each man took her into his arms. When the bombardier, already more drunk than sober, decided to extend his kissing rights to the maid of honor, Janice deflected him with the little side step she'd learned in the café, and said, "Whoa cowboy, not this filly."

Charlie Morgan moved immediately to position himself between Janice and the inebriated lieutenant, and stiff-armed his crewmate out of the way.

"Sorry about that," Charlie said to Janice, "everyone wanted to see Clara since Bill talks about her all the time. I guess Tony thought you came along with the deal. I'm sorry."

"You must think I'm a good deal more delicate than I am," Janice responded.

"Not really," Charlie admitted, "I was just hoping to look like a knight in shining armor."

"Well," Janice replied looking him up and down, "do you have a buffer with you?"

Charlie laughed.

II

From the moment they picked up the two aviators at the Tinker Field gate, until Clara and Bill were to climb the steps of the Pullman car to Texas, Clara had planned every minute. The evening started with dinner at the Skirvin Towers

Hotel. The band was terrific, and both couples danced and with the exception of Janice, drank heavily from a brown-bagged bottle Clara had brought with her. The rules of the hotel required that the bottle be kept on the floor, so the couples ordered "mixers" from the waiter and then "charged" the drinks from their bottle.

"You're a much better dancer than the last time we were together. How did that happen so quick?" Charlie asked.

"Thank the American Red Cross," Janice replied. "Mrs. Phelps finally caught me. She is the chaperone for Edmond girls who attend the dances sponsored by the Red Cross. There are also USO dances, of course, but they tend to draw their girls from the city, and colleges. In any case, with so many military bases in the Oklahoma City area, helping maintain the men's morale has become a big deal. I wanted to help, and dancing is the one thing the guys really want to do. In the last three weeks I have been to six dances. What can I say, she made an appeal to my patriotism."

"Is that what it took," Charlie asked, "an appeal to your patriotism? I'll need to store that little tidbit away for future reference."

"Don't hold your breath, Charlie." Janice retorted, then returned to speaking about the Red Cross dances, "You know, it's not like it is some horribly hard job or something. I enjoy it. Besides, we get everybody here. In three weeks I have already seen some really great bands. Benny Goodman is coming, and Vaughan Monroe was here earlier. I love the music and I've had fun."

"What about all of those fella's?" Charlie prodded.

"That's a laugh. The boys come and go so fast I probably couldn't remember two of their names at the end of the evening. There's no hanky panky, you know. The girls cannot leave the dance even for a minute. We just dance with one fella after another all evening and then ride the bus back home. I feel sorta' sorry for them, the GIs I mean. Most of them are so young, and they're lonesome. Dancing is something fun that reminds them of home," Janice concluded.

"And what they are fighting for," Charlie added.

"Oh you," Janice pinched Charlie's ear gently. "Nothing like that goes on." Janice paused for a moment and made a face as she thought of Tina. "Well, very little, anyway. Sure, some of the girls give a special boy their phone numbers occasionally, even though it's supposedly against the rules. I haven't done that, but still, the guys are wonderful and many of them are really sweet."

"That's what I want to be known as," Charlie confided.

"What?" Janice asked.

"Sweet," Charlie replied completely deadpan. "I've just spent a year and a half learning how to operate the most awesome fighting machine the world has ever known, but I'd really rather be known as sweet. I've been working very hard on it."

Janice leaned back in his arms and considered Charlie for a moment. "That's what I've always thought about you," she finally replied with a hint of sarcasm. "A sweetness that's almost feminine, actually."

"Well, there you go," he replied as though he believed her, "you see, it's already working."

They danced without talking for a moment. Janice considered how well that feminine crack would have gone over with most of the boys she knew. Charlie had the confidence to just play right along, and even extend the joke. She couldn't remember why she'd been less than thrilled with Charlie on their last date. Tonight she was having a great time, and Charlie was the reason.

"You're a funny guy, Charlie Morgan," Janice said at last.

"Wow, what a night, there is another of my goals met," Charlie allowed as he gathered Janice even closer in his arms. "My dad always says its better to be funny than romantic, it lasts forever, and in the long run women like it better. Remember that."

"I'll try," Janice replied.

By 10:30, the bottle was empty, and Janice knew they needed to leave if they were going to be back home by midnight. Although not normally superstitious, she wasn't going to take the chance of allowing Bill to see his bride on their wedding day until they were at the altar.

"Let's get this show on the road," Janice ordered. "It's bad luck if we allow Bill to see his bride on their wedding day, and if we don't get going, it will be after midnight before we can drop Clara off at home."

Everyone else groaned, and made catcalls that amounted to referring to Janice as a killjoy. Finally Charlie rose somewhat shakily to his feet and raised his glass.

"I want to propose a toast," he said.

"Hear, hear," Bill responded.

"To my old buddy, Bill," Charlie began, "and my new friends, Clara and Janice. May the wedding we celebrate tomorrow mark the beginning of a lifetime of health, wealth, and happiness. May you see your children, grandchildren, and great-grandchildren prosper, and may we all be friends for fifty years."

Everyone stood and clinked their glasses over the center of the table. Clara then turned to Janice.

"OK, it's you're turn now, Janice," Clara demanded.

"Yikes," Janice replied, "OK, how's this, Ditto." Then Janice tried to sit down.

"Boo," all three of the others said at once.

"Come on Janice," Bill called out, "you can do better than that."

"OK, OK," Janice yielded, "give a girl a chance to collect her thoughts."

Janice then looked at the expectant faces around the table, raised her glass, and said, "We live in a world, and during a time when just about every physical thing is in short supply. We ration gas, sugar, meat, and even shoes. At the same time, we also collect metal, brass, and rubber. We use it up and wear it out. What we have in abundance in this country, it seems to me, are spiritual things, things like commitment and of course, love. I think the reason we have so much of those things in America is because the more profligate we are in commitment and love, the more of them we have. So, that's what I wish for you: love and commitment. Spend it on each other without regard, lavish it, and pour it into your marriage like Niagra Falls. I hope you'll make a river of your love that flows and ebbs around you forever."

Janice held out her glass, and the others clinked their drinks with hers. For a moment the table was silent, then Clara, her eyes lit with tears, put down her drink and began to clap. "Oh Janice, that was beautiful."

Janice grabbed her purse and said, "OK you guys, that's that. Let's get this show on the road. It really is time for us to go."

On the way out of the restaurant, Charlie took Janice's arm and slipped her hand into the crook of his elbow. He then patted her hand with his own.

"Niagra Falls," he whispered into her ear, "what was that, this Sunday's sermon?"

"Oh hush," Janice replied. "I just wanted somebody to bless this union. Besides, I'm not any good at that sort of stuff."

"On the contrary, Missy," Charlie replied, "quite on the contrary. Not only did you do fine, you also showed me a romantic side of you I had overlooked until then."

"What made you think I don't have a romantic side?" she wanted to know.

"I didn't say you didn't have one, I just hadn't seen it," he replied.

"Let's go, Charlie," she concluded firmly.

III

Less than an hour later the Lookabaugh's Chevrolet was parked in front of the Beech's tiny white frame house located on Edmond's west side. The structure was in need of paint, and there was a ringer type washing machine on the sagging front porch. Bill and Clara were locked together under the single yellow light bulb suspended from the porch's roof. Its light cast a halo around their heads, and made Clara's hair seem to shine. Janice and Charlie were alone on the front seat of the car.

"Penny," Charlie said.

"What?" Janice answered, shaking her head slightly as she returned from her reverie.

"Penny for your thoughts," he explained.

"I'm not sure they are worth a penny," Janice replied. "I was just watching them and wondering what sort of life together they will make."

"Who's to say," Charlie observed, "maybe it will be great."

"Maybe," Janice agreed without enthusiasm.

"Let me ask you something," Charlie continued.

"OK," Janice said.

"Are you and Clara best friends?" he wanted to know.

"What?" Janice replied in confusion.

"All this worry about her. I keep wondering why this is all so important to you?"

"I just hate to see someone, anyone, make a mistake that will last them a lifetime," Janice explained.

"A lifetime," Charlie ruminated, "and just how long is that, Janice?"

Janice had her mouth open to answer and turned towards Charlie. As she did so he shifted in the seat and the glow from the light bulb on the Beech's front porch glinted off the wings above his left breast pocket. In an instant, Janice realized what Charlie was trying to make her see. Janice remained silent for several moments. Finally she turned on Charlie.

"So," she began, "since we're in a war do we just forget everything we have all been raised to believe and just quit worrying about the future."

"Well," Charlie replied softly, "maybe 'quit' is too strong a word. Maybe just suspend worrying about things which are out of our control for the duration."

"That doesn't make sense, Charlie," Janice insisted. "Everyone isn't going to die. What about the ones who live? Do they just go on and live with the results of goofy decisions they made when they thought there would never be any consequences?"

"There will be a time for that later," Charlie replied. "Janice, there is just too much right now, right now to spend time worrying about a future that may never arrive. I think you need to relax and let your guard down a little. Carrying the worries of the whole world on your shoulders must be exhausting to you. Bill and Clara are going to have a few weeks of 'right now' and then we're going overseas. After that, if this was all a big mistake, they can fix it."

"You mean like a divorce?" Janice asked, her voice making it sound like she was talking about rape or murder.

Charlie laughed. "Yes, divorce, if that is what it comes to. Janice, this is 1943 not 1743. Nobody is going to make them wear scarlet "A"s emblazoned on their chests if they wind up divorced. But divorce is just one option. Another is for them to grow up. Maybe they'll develop a little of that love and commitment you were talking about earlier. After all, they say that absence makes the heart grow fonder."

"When have you seen that work?" Janice asked sarcastically. She wasn't about to tell Charlie about the Navy lieutenant who's proposal Clara had rejected 24 hours earlier, but she couldn't leave it alone either. "Do you want to fly to Germany every day with somebody who's worried about his marriage?"

"Well," Charlie acknowledged, "now that's an interesting point isn't it. It doesn't change anything, but it is interesting."

Janice turned a little more towards Charlie and considered his profile in silence for a moment. Finally she said, "OK, so if you're one of those who doesn't consider the future, what do you think about."

Charlie pursed his lips slightly and Janice had a brief premonition of what he would look like twenty or thirty years in the future. When he didn't speak, she thought maybe she'd gotten too personal, that he wasn't going to answer. Finally, without turning towards her he rubbed his face, and then said, "Right now, pretty much."

"Right now? What is that, a philosophy? What does it mean?" she asked. "Like whatever you're doing right that moment?"

Charlie delayed answering again. Finally, he said, "Our days are pretty full, Janice. When I strap that bomber to my butt I have my life and the lives of nine other men riding on many of the decisions I make. The reason I'm the aircraft commander is because somebody decided I had that level of focus. I - I do have it, but remember that two years ago I'd never even been in an airplane. Now I command a plane that killed one of the most experienced test pilots in America when he first tried to fly it. I'm no great stick. I'm just a guy who wants to go over there do my bit and then come back. To do that, I gotta' fly when I'm flying. When I'm in the plane I think about that and darned little else. When it comes to flying, there is nothing else.

"As far as that other junk goes, I don't spend time on it because it's pointless. It's when I'm not in the plane that I really think about right this minute."

"But everyone thinks about the future, Charlie," Janice insisted, "it's human nature. We make plans, we pursue goals, it's . . . it's what we do."

"It's what you do, Janice. Some of us lack your ambition and drive. After the war, maybe it'll be up to people like you to get the rest of us back on track."

Charlie could tell that Janice wasn't satisfied. "Janice," he began again, "if this war has any redeeming qualities at all, it's that it has allowed a whole generation of guys like me avoid having to decide what it is we're going to 'do' with the rest of our lives. I hated thinking about that even before Pearl Harbor and I don't like it any better right now. If the war hadn't come along I'd be in college right now and I'd probably still not be thinking any further into the future than next Friday night. If I'm playing poker, then I'm thinking about poker. If I'm drinking, then I'm thinking about drinking. If I'm just on my own, then I'm thinking about this very minute."

"This conversation is getting circular," Janice said, exasperated, "then it's whatever you're doing right then, is that right?"

Charlie looked at her before he replied. "No, Janice," he finally said, "I mean right this minute. Right here, right now . . . with you."

Janice was too stunned to respond for a few moments. Finally she looked down at the horn button in the middle of the steering wheel. "Me?" she asked incredulously, "you can't be serious. Why me?"

"Why not you? I know you. You're age appropriate, smart, good looking, unmarried, and sufficiently mysterious to be intriguing. I haven't decided if you're really as serious as you seem when we're together, or just afraid of my devilish charm, and shy as a result."

"Well, shy certainly describes me," Janice acknowledged. "It's my shyness that helps me keep all of those truck drivers and students in line at the café."

"Oh, and I almost forgot," Charlie amended, "you're sort of funny in a self-effacing kind of way, that's one of my favorite traits."

"We're both a couple of riots," Janice acknowledged glumly. "Don't get off the subject. You scarcely even know me, and the little I know about you would lead me to believe that we aren't all that much alike. You never think about the future, and it's all I think about. You even told me that I go around all the time with the weight of the world on my shoulders, and you think we shouldn't worry about anything."

"That's not true," Charlie responded reasonably, "I worry about whether the fuel lines to the cylinder heads are securely fastened, or that every item on the checklist is properly completed before we start engines. I can do something about those things. I'm just not going to worry about what happens to poor Poland, or what we'll all be like after the war. Those things are out of my pay-grade, Janice, they are too big for me and I can't fix 'em.

"Right this minute, on the other hand, was something I could do something about, and from way down in Texas, lo and behold, here I am. Sitting in a car, alone with you, exactly the thing I was thinking about. Pretty neat trick, huh?"

"You're a regular Houdini," Janice allowed dryly. For a moment she studied her hands as though she found them to be a good deal more interesting than she actually did, studiously avoiding making eye contact with Charlie.

"Well, so much for honesty," Charlie interrupted her thoughts. "By now I must seem a little scary to you. Let me put it a different way. When we first met, I liked you. I liked your "way." I bet the French have a word for that, but I don't know what it is. If I'd sat next to you in class, we'd have had a whole semester to get to know each other and if I'd wanted to get to know you better, I'd have had a friend of mine talk to a friend of yours, and we might have gone out. I liked you, and wanted to see you again. That's all it amounts to."

"Tomorrow at noon," Janice began, "it's going to amount to a heck of a lot more than that. Two people are going to get married who have known each other for only a few months and who, for all I've seen couldn't raise a house plant between them."

"What should I have done, Janice? Try to talk him out of it? I've learned a couple of things in my life. One is you can't make anybody do anything they don't want to do. The second is that you can rarely stop somebody from doing something they're really determined to do. Bill wanted to get married so much it was about to start making his teeth hurt. I didn't make that happen. Trust me on that one, O.K?"

There was a momentary pause before Charlie continued. "I might have tried though," he admitted. "If I could have talked him into it, it would have been worth it to be here with you tonight, to see you again. Short of murder, I'd have done a lot to be right here right now." Janice continued looking down at the steering wheel. She was unused to having a boy try to romance her. Since Tommy had left for the Pacific Janice had avoided situations where that might occur. Situations, she realized, just like this one. Janice knew Charlie's words were having an effect on her; it just wasn't one she understood.

Finally Charlie gently used the tips of his fingers to turn her face towards him. He was looking into her eyes. To Janice, Charlie's fingers felt like they were discharging a high voltage electric current that was shooting through her body. In combination with his words of a few moments earlier, his touch was making her dizzy. She had trouble returning his gaze. *He's going to kiss me,* she thought, *I'm as afraid that he will as I'm scared that he won't. What the hell am I going to do?*

Torn about half way between jumping out of her own family's car and running home and throwing herself into Charlie's arms, Janice's subconscious began searching for something that would constitute safer ground. In the midst of this emotional swirl, the face of Tommy Morrison appeared in her mind's eye. In an instant, Janice realized how high the war's price had been in the years since Tommy had been gone. It wasn't easy, but finally, Janice gently took the young aviator's hand from her face, and as though it were an appendage that had somehow become separated from the remainder of his body, used both of her hands to return Charlie's hand to him. Quietly, carefully, she began, "You're a nice guy, Charlie." And with those words, the magic of a few moments earlier was as gone as if somebody had poured a bucket of cold water on the couple in the old Chevy's front seat.

"Oh, oh," Charlie interrupted, "here it comes."

"Now, wait," Janice held up her hand, "you are a nice guy, Charlie. Last year I met a boy who was on his way to flight school. I wasn't interested, but we still got to be friends. When he writes me, I write him back, but nothing is ever going to come of it. Just like him, Charlie, you're going to be gone soon. I'd be happy to write you while you're overseas, O.K., but somehow, I don't think you're looking for a pen pal."

"Could I possibly have communicated that to you?" Charlie said. "We have an expression on the flight line when somebody belabors the obvious, it's 'No shit, Sherlock.' I guess that would fit here as well."

"Men," Janice sputtered, "the moment a girl doesn't just throw herself into your arms you get your feelings hurt. I told you when we first met why I wasn't free to be interested in you. I also told you that you're a nice guy; I'm just not looking for anything more than a casual friendship. Your problem is that you won't take no for an answer."

"Yeah, well forget it," Charlie responded sarcastically, "at this point I wouldn't even take yes for an answer."

"That's fine with me," Janice began when suddenly the door of the car opened and Bill stepped inside, shoving Charlie across the front seat towards the middle.

"OK, you two, break it up and let's get this show on the road," Bill said once he was settled, pulling his hat down over his eyes and feigning sleep. He was unaware that he was interrupting their argument. "I am going to need some shut-eye tonight and a chance to sober up. I don't want to have to confess to my grandchildren that I was drunk when I married their grandma."

The mood was broken, but there was only so much room in the front seat of the car, and Janice noticed Charlie's leg pressed against her own. She could feel the worsted wool of his trousers through the thin cloth of her dress and slip. Charlie affected that he was unaware of the pressure of his leg, but before they had driven the seven blocks to her home, Janice noticed the peculiarly male phenomenon she had observed only rarely in the past. It took Charlie a couple of minutes to exit the car when they arrived at the Lookabaugh home.

Once the two aviators had been shown to John Junior's room, Bill was asleep and snoring loudly within moments, but Charlie lay awake for a very long time.

"Damn," he said aloud.

"Wha...," Bill replied groggily.

"Roll over, Bill, you need your beauty sleep. God knows you're ugly enough right now," Charlie replied.

"You're right Charlie," Bill mumbled, "you're right."

A few feet down the hall, Janice lay in her bed, eyes wide open. For a long time, she considered Charlie Morgan. He was totally different from every boy she knew. As soon as that thought crossed her mind, it occurred to her that with the exception of poor Seth Little, who had lost his right arm in a washing machine when he was two years old, she didn't really know what any of the boys she knew were like any more. Almost all of them were in the service, spread all over the world. Many had been gone for years. Maybe they were all like Charlie now, insouciant, suave, cynical, and self-assured. Janice thought of the words to the song, "either too young or too old."

Tonight was different. Even with Tommy, she had never felt like this before. It wasn't the same as it had been when he was home because she had been a seventeen year old girl, and that was no longer true. Janice had to admit to herself that while she didn't know just exactly what she wanted, she did know that she didn't have it.

"Damn," she said aloud.

IV

The next morning dawned clear and bright and Charlie awoke to the smell of coffee and bacon. When he wandered into the kitchen, shaved and showered, Marge Lookabaugh looked up from her biscuit bowl and asked him how he liked his eggs. In a few minutes, Charlie was seated in front of a plate piled high with eggs, biscuits, bacon and a slice of ham.

"I think I might just have died and gone to heaven, Mrs. Lookabaugh," Charlie acknowledged as he set about demolishing the plateful of food.

"What about Bill?" Marge asked.

"I'll go check on him in a minute, ma'am, but I think if I was you, I'd start washing up. Bill's not much for the morning after, if you get my drift."

Marge nodded, and put the frying pan in the sink.

Janice entered the kitchen at that moment, pointedly not looking Charlie's way. The young pilot caught his breath and watched her as she passed, dressed for the morning in a plaid skirt and white blouse under a light blue cotton sweater. She was wearing white socks and Mary Jane style shoes. Charlie forgot how hopeless she'd made him feel the night before as he strove to memorize everything about her that he could. She grabbed a piece of toast from the top of the stove, and stuck it into her mouth, grabbed a piece of paper from the side of the refrigerator Charlie could tell was a list and kept walking towards the door. She was almost out the door before Charlie called to her.

"Hey, can I go with you?"

"To the grocery store?" the girl replied. "It probably won't be very exciting."

"Who's to say? Give me a minute to wind up here," he requested.

"Hmmph," Janice snorted. Marge Lookabaugh looked at her daughter with a quizzical expression on her face, which Janice returned by making a face of her own, but neither woman said anything.

When the two young people walked out of the house, Charlie was wearing his full uniform, and in the enclosed environment of Edmond, he caused quite a stir. Almost immediately, they encounterd old Mrs. Pierce, working in her garden. She hallooed the couple and Charlie led the way to her fence. Janice tugged at his sleeve, but Charlie wouldn't be deterred.

"Hello," he said, "I'm Charlie Morgan. There is going to be a wedding this afternoon, and," Charlie paused for dramatic effect, "and Janice and I are going to be in it." Mrs. Pierce almost choked on her tongue in the moments before Janice leapt in and explained what was actually occurring.

"Charlie, for crying out loud, behave yourself," Janice hissed at him when she had finally dragged the aviator out of the old woman's hearing.

"Or what," Charlie asked feigning innocence, "are you going to spank me if I refuse?"

"I will if I have to," she snapped back at him.

"Oh man," Charlie replied pretending to shiver with excitement. "Look, Janice, don't tease me, O.K? There's only so much of that a guy can take."

"Oh for goodness sakes, Charlie," she replied exasperated, "act your age, OK?"

Of course, that wasn't the end of it. On the way to and from the store, Janice was required to introduce Charlie to every human being they encountered along the way. Each time he would react as a totally different persona. Once he proclaimed himself a Field Marshall in the Czechoslovakian Army, another as Crown Prince of Batislava, both times complete with an accent. Later he told his mark he was a Boy Scout helping an elderly lady to the store and back and one time each he introduced himself as Janice's fiancee, confidant, and guard. Each time there would be an awkward silence before the target of that particular scam would laugh, clap him on the shoulder, and wish him well "over there." The trip to the store, one Janice had made dozens of times in less than 15 minutes, took over an hour. When they arrived back at home, Janice retrieved the small bag of groceries, handed them to her mother with the admonition to ignore everything anybody said to her at church the next morning, and then collapsed onto the couch.

"I thought you said you didn't think a trip to the store would be very exciting," Charlie interrupted her thoughts, "that was great. Let's go again," he prompted.

"Unhhhh," Janice replied.

V

The wedding, planned to allow for a reception afterwards before Bill and Clara needed to meet the train for Texas just after 3 p.m., was scheduled for noon. At 10:15, Janice threw her suit into the car and headed to the Beech's home to get Clara. To give everyone else a better chance of being ready on time, the two girls had decided to dress for the wedding at the church. Their families and the aviators would simply walk the few blocks, leaving early enough to be there on time.

Clara looked at Janice's reflection in the mirror in the Church's ladies room. "Thanks," she said when they'd made eye contact.

"For what?" Janice asked.

"Everything, of course, but mostly for giving me hell on Thursday. I needed it. I wasn't really prepared to give up on Bill and take up with that lieutenant or anything, but I just don't know what I was ready to do. I know you can't understand that, and I know it's wrong. But here you are, still willing to stand up with me. I appreciate that, and I will forever."

"Forever is a long time," Janice observed. "The day may come when you wish I'd hit you on the head and dumped you into a slow freight train heading to Tucumcari or somewhere. Even in the best of marriages it isn't perfect all the time, Clara. Married people have to compromise. My grandmother said that marriages aren't really 50-50 propositions. They are more like 70-30, and both people always feel like they are the 30."

"Your grandmother was pretty smart," Clara allowed.

"I always thought so," Janice agreed. "You look really pretty, Clara. I know Bill is going to feel like the luckiest guy in the world when he sees you coming down the aisle."

"I've been dreaming of this my whole life, Janice. Falling in love, getting engaged, my very own wedding. So far it's been better than I had the brains to dream up. But the easy part is over. I realized this mornin' I'm gonna' have to shift from wedding to marriage after today. I don't know that I ever really dreamed of that part before. I know that's what you've been worried about - my commitment I guess." Clara turned away from the mirror and faced Janice, took the other girl's hand in her own and looked into her eyes, "I want you to know that I am going to do everything I can think of to make Bill happy that he did this. I swear I will."

"I hope you're both really happy," Janice responded and hugged her.

"Oh nuts," Clara laughed as tears filled her eyes, "now I'm gonna' have to do my mascara all over again."

Clara's mother and sisters entered the room at that point, and their chatter drowned out any further talk between the two girls. A few minutes later, the photographer came in and took a few standard shots of Clara getting ready and Janice helping her. Finally, it was time to go, there was nothing else left to do. Clara and her family members bustled out and headed to the church vestibule to await the bridal song. After the others were gone, Janice wandered around the room collecting Clara's discarded clothing and toiletries and placed them in the other girl's suitcase. At the door, she took a final look around the tiny room, snapped off the light and followed the others.

VI

The minister droned on a little longer than Janice's attention span when he was describing the sanctity of marriage and her mind wandered a bit. Near the front of the groom's side of the church the members of the Scarlet Woman's crew who were not in the wedding party filled an entire pew. Seated squarely in the middle of the airmen was Janice's little brother, John, Junior, wearing the most preposterous smile Janice had ever seen. In the row behind them, Janice's parents shared a pew with old Mrs. Pierce, who as near as Janice could remember hadn't even been invited. Janice was convinced the old woman had attended the wedding to see for herself if Janice was getting married as Charlie had suggested earlier in the day. Finally, about a dozen little boys had crowded over on that side to be near the heroes of the Army Air Corps.

On the bride's side of the sanctuary sat the Beech's. Janice quit counting when she got to 50 of them, and they ran curiously to type - large. There wasn't a single suit among the men, and several were wearing denim overalls. One of the Beech men was already asleep, gently punctuating the minister's sermon with his snores. Janice smiled as she remembered that Clara had wanted to keep Bill from knowing too much about her family until it was "too late." As Janice's eyes played over the group, she decided it had been a good idea.

Next, Janice studied the wedding couple. Clara was nervous, and her responses to the minister's questions tended to be in a wavering voice that was probably inaudible on the back row of the church. Bill's answers were more easily heard, and while his voice did not quaver, he was sweating, and the collar of his shirt was damp above his tie.

Finally, there was Charlie Morgan. He was fun to look at, Janice decided. He was as handsome and collected in his tropical worsted summer uniform as Bill was mussed and stressed in his. While she was studying him, Charlie caught her eye and winked at her. This embarrassed Janice, and she quickly averted her eyes, but a moment later she was staring at him again, just as he was staring at her. *What is it about this guy,* Janice thought to herself, *he's like poison ivy or something. He kept me up half the night fretting about our conversation and now I can't take my eyes off him.*

Janice's thoughts were interrupted as Clara turned to hand her the bouquet. *Good Lord,* she thought in sudden panic, *I only have this one thing to do, and I just messed it up.* Janice took the bouquet so that Clara could receive her ring. The old minister spoke on for a few more minutes and finally the thing was done. Clara and Bill walked down the aisle, and a moment later, Janice and Charlie followed them. The wedding was over, and for better or worse, Clara was married.

The reception that followed the wedding was held in the Beech's backyard. If the fact that it was a Baptist Church wedding was supposed to preclude alcohol, that proscription had been lost on the Beech's. There was a keg of beer in a tub of ice as well as a wide variety of bottles. While everyone awaited the appearance of the bride in her traveling clothes, those who were inclined began to partake. The airmen, who had brought most of the bottles themselves, could scarcely finish one drink before somebody was offering them another.

Janice had offered their somewhat larger yard for the reception, but the Beech's house was chosen because it was close to the Santa Fe Railroad station and would be an easy walk for the couple when it became time to catch their train. Before long, the small yard was filled with people, mostly relatives of the bride, feeling the effects of liberal amounts of alcohol. Janice smiled as she looked around, pleased that she wouldn't be cleaning up after this party. The photographer reappeared with the bride and groom. He posed the wedding party in front of the small cake. After the flash of the bulb, Charlie asked him to take another, confessing he had moved at the crucial moment. When the photo was posed and taken again, the photographer turned to Charlie, "Well, what do ya' think there, Admiral? Will that one work?"

"Perfect," Charlie answered.

The band had fit the budget for the wedding precisely: free and almost worth it. It comprised three old drunks, relatives of the bride's, who came close to carrying a tune several times during the dancing. Janice laughed in surprise every time she heard a few bars that betrayed the identity of the song they were performing. After they began, Bill and Clara danced first, and then Clara danced with her Dad. For the third number, Charlie led Janice onto the dancing area.

"You couldn't take your eyes off me in there, could you," Charlie began.

"What?" Janice replied as though it was the most outrageous thing she'd ever heard.

"Don't deny it. The truth is I couldn't take my eyes off of you either," he admitted. "Look, Janice, I just want to say I'm sorry we got into that little spat last night. I wanted to get to know you better, and I'm really glad we all came up here."

"Thanks," Janice replied for want of anything better to say and embarrassed that he had caught her blatantly staring at him during the ceremony.

One of the other airmen cut in at that point, and Janice wound up dancing with every member of the bomber's crew. By the time Charlie had worked his way back to the front of the rotation again, it was almost 2:30 and time for Clara, Bill, and the others to leave. The men of the Scarlet Woman were going to ride the train to the Oklahoma City station and then take a cab to Tinker Field from there.

"I've been thinking about the future," Charlie offered.

"I'll bet," Janice responded.

"No really, do you want to know what I've been thinking about?"

"What? No, wait, no I don't want to know," then after the slightest pause she continued, "OK, I do want to know."

"I've been thinking that we're going to see each other again. I made this one happen by thinking about it. I think I can do it again." With that he leaned forward and surprised Janice by kissing her lightly on the lips. Almost involuntarily, Janice leaned into the kiss before she caught herself and jerked away from Charlie like she'd been burned. Janice almost slapped Charlie, but stopped because she didn't want to cause a scene. Instead she brought up her hands and pushed him away. He caught her wrists easily and held them gently at his chest.

"The way you telegraphed that slap you never quite got around to delivering," Charlie said with a smile, "a fella'd think you weren't too upset about that kiss. Unfortunately, Janice, I can't stand here waiting for you to tell me to do it again. I've gotta' go." He kissed her again, lightly on the cheek this time and left her standing on the dance floor. As the Scarlet Woman's crew members began the short walk to the train station, Charlie grabbed his small travel bag and followed them out of the yard.

Janice was watching them go when Clara grabbed her from behind. The two girls hugged, and Clara said, "Guess what Bill told me when we were dancing a minute ago?"

"He's pregnant," Janice guessed.

"No silly," Clara responded as though Janice's answer might have occurred. "He explained why he wouldn't let me come down there to get married."

"Why was that?" Janice wanted to know.

"Because of Charlie," Clara replied with a smile like the cat that ate the canary.

"Charlie?" Janice replied, confused for a moment. Then suddenly she realized what she was getting at. "Charlie?" she repeated. He had told her as much the night before when he said he made this whole trip happen. Now Clara and Bill were in this ridiculous marriage, and she was furious at him all over again.

"He wanted to come up here and see you again," Clara added superfluously. "Look, Janice, if you need a matron of honor when you get married, I'll try to be available." Clara hugged Janice one last time and then was gone.

Janice stood and watched Clara and the others as they walked away. She could feel Charlie's lips where they had touched her own and again where he'd kissed her cheek. She reached up and touched her own lips with her fingertips - torn between savoring and begrudging his kisses. When everyone was finally out of sight she shook her head. "Damn, Charlie," she whispered, scarcely audible, "just what I didn't need."

Chapter Fourteen

Bertha

The Wide-A-Wake Café
Wednesday, July 21, 1943
2:20 p.m.

I

$\mathcal{P}$hilip Potts, Sr. opened the screen door to the Wide-A-Wake Café and stood in the opening as his eyes adjusted from the blinding glare of the afternoon sun. Bertha Potts saw her husband the instant he opened the door. In the eight years she had worked in the café, Phil had been there only twice. Once to report the death of her mother in a house fire, and the other to eat lunch. It wasn't noon.

Bertha Potts was a large woman, tall and rawboned. Her callused hands and grim face bespoke a lifetime of hard work and tough conditions. To those who knew her, Bertha's most consistent characteristic was her unflinching piety, and an unwavering faith in God. To those who did not, she could seem harsh and humorless. She now stood frozen, holding a plastic tray with four glasses of water and two cups of coffee. The pain in Philip's eyes when his gaze met hers caused Bertha's hands to go numb and the heavy tray dropped straight to the café's linoleum floor.

The resulting explosion sounded like the detonation of a bomb in the close quarters of the small restaurant. Every eye in the café was instantly riveted on Bertha who was rapidly going into shock. Philip walked past the wreckage of the cups and glasses and put his arms around her.

Bertha was shaking, bent slightly at the waist, hands about halfway to her face, and totally stiff. She was staring vacantly into one of the corners of the café's dining room. Philip was holding her awkwardly. Close physical contact wasn't common between them, with Phil Potts as unused to providing comfort as his wife was to receiving it.

"Which one was it?" she croaked in a voice so filled with anguish she could scarcely be understood.

"Junie," he answered quietly. Philip Potts, Junior, called Junie by his family and P.P. by his classmates and friends was their third child and second son.

Their first son, James Robert, named in honor of Phil's father, and his brother, Junie, were soldiers serving with the U.S. Army's 45th Infantry Division (Texas and Oklahoma National Guard) fighting at the port of Gela in Sicily. Young Philip was killed during an air raid.

"Oh no-o-o-o!" She cried and buried her face in his shoulder. On the day he died, Philip Potts, Junior was eighteen years, nine months and four days of age.

II

"Janice," Ellen Rogers voice sounded strained as it came through the earpiece in the Lookabaugh's phone, "Bertha had to leave. Can you come in early and finish her shift."

"Of course," Janice answered, "give me a few minutes to change and walk over there. Is Bertha all right?"

"P.P. was killed in Italy. Phil, Senior came and got her."

"Oh no," Janice replied, then, "hang on Ellen, I'll be there as quickly as I can." P.P. Potts had been two years behind Janice in school. Janice remembered how upset Bertha had been when P.P. dropped out of high school shortly after his seventeenth birthday and followed his brother into the Oklahoma National Guard. Now he was dead.

III

Three days later, following the memorial service at the Baptist Church, Janice, her younger brother, and her parents walked onto the porch of the Potts' modest home carrying a covered dish and an apple pie.

Once the food was arranged, Philip Senior quietly asked Marge and Janice if he could speak with them alone. He then led them into the kitchen.

"Bertha went into the bathroom when we got home from the church and won't come out. Can you talk to her?" he asked, looking at Mrs. Lookabaugh.

Marge looked at Janice before returning her gaze to Philip, Senior. "Philip, I would, but I scarcely know what I'd even say to her." She then looked uncomfortably at her daughter.

"Let me try, Mr. Potts," Janice suggested.

"Please do what you can," he asked.

Janice nodded her head then walked to the bathroom door and knocked.

"Bertha," she said quietly, "it's me, Janice." There was no response.

"Bertha, will you open the door?" Janice asked. "Everybody is worried about you."

After a long moment, Janice heard the lock, a simple eyelet and hook, being released on the other side. She opened the door and walked in. When Janice entered the small bathroom, Bertha was using the toilet as a chair. In her hand was a wad of tissue paper she'd been using to soak up her tears.

Janice seated herself on the edge of the tub and took Bertha's hand. She didn't say anything. She just sat.

After a few minutes, Bertha said, "He was only a baby. He didn't have no business in the army."

Janice squeezed her hand.

"Do you remember my son, Janice?" Bertha asked, her voice seemingly coming from far away.

"Of course I do, Bertha, you know I do. P.P. was only two years behind me in school," Janice answered.

"His daddy and me called him Junie, 'cause we di'nt need more'n one Philip around the house." Bertha's eyes seemed focused on something far away. She smiled wistfully as she spoke. "He was a pistol, Janice. He was three years younger than James Robert, but he didn't know that. If James Robert could climb a tree, then Junie could too. If James Robert was ready to go swimming in the pond, then Junie was right with him. It just didn't ever occur to him that he couldn't go everywhere with his brother. James Robert was real good to let him tag along all of the time when they was growin' up.

"Once when Phil was out of work, Junie was probably five or six, we stayed with my folks on the farm. I come back home from my job at the cannery, and the boys, our two and my sister's three, was jumping out of the hayloft onto a big ol' pile of straw they'd kicked out to make a soft place to land on. They was jumping twenty feet if it was an inch, and there was Junie, ready to take his turn just like them bigger boys; laughing like crazy, and so excited he could just barely stay inside his skin. It scared me to death, but before I could stop him he took this huge jump and it seemed like he was in the air for two minutes, although I know it wa'nt.

"When they come back from the fields, Phil and my Pa was so mad at them boys they made 'em carry all that hay back up there 'thout any help. Junie did his part right with the others, even though I was afraid to have him around all them boys carryin' pitch forks. When they was finished, Philip took a switch to James Robert, and when he was done Junie said, 'Me too Pa, I was right there with 'em, give me what I got coming too.' So he did.

"I was scared when I seen 'em jumpin', Janice, and they ruined some of that hay, but I wouldn't take $100 for the sight of Junie's face when he'd jumped from that hayloft. He was so happy and so proud of hisself.

"When James Robert joined the Guard, we knew Junie'd be right behind. We tried to get him to wait, but he was rarin' to go. He wanted to be with his brother. The army di'nt agree, and they wasn't even in the same outfit." Bertha's composure cracked at this point and she continued in tears, her face screwed up in pain. "Janice, he was all alone when he died. He was afraid of the dark when he was alone, and he di'nt have any kin with him at all. He was alone an' I bet he was scared."

Bertha broke down again. The toilet paper she was holding was dissolving and Janice got her some more and handed it to her. After a moment, Bertha resumed, almost squeezing out the words in her grief.

"He was so young. And he was so far away. If I coulda' just been there, Janice, just for one moment, I could have held his hand and told him I loved him."

"He knew you loved him," Janice said softly, "you're such a wonderful momma."

"How would he know?" Bertha snapped. "I didn't tell him often enough, his Pa never told him at all, that ain't Phil's way." Bertha turned to Janice with grief stricken eyes and took hold of the girl's shoulders in her large hands before she continued. "What if he didn't know?"

"He knew, Bertha," Janice reassured her as tears began spilling from her own eyes.

Bertha put her hands on her stomach, then said softly, "I carried him right here under my heart. Now I'm never going to see him again, and all I got left is empty and hurtin'. My heart won't work, Janice. I cain't hardly breath 'cause my ribs have closed in on my lungs and I cain't bring in any air. My skin hurts, my fingers hurt, my eyes hurt. I cain't barely stand how much I hurt." Bertha wasn't looking at Janice. She was speaking through clenched teeth as she stared at the floor near Janice's feet. She blew her nose loudly.

"He was a good son, and you are a good momma. You loved him every day of his life. He's with God now, and there isn't anything he doesn't know. Take comfort in that if you can."

"I cain't Janice," Bertha insisted, "I just cain't."

"Maybe not yet. Maybe in time," Janice suggested.

"You don't understand," Bertha interrupted in a voice that made it seem hopeless. Then, Janice could almost see a sudden resolve form on Bertha's face. She made a decision, then as if eager to get it off her chest before she could change her mind, Bertha cried out in a rush, "You cain't understand. I'm never going to get over this because I killed him, I killed my boy!"

"What?" Janice responded in confusion.

"I killed him," Bertha insisted.

"What are you talking about, Bertha? You didn't kill P.P., he died in the war, thousands of miles from here. You didn't have anything to do with it," Janice reassured her.

"I did too. I killed him 'cause I didn't do right. Every day I'd get up, prepare breakfast an' get ever'body off to school or work. Then I'd pray to God to protect my boys. I made deals with Him. 'If You'll keep my boys alive, I'll smile at every customer all day long,' or 'If You'll keep my boys alive today I won't eat any meat all day.' It was the last thing I did every morning before I left for the café. It was working, Janice. I prayed every day, and they lived every day.

"Then Wednesday I overslept. I don't know why, I never do that. I was rushed though, and I was almost late to work. I got behind, and I didn't pray, Janice. I didn't pray on Wednesday and God killed one of my boys."

"Bertha," Janice snapped impatiently, "Bertha look at me!" Janice grabbed the older woman's shoulders and turned her until they were facing one another. "Philip, Junior didn't die on Wednesday. You just heard about it on Wednesday. He was already dead when you got up that morning. You didn't kill him. The war did. This damnable war. God isn't punishing you for not praying on Wednesday. If God protected people's children based upon how Godly they are, your boys woulda' been the safest soldiers in Europe. There may be no comfort in it, but the reason Philip died is because he was a soldier in a war, and soldiers die in wars.

"Bertha," Janice continued in a softer voice, "I know you're hurting real bad, but if you convince yourself it's your fault he died, you'll do nothing but give yourself a nervous breakdown. You have two more children here and James Robert still in the war. They all need you. You cannot do this to yourself or to them. It's right for you to grieve, Bertha, but you've gotta' snap out of this desire to blame yourself. It's crazy, and it'll make you crazy if you keep it up."

Bertha was silent for almost a minute before she said, "If I'm not being punished, then why my son?"

"You know I don't know that. I do know that God answers prayers, He just said no this time, and you and I may never know why."

"What if God takes James Robert? My boys were supposed to be there when I get old. They are supposed to come to my memorial service, not me to theirs. What if God takes all of my children?" Bertha sounded rational, but her eyes were wild like she was getting ready to run.

"Bertha," Janice interjected softly, "don't borrow trouble. You're not in charge of who lives or dies. If God takes all of your kids it'll be because it was in his plans not yours. There isn't anything you can do except pray. Do you remember Job? God took all he had, but Job didn't turn away from Him. God rewarded him for his faithfulness ten fold. This is part of God's plan, but you and I don't know what it is or how it will fit. We just have to accept it by and by."

"Then what do I do now?" Bertha asked.

Janice patted Bertha's hand while she thought. Finally she admitted, "I don't know exactly, but I do believe you can't quit doing the things you've been doing. Keep asking God to protect your family. James Robert still needs your prayers, he's going to need them the whole rest of your life. As for everything else, you just keep living, you keep right on loving your family. If you're afraid they don't all know you love them then don't waste another day before you tell them, tell 'em today, tomorrow, and every day from now on. There's nobody doesn't want to hear that from time to time. Keep writing James Robert, write him today and tell him you love him, too. Also, keep smiling at the customers at the Wide-A-Wake, ain't nobody doesn't like a friendly smile, don't save those to try to bribe God, just give 'em away! In a month, you won't think about Junie every minute. Later, you will start remembering what it was like in better times. Eventually, you'll laugh about something again, and you won't cry every time you think about him. It's never going to be OK, but I bet it'll get better.

"My Uncle Frank got killed on an oil rig over in Seminole. After he died, my grandma told me that parents expect to be buried by their children. When it's the other way around, she said it leaves a hole that never heals. She died missing my Uncle Frank; she never got over it completely and maybe you won't either. She may have been sad about her boy, but I remember Gramma as cheerful and happy. She lost her son, but she went right on living and loving everyday 'til she died. That's what you have to do too, Bertha." Janice squeezed back the tears in her own eyes.

Bertha sat silently for a long time, finally she smiled sadly and hugged Janice before she said, "How'd you get so many smarts into a head that young?"

"I'm not that smart Bertha." Janice answered ruefully, "I'm just getting like everybody else in this town. I'm learning from experience,"

Bertha hugged Janice again, then she stood, took a deep breath and said, "Honey, I've got guests here. I need to see to them."

Janice smiled at Bertha and followed her out of the tiny room. Bertha walked straight to her husband and kissed him lightly, "I love you Philip," she said for the first time in years.

Surprised, Philip answered awkwardly, "I - I love you too, Bertha."

"Well good," she replied, "then I'm gonna' expect to hear it from time to time. Don't worry Phil, you'll get better at it once you've practiced some." She then turned to Janice's mother and said, "Hello Marge, thank you for being here."

Chapter Fifteen

Terrible Resolve

"I feel all we have done is awaken a sleeping giant and fill him with a terrible resolve."
Admiral Isoroku Yamamoto following the Japanese attack on Pearl Harbor

Central State College
Thursday: 25 May 1944
11:55 am

I

"*Janice!*" Cynthia Butler called out to Janice Lookabaugh as she was leaving the business college classroom building one day before the end of finals. Janice hadn't seen Cynthia since she graduated from Central State with the class of 1942. Cynthia was dressed in a smart, yet simple navy blue suit with contrasting blue piping and a white blouse. Shoes and a purse in the exact color of blue as the piping on her dress set off the outfit.

"My gosh, Cynthia," Janice exclaimed as she hugged her friend, "you look wonderful! What are you doing here?"

"Actually, I'm looking for you," Cynthia responded, "I went by your house and your Mom told me where I might find you."

"Me?" Janice responded. "Well I'm glad to see you, but why?"

By this time the girls were walking arm in arm across campus toward the University Center where Janice had been headed before Cynthia had joined her.

"Are you in a hurry?" Cynthia asked. "If not, let me buy you a coke."

"I just finished my exam for today. Ultimately, I need to get started on tomorrow's test in English Lit, but short of an air raid, I'd love to have something provide me with a reason to delay getting started," Janice responded with a smile.

The two girls entered the college's student union, got into line in the snack bar and once they'd received their drinks, Cynthia handed a dime to the cashier and they found a table. This late in the semester, there were very few students still on campus, and the cafeteria was almost empty.

"First," Cynthia began, "let me ask you how committed you are to the Wide-A-Wake?"

"Are you kidding?" Janice responded, "it's the primary reason I study so hard. If I never see ham or eggs again after I graduate it will be too soon for me. Are you offering me a job of some sort?"

"Actually," Cynthia replied, "I am. I work for the standards office in the bomber rework facility out at Tinker Field. We need someone who can work as an inventory specialist. Mostly you just count rivets or whatever they have in the supply room to insure we don't run out of something that might result in a delay in the repair work. One of the most important parts of the job is the requirement that the specialist make computations of aircraft weight. We have to know how much every airplane they send out of there weighs, or "grosses out," as the Air Corps types call it. About the only way to do that is by actually weighing the parts themselves to make sure they are consistent in size and weight from lot to lot so this B-24 or B-17 weighs about the same as the others of its type."

"Would you be offended," Janice interjected, "if I mentioned that this sounds about as exciting as watching paint dry?"

"It's mind numbing," Cynthia confirmed before she continued, "but here is why we do it. The gross weight and the fuel it's carrying determine the range of a bomber. If they don't know how much the plane weighs, they might overload it with fuel and bombs and it wouldn't be able to take off. With too much weight, the range is shortened and even if it did take off, it might not have enough fuel to make it back after a mission. If you consider the thousands of rivets and the miles of wire and tubing aboard one of those monsters, you can see that even a small amount of weight difference in some parts could make a big difference in how much the plane weighs. It may not be the most exciting job in the world Janice, but it is important. Most of the jobs people are doing out there are.

"My boss is an Air Force officer and he asked me if I knew anybody who could do that job."

"And you told him about me?" Janice asked.

"Oh heck no," Cynthia responded, "I told him I didn't know anybody like that. I did tell him I knew a girl who could carry six cups of coffee on a tray, add three lunch tabs in her head, and sweat like a field hand without dripping on the pork chops. It turns out THAT is just what the job requires. Of course, I told him about you, silly. The job pays thirty-five dollars a week. When is your last final?"

After a moment's silence in which Janice's mind registered the sum Cynthia had just quoted to her, she responded, "Tomorrow," then, "did I hear you correctly? Did you say $35 a week, and not a hash brown in the whole deal?"

"That's right," Cynthia responded, then she lifted her coke and took a sip through the straw while she watched Janice for a reaction.

154

Before the war, Janice had made one dollar a day at the café. Sometimes her tips would equal that amount, literally doubling her pay, but not often. Since the war had begun, the difficulty of keeping help had driven up wages until she now earned twenty-five cents an hour, plus tips. People had more money now and tips were better, sometimes she worked a six-hour shift and left with $2 even $2.50 in tips. Even yet though, a nickel or a dime was the most common, and nickels were far more common than dimes.

"I'll have to tell the Noe's," she finally responded. "They are thinking I'll be there this summer to work full-time. . ." Suddenly it occurred to Janice that she was planning on leaving the café without so much as a rearward glance. She had worked there since she was 16. The Noe's had been wonderful to her, almost like extra parents, but thirty-five dollars a week would double, maybe even triple what she could earn at the café.

"Are you sure I'll get the job?" she asked.

"Trust me on this one, OK?"

"OK."

Janice got the job.

II

At 5:45 am on Monday Janice boarded Fred Weibel's bus for the twenty-mile ride to Tinker Field. On Cynthia's advice, she was carrying her lunch and wearing a suit consisting of pants and a short "Ike" jacket of lightweight khaki colored material. With the exception of some blue jeans, she was wearing the only trousers she owned. She dismounted at the stop Cynthia had told her about and entered the base's administration building at the door marked: "New Employees." The next two hours were spent filling out forms and checking onto the base. Finally, she reported to the hangar in which she was going to work and handed all of the forms she'd been carrying around to the civilian personnel clerk of the rework facility. She was then interviewed as part of a group of seven other new workers by an ancient Master Sergeant who said, "Excuse my French," every time he swore. When he was finished, he introduced Colonel Clark who commanded the rework facility in which Janice was to be employed.

If nothing else, the Colonel served to make the Master Sergeant look young. He was a retread from the First War who'd apparently been pretty old even then. He had been returned to active duty after almost twenty years as a civilian. His tunic, or blouse as Janice soon learned it was called, was festooned with ribbons from campaigns of another era, but he was all business about the war in which he was now involved. Janice got the impression during the talk that, at least to the colonel, the fate of the free world was intricately woven into the fabric of rivets, tubing, wires, and spark plugs.

When the colonel was finished, the Master Sergeant resumed the floor and called the names of each of the new workers, and handed them a small sheet of paper with instructions on how to find their workstation.

"You'll be met by your shift supervisor when you get there. If he or she ain't there, try not to start a damn fire, excuse my French, or blow up the building 'fore they do, OK?" Janice couldn't tell from his face whether he was kidding or not.

When Janice arrived at her workstation, her supervisor, Nadine Thomas, met her. Within ten seconds, Nadine told Janice she was married to a sergeant in the 45th Division, currently serving in Europe with an infantry company. She was an attractive woman in her late 20's, friendly, helpful, and dressed in a practical coverall similar to one she handed to Janice.

"Draw another one before you go home. It's your job to keep them clean. If you come in here dressed like you are, somebody will drive a forklift or a tractor into a wall every hour all day long and we'll never get anything done. The informal rule among the women around here is to keep it covered. Unfortunately, the less you look like a woman, the more women are going to be able to do to help win this war."

Janice smiled ruefully, "Tell me about it," she acknowledged, "I have been working as a waitress since I was sixteen."

"Well, then you know," Nadine agreed. "It would be one thing, I suppose if we were all off in the Pacific someplace, but these guys go home to their wives every night and they still act like they haven't seen a woman in months."

Janice nodded in acknowledgment.

"You ought to see 'em when Princess Cynthia comes down here pretty as a movie star and dressed like a million bucks," Nadine added. Involuntarily, Janice stiffened to have her benefactor subjected to what seemed like a disparaging reference. Nadine noticed. "Don't get your panties into a knot, Sweety, I don't mean anything by that Princess stuff, but she is sort of like royalty around here. She runs this facility a damn site better'n that old Spanish American War reject ever did. The day she showed up was the luckiest one of his life, and thank goodness he's smart enough to know it. He don't visit the latrine without the Princess' say so. She's one of the good ones, Janice, but when she's on the floor down here, she's just another skirt to this bunch of tomcats we work with. Anyhow, if you can live with that, this is a great job. I guarantee ya', it's the best one I've ever had."

For about thirty minutes, Nadine showed Janice how to enter inventory items on the worksheets, when and where to carry the parts she was responsible for loading onto carts, and things like the difference between an aluminum and a steel rivet. She explained the importance of what they were doing, although using more time and with less information than when Cynthia had explained the same thing to her at the student union. Finally, Nadine demonstrated how to

156

weigh and record the data from her spot checks. It occurred to Janice that the demonstration was about 10 minutes too long.

For the remainder of the morning, Janice mostly counted out boxes of rivets, screws and assorted airplane parts. She also loaded crates, made inventory entries, submitted orders, and in general made herself as useful as her limited experience allowed. Suddenly, she was startled to hear a loud whistle. Surrounded as she was by bombers, the sound made her think for a moment they might be under attack. The sound hadn't even died away, when the other workers began leaving the floor, putting down their tools and stopping immediately whatever they had been doing.

"Come on, kiddo," Nadine hollered with a wave of her hand, "it's lunch time. I'll introduce you to everybody."

"Everybody" turned into a group of about 15 women who were also working in the giant hangar that housed the rework facility. They occupied a table in the lunchroom while everyone looked expectantly at Nadine while she did the honors. As soon as Janice had been introduced around the table everyone attacked their brown bag lunches.

"Lunch 'hour' is 20 minutes, Janice, go to it," Nadine instructed.

For the next few minutes there was only the sound of rustling paper bags and wax paper coming off sandwiches. When they were finished, a few of the girls lit cigarettes while others left for the restroom.

"I know you probably feel a little lost right now," Nadine began, "but you'll soon get the hang of it." She paused a moment for emphasis and then continued, "Janice, what we're doing here is really important. The bombers usually arrive here almost worn out. God knows what sort of horrors they have been through. When they leave they are either as good as new, or even better. I'm really proud of what we're doing, but you know the best part?"

"The paycheck?" Janice answered facetiously, "no really, what?"

"I have six men working for me, and other than trying to get into my pants, none of them really questions my right to be in charge. Things are changing, Janice, and I am damned if I ever plan to let them go back the way they were. I like working, and I like being in charge. Look around you. There are dozens of facilities just like this one in the country, and then there are the factories that make these planes in the first place. There are others making the ships, guns, tanks, everything America and our allies need to fight this war. All of them have to have women like us in order to operate. When this war is over, nobody is going to be able to say that it was just men who won it. If it wasn't for women, every one of these places would grind to a halt PDQ."

"PDQ?" Janice asked.

"Pretty darn quick," one of the other girls explained, Janice thought she recalled that her name was Colleen.

"Pretty damned quick," another girl, named Teresa, corrected spitting out the words from around the cigarette jammed in her mouth.

"To each his own," Colleen said.

"As I was saying before Miss Holy-roller and Miss Pottymouth over here got involved," Nadine looked at the two girls who had interrupted her with a withering glance before she continued, "most of the women in this place have no intention of meekly returning to their kitchens and turning everything back over to the men after the war. I don't know about the other husbands represented here, but when HE gets back, Elliot isn't going to know what hit him."

"Is Elliot your husband?" Janice wanted to know.

"Yep. He's a great guy in a lot of ways, and I love him, but his idea of helping out around the house is to get out of it. The next time Elliot picks up a glass or plate will be the first time he's ever done it. I have been putting little hints into my letters to him, but we're gonna' have a real come to Jesus meetin' when he gets home."

"I thought we were just fixing broken bombers around here," Janice remarked. "Are we really changing the world?"

"Don't mock," Nadine responded, but she smiled at Janice to show she wasn't offended. "Just you wait. We're going to have a hell of a fight on our hands; there is no doubt about that. America will need jobs for all of us after this war is over and the veterans are going to be right to expect some consideration. They are, after all, the ones who got shot at. But there are also going to be thousands of widows, single women who are independent and young women like you who are educated and ready to take a real place in the world. What are we all supposed to do? There's no way we're going to give up what we have won, so we're going to have to be ready to fight to keep what we have right now, and what we should always have had. It's a brave new world ahead of us. I know it's gonna' be tough to make this country accept us for our abilities, but to tell you the truth, I can't wait."

Janice let her eyes travel around the circle of women at the table. They looked like any cross section of distaff Americans, different ages, sizes, and shapes. Superficially, their similarity lay in the coveralls and bandanna wrapped hair sported by each of them. But in their eyes was a glow of commitment they all seemed to share.

Jeez, Janice thought, almost as spooked as she was inspired, *what if there is a group like this in every war plant in America?*

During the course of the week that followed, Janice allowed the rhythms of the work in the hangar to direct her efforts. She discovered how quickly certain jobs would require certain parts, what the difference was between a 16-ohm and a 32-ohm resister, and dozens of other pieces of arcana she needed to do her job. She could not help but be impressed with the work being done. She never stopped being surprised when she would look up to see one of the other women dangling from an aircraft wing, or reaching high on the tail assembly of one of the giant bombers to replace damaged aluminum or drive rivets.

III

Just before quitting time on Friday, Janice saw Cynthia Butler crossing the floor of the hangar. Cynthia waved, and Janice straightened; waiting while she approached, accompanied by the catcalls and whistles from the men working on the floor.

Cynthia was not intimidated by the behavior of the male workers. Instead she walked with her head held high, waving at one of the men.

"Hey, Sam," she called out, "I'm glad you like the dress. I'll let your wife know next time I see her. She'll probably want one like it." Sam lowered his head as the red from a near lethal blush climbed up his neck. Cynthia finished her walk to Janice's workstation in relative silence.

"When you've changed, come by my office and we'll ride home together," Cynthia invited Janice, "It'll save you the bus fare."

"OK," Janice responded, "thanks," then, "I think you scared the heck out of old Sam there."

"Oh yeah," Cynthia replied matter of factly over her shoulder as she headed back to her office, "he's so scared he'll be on his best behavior for the best part of ten minutes now."

Janice smiled and shook her head.

A few minutes later Janice walked across the hangar floor towards the administrative headquarters of the hangar. Cynthia's office was one of several located up one very long flight of stairs from the hangar floor. When she arrived, Cynthia was seated at a wooden desk, surrounded by logbooks into which she was transcribing numbers and data. The older girl looked up, smiled at Janice and held her index finger in the air in the "wait a minute" signal that would be discernible to anyone, and finished what she was doing. After that, she closed the book, carried it and its twins to a substantial file cabinet with a combination dial on the drawer, put them inside, closed the drawer, twirled the dial, tested the lock, and then reversed the card on the front from its red side which said "OPEN" to its green side which read "LOCKED."

"Let's go," Cynthia said, "my brain has turned to jelly."

"Tell me about it," Janice agreed, "I have this horrible feeling that I may already know everything there is to know about being an inventory specialist. By the time I go back to school I'll probably be untrainable due to brain damage."

"Nadine tells me that you're doing a great job, and more importantly to that crowd, that you fit right in. She says you're funny to boot."

"That's me," Janice responded, "a regular Little Snooks," she allowed referring to the radio character portrayed by comedienne Fanny Brice.

"Well, maybe not that funny, but you're fitting in. A sense of humor goes a long way around here. It's one of the reasons I wanted you to work here."

"Not that I don't appreciate it," Janice responded, "but clearly, any well-trained monkey could do what I do."

"Is it as bad as all that?" Cynthia asked.

"Wait a minute," Janice responded, "I guess I was close to sounding ungrateful, and I am $35 whole dollars away from feeling that way. It's just that I would think filling this job wouldn't be that tough. Why go to the trouble to recruit me?"

"Janice, we have about forty four thousand people working here on this base. There are actually folks commuting to work from a hundred miles away, and hundreds of new applicants try to get jobs here every week. Whenever you hire somebody new, you're always getting a pig in a poke. We have discovered that if we hire somebody we already know something about, we have fewer problems. I worked with you for a year in the café, and you never slacked off. It's a valuable trait, and one we need out here."

"So is that it?" Janice asked.

"You're the one who is setting the agenda, Janice, if you return to college in three months, then yes. Look, there will be plenty of time for what comes next. It's Friday night. Let's leave work behind for a couple days, what do you say?"

"OK," Janice agreed.

By now the women had left the building and were on their way to the small parking lot near the hangar's massive sliding doors. Janice saw the prewar Oldsmobile that had belonged to the Butlers since the mid-30s. There was a "C" sticker in the windshield. In the war-directed rationing of the time, "C" coupons allowed for unlimited gasoline. Janice took note and was impressed. Cynthia climbed in under the wheel and Janice entered on the passenger side. Once the car was started, Cynthia confidently shifted into gear and drove towards the main gate.

"I appreciate the ride." Janice commented as though silence was illegal.

"Sure," Cynthia answered.

"Tell me something," Janice requested.

"OK," Cynthia responded, "what do you want to know?"

"How did you get started here? I thought you went off to Macomb or someplace and were going to teach school."

"I did. Actually it was in the Caddo County schools. I was being paid $60 a month for nine months. I was expected to save enough from that sum to support myself during the summer when I wasn't teaching. It was my first job and I didn't save any money. When summer came I had to move back home and I needed a job. Col. Clark, our boss, was a partner in the firm Daddy went to work for right after he graduated from law school. Daddy knew he'd been recalled to do this job, so he called him and he told Daddy he needed a secretary. I took the job, and I was glad to get it, but he didn't anymore need a secretary than my old Aunt Hattie. What he needed was an executive assistant."

"A what?" Janice asked.

"Executive assistant, someone to help him implement policy around the place, make stuff happen, but in his name."

"So is that what you do now?"

"Nope," Cynthia answered.

"Why?"

"Two reasons, really. For over a year I was a secretary in name, and even worse, in pay. Old Clarksie was happy as hell to have it the way it was. He got all of the credit, and after I finally figured out what it was we were doing around that place, I did all his work."

"A year?" Janice asked. "So you didn't go back to teaching after the summer."

"Are you nuts? Of course not. I hated teaching, even worse, I was lousy at it. Besides, $60 a month for nine months, heck I was making twice that a month as a secretary, and I got paid for twelve months."

"So what happened?" Janice wanted to know.

"First, even the Air Force realized this was too big for one guy and a Master Sergeant to administer, so they opened up the staff for an assistant director. Second, Col. Clark starts interviewing completely inexperienced men for the job without so much as a 'how do you do' to me. He didn't even consider me. What's worse, he wanted me to do the interviewing, and then train the man we hired. I stormed into his office and told him that if I didn't get that job I was walking. He believed me, and I got the job. I'll say this for him. Once I convinced him, he really stood by his decision. We walked right into a firestorm on that one, but he stood by me. It took some convincing, but the Base Commander finally agreed. I was almost the first woman on this base to work at the executive level. Maybe in the whole Air Force."

"Cynthia Butler," Janice acknowledged, "trail blazer."

"I am, but why does a woman with a college degree have to start at the secretarial level all the time just to have a chance to do what I did?"

"I can think of one reason," Janice opined, "you didn't have an engineering or production management degree. It doesn't surprise me that they don't turn multi-million dollar rework facilities over to retiring first grade teachers. Goodness, Cynthia, why can't anyone around here just enjoy their success without making everything so political all of the time?"

"God, how naïve are you?" Cynthia demanded. "The reason is because everything IS political, that's why. You can't just sit around waiting for a miracle, sometimes you've got to go make one by grabbing what is by the nape of the neck and shaking it until it's what it should be. Look around you on Monday, Janice. Half of the girls in there are the product of one sort of miracle or another. Most of them overcame resistance from their parents, or husbands just to apply for their jobs. A couple of years ago, women couldn't even get jobs as streetcar conductors. Now you have Teresa and Colleen working heavy equipment, and Nadine supervising some of the most complicated work in the world. It is a miracle, and the sooner we recognize it, the more likely we are to retain these advances after the war."

"Who are you?" Janice asked.

"What do you mean?" Cynthia responded.

"Where did all of this awareness come from? You were the quintessential doyen three years ago, getting your education and hoping for Mr. Right to come galloping up on a white charger. Now look at you. You're not even the same person."

"Thank God," Cynthia answered, and let it drop.

IV

The summer of 1944 dragged slowly into the dog days of August as one day of startling war news and unending heat and humidity followed another. The hangar in which they labored was a gigantic sauna. Two things offset the stultifying boredom of Janice's job. First was the underlying optimism that followed the D-Day invasion of continental Europe. Suddenly, Janice began to believe the end of the war was in sight. Second, was the approaching resumption of classes at Central State College. Janice was eager to go back to school. Nadine and Cynthia had calendars as well and seemed to be on a non-stop recruiting effort to get her to postpone her return to class. As a result, Janice kept quiet about her plans.

Although she was bored with the work she was doing, the one element of her job with which she never tired was the planes themselves. Janice's hangar worked only on Flying Fortresses and Janice came to look upon them as gallant steeds in some mythic fable. Part of her fascination lay in the idea that she knew men, Jerry Harper, now dead, Charlie Morgan, and Bill Otis, Clara's husband, who piloted these gigantic planes. Even more interesting to her was the idea that many of the planes on which the crew she supported worked had completed twenty-five or more missions flying from bases in England to France, Germany, Belgium, and other targets controlled by the Nazis. *What stories they could tell, if they could only speak,* she frequently thought, but never said aloud for fear of being ridiculed by the others.

Finally, early on Monday, the day she planned to give notice she was quitting, Janice delivered a crate of aluminum rivets to Teresa Wright. Teresa was the woman Nadine had referred to as "Miss Pottymouth" when Janice had asked what "PDQ" meant on her first day. Teresa was a tough young woman with arms made strong from hours of handling a rivet gun and the other heavy tools used in her job. She was a strong woman and very direct, frequently using language to match. Teresa climbed down from her ladder and thanked Janice for anticipating her needs. She then reached out and patted the side of the bomber with her gloved hand.

"Keep those rivets and alclad coming, Janice. This baby's gonna' need a lot of work."

"I really like being out here around the planes." Janice remarked, "I think it would be wonderful if they were able to report what they had accomplished and what they have seen."

"What the hell are you talking about?" Teresa challenged her with a quizzical chuckle.

"Nothing really, except it's a shame none of these planes will ever be able to tell their own stories."

"Buuull shit," Teresa responded, stretching out the pronunciation of the first word to add to the disdain with which she said it, "they tell us all the time. It's clear you need another tour of the world famous Boeing B-17, Flying Fortress."

With that Teresa grabbed Janice's arm and led her to the principal workstation on the hangar floor. She grabbed a bound ledger from a row of them on the shelf above the desk.

"Janice," she began, holding the book in one hand and pointing to the bomber with the other, "this is the log book for that aircraft right there. Every bit of maintenance that has ever been performed on that plane is recorded in this book. Every spark plug, every bit of caulk, every guy wire that was ever replaced. Our job is to go back in there and make sure there were no shortcuts, no pieces about to go, to replace the parts that can't take two tours and to look for damage that was somehow overlooked. Let me give you a few examples."

Teresa flipped impatiently through the pages until she found an entry she wanted to read.

"August 17, 1943, flight to Schweinfurt ball bearing factory. Caulked 67 bullet holes in tail section, 113 bullet holes in waist gunner positions and 62 in the radio room. Replaced radio gear. Hosed down the interior of the radio room.

"Here's another, October 10, 1943, Munster. Caulked 403 bullet holes in tail section, waist gunner's position, and nose. Replaced Number 3 and number 4 engines. Replaced horizontal stabilizer, right side, replaced rudder due to battle damage. Replaced ball turret. Hosed down waist station. Plane down two weeks for parts and repairs."

"Oh, here's a good one. February 3, 1944, Frankfurt. Caulked 116 bullet holes in tail section and waist gunner position. Replaced Plexiglas in cockpit, co-pilot's side. Replaced copilot's seat. Replaced actuator on top turret. Hosed out cockpit and access ramp.

"Believe me, Janice, these babies are telling their stories all right. They tell them through these logbooks, and it's the truth, not that bullshit you see in the newsreels. The twelve-hour flights, the constant attacks from German fighters, the bullet holes, the blood that needs to be hosed out of the plane after it lands, the ball turret that got shot completely off the bottom of the bomber with some poor slob still locked inside a position too tiny for a parachute that probably wouldn't have saved his life anyway. They also tell about the miracle of this plane's design and manufacture. How does a plane return to base without its horizontal stabilizer? Without its rudder?

"Last fall the crew of the Memphis Belle was right here in Oklahoma City on a bond tour. Do you know who they are?"

"No," Janice responded quietly, overwhelmed with the picture of the ball turret gunner falling to his death from five or six miles up in the air. She shook involuntarily.

"The crew of the Memphis Belle was the first crew in the 8th Air Force to complete their allotment of twenty-five missions. We sent our first crews over there in June of 1942 and in a year exactly one crew lived through their entire tour without getting shot down or chopped to pieces in the sky.

"You know, that reminds me of the other place these planes are telling their stories," Teresa continued. "It's on the faces of the men who fly them. More crews have survived their tours now than a year ago, but the fliers who come back are different from the ones we sent to war. They aren't boys anymore when they come home. They're old men, old men at 19 or 20. Old men who have seen too much, not only of the missions they survived, but also the ones their friends did not.

"I met a tail gunner last month who is a little less secretive than the Air Corps, Janice. He told me about the mission to Schweinfurt, when they lost 60 bombers on one mission. That's 600 guys Janice. Six hundred men who were at breakfast and were missing at dinner. Then a few days later, the survivors had to go up and do it again."

"Show me," Janice asked, her voice tight and dry.

"Show you what?" Teresa replied.

"Show me the damage on the inside of the plane."

"Follow me." Teresa turned and walked to the plane, opened the crew door just aft of the waist gunner's station, and ushered Janice into the body of the bomber.

Despite working around them every day, this was only the second time Janice had been in a B-17. Shortly after coming to work at the facility she had toured one of the bombers to help her learn enough about the aircraft to know the turrets from the bombsight, and the horizontal stabilizers by their name instead of "those wing looking things on the tail." That plane had been on its way out of the hangar after a successful rework. It had literally been as good as new. This bomber, with it's nickname, "The Salty Dog" still painted in fading pigments on the fuselage beneath the navigator's window had just been wheeled in that morning.

Janice's first reaction was of how small it was, how tight the space. Her impression three months earlier had been that the bomber was huge. Now she was trying to imagine where the two gunners located in the waist of the plane would have hidden from 403 machine gun bullets that penetrated the skin of the aircraft during a single mission. She finally determined it was not possible. At that moment, she noticed something even more dramatic. The skin of the plane was pockmarked with hundreds of light brown spots on the interior of the plane. They were of dried caulking compound. This was the caulk the maintenance reports had coldly recorded as the repair for having bullets pass through the skin of the bomber. They were everywhere.

"How could the gunners have lived through this?" Janice asked, almost of herself.

"Who says they did?" Teresa responded. "What do you think the crew chief meant when he wrote, 'hosed out the waist gunner position?' Those logbooks are for repairs to the plane, Janice, they don't say anything about the men who flew back here."

Instantly Janice's mind leapt to the cockpit, and the terse entry about replacing the co-pilots' windscreen and seat, followed by hosing out the cockpit. She thought of Bill Otis and Charlie Morgan as she struggled to recall the name of their plane until she remembered it was "The Scarlet Woman" not "The Salty Dog." Janice sat down heavily along the fuselage and began studying the inside of the plane. Teresa stood with her arms crossed at her chest and watched Janice for a moment.

"Nadine tells me we're about to lose you. That's a shame, but I guess we're going to need college graduates after this war is over," Teresa commented in a tone that clearly showed she thought no such thing. She followed Janice's gaze around the interior of the bomber's waist for a few moments before she continued.

"There are ten men flying in every one of these planes and America is makin' 'em by the thousands. I hear that to qualify to be a flight crewman requires the same test scores and abilities that would get you into officer's candidate school in the infantry. Somebody is going to have to take the place of all of the fellas who go up in one of these and don't come back; guys who'll never get a chance to go to college or have a family, or anything else.

"I don't give a damn about college, Janice. My job is to make sure every bomber that rolls out of here is as good as we can make it. I want to know that every airman flying in a plane we worked on has every chance we can give him of flying it back home after his tour is over.

"I'll tell you something else, Janice, I am a veteran of this war. I'm a veteran every bit as much as that antique Master Sergeant who works for Colonel Clark. Every bit as much as any of the thousands of men and women who wear a uniform, but will never go over seas. I am proud that I'm helping to win this damn thing.

"Thirty years from now you'll probably be telling people that you were a defense worker during the war, but to me, if I left here to pursue something unrelated to the fightin', I'd consider myself no different from a draft dodger.

"I don't know what you're studyin' in college, Janice. I just hope you'll make damned sure you learn stuff that will make up for some of the guys we lose because people here in the states were unwilling to put their lives on hold while we kicked those Axis bastard's asses. OK?"

Teresa turned and left Janice in the aircraft. The muscular girl's words had struck at Janice like hammer blows and they hurt. For a moment she sat silently, but before Teresa could get away, Janice called to her. Teresa turned and looked at Janice.

"Thanks for the tour," Janice said quietly, "thanks a lot."

Teresa raised her chin at Janice in acknowledgment. It was a gesture Janice recognized from her father and uncles. She'd never seen a woman use it before.

It was hotter than the gates of hell in that plane and Janice had begun to sweat the moment she entered, but she made no move to leave. Instead, she let her eyes travel to each of the battle stations she could see from her vantage point. After a few moments she stood and carefully worked her way to the front of the aircraft. She passed through the bulkhead that led into the radio room. The radios had been removed but she didn't need much imagination to see the damage 60 machine gun bullets would have created as they smashed through that tiny space. Janice made her way across the catwalk that spanned the bomb bay and looked up into the cockpit. She could almost see the copilot, strapped into that seat for ten or twelve hours with his brains blown out as the pilot struggled to fly the plane alone. Involuntarily, Janice shuddered as she considered what had to be going through the pilot's mind as the frigid wind howling through the hole in the windscreen at almost two hundred miles an hour buffeted the lifeless body in the seat next to his.

Janice thought of Jerry Harper, the boyish B-17 pilot from Weatherford. Had his final flight been similar to those "The Salty Dog" had somehow survived? Had calamity piled onto calamity while the crew fought for their lives until the aircraft finally exploded, taking Jerry and his men to their deaths in a violent fireball? What of Charlie Morgan and Bill Otis? Would she someday see "The Scarlet Woman" wheeled into the hangar, a battered survivor of the war, or was its broken carcass already lying along the flight path to Berlin?

Janice's last stop was the nose, the "office" for the bombardier and the navigator. She brushed the dust from the navigator's stool and sat down. She stared out the Plexiglas and could almost see the approach of a German fighter with its guns blazing directly at the nose of the plane. For an instant, the image was so real, Janice had to close and rub her eyes to make it go away.

Janice tried to slow her breathing, but she couldn't do it. For five minutes, longer than any break she had taken since she came to work at Tinker Field, Janice sat on the navigator's stool and cried. Janice grieved. Her tears were for everything she wished she didn't know. All the experiences she wished she'd never had. She cried about the loss of innocence, the years when she should have been a carefree kid, able to pursue love and life and her own hopes for the future. She grieved for the years that had been sucked up by a war so far away geographically, but which snatched at every aspect of her life, even her dreams. When she was finished, she crawled out of the bomber's nose, walked slowly to the crew door, squared her shoulders, and let herself down onto the cement floor of the hangar.

After she washed her face, Janice worked her way up the long flight of stairs to the rework hangar's offices. Having a college education had been the most important goal in her life from as far back as she could remember. No one in her family had ever earned a degree before. Whenever her mother mentioned college, it was always in a reverential whisper as though she was referring to the church or the White House where Franklin Roosevelt lived. Janice entered Cynthia's office without knocking.

Cynthia looked up when she stuck her head around the door.

"If you'll have me," Janice told her, "I'm here for the duration. College is gonna' have to wait."

Chapter Sixteen

Charlie

Aviation Rework Facility
Building 5056
Tinker Field Army Air Force Base
Friday: October 13, 1944
4:48 pm

I

*J*ust before quitting time, Janice saw Cynthia Butler crossing the floor of the hangar. Cynthia waved, and Janice straightened, wiped her hands on her coveralls, and walked towards her friend.

"When you've changed, come by my office and we'll ride home together," Cynthia invited.

"OK," Janice responded.

"Oh, and brush your hair," Cynthia called over her shoulder as she walked away, "we're making a stop first."

A few minutes later, hair neatly brushed to remove the effect of the bandanna she wore all day and wearing a dress she had more or less remade from one of her mother's, Janice met Cynthia and the two girls walked out of the building. Once they were in the car and it was started, Cynthia drove onto the main road towards the officer's club.

"Where are we going?" Janice asked.

"The O'Club," Cynthia replied, "I want you to meet somebody."

"I hope this isn't a blind date," Janice countered.

"It better not be," Cynthia answered, "or our friendship is over. This one is mine."

"Yours," Janice responded, emphasizing the word, "have you got a fella' Cynthia?"

"And how," she answered, "wait until you meet him. I don't know what I have been waiting for all these years, Janice, but if this ain't it, I'm finished as a woman. He's coming to Edmond to spend the weekend at my house and meet my family. He has to return on Sunday afternoon, so he's driving his LaSalle. I need someone to drive my car home. I hope you don't mind being a beard for me, but I want to ride up there with him."

"A LaSalle? Gee, Cynthia," Janice responded deadpan as she pretended to smooth her hair, "I've never driven anything this large before. Maybe I better not. Tell you what, why don't I ride up with Lover Boy to make sure he doesn't get lost, and you can drive this big old boat home tonight."

Cynthia jerked her head to the side, almost driving into the ditch as her hands followed her eyes. Quickly righting the car, and simultaneously deciding that Janice was only joking, she responded, "That'll be the day. You know, when Nadine said you were funny, I just thought she was talking about how you looked in those coveralls you wear all day. By golly, you <u>are</u> a regular Fanny Brice."

Both girls laughed as Cynthia pulled the Olds into the parking lot at the Officer's Club, switched off the engine, and began the walk towards the front door.

"Tell me about him," Janice asked, "including the LaSalle."

"I must say, I never took you for a car crazy, but OK, he's a major…"

"A major," Janice interrupted, "my gosh Cynthia, how old is this guy?"

"He's 27, smarty-pants, just the right age for me. He was commissioned just before the war from ROTC, because he wanted to learn to fly. If he hadn't been wounded, he might even be a light colonel by now. The Air Corps promotes pretty fast these days. You might have heard something about a war," she finished while wrinkling her nose.

"Anyway, if I may continue, he flew B-24's from North Africa into Italy and Eastern Europe early in the war. He was wounded at Ploesti and barely survived the flight back to his base. After he recovered from that he was assigned to Kelly Field in Texas to help train flight crews in long distance navigation and bomber tactics. Finally, he came up here to work on the design of defensive armor and navigation systems. He has a degree in aeronautical engineering from, get this, MIT."

"Murray in Tishomingo?" Janice asked with a straight face, referring to the tiny Oklahoma agricultural college.

"No wise guy, the Massachusetts Institute of Technology, of course."

"Wow," Janice responded, "he sounds perfect for me I - I mean you."

Cynthia smiled. "You know, it does me good to hear you cracking wise about men. I thought you were going to be a nun there for a while."

"Nothing's changed," Janice confessed, "in fact my mother calls me, 'Sister Janice, the first Methodist nun'."

"Boy, you know you're boring when your own mother wants you to go out more." Cynthia observed dryly. "Not that I don't admire loyalty like yours, I really do. In fact, if Larry is sent back out, I am going to expect it of him as well."

"Is that his name?"

"Lawrence Remington Carmichael, soon, hopefully to be the Mister of Mr. and Mrs. Larry Carmichael."

"Soon?" Janice asked.

"Well, we'll see," Cynthia responded, "he did want to meet my family."

"Wow," Janice responded for the second time in as many minutes as they walked up the steps to the club, "these are big developments."

II

When Janice saw Larry Carmichael for the first time, her reaction was, "Oh my gosh, this guy was sent up straight from Central Casting to play Cynthia's beau." He stood about a head taller than Cynthia, but he looked even taller due to his slim build and erect carriage. His beautifully tailored summer service tropical worsted wool uniform was colorfully splashed with ribbons and devices. He was wearing beautifully polished brown leather shoes, and his frame cap was tucked carefully under his arm. Not handsome in the manner of movie stars maybe, he was still attractive, almost elegant, Janice realized, but in a manly instead of foppish sort of way. His demeanor made him a match even for Cynthia's good looks; in short, they looked like they were made for each other.

"Janice," Cynthia gushed as she intertwined her arm all the way to the fingertips with those of the man, "this is Larry Carmichael. Larry, this is Janice Lookabaugh who has agreed to drive my car home tonight so I can ride with you."

"Ah, wonderful," Larry responded, "Janice we are going to have dinner before we start out, will you join us?"

Just as Janice was about to say no, and excuse herself, she heard her name being called. Cynthia heard it as well, and both girls turned towards the sound.

"Janice," the speaker repeated and suddenly she knew to whom the voice belonged. Janice began searching the crowd until she saw him. It was Charlie Morgan, Bill Otis' best man from Clara Beech's wedding.

Charlie was dressed the same as Larry, except that he was wearing the railroad tracks of a captain. His combat decorations were topped with the Distinguished Flying Cross, the Air Medal with numerous oak leaf clusters, and the Purple Heart.

"Oh my gosh, Charlie," Janice said in shock, "what are you doing here? I thought you would still be in Europe."

"Well, we did our twenty-five and got out alive," Charlie responded in the axiom of aviators in all theaters of the war. "We came home two months ago. Since then I have been ferrying bombers around. I was standing in line over there to try to place a call to you tonight. I can't believe I just bumped into you like this."

"You were going to call Sister Janice, the first Methodist nun?" Cynthia asked archly. She tapped her index finger on the point of her chin as she fixed her gaze on Janice in a blatant attempt to force a reaction out of her. She got one too. Janice pinched Cynthia, but the older girl just elbowed her aside and moved to block any escape Charlie might try to mount. "Well, Captain, clearly you're someone we all need to know."

"Charlie Morgan," Charlie announced, offering his hand first to Larry and then taking Cynthia's offered hand in his.

When introductions were finished, Larry did the gentlemanly thing and announced to Charlie that they were about to eat dinner and they'd be delighted if he joined them. It was clear from Larry's face that he was not going to be delighted, and Janice immediately demurred. Charlie, assessing the situation, and knowing that if he didn't secure this invitation Janice was going to leave, immediately agreed. Cynthia, by now more interested in the sudden appearance of a man in Janice's life than in being alone with her almost-fiancée insisted as well, and finally Janice gave up. While they were waiting for a table, Janice got into line in front of the phones. When it was finally her turn, she called her mother and told her she wouldn't be home for dinner. Soon after that, they had a table and the four of them entered the dining room together.

III

Janice had never seen two men with combat experience in different aircraft types square off against each other, so dinner was very educational for her. Larry and Charlie spent the first 30 minutes comparing respective information such as aircraft types flown, missions accomplished, theaters fought in, and cities bombed. If Hazel was alive, Janice realized, she would say they were so busy measuring their peckers, they forgot there were ladies present. There were cocktails before dinner, wine with it and Scotch afterwards. Even the drinking took on the form of competition as the aviators scrupulously matched one another drink for drink. During the evening, Janice watched as Larry's reserve melted under the combined effects of bon homie and booze. The men kept everyone laughing by topping one another with outrageous stories, reported as gospel, in which the tenets of human nature and the laws of physics were routinely violated. Janice laughed more often than she had in years, suddenly realizing that the last time she'd had this much fun was Clara's wedding, and before that, her original date with Charlie.

When they had paid the tab, Cynthia and Janice half dragged the two drunk men from the club and out to the parking lot. The cool, smoke-free air of the night was bracing to Janice, but it visibly staggered Larry. As Janice watched Charlie assist Cynthia's beau to the cars, she realized it was going to take a lot longer than any trip to Edmond for Larry to sober up. She hoped Cynthia was prepared to drive the LaSalle. To Janice's amazement, Charlie was still coherent and upright, a fact she attributed to practice as much as anything, although she was sure he must be feeling some effects from that much booze.

"'M serious, Larry old buddy," Charlie said as he helped the Major towards the parking lot, "I've always really admired you B-24 jocks. Shit, the first time I ever saw a Liberator I thought it was the box they shipped the B-17s overseas in. You gotta' be a terrific flyer to get something that ugly off the ground."

"B-24's a fine aircraft," Larry slurred back at Charlie, "precision high altitude bomber, goes faster, carries more, hell of an aircraft."

"When you're right, you're right Larry," Charlie agreed, "only thing that could improve it would be to make 'em a night bomber, then nobody'd have to look at that nasty thing."

Both girls laughed at Charlie's needling as they maneuvered the men towards the cars. Cynthia handed the keys to the Olds to Janice and made Larry give her the keys to the LaSalle.

Larry shook off Charlie's arm and straightened to his full height.

"I'll have you know," Larry pointed out formally. "I'm perfec ally cabable, no wait, cap'ble, oh what the hell, I CAN drive - but I choose to let you do it in order to humor you." He then began leaning towards the other man until Charlie finally put Larry's arm back over his shoulder to keep him from falling.

"Yes, dear," Cynthia agreed, "but if it's OK, I prefer to make the whole trip with the tires on the down side of the car. Just call me an old fuss-budget."

"Yes - you - are," Larry remarked with extra emphasis, "but you're my old fuss-budget, and by God, you'll do."

"Yes dear," Cynthia repeated. Then to Janice, "Maybe you'd better drop Charlie off at the Bachelor Officer's Quarters before you drive home. He looks better than Larry, but he can't be in any shape to be walking around on an unfamiliar base trying to find his room."

"Thank you, dear lady," Charlie responded, his speech only slightly affected by the load he was carrying, "but first, let's get old Larry parked into the LaSalle." Then turning his attention to the Major, he continued, "Tell me, ol' buddy, would you prefer to throw up before you get in the car, or afterwards."

Larry seemed to think that one over for a moment before he responded, "Afterwards, I think. It seems more practical from an engineering perspective."

"Very well," Charlie agreed and opened the passenger door and poured the inebriated major into the front seat.

"Thin kew, Captain Morgan," Larry said with exaggerated formality, "I wish you all a most pleasant evening." No sooner was Larry finished speaking than he passed out cold.

"Well," Cynthia remarked, "he should make quite the impression on my parents tonight. It's a good thing I already told them he graduated from MIT."

"Don't even worry about it," Janice advised, "when you get to Edmond, if he isn't sober yet, take him to the Wide-A-Wake and make him drink coffee."

"Does that really sober people up?" Cynthia asked.

"No," Charlie interjected, "but at least you'll have an alert drunk on your hands."

"You stay out of this," Cynthia said with a laugh, "this is all your fault."

"Nope, nope, nope," Charlie insisted as he wavered at a highly stylized position of attention. "In the service, the senior man present is responsible for everything the unit does or fails to do. The Major is clearly senior to me in rank so this is all HIS fault." With that he saluted the unconscious Larry, palm up in the British fashion. "Carry on, sir, you're a good old bean for a B-24 type, I shit you not."

At that moment, the door on Larry's side of the car opened, he leaned out and vomited everything in his stomach onto the asphalt of the parking lot.

"Well," Charlie observed clinically, "that should help. He won't have as much booze to process now. It's my professional judgment he should be sober enough by the time you get home to stand upright for at least . . . ," Charlie looked skyward and counted on his fingers, "forty-five seconds before he throws up again. Cynthia, I suggest you make the introductions to your parents really really brief."

"Thank you, Dr. Morgan," Cynthia responded with another laugh, "OK, you two get out of here. I have a drunk to transport." Cynthia hugged Janice and as she shook Charlie's hand she said, "I actually had a very good time tonight. It was fun to meet you, despite the mess you made out of my boyfriend."

"I am always pleased to be of whatever service I can provide," Charlie answered. "You know, I've always thought of B-24 pilots almost like they were allies."

Cynthia laughed and hugged him. She then got behind the wheel of the LaSalle, fired up the engine and with considerably less assurance than she'd shown with the Olds, pulled it out of the parking lot and began driving towards the gate.

"That is a completely different Cynthia than the one with whom I used to work," Janice remarked.

"How's that?" Charlie asked.

"She was always such a stickler. Everything always had to be just so. She's still like that at work, but now, here she is driving off with a drunk boyfriend on her hands on their way to meet her parents for the very first time and she's laughing about it."

"She's old enough to know her own mind," Charlie observed, "and unless I'm crazy, she's really in love with that guy. Her parent's opinion of him won't change that. Anyway, even if he's drunk for a few hours, it won't change the sort of man he is."

"What sort of man is that?" Janice asked.

"Did you hear him say he went to Ploesti?"

"Was that one rough?"

"There weren't any rougher ones," Charlie observed. "The 15th Air Force actually attacked Ploesti earlier, but the first time they didn't take enough planes, so those poor bastards had to go back. They had to fly all the way across the Mediterranean from Africa and about half of the bombers got lost, others became disoriented and made their attack runs from the wrong direction. When the bombers on the correct heading came in they had B-24s crisscrossing each other right above the city dropping bombs right through the other formations from their own group. To make matters worse, the Germans knew where they were going long before they arrived because the oil refinery at Ploesti was the only strategic target in the whole area. The Germans knew they had to protect it so they threw everything they had at those guys: fighters, flak, flushing toilets, you name it. The crews could see the flak for a hundred miles before they got to the refinery. One of the pilots who was there told me that the smoke and flying metal from the anti-aircraft fires was so thick above the target it looked like a huge black tornado that they had to fly right through. It was murderous all the way in and all the way out. You could have navigated from Ploesti to the Med by just following the line of wrecked planes on the ground. Even the bombers that made it back to Libya were beaten to a pulp. My buddy who was there told me that of the 178 planes that went on that raid only 30 ever flew again.

"This war has been tough on bomber crews, Janice, but nobody's faced a worse mission than that guy. Do you remember me telling you the first night we met about not believing in heroes anymore?"

"Sort of," Janice acknowledged.

"Well, I was dead wrong. I thought wars were too big for heroes now, too impersonal. My problem was I just didn't know what heroism was. Now I know heroes are the ones who know they're going to get their asses kicked, are scared to death, and go in anyway. That guy is a hero."

Janice's eyes were filled with tears and she didn't know what to say as they stood there and watched until the LaSalle's taillights faded from view. Finally she reached over and squeezed Charlie's hand. It only lasted a moment before she released him.

"What's with you," Charlie asked Janice after the silence became deafening.

Janice looked at Charlie for several moments before she answered, "I guess I'm a little surprised to hear you this poetic after so much booze."

"I'm part Irish," Charlie acknowledged, "it's only when I'm drunk that I'm poetic. If I wasn't, there's no way I'd say anything nice about that B-24 pansy. Come on, let's go back inside and I'll buy you a lemonade or something while I finish what ol' Larry and I started."

"No thanks," Janice responded, "and if you want me to drive you back to the BOQ, the bus is leaving now. You've had enough, and I need to get home."

"Party pooper," Charlie complained, but he got into the car and sat while Janice started the motor and figured out the gearshift before lurching out of the parking lot and finally getting smoothly under way.

"Well," Charlie observed wryly, "that was exciting."

"Oh hush," Janice responded, "I've never driven this car before."

"You don't have to convince me," he replied. He then proceeded to give Janice a series of mostly useless directions on how to find the BOQ while they negotiated the few blocks to the building in which he was temporarily housed. When they pulled into the parking lot, he reached over and turned off the key.

"Let's talk for a minute, OK?"

"OK, but for just a minute. It's going to take an hour for me to get home, Charlie and I need to get going."

"I understand." They sat silently and Janice stared out of the windshield for a long enough period of time for her to wonder if the booze hadn't finally caused Charlie to pass out. When she turned to look at him, she realized he was staring at her in profile. Shocked into action at being caught, he finally began to speak.

"I was going to call you tonight. I was in line to use one of the phones at the O'Club when I saw you."

"So you said earlier."

"I wonder what would have happened if I hadn't seen you in the foyer of the club?"

"Well," Janice suggested, "for starters, Larry probably wouldn't be about to meet Cynthia's parents for the first time pretty much dead drunk."

"Well, maybe," Charlie responded, "bu-u-u-t he might have met another B-17 pilot, and then it would have been that guy's job to drink his candy-ass under the table. Actually, though, I was thinking about you and me. What if I'd called you? Would you have been willing to talk to me?"

"Sure," Janice replied, "talk is pretty safe."

"Not to me its not," Charlie said. "Every time I see you I'm always ready to say the dumbest things possible."

"Like what?" Janice asked.

"I've been out with you three times now: our blind date, the wedding party, and now tonight. I feel like I know you."

"How do you think I feel," Janice responded, "three meetings, and you're the steadiest relationship I've had since the war started." Janice was silent for a moment before she continued, "Charlie, I'm a little uncomfortable with the direction we're taking. I'm afraid I know where you're going with this and maybe you shouldn't."

"You're probably right," he agreed, "but before I shut up, let me show you something." With that, Charlie reached into his blouse and pulled his wallet from the inside pocket. When he opened it there was a picture. It was the photo from Clara and Bill Otis' wedding that showed the bride, groom, best man and the maid of honor.

"That's the only picture of you that I have. Do you remember when I told the photographer to take two of the four of us standing up front? That is the second one. I knew then that I was going to want it. I've been carrying it over my heart for a year."

Janice was silent for several seconds before she replied, "I don't know what to say, Charlie."

"That's the beauty of this. You don't have to say anything. You tried to get me to shut up but I wouldn't do it. I know I've already said too much, but I need to finish. I may never have another chance. Janice, I know you don't have room for me in your heart right now. But I've learned that life is short, really fragile, and unhappy way too often. I don't want to spend my life regretting the stuff I didn't say. I'm in this world, Janice, same as you. If you ever need somebody, I'd hate to think you might just look around and settle for one of the thousands of guys who'd love to have a girl like you and not even know that I'm one of them."

Charlie opened the door and left the car. He walked slowly away.

Janice sat for a moment. Her hands were on the steering wheel and slowly she lowered her face onto the backs of her wrists and exhaled all of the air she'd been keeping in her lungs. It took every bit of willpower she could muster not to beep the horn on the car and call him back. If she had raised her head, she would still have been able to see Charlie as he walked away, but she missed him already.

"Man, oh man, Tommy," she said, "that one was close."

Chapter Seventeen

Christmas 1944

410 E. Third Street
Edmond, Ok.
December 8, 1944

I

*A*lthough Janice had quit working at the Wide-A-Wake Café six months earlier, she still planned to attend the annual Christmas party hosted by the Noes. She wasn't the only former waitress who found her way to the warmth and friendship of the Christmas Eve celebration every year and not just for the companionship. Everybody in town knew the party was the best gossip mill in Edmond. What the waitresses didn't know after feeding half the town's citizens every week was simply not worth knowing. The party provided the waitresses with a great opportunity to discover who was getting married, or having babies, or who had been sick.

The party also gave Janice a chance to catch up with Hazel's Nutt's children. Despite her vow to spend time with the kids, she hadn't done it. She had been able to take the children to the 1943 party, but when she started working at Tinker Field, Janice began a regimen of almost 60 hours a week either working or just riding back and forth on the bus. When she finally did get home she was almost always exhausted. Her weekends were filled with laundry, helping her mother work the victory garden, canning vegetables, and otherwise helping to maintain the home.

Janice had never promised anyone but herself that she would be a better friend to Hazel's kids, but she still felt guilty about it. She knew she could have called on the children, she just didn't. Her shame at having to face them after not being any part of their lives for the past year almost prevented her from calling Mildred Price, their aunt, to ask her if she could take them to the 1944 party. She debated the issue with herself for days before she finally picked up the phone about two weeks before the party. When Janice finally had Mildred on the phone, her reply to Janice's request chilled her to the bone.

"They don't live here anymore," Mildred announced.

"They don't," Janice replied too stunned to keep the surprise out of her voice, "I uhh, I thought you were their only family."

"I couldn't keep them," Mildred confessed.

Janice waited so long to reply there was more judgment in the silence than in anything she might have said. Finally she murmured, "I see."

"I couldn't keep them," Mildred said again.

"I'm sorry," Janice replied as quickly as she could, "can you tell me where they are?"

"The county has them."

"The county?" Janice repeated. If she'd done a poor job of keeping the surprise out of her voice a moment earlier, she did even worse at hiding her dread at this confession.

"Is there something wrong with your telephone, Miss Lookabaugh?" Mildred demanded.

"I'm sorry, Mrs. Price," Janice answered, "I'm just trying to determine if I should try to find them for the Christmas party at the café or if that won't be possible. Can you please tell me where they are?"

"I would have kept them if I could," Mildred insisted defensively, "I – I have children of my own and no more money or space just because they were here."

"Can you help me find them Mrs. Price?"

"Haley is with the Pucci family right here in Edmond," Mildred finally replied, "and Jimmy is out ta' the Boy's ranch. Ruth has been with a couple of families. I don't rightly know where she is right now."

Janice counted silently for a few moments before she trusted herself to speak. In the 1940s, "the county" and "the boogeyman" meant exactly the same thing. Parents sometimes used state funded care as a threat of last resort. ("If you kids don't quit that, I swear, I'm gonna' put you in the children's home. Then you just see what happens!") No children ever wanted to see what happened. What Janice wanted to do was to scream at Mildred Price, "What do you mean you don't "rightly know" where she is? You're her only adult relative for crying out loud. How could you not know?" But as it was she didn't know what to say, so she said nothing.

Orphan care didn't just occupy space in Janice Lookabaugh's imagination, it was one of the few things that haunted it. When she was eight, her family had gone to the Oklahoma Methodist Home in Bethany one Sunday afternoon to visit a boy from their church whose caretaker grandparents had been killed in a house fire. His closest family lived in California, and while they were making arrangements to send for him, he had been placed in the home temporarily. The Methodist Home wasn't even in Bethany any more. It moved to a beautiful campus in Tahlequah, in Northeastern Oklahoma less than two years after Janice visited. But for the rest of her life, the image of the threadbare, paint starved, two story structure and its silent denizens left Janice with an image of institutional childcare that was decidedly more Dickensian than Oklahoman.

"Thank you, Mrs. Price," she finally said with a minimum of sincerity.

The first county sponsored foster home in Oklahoma wasn't even established until 1936. In the few intervening years, the children who found themselves in the state's foster care system experienced results that were decidedly mixed. Many children lucked out and found themselves with wonderful and caring families that provided them with loving, safe, and warm homes. Others were placed with families who somehow managed to turn a profit from the dollar a day stipend paid by the state. In rural areas, some foster families saw the children as free labor for their farms and ranches. In the worst cases, abusive adults and even vicious predators found their way into the system as care providers with typically dire and notorious results. Younger more "adoptable" children were usually placed with families while older children found themselves in orphan homes, workhouses, or for even the most minor of offenses, the state training school. Siblings not only frequently, but routinely were separated from their brothers and sisters. Naturally, the many wonderful foster parents never appeared in the folklore or newspaper articles, while the more salacious stories were told and retold until they seemed more common than they were.

"I couldn't keep them," Mildred repeated for the last time as Janice tapped the phone's hook to get the operator back to break down the call. Mildred's voice was still ringing in Janice's ears when she finally hung up the phone.

Practically everything anybody did to occupy themselves in rural Oklahoma in the 30s and 40s could get them seriously injured or killed. As a result, Janice had known several orphans in her life even before Jimmy, Ruth, and Haley Nutt. People routinely died from farm accidents, the primitive and therefore hazardous industrial base, driving country roads, hunting, fishing from primitive skiffs and canoes, working the oil rigs, even childbirth. It was all life threatening. People died. Sometimes they even killed one another. Just like Hazel and Jimmy Nutt had done. Orphaned children, however, rarely became the responsibility of the state. There was almost always somebody, an aunt, a grandparent, grown brothers and sisters, somebody to care for orphaned children.

Abandonment by a living relative was so rare it was not only difficult for Janice to accept, it was scary. At age 21, and although she was already making a living, Janice still lived at home and the prospect of losing her parents terrified her. Ruth Nutt's situation was even worse. She had lost her parents and now, separated from her brother and sister, she was being passed from family to family. To make matters worse, her only adult relative had no idea where she was. A cold shiver worked its frigid way up Janice's spine.

II

Getting permission for Jimmy and Haley to attend the Christmas Eve party required exactly three calls. Janice recognized the name of the family Mildred Price had told her was keeping Haley and she knew where they lived. She made a personal call on the Pucci's and they quickly agreed to the Christmas Eve visit. When she got home, she called the long distance operator to get the number for the Boy's ranch. She then called the director who quickly agreed to what he referred to as "the furlough".

After she hung up, Janice sat and studied the phone while she considered what to do next. All she knew was that Ruth was "with the county" and she finally had to admit to herself that she had no idea of where to even begin her search for Hazel Nutt's middle child. After several false starts, Janice's search led her to the Oklahoma County Child Welfare Division of the Oklahoma Department of Public Welfare. Its staff of social workers served as the advocate for children in need of assistance. Additionally, in the case of foster care, they had follow-on responsibility to insure those situations remained safe as well as in the child's best interest. When a foster or adoptive placement couldn't be found, an institutional situation was the next resort. Because he was older, institutional placement was what had happened to Jimmy. As Janice worked her way through the labyrinth of the system, she finally found Miss Helen Goodman, the social worker who had been assigned the case of Hazel Nutt's orphaned children after Mildred Price determined that she could care for them no longer. Miss Goodman provided Janice with the name and address of the family that had accepted Ruth. They didn't have a phone.

When Janice attempted to call on the family she discovered that Ruth was no longer there. The trail led back to the Child Welfare Office, but it was late Sunday afternoon when Janice got back home from searching for the family, and she didn't have time Monday morning to make another call. Because her work schedule coincided with the agency's, further calling would require that she do it from work. Once again, Janice climbed the long staircase to Cynthia's office.

"What's up, kiddo," Cynthia asked.

"I need some slack and a little help," Janice told her.

"Name it," Cynthia replied.

"I need to use your phone, and I need to use it before noon. Can I take my lunch now and make some calls."

"What's going on," Cynthia began and then stopped herself, "first, OK, you can do it as long as you can tell me that nobody is going to stop doing their jobs on a multimillion dollar rework facility while you're up here using the phone." Janice nodded her head to insure Cynthia that her requirements on the floor below were under control.

"Now," Cynthia continued, "with an eye towards seeing if I can help, and not so you can get my permission, tell me what you're trying to do. "

So Janice told Cynthia about her problems finding Hazel's middle daughter, finishing with, "If I wait for lunch time, then find a phone to make my calls, the people at the Child Welfare Office will be gone to their lunches as well. It is one of those double whammies you hear about."

Cynthia studied Janice for a moment then shook her head as she recalled a long ago conversation with Janice in the break area behind the Wide-A-Wake. "Tell me what this is all about. After all these years are you still feeling guilty somehow for what happened to Hazel?"

"No, I swear Cyn, its nothing like that at all. I - I just want to take those kids to a party." Janice hadn't even considered that she might feel anything more than friendly concern for the children of a dead friend. After a moment's reflection, Janice realized she was going to have to think about what Cynthia had said. She had known that Hazel was in danger, could she have stopped this whole nightmare. Janice shook her head and continued, "They had such a good time last year, and now that they aren't together anymore, it will be an even bigger deal for them.

"If I seem to be making a mountain out of this mole hill I apologize, but I'm worried about Ruthie. It's probably nothing, but she's just a little girl out there someplace. I can't find her, Cynthia, and it's bothering me something awful. The child welfare people are giving me the run-around, and even her own aunt doesn't know where she is. I just need to see this thing through. Nadine promised to keep things moving down there, and if I take more than my 20 minutes I promise I'll make it up."

Cynthia stood and walked around her desk. "Come with me," she ordered. "My phone is only a class C line. Colonel Clark has a class A phone just like the kind people in Oklahoma City have in their homes. With mine you can call anybody here on base, but to get off base you have to call the operator. With his phone you just dial any local number and it rings 'em up."

"Wow," Janice replied. All the phones in Edmond were still served by an operator in 1943. Callers tapped the hook to ring up the operator, told her the number, and the call was connected. Numbers were usually two or three digits. In her entire life, Janice had never used a dial phone. She confessed as much to Cynthia.

"Nothing to it," Cynthia assured her, "I'll show you how it's done." With that she led the way to the inner door that led to Colonel Clark's office. When they opened the door, Janice was surprised to see Colonel Clark sitting behind his desk. Her heart sank, but Cynthia didn't even slow down.

"Colonel," Cynthia began, "you need to head to the club for your lunch."

"I do?" he replied.

"Yes sir," Cynthia confirmed.

"Do I have an appointment or something?"

"No, but I need to use your phone and if I wait until you leave at noon, the people I need to talk to will be gone to their own lunches." She didn't plead with him or ask for permission. She just started moving around the side of the desk and stood there while the Colonel made up his mind, grabbed his hat and left his own office.

Janice's eyes were practically bugging out of her head.

"Oh my gosh," Janice finally gasped after the Colonel was gone, "if I hadn't seen that with my own eyes, I wouldn't have believed it. Who runs this place – as if I didn't already know."

"Janice," Cynthia explained, "if I waited for him to make all of the decisions he's getting paid to make around here, we'd still be flying biplanes in combat. It's taken a while, but we have worked out a system. He does what I tell him, and I do every damned thing else. It is better that way, and he knows it, but don't kid yourself, I'm always one screw-up from being launched out of here on my fanny. Until that happens, if I tell him to go to lunch, and as long as I say 'sir' when I do it, he goes to lunch."

"Wow," Janice repeated.

"One more thing," Cynthia added, "the whole deal will continue to work as long as he trusts me. I can't just mess with him. I did this because I knew it was important. Make your calls Janice."

"Thank you," Janice replied. After a ten second demonstration, Janice was left alone at the Colonel's desk.

Janice began her calling by dialing the number for Miss Goodman, the social worker who had been assigned to the case originally and who had referred Janice to the incorrect home.

"Miss Goodman," the woman said into the phone.

"Miss Goodman, this is Janice Lookabaugh. I spoke to you earlier about the children of Hazel Nutt. I appreciate your help and I found Jimmy and Haley, but the family you told me have Ruth didn't keep her. Can you check and tell me where she is."

There was a long pause on the other end of the line. Janice glanced at the clock; her twenty minutes were flying by.

"Miss Lookabaugh," she finally replied, "I was unaware that Ruth had not stayed with the first family with whom she was sheltered. Typically, our problem placements are referred to Mrs. Phillips. Ardalene Phillips is her name."

Janice's attention was snagged by the term, "problem placement." She tried to imagine the talkative little girl who had been walking down the lane to the Nutt's house less than three years earlier as a problem placement.

Janice was referred to Mrs. Phillips. When Janice finally had her on the line, she told her what she wanted.

"I have no idea who you're talking about, Miss," the social worker told her.

"You don't have a Ruth Nutt among your clients," Janice asked.

"No," Mrs. Phillips replied.

"I don't understand that," Janice responded, "if Miss Goodman says you have her file, and you say you don't even know Ruth, is it possible that after you she was transferred to another caseworker, or that her new family has changed her name? Do you have any children named Ruth in your files?"

For the second time, she began to explain what she was trying to do. Before she had scarcely begun, the woman on the other end of the line stopped her.

"Uh, Miss Lookabaugh is that correct?" the woman asked. Janice affirmed that it was. "Miss Lookabaugh, what exactly is the nature of your relationship with the girl in question?"

"I'm a friend of her mother's," Janice repeated. Janice had told her this earlier.

"Well," the woman replied dismissively, "then you have no standing with the child in question, no legal or blood relationship is that correct?"

"No," Janice agreed, "as I told you, I am a friend of her mother's."

"I see," the woman said to her in a perfunctory way, "since you have no standing with the child and her mother, as I'm sure you know, is dead, I must tell you it is our policy not to give that sort of information to the public at large."

"Mrs. Phillips," Janice tried to keep any emotion from her voice, "I am not the public at large. I told you, I am," Janice paused, "I was a friend of her mother's."

"Well," the woman said dismissively, "I don't see how you could have any reason to have access to information about this child."

"Don't tell me that," Janice snapped, "I'd be more willing to buy that load of malarky about agency policy if you hadn't already told me that you didn't even know the child. Miss Goodman told me she had no idea where Ruth was. You don't know either do you? You've lost her, haven't you? A little girl, lost in the bureaucracy, and you want to hide behind some bogus policy you just made up to keep from admitting it!"

"I told you that it is our policy not to discuss cases with the public," Mrs. Phillips replied.

"If you can't help me, tell me who can. Who is your boss, Mrs. Phillips? Tell me who else I can speak with. I want to know that Ruth Nutt is OK."

"Miss, I have told you all I can, good day." The phone went dead in Janice's ear.

"Damn!" Janice shouted at the phone. She looked up in alarm as she realized she had used bad language in the Colonel's office. She was doubly shocked to see Cynthia standing in the doorway.

"Remind me not to put you on the phones around here, Janice," Cynthia Butler observed dryly, "I just stuck my head in to see how it was going. Not too good I gather."

"That horrible woman just hung up on me," Janice was almost in tears. "I spent almost all of my time just trying to get to her, and then after she admitted she didn't know Ruth she tells me it's their policy not to discuss the children with the public at large."

"It sounds like a good policy, Janice."

"I'm not the public at large," Janice almost sobbed. "I started this just wanting to get those kids to a Christmas party, now I'm in this up to my elbows, and I can't find Ruth. She's probably fine," Janice said to the phone but then looked up at Cynthia before she continued, "but what if she isn't?"

"Go back to work, Janice," Cynthia tried to reassure her, "let me give it a try."

"They don't even know where she is, Cyn," Janice remarked as she stood and walked out from behind the large wooden desk, "they don't even know where she is."

III

Over the next two days, Cynthia called the Oklahoma County Child Welfare Agency no less than fifteen times. In turns she tried cajoling, pleading, badgering, and threatening. She got nowhere. When Colonel Clark returned from his lunch on Wednesday, December 20th, he entered his office to find Cynthia had advanced from threatening to shouting, but still to no avail. Cynthia slammed the phone into the receiver.

"Damn!" she shouted at the phone.

"Cynthia," Col. Clark gasped, surprised, "what's going on here?"

For a moment, Cynthia thought about just apologizing for using his phone on personal business and returning to her desk. She reminded herself that she'd scarcely known Hazel Nutt. After she stood she remembered the first rule of problem solution in the U.S. Army Air Corps: The best way to make your problem your boss' problem is to tell him about it. *What the heck*, she thought, and told him what she was doing.

"Cynthia," he said, "did you forget that I was a lawyer when your daddy was in short pants? I hired him for his very first job. I may not know too much about aviation rework and facilities management, but I'm one hell of an attorney. More important in this case, is the fact that when the war started and I wanted to help, I had the contacts here in this state and in Washington D.C. to get myself recalled. How effective do you think those pissants at county are going to be at telling me to go to hell?"

Col. Clark picked up the phone and from memory called State Senator Philbin Black. Senator Black's district included Oklahoma City and Oklahoma County. It took Col. Clark less than two minutes to tell the Senator what he knew about Ruth Nutt and what he wanted.

"Now what, sir?" Cynthia asked.

"You go back to work. I should be receiving a phone call sometime this afternoon. Senator Black told me the Department of Public Welfare's Director's name is Dr. Eustus Carling. I'm pretty sure Dr. Carling isn't going to enjoy his call from the Senator, but I bet it'll make him very malleable."

Senator Black was even more effective than Col. Clark had predicted. Less than fifteen minutes had elapsed when Dr. Carling called. Col. Clark buzzed Cynthia's intercom to have her come in and hear the conversation.

"Col. Clark," the director began, "I understand we're missing a little girl."

Clark was surprised. He had expected a layer of denial he would have to pick apart. Philbin Black had done his job.

"Why, Doctor?"

"It's a good question. I wish I had a really great answer for you. Sometimes we place a child with a family that leaves the jurisdiction. Sometimes it is something else, and to tell you the truth, sometimes, we just drop the ball on the paperwork. I know that doesn't make this any easier for the young woman who started all of this, she just wants to know where her friend's daughter is. I don't know yet, but I will find out. I bet she's fine, and one of us just put her file in the wrong place."

"How often does something like this happen?" Col. Clark asked.

"Not often, almost never in fact, but it does happen."

"OK," Clark continued, "when will we know where little Miss Nutt is located?"

"Well, Colonel, I don't exactly know. Several of our staff members are already on Christmas vacation. Friday is the last work day before Christmas. Tell you what, we'll make a real full court press on this as soon as everybody is back in the office. I will do my best to get that information to you early next week."

"Hell, Doctor," Col. Clark chuckled and then continued in the voice he'd used to dismantle witnesses in court, "I gotta' tell you how much I appreciate your candor. For a moment there I thought your conversation with Senator Black had done all I hoped, but apparently it didn't. For your benefit, let me just review the bidding here. First, you've already outlined several examples of how you

will extract a pound of flesh from back around your posterior. Good day, sir."
Col. Clark did not hang up the phone.

"Colonel Clark," Dr. Carling said loudly enough for Cynthia to hear, "wait.
Perhaps we should restart this conversation. Let me assure you we are going to
start right now and do everything in our power to find little Miss Nutt. What say
I call you with a report of our progress at four?"

"Well, let's see," Col. Clark replied, "it is now 1:17 p.m, four is more than
two hours from now so that won't do. Call me with the first report of your
progress at three instead." Clark hung up the phone.

"Damn!" Dr. Carling shouted at his phone as he slammed the phone into the
receiver.

"Damn," echoed Col. Clark in his own office as he looked at Cynthia, but he
appended, "that was fun!"

"Colonel," Cynthia asked when the expression of satisfaction on the old
man's face had mellowed somewhat, "who were you going to call?"

"I have no idea," the colonel replied, "but fortunately neither does Dr.
Carling."

IV

The rework facility was scheduled to shut down for Christmas at noon on
Friday December 22nd. Just before quitting time, Cynthia found Janice on the
floor of the rework facility.

"Colonel Clark wants to see you, actually both of us," Cynthia said.

"Now?" Janice asked.

"Come up as soon as you clock out," Cynthia replied.

When the girls walked into the Colonel's office he was sitting behind his
desk, tie pulled down, a smug and satisfied look on his face. He held up a
buck sheet, the form used by the office to record phone messages, and gestured
for Janice to take it. Janice took it and read the form. It included two names,
Cletus Preble and Miss Croman and an address on 1st and Harvey Boulevard in
Oklahoma City.

"That address is the county office. Cletus Preble is the foster parent who has
Ruth," the Colonel reported, "Miss Croman is Ruth's **new** caseworker. She will
meet you at that address on Sunday afternoon whenever you tell her to be there.
I've taken the liberty of asking Cynthia to drive you over to the agency office.
Miss Croman will get you and little Miss Nutt to the party after you go get her."

"Colonel," Janice began, "I scarcely know how to even tell you how much I
appreciate what you've done."

"Nonsense," the old lawyer replied, "this whole business has been the most
fun I've had since Pearl Harbor. I'm just glad I could help."

"Thank you, Colonel, thank you so much."
"You're welcome, Miss Lookabaugh."

Chapter Eighteen

Ruthie

Office of the Oklahoma County
Child Welfare Office
Lincoln Blvd, Oklahoma City, Ok
December 24, 1944
1:30 p.m.

I

$\mathcal{W}$ill Rogers, Oolagah, Oklahoma's favorite son once said, "If you don't like the weather in Oklahoma, just wait a minute." Sunday, December 24, 1944 was just such a day. After a week of cold wet weather, the day dawned cool and clear. A warm front was bringing clouds from the gulf coast, but they hadn't yet arrived. The sky was a flawless blue and by mid-afternoon it was almost 60 degrees.

Cynthia Butler pulled her family's Buick into the lot in front of the Oklahoma County Court House on 1st and Harvey in Oklahoma City in which the Child Welfare Office had space.

"I'll wait and make sure you're met," she told Janice as the other girl climbed out of the car.

"Thanks Cyn," Janice replied, but she didn't need it. There was a tall, very slender young woman standing next to an old Ford Coupe in the lot.

"Miss Lookabaugh?" the young woman asked. Janice nodded. "I'm Gwynn Croman," she continued and offered her hand. "I'll be driving you out to the Preble home to see if we can't get Ruth for the party."

"It's nice to meet you, Miss Croman," Janice answered and then continued, "and since you're here as advertised, let me signal to my friend to go on home." Janice then turned and waved to Cynthia.

"Sure," the young woman replied with a chuckle as she watched Cynthia return Janice's wave and then drive off, "but you didn't have much to worry about there." Janice eyed her with a quizzical look as she turned away.

"Thank you, by the way," Miss Croman remarked when Janice had returned.

"Thank you?" Janice questioned her. "I have to admit, I wasn't expecting that."

"Well, you inspired quite a beehive of activity around the office in the past few days," Miss Croman continued a trifle dryly, "it's the cleanest and most organized this place has been since I began working here two years ago."

"I had a feeling about that," Janice acknowledged.

The young social worker finally smiled, "Well," she said, "at least you haven't apologized."

"No," Janice acknowledged, "I never wanted to cause this big ruckus, Miss Croman, I just wanted to find Ruth. If I'd been able to get the information I needed more easily, we'd have all been a lot less stressed the past few days."

The two women looked at each other silently for a moment while Janice considered how difficult the young woman beside her was going to be. Finally, Miss Croman visibly relaxed and said, "You're right of course. Your Col. Clark caught us in a mess here." Miss Croman then climbed into the Coupe and released the lock on the passenger side so Janice could get in. The car started immediately and Miss Croman pulled smoothly onto the street. Janice could hear the uneven thrum of the old Ford flat head motor but she still had questions and Miss Croman had obviously been instructed to be as forthcoming as needed.

Janice leaned over and said loudly enough to be heard,

"What happened," Janice wanted to know.

"What can I say?" Miss Croman replied. "Her file got lost. It's inexcusable, I know, but it happens sometimes. Ruth was a problem placement. . ."

"Wait a minute," Janice interrupted, "that's the second time I've heard that term in the past few days. Tell me what that means."

"Ruth was returned to the agency. That automatically puts her in the problem placement category. Her file was transferred to Mrs. Phillips and somewhere in there her file got misplaced."

"Miss Croman," Janice began, "I know that child. There isn't a sweeter disposition on the planet. I just can't understand why she was even returned to the agency."

"Call me Gwynn, OK?" Miss Croman responded, "It'll make me feel better when I start confessing the agency's sins."

"I'm Janice."

"As I was saying, Janice, your Col. Clark caught us in an awful mess. The population in Oklahoma County has grown unbelievably since the war started. Lots of those people have moved from other parts of this state or even other parts of the country. The old network or grandparents, aunts and uncles doesn't exist for those families. We get a larger percentage of a much bigger population, and we have the same number of caseworkers today that we had in 1942.

"We have caseworkers in this agency with literally hundreds of children for whom we provide all sorts of help. Sometimes the child needs medical care and we literally go negotiate with the doctors to help the child for free. Sometimes the child needs an attorney, and sometimes it's foster care. Even after we find the child a home, we then must insure that those homes stay safe and stable. We aren't a war industry, Janice. We're just a bunch of understaffed, overworked civil servants. Nobody in this agency is superhuman, and too darned many of us are just barely average. There are great jobs out there right now for people with the same qualifications you have to have to get this one, jobs that pay a whole lot more. Anybody who would take this job has to either really love kids or be crazy. I like to think I know which one of those I am, but you can't always tell if you're crazy."

Janice smiled, but then asked, "Tell me about the 'problem placement.'"

"That's what I was getting ready to confess," Gwynn replied. "Whenever a placement doesn't work out, it's much more difficult to find another. Those children usually wind up in a state home of some sort. Mrs. Phillips has the responsibility to keep trying to find placements for those kids. In my mind she has the toughest job in the agency, and she tends to be harried and under pressure as a result. When Ruth came back to us, it was right at Thanksgiving. Mrs. Phillips was already gone for the holiday and one of the other caseworkers made the arrangements from her list of last resort families."

"Last resort families?" Janice interrupted.

"It sounds ominous, and they aren't usually our first choices. Usually it's families that need the money, and when they want boys, it's usually because they have a small farm that needs tending. But, she's still out there, so I guess it's working out OK, but I really don't know that for sure because in the month Ruth has been with the Prebles, nobody has been to see her. Her folder fell down between two cabinets in the file room and the caseworker who placed her never even mentioned it to Mrs. Phillips. Try to imagine how many places we'd already looked before we got around to moving the file cabinets, Janice, and you'll have a good idea of what it's been like to work in the Child Welfare Division for the past few days."

Janice smiled wanly, and to her credit, Gwynn Croman did as well.

"I'll bet you were cussing me," Janice allowed.

"For a while," Miss Croman acknowledged.

"You still haven't told me about the 'problem placement.'"

"I kept hoping you'd forget," Gwynn confessed, "but that's maybe the worst part of all of this. When Ruth was returned to us it was not a traditional return. The family that had her was moving to follow war work to California. That's it. Ruth hadn't been a delinquent or a problem in any way. We just plain dropped the ball on that one.

"As far as the Prebles go, we always try to keep the kids and families together as much as we can. Too much instability is bad for them, so I hope this placement is working out. I'd hate for her to have three families in a month, although that happens too, sometimes. If we'd been on the ball, though, she'd not have gone to the Prebles on a return like hers."

Janice rarely had premonitions but the litany of errors that had her in this car on this day going to this house sent a chill up her spine. It took almost 30 minutes to arrive at the small farm to which young Ruth Nutt had been sent. When the road bisected the boundary onto the property, Janice stepped out of the Ford and opened the gate, waited while Gwynn Croman drove through and then refastened the gate before climbing back into the old car.

"Thanks," Gwynn said after Janice was seated again, "how'd you like to come to work with me every day. That's the part of this job I hate the most."

"I think I'll pass," Janice replied, "I was raised on a farm 'til I was fourteen. Whenever Daddy wanted one of us to go with him to check the cows or something, we always knew the real reason was to have somebody to open the gates. I can imagine how big a hassle that is for you out here alone all the time."

"Not to mention what it does to my shoes," Gwynn allowed. Janice chuckled, then true to her gender and almost against her will, furtively evaluated the other woman's footwear.

When they reached the farmhouse Janice shook her head in disbelief. The little chill she'd felt earlier turned into an icy vibration in her spine. The house was beyond tiny, no more than three rooms built with a crawl space underneath. It had never been painted. There was a porch along the front, but one of the steps leading to it was missing. A large hole in the wooden flooring of the porch appeared big enough for a good-sized dog to pass through easily. The front door was ajar in deference to the unseasonable warmth of the day. The resulting access to the pathetic little house was guarded by a screen door with so little mesh remaining that its condition belied any function at all. Janice looked at Gwynn Croman, but the other woman's face gave nothing away. Janice recalled the tiny unpainted house in which Ruth had lived with her parents. That place had been a palace compared to this.

Gwynn pulled the Ford to a stop on the grassless front yard and stepped quickly from the car and climbed carefully but purposefully onto the porch. A small woman in a pale smock appeared in the door before she reached it.

"Merry Christmas," the social worker announced, "I'm Miss Croman with the Child Welfare Division. I have been assigned to check on Ruth Nutt from time to time."

"What happened to the other lady?" the woman asked.

"Are you Mrs. Preble?" Gwynn asked, ignoring her question. The woman nodded laconically, almost a shrug.

194

"My husband is in the field," the woman replied.

"Is Ruth here?" Gwynn asked.

"My husband is in the field," the woman replied again.

"Mrs. Preble," Miss Croman emphasized, "I am here to see Ruth. Is she in the house?" Gwynn crossed the porch and reached towards the handle to the screen door. She didn't touch it but her actions got the response she sought and Janice had time to reflect on how impressed she was with the young social workers professional skills in the moments before Mrs. Preble pushed open the door and led Ruth onto the porch.

Janice was trying to take her lead from Miss Croman. Despite her youth, it was obvious to Janice that Gwynn knew her business and how to get things accomplished. But when Ruth walked out onto the porch Janice couldn't stifle her gasp.

The child was filthy. Her hair was disheveled and matted, and finally, unbelievably, Ruth was wearing a feed sack. Janice could scarcely believe the apparition the child had become. Gwynn never hesitated for a second. She crossed the porch and knelt in front of Ruth. It appeared as though she hadn't even noticed the inappropriate clothes and how dirty the child was. "Hello, Ruth," Gwynn said in a friendly voice, "I'm Miss Croman. I work with the child care agency in Oklahoma City. I'm glad to meet you."

Ruth said nothing.

"There wa'nt no school today," Mrs. Preble announced, "it be'in Sunday an' all. We save her good clothes for school days."

"Of course," Miss Croman replied. There was neither inflection nor judgment in her tone or manner. Janice couldn't tell if Gwynn normally saw children in gunny sacks or if she was just being careful.

"Mrs. Preble," the social worker continued, "this is Miss Lookabaugh," Janice saw Ruth jerk and turn to look at her, "she is, or was, a friend of Ruth's mother. She would like to take Ruth to Edmond this afternoon for a Christmas party with her mother's former co-workers. Ruth will also be able to see her brother and sister. We will bring her back tonight by 8 p.m. She'll have eaten and will probably have a couple of new clothing items when she gets back."

"My husband is in the fields," the woman said again.

"Very well," Gwynn said, "perhaps you could direct me."

"I'll walk wi't chew," Mrs. Preble said and began leading Ruth from the porch, "come on Ruth."

"No," the girl said firmly, it was the only word she'd spoken since they'd arrived.

"Girl," the woman said, there was menace in the tone.

"She'll be fine right here with Miss Lookabaugh," Miss Croman promised and then began walking in the direction Mrs. Preble had been leaning when

Ruth decided not to follow. The foster-mother turned between the child and Miss Croman made a face at Ruth and then followed the social worker.

After they had disappeared from view, Janice walked to the porch and sat gingerly down on its edge. She looked up at the child and then patted the edge of the porch

"Come sit next to me," Janice said. The little girl came and sat down.

"Are you doing OK, Ruth," Janice asked. The girl looked down and hunched her shoulders.

"Tell me about your school," Janice continued as though the previous response had been adequate.

"S' OK," the child replied.

"Do you remember me, Ruth?" Janice asked.

The little girl nodded her head. Janice was eager to draw her out and get her talking. She could tell that the situation was horrible, what Janice didn't know was if it was safe. There were lots of homes in Oklahoma without paint, lots without bathrooms, lots with rotted steps and holes in the porches. The home that Ruth had been born in had most of those things wrong with it. Those weren't the things that made it unsafe for her momma though, it was the presence of Jimmy Nutt, Senior that had done that. If a house had love in it, Janice believed, you could raise good kids in it. She'd seen little so far to make her believe this house would pass that test.

"Where are we going to go tonight?" Janice asked her.

"Party," the little girl replied.

"Do you know who we'll see there?"

The girl's eyes filled with tears. Her tiny shoulders began heaving and finally she said between gasps, "Jimmy an' Haley."

"I know you miss them," Janice began, as she wrapped her arm around the little girl's shoulder. Her heart was breaking as she watched the little girl struggle to find her voice.

"I miss my momma," she finally blurted out and then collapsed onto Janice's lap.

Now Janice's eyes filled with tears. "I know you do," she whispered huskily.

For a long time Janice and the girl sat while Ruth cried herself out. When she was finished, the old Ruth began to emerge. Living with the Prebles had cowed the girl to the point where she was becoming non-verbal. After the cry and the warmth of Janice's arms around her, the little girl clung to the caring presence of her mother's old friend. When Ruthie spoke again, she dispelled any thought Janice had about the possibility that this might be an OK home for her.

"Don't want to stay here," Ruth said emphatically.

"Tell me why," Janice asked her.

"He's not nice to me," Ruth said.

196

"Mr. Preble?" Janice asked. Ruth nodded her head.

"What does he do?" Janice asked.

The little girl put her head down and hugged Janice. She communicated fear with every gesture. "He's mean," she said.

"What does he do that makes him mean, Ruthie?" Janice asked gently, "does he spank you or hit you?"

Finally, the little girl climbed onto her knees and whispered into the older girl's ear. As she spoke, the blood drained from Janice's face. To her credit, the shocked girl didn't react.

"Ruthie, honey, go get in Miss Croman's car," Janice said in the same voice she'd been using since she sat down with Ruthie on the porch.

"Mr. Preble hasn't said OK, yet," Ruth replied.

"Do as I say, Ruthie, right now, OK." Janice stood and led the girl by the hand to the old Ford. The door wasn't locked and the keys were still in the starter lock on the dashboard. Janice hadn't expected to see the keys in the car but she made a decision immediately. She helped Ruth into the small back seat. Janice then climbed behind the wheel and looked skyward for deliverance before she started the car and drove off in the direction Gwynn and Mrs. Preble had walked a few minutes earlier.

"Where is Mr. Preble?" Janice asked when they had gotten as far as she'd been able to follow the progress of the other women from the porch.

"Corn field," the child replied, "the cows are in it. He was over there feeding 'em."

"Where, honey," Janice asked again, the child pointed and Janice drove in that direction. By following Ruth's directions, Janice finally arrived at the field she was seeking. She could see an old Dodge pickup parked about 200 yards away. The back of the truck held several large sacks of the sort used to carry grain. A burly dark-haired man stood on the truck bed shoveling feed to the cows that had gathered around the vehicle. Gwynn and Mrs. Preble were already walking back across the field towards the fence behind which Janice had parked.

"Ruth, listen to me, OK? I want you to lie down on the back seat. Don't sit up, no matter what you hear. OK?" The child nodded her head and curled into a tiny ball on the rear seat.

"I'll be right back," Janice promised.

"OK," Ruth squeaked in reply.

Janice left the car and separated the barbed wire on the fence and by carefully gathering her skirt in her hands and raising it almost to the top of her thighs was able to climb through the strands into the field.

The ground was covered with the stubble left from the corn harvest. The field had been roughly cultivated before that and the going was made difficult by the large dirt clods that hampered Janice's progress as she walked towards the women.

When she got close enough to be heard, Janice said, "Let's go, Miss Croman."

"I'm afraid Mr. Preble has said no," Gwynn responded.

"Fine," Janice replied, "well, we tried, let's go."

"Where's Ruthie," Mrs. Preble demanded suspiciously.

"She's fine," Janice told her.

The woman's eyes shifted to the Coupe. Janice let her own eyes follow those of the woman. Ruth wasn't visible, but the look of guilt on Janice's face told the other woman everything.

"Miss Croman," Janice voice was strident, "we need to be going. I still have to retrieve the other children and have them at the party by five."

"Cletus!" the woman shouted.

As soon as Mrs. Preble called her husband's name, Janice started pulling on Miss Croman's arm. If anything, Gwynn Croman was even more unused to subterfuge than Janice. She looked at Janice in surprise and stopped walking. Janice jerked on Gwynn's hand and tried to hurry her along. None of this was lost on the other woman.

"Cletus," Mrs. Preble called her husband, "Cletus, they have the girl in their car!"

"What," Miss Croman asked, "no, no she isn't. I have to have your permission to take Ruth. Your husband said 'no.'" Gwynn was totally dumbfounded and Janice found herself unable to get the other woman to walk towards the fence.

"Come on, Gwynn," Janice urged her.

Until that moment it hadn't dawned on Miss Croman that something was wrong. When she finally realized that Ruth Nutt really was hiding in the Ford, Gwynn had the same look as a deer caught in the headlights of a car.

"CLETUS," the woman screamed, "they got the girl! They gone take 'er!" This time the farmer heard. He looked up from his labors and saw the confusion over by the fence. He dropped the shovel he was using and jumped lightly down from the back of the truck and began running towards them.

Janice was pulling Miss Croman' arm. "We're leaving," she insisted.

"What are you talking about?" Miss Croman demanded as she shook her arm free from Janice's hand, "what the heck is going on?"

"Miss Croman," Janice said exasperated, "get moving and I mean do it right now. I'm not leaving that child!"

"Cletus," Mrs. Preble shouted again, "they do have her. Come quick!"

"Like hell," the man shouted, "you leave that little gal alone. Get the hell off o' my place, damn you!"

"Miss Croman," Janice called over her shoulder as calmly as a running woman could muster, "when I get to your car, I am leaving in it. You can go with me or stay here, but if you want to go when I do you'd better be in that car when I get to it. I AM NOT LEAVING THAT LITTLE GIRL!"

Gwynn Croman had been warned that Janice had political connections and to do anything that was legal to assist her, but this was way beyond legal. She jogged to catch up with Janice.

"Miss Lookabaugh," she gasped, "we cannot do that. Mr. Preble said no."

Janice had reached the fence at this point and she stopped, gathered up her skirt and separated the strands of barbed wire and stepped through. Once she was on the other side, she held the wire open for the befuddled social worker who was being paced by the irate foster mother clutching at Miss Croman in an attempt to impede her departure. Janice gestured for Gwynn Croman to come on as she looked across the field at the rapidly approaching farmer, running as fast as he could over the broken earth. Janice looked at the bewildered young woman and the foster mother and finally made a decision.

"He molested her!" Janice shouted at the social worker.

Both Miss Croman and Mrs. Preble looked like they'd just been struck. "Are you sure?" Gwynn asked, shaken.

"Ask her," the frantic girl responded, "she's in your car right now, and YOUR HUSBAND," Janice screamed at Mrs. Preble who had stopped in her tracks when Janice spoke but was still standing nearby, "YOUR HUSBAND DID IT TO HER!"

Gwynn Croman looked at Janice, the car, and then back over her shoulder at Cletus Preble. Her situation was impossible. She had no information at all. She knew neither the family with custody, nor the woman who'd accused Cletus Preble of this heinous crime. She looked at the fence, and the strands of wire Janice was holding open, then back over her shoulder at the furious and quickly approaching man. The social worker gathered her skirt in her hand and stepped through the wire. Unfortunately, she didn't grab enough cloth and the skirt got hung on one of the barbs.

"Step the rest of the way through," Janice ordered, "you can unhook it from this side." When Gwynn tried, she straightened too early and hooked her sweater in the top strand. She was hooked. Janice reached over and freed the other woman's sweater but Cletus was about to reach them.

"Stop, damn you!" he shouted just as he caught the toe of his boot on one of the furrows and fell to his knees. His momentum carried him forward, and the women watched as he rolled over his shoulder and landed flat on his back. The man cursed and jumped quickly back to his feet and continued his advance. Janice released both strands of the wire and bent down. She picked up several dirt clods from the ground and turned to the man, angrily heaving them at him.

"You bastard!" Janice screamed at him, defiantly standing her ground by the fence while throwing rocks and dirt clods as fast as she could retrieve them from the rocky ground at her feet. When she hit the man, puffs of dust exploded on his chest and arms as the clods broke into bits. Although back on his feet, the farmer wasn't running anymore. Instead, he bent over and raised his arm to protect himself from the hail of detritus Janice was directing at him while he screamed imprecations back at her.

"That gal is our'n, damn you, leave her be!" he shouted.

"I'll see you in hell, first!" Janice shouted back at him and let fly with a good sized rock that almost hit him. By now Gwynn Croman, free of the fence, was running towards the car.

"Let's go!" she shouted at Janice.

Janice looked at her with the look common among combat troops right after a fight. She'd been throwing things at the farmer in a furious frenzy, and it took Gwynn's words to remind her that this was not just about imposing her will on Cletus Preble. It was an attempt to get Ruth away from the place. Janice looked at the car, bent over picked up one more rock and began running to the Ford.

"Stop, damn you," Cletus shouted again when the storm of rocks and clods had stopped, "that girl is mine. I won't have you take her away 'cause of some stupid lie!"

During the whole time Janice had been trying to get Gwynn Croman through the fence and had been throwing rocks and dirt clods at Cletus Preble, his wife had been standing right where she was when Janice had told Gwynn that Ruth had been molested. The woman was now near the fence and right where her husband was heading at a full run, obviously intending to vault the wire somehow. When he got to the barrier, he put one hand on top of the fence post and pushed off with his left leg. Just as he left the ground, Mrs. Preble reached out and grabbed the cuff of his coveralls. Her husband, momentum lost, tumbled into the wire, hanging up on the barbs along the top strand, and swinging, top heavy until he was hanging upside down on the fence.

"You bitch," he screamed at his wife as he fought to get free, "what the hell did you do that for?"

If the little woman said anything, Janice couldn't hear it. The woman simply turned away from Cletus Preble and squatted down almost into a sitting position wrapping her arms around her head in a gesture that communicated her own shame and anger. She left her husband to struggle as he hung upside down on the wire.

"Janice!" Gwynn screamed, "come on!"

Janice jumped onto the running board of the already moving car. She swung open the door and hurled herself into the seat just as the door swung completely open to the full extent of its hinges and then slammed shut just as Janice got out of the way. The car sped through a tight circle as it threw up dirt, mud, and gravel behind its wheels.

"Miss Lookabaugh," Gwynn finally said when they had reached the gate, opened it and then closed it again before they sped away, "if you're wrong about this, I'm finished."

"Ask her," Janice replied grimly as she looked through the rear window of the car. There was no sign of the Dodge pickup and she began to relax.

"I plan to," she said. Several minutes later, the car bumped up onto the macadam surface of the highway, and Miss Croman turned north towards Edmond. "What the hell do we do now?" she asked almost rhetorically.

"Drive to my house," Janice replied.

"But what about the molestation, what about what we just did to that man back there? We just kidnapped a little girl. What do we do about all of that?"

"Miss Croman," Janice replied, "I have a friend who says that when she has a problem, she just figures out what parts of it she can do something about and then ignores the rest. That is good advice for us right now. Drive up the Broadway Extension until you get to Edmond. I'll give you more instructions when you need them. Ruth is going to need something else to wear tonight and whatever else is true, it's still Christmas Eve and we can still take her to see her brother and sister. As God is my witness, Gwynn, that is just what I plan to do."

"OK, Miss Scarlet," Gwynn smiled at the fiery woman in the seat next to hers, "just give me instructions to Tara, OK?"

"Janice," a voice called to her from the back seat, "can I come up there with you now?"

"You bet, Ruthie," Janice replied, cheerfully oblivious to the chaos she'd left in her wake a few minutes earlier, "come on up."

II

They drove in silence for several moments as Janice held the frightened child at her side. Other than asking for permission to sit with her, Ruth had said nothing since she'd told Janice about Cletus Preble touching her "down there where I potty." After they had crossed the Edmond city limits Janice confessed, "My heart is still beating like a trip hammer."

"Me too," Miss Croman confessed, "I've been sitting here trying to figure out what I'm going to do next. It's almost five already. The office is closed until Tuesday of course. There is nobody to report anything to. I could call the director at home, but other than ruin his Christmas, what else would it accomplish?"

"That's easy," Janice answered, "another of my friends told me when I was starting to work on this that the one way to make your problem your boss' problem is to tell him about it. Bad news is just like fish, Gwynn. It never gets better with age."

"You seem to have a lot of friends," Gwynn observed.

"Not really," Janice allowed, "but I guess I am kinda' proud of the ones I have."

"After watching you at that fence today, I'd say you make a better friend than enemy. I hope you'll consider me one of that former number," the social worker requested.

"It would be my great pleasure," Janice promised with a smile.

Gwynn smiled back before she continued, "But what next for Ruthie Nutt?"

"Well," Janice assured her, "for tonight she can stay with me."

Gwynn chuckled, "I suppose that works. Tomorrow is Christmas. Can you keep her until Tuesday?"

"Sure," Janice nodded in confirmation, "but what happens then?"

"I don't know, Janice," Gwynn replied resignedly, "I don't have the authority to do a tenth of the stuff I've already done this afternoon. I can't make a spontaneous assignment of a child to somebody else – and I just did it. I didn't have permission to snatch Ruth from the Prebles either, although based on the allegations in this case, I will probably be able to invoke some sort of emergency provision, but what difference does that make? As soon as my boss hears about this afternoon I'm going to be fired anyway. Of course, even that's not so bad. At least if I'm fired I won't have to be the one to place Ruth with another stranger."

"They're not going to fire you," Janice predicted, "you were protecting her."

"Well if they don't, then by Tuesday I will have to find her another situation. And that may not even be the half of it. She may need other kinds of help. This has been a nightmare for her and who knows what kind of injuries she's suffered."

"We may not know for a long time," Janice opined, roughly quoting one of her college psychology text books, "but her momma sure was tough, maybe she'll be fine."

Gwynn looked down at Ruth and arched her eyebrows at Janice in warning.

"She's asleep," Janice assured the other woman, "she dropped off almost immediately after she put her head down on my lap." Ruth stirred slightly at that point and rubbed her eyes.

"We're almost back to Edmond," Janice told the child, "we're gonna' go by my house and get you a nice bath. After that we're gonna' see Jimmy and Haley, OK?" The little girl hugged her arm and almost immediately drifted off to sleep again.

III

Marge Lookabaugh welcomed her daughter and her two guests into the house exactly as though she'd been expecting a gunny sack clad child to suddenly show up for Christmas. Once the introductions were made, Janice headed up the stairs with the little girl.

"We're going to go get Ruthie cleaned up, Momma. When we're done, we're going to need something for her to wear. Do we still have something of mine or Karen's up in the attic?"

"Land sakes child, we would have given anything like that to the church years ago," Marge replied with a chuckle. "But the Miller's little girl isn't much bigger than Ruthie. Maybe she has a dress and some underwear we can borrow until after Christmas."

"Momma, would you go see, please?" Janice called down the stairs.

"I was just getting my coat," Marge replied.

After never having even met Janice before a couple of hours earlier, Gwynn Croman suddenly found herself alone in the Lookabaugh's orderly living room. Rather than sit or leave, she followed the sound of running water up the stairs and to the door of the bathroom.

"May I come in?" she asked from the doorway.

"Of course," Janice agreed.

"Look," Ruthie called out and demonstrated her mastery of the faucet extending over the ceramic covered tub, "water comes right out of the wall!" She then filled a small rubber pitcher with water and poured it over her own head.

"She told me she's never been in a tub that didn't have to be filled with buckets of water heated up on the stove," Janice told Gwynn who simply nodded. The same could be said of any number of her charges. "We're having fun up here aren't we?" Janice said to the child.

"Yes," the little girl replied. Her hair was filled with shampoo and was piled on top of her head. Ruth was occupied with a rubber duck that belonged to John Junior. As carefully as she could, Janice began working a comb through the child's hair. Occasionally, Ruth winced, but for the most part she sat patiently while Janice pulled the comb through her wet hair. It took some time, but finally she was smoothly pulling the comb through without tangling.

"OK, kiddo," Janice said cheerfully, "let's get you rinsed off and out of this tub."

The child stood and Janice used the rubber pitcher to rinse the remaining shampoo and soap from her hair and thin little body. There were bruises on her arms and legs. Gwynn was tempted to ask about them, but kept her counsel. It didn't take too much detective work to determine the origin of the bruises and the child was relaxed and happy standing there in the tub being fussed over by somebody she trusted. She could drag her back to the nightmare later. Right now it was Christmas Eve and for a little while, Ruth was just a little girl on her way to a party.

Gwynn wasn't in charge of the questions Janice asked however, and after she had finished rinsing the child she asked her where she'd gotten the bruises.

"Mr. Preble," Ruthie answered, "he's a bad man."

"Well," Janice assured her as she wrapped a large white towel around the little girl and another around her head, "you're never going to have to see him again. Miss Croman is gonna' find you a wonderful new home, aren't you Miss Croman."

Gwynn was surprised to hear her name. She'd felt almost invisible standing there at this sight of domestic ordinariness. What was she going to do? The onus of this little girl's future was back on her.

"Janice, Ruthie," Marge called up the stairs, interrupting her thoughts, "come see what I've got."

Janice made a face at the little girl that mimed excitement. "It sounds like she must have found you a dress to wear, let's go see Ruthie," she said.

"OK," the child replied excitedly.

Gwynn was dumbstruck. Could this be the same scared, monosyllabic child she'd met on the porch of the Preble farmhouse a few hours earlier? All of her study showed her that children had marvelous recuperative powers, but this seemed more like a miracle. The problem Gwynn Croman admitted to herself was that long ago she became a woman who didn't believe in miracles. She was much more inclined to describe what she was seeing with her own eyes as simply a manic episode and if it was, there was going to be hell to pay. Only time would tell.

The two women led the towel wrapped child down the hall to the stairs. At the bottom, Marge Lookabaugh smiled up at them. Her arms were literally filled with clothing.

"They gave me all of these," Marge reported, "they've been meaning to deliver clothes to the church ever since Thanksgiving but got too busy. Shelly Miller has outgrown these, Ruthie, so you can have any of them that fit."

The child was too overwhelmed to respond. She had never owned more than three outfits at once in her life. Marge was holding at least six dresses or skirts, plus blouses, shoes, underwear, even a coat, gloves and a hat.

"Oh," the child finally responded, "oh, oh, oh."

Two of the outfits were too large for Ruth, one was too little, but Janice suspected it might work perfectly for Haley. Marge set it aside to wrap as a gift that Ruth could present to her little sister. Marge and Janice began dressing the little girl in the clothes that had the best chance of fitting. The first was a little loose, perhaps, since Ruth was much thinner than the little girl who lived next door, but the length worked and Ruth looked beautiful in it.

As she studied the little girl in her new finery, Gwynn Croman could tell how pleased Ruthie Nutt was and that she knew she looked like a million bucks in the clean used outfits she'd inherited from the child next door. Gwynn hoped all of this fussing over her would be a little bit more of the currency needed for her road to recovery. She smiled at her happy charge.

"Well, what do you think, Ruthie?" Gwynn asked.

"Everything is perfect," the child responded, her voice a tad muffled as Marge pulled one of the dresses over her head so they could try on another.

A few minutes later, Janice sat with Gwynn Croman while Ruth and Marge left to hang the small clothes she wasn't going to wear that day on hangers in the closet in Janice's room.

"What happens next?" Janice asked.

"I'm going home," Gwynn replied, "there's going to be hell to pay when I make my report on Tuesday. I may need you to testify if the agency brings charges against Mr. Preble, but I wouldn't hold my breath on that one. The word of a child against two adults. . ." Gwynn left the thought hanging in the air and sighed. "But after all that, I still have to find another situation – another family," she corrected herself, "for Ruth. I don't suppose you'd be interested? You seem to have a way with children, or at least that one."

"I can't make commitments my parents would have to honor. I want what's best for her, but I work full time out at Tinker Field. I can't do this to my mother." Janice paused for a moment and smiled slightly before she continued.

"However, I can tell you this; when we lived out on the farm we always had a collection of cats and dogs on the place. They would just wander up as strays. It drove my daddy crazy, but by the time the animals had been on the place for a few days Mom would be fretting about them like they were pedigreed pets. By Tuesday, who knows? Ruthie's a lot more precious than a cat.

"But for right now," Janice interrupted herself, "I need to go get the other kids. What else can I do for you?"

Gwynn smiled and shook her head slightly.

"Nothing," she replied. "You know, Janice, I'd like to think that something like this is never going to happen to me again, but if it does, I hope I'll have the guts to see it through the way you did today."

Janice smiled, "Thanks."

"This has been quite a day, Janice, I don't think I'll ever forget it. Especially the part where you were standing at the fence or hanging on the running board of my car hurling rocks and curses at that horrible man. You really do have guts, girl."

Janice smiled again, "With the danger of destroying your image of me, I think I can tell you I was about to wet my pants when all that was going on."

Gwynn chuckled. "I wondered if I was the only one," she confessed.

Janice smiled back at her.

"I'm out of here," Miss Croman announced and stood. "Janice, this is my card. My home phone number is on the back. If something happens tonight or before Monday and you need me, just call, OK?"

"OK," Janice promised and then walked her to the door.

It wasn't until they were shaking hands at the door that Gwynn Croman realized she was looking down at Janice.

"Somehow, after all that's happened today I'm surprised to notice that I'm taller than you," she observed, "I have the feeling that if somebody had asked me to describe you later I'd have said you were more Amazon than petite."

"Five foot two," Janice admitted, "but Momma always says I like to think I'm big enough up here," she added as she tapped the side of her head.

"She'll get no argument from me," Gwynn agreed and left into the gathering night.

IV

When Janice returned with Haley and Jimmy Nutt it was dark. The clouds had moved in and it was cold again. When they entered the house Ruth was fully dressed in one of her new outfits. Her face was radiant. She looked so much like her mother that tears sprang into Janice's eyes.

"Ruthie, Ruthie, Ruthie," Haley cried out as she ran to her sister with outstretched arms, "you look just like a princess."

"I feel just like a Princess," Ruth replied as she hugged her sister and brother. "Merry Christmas Haley, Merry Christmas Jimmy, I am so very happy to see you!"

V

When Janice arrived at the Café with Hazel's children, Bertha Potts greeted her and crossed the little room to hug her and the kids. In the almost eighteen months since the memorial service for Phil Potts, Junior, Janice had seen Bertha only a few times. Nonetheless, the events of that day had joined them together in a way that just working with one another never would have done. Despite her grief over the death of her son, almost everyone agreed that Bertha was a completely different person since her loss. In the year and a half that had elapsed, her coworkers had begun to notice her face was frequently creased with smiles, and as time passed, they became less awkward and more spontaneous.

"Hello Bertha," Janice greeted her after they'd hugged.

"And who are these young adults?" Bertha asked as she turned her attention to the kids.

"I'm Haley," the youngest of the children responded.

"Oh, you can't be Haley," Bertha said with an exaggerated doubt in her voice, "I just saw Haley here last year at this very same party and she was just a little girl. You must be Ruth."

"No," Ruth said delightedly, "I'm Ruth."

"You," Bertha said feigning shock, "why you're practically grown. You can't be Ruth, the next thing you'll be telling me that this young man here is Jimmy."

"I AM Jimmy," the boy replied.

"Well that just doesn't seem possible," Bertha claimed, "but whoever you are, I bet you'd like some turkey and mashed potatoes. Why don't you kids go sit at the counter over there and I'll bring you something to eat."

Janice smiled at Bertha's manner. Sharing her love of life and friends was getting to be a real habit with Bertha.

The party was even more of a success this year than it had been in 1942. At first, Ruth would scarcely let Janice leave her side, but as the evening wore on and she began to realize that she really was among friends, the little girl became more and more confident. At one point while Janice was trying to tell Cleo Noe something of what had happened during the afternoon, she looked up at the sound of little girl laughter to see Ruth and Haley kneeling on stools at the U shaped counter of the café conducting a double jump at checkers against the about to be defeated Bertha.

"Bertha's smiled more tonight than normal," Cleo remarked, "those kids have been a tonic for this whole place. Thank you for caring about them Janice."

"They make that pretty easy to do," Janice replied.

"It doesn't sound like it was too easy today," the older woman answered.

"Caring about them is easy," Janice promised, "doing something is hard."

Cleo patted Janice on the shoulder and left to see to her other guests.

"OK, you three," Janice said to the children, "let's get your coats. We need to leave or we're gonna' be late for church."

"Aw, Janice," Ruthie complained looking over her shoulder, "Haley and me are about to whip Miss Bertha."

"I'm already whipped," Bertha admitted and rearranged the checkers in a sign of surrender, "you kids go get your coats on. I don't want you to be late for church. Anyhow, I gotta' go too. My husband will be here any minute."

When the family emerged from the church, there was a small panel truck parked outside with the Oklahoma Boy's Town and Ranch logo on the side.

"My chariot awaits," Jimmy said to the others. He hugged his sisters and then Janice.

"Thank you," he said to her, "you just keep rescuing us, Janice, OK? I don't know what would have happened to us if it wasn't for you. I hope it won't be so long till I see them again. But if it is, please remember us next year."

"I promise," Janice pledged, "I won't allow such a long period to go by again." She hugged Jimmy, now almost a head taller than she was herself.

After that, John Lookabaugh helped load the girls into the car. Haley had to be returned to the Pucci household. When they arrived at the younger girl's foster home, the girls cried and clung to each other. Separating them was the toughest thing Janice had had to do during a particularly tough day. Marge Lookabaugh couldn't even talk after they were back on the road and she hugged John Junior to her until the boy finally made gurgling noises like he was being choked.

"Mom," he squawked, "let a fella' breath."

"Oh hush," Marge responded, and pulled him even closer.

In the back seat, Ruth had curled up under the crook of Janice's arm.

"Am I really here, Janice," the little girl asked.

"You're really here," Janice confirmed, "and nobody is ever going to make you go back there. You're going to be safe from now on. I promise," she finished with no idea of how that promise was going to be fulfilled.'

"Look," John, Junior cried out, "it's snowing."

"Only in Oklahoma," John, Senior remarked, "sixty degrees in mid-afternoon, and snow before midnight."

"Well, I'll be," Janice said quietly from the back seat, "a white Christmas."

The next morning the family arose at the insistence of ten year old John, Jr. and opened the packages under the tree. There were two gifts for Ruth. A doll that Shelly Miller had provided and a baby carriage that Janice remembered as part of her own childhood. She wondered when in the previous night her father had gotten it down from the space above the garage and cleaned it so thoroughly. Ruthie was thrilled with both gifts.

They ate breakfast a little before nine o'clock and left for church. After they returned and ate a light lunch in preparation for the huge family feast that was to come later in the afternoon, John, Jr. left to explore the snow which was rapidly melting on the too warm ground outside.

A few minutes before 2 p.m. there was a knock at the door. When Janice opened it, Phil and Bertha Potts were standing outside. They had gaily wrapped packages in their arms. Janice opened the door and welcomed them in.

"Merry Christmas, Mr. Potts, Merry Christmas Bertha," Janice greeted them.

"Merry Christmas, Janice," Bertha answered, "is Ruthie still here?"

"Miss Bertha," Ruthie called from the door to the kitchen, she was wearing an apron and holding a wooden spoon with batter of some kind on it. The little girl ran across the living room and hugged the new arrival.

"This is for you," Phil Potts said to her, "Merry Christmas."

"Oh, thank you," Ruth said delightedly, "I've never had so many gifts before. You're too good to me."

"Aw it ain't much," Phil said, "but Bertha said you was a real gem at Checkers. I figured you might could use your own board."

"Is this checkers?" Ruth asked.

"Yes'm," the man replied sheepishly.

"Oh, play a game with me, please," Ruthie begged.

"You be careful playing with her," Bertha warned her husband, "she could wind up owning our truck or somethin'." Ruth laughed and led the way to the dining room table.

Bertha stood with Janice as they watched the child set up the board. Phil seated himself and put his chin in his hand to study the layout.

"Cleo told me somethin' of what you went through yesterday," Bertha began. "Seems like they oughta' have you in the Marines or something. We'd probably be in Tokyo by now."

"Anybody would have done it," Janice demurred.

"Not likely," Bertha disagreed, "seems like you always wind up rescuing the rest of us when we really need it, Janice."

"Not their momma," Janice pointed out.

"That weren't none of your doing, Janice, and you can't spend the rest of your life worrying about it neither. But what about them kids? What will happen to 'em now?"

"I don't know," Janice replied, "the social worker told me last night she needs to find a new 'situation' for Ruthie. The other kids seem to be in stable 'situations' now," Janice used the hated word twice in close proximity. She screwed up her mouth in distaste.

"So they need a home for Ruthie?" Bertha asked.

"Yes they do," Janice answered a smile playing at the corners of her mouth as she looked sidelong at the woman next to her. "Do you want the job?"

"Well," Bertha allowed with an embarrassed smile as she realized Janice had already figured out her scheme, "Helen's our baby and she's gonna' get married this spring. When James Robert comes home he won't be no kid anymore. He won't wanna' live with his folks for long. I'm only 39 Janice. I'm too young to retire as a Momma, an' I'm too old to start over again with kids of my own. Hazel's children look like a perfect fit for us."

Janice had been so certain she knew where Bertha was leading her, it took a moment before she realized her friend wasn't talking about 'just' Ruth.

"All of them?" Janice finally said with amazement, "you want them all?"

"There a good set Janice, it'd be a shame to break up a good set like that."

"Oh Bertha," Janice hesitated for a moment before she continued, her emotions almost costing her the ability to speak, "oh thank you, thank you, this is so wonderful."

"I'd have never brought more children into the household we had before . . . well, before we lost Junie," Bertha said with a small rueful smile, "I didn't think there was enough love in it. Turned out there was plenty, we just di'nt ever tell each other. I got room in my heart for three more young'uns, Janice. I want 'em. Phil wants 'em, and when we told Helen she wanted 'em too. We owe all of that to you, Janice."

Bertha paused for a few moments before she continued, a wistful hint of sadness in her voice, "I ain't never gonna' get over losin' Junie over there in the war. I know that part of me will never heal. But if you hadn't took me aside in the bathroom that day, I'd have never known what kind of family I had left. I only needed to tell 'em, and God help me, it just never occurred to me. I wasted so many years with my family, Janice, wondering if they knew how much I loved them. I won't do that again."

Janice hugged Bertha, "I'm turning into such a big crybaby," she whispered, almost unable to stifle a sob.

"Bertha," Phil admitted from the dining room table, "I believe she's already got me."

"I believe she does," Bertha agreed without being able to see the pieces on the board. She began crossing the room to the table while Janice headed to the kitchen.

"Where are you going, Janice?" Ruthie cried out happily, "I'm getting ready to win."

"I'll be right back," Janice promised, but she'd just remembered the business card Gwynn Croman had given her the previous day with her home phone number on it, "I have an important phone call to make."

Chapter Nineteen

Homecoming

410 E. Third Street
Edmond, Ok.
Thursday: August 6, 1945
5:30 a.m.

I

*J*anice sat on a small stool in front of the freestanding wood framed, full-length mirror she had inherited from her grandmother. She'd been sitting like this for several minutes, time she didn't really have to waste. Very soon she knew she had to leave for work. Still she sat.

Her hair was parted in the middle and gathered and pinned into a bun at the back of her head. She was bare foot and wearing her slip. In her right hand she held a plastic lipstick tube, in her left a tissue with a peach colored smear at its center. Twice already she had applied and then removed lipstick. She applied it a third time, sighed nervously and stood. She walked to the closet, removed her Wide-A-Wake Café uniform and examined it. Comprising a plaid skirt and vest worn over a white blouse and an apron, it was a far cry from the stiff one-piece jumper she had worn before she had quit to work at Tinker Field. Now she was back. With the victory in Europe a few months earlier, the B-17 rework line had slowed and finally stopped. After that, only P-51 fighters and C-47 transport aircraft were undergoing rework in the giant hangars at Tinker. The slow down had resulted in numerous layoffs, and Janice had reneged on her promise to stay for the duration when she realized that if she remained someone else would lose their job.

After she quit her job at Tinker Field, Janice returned to Central State College with a good deal of relief. Ever since she'd agreed to stay on at the airfield, she'd been terrified that something else would happen and then something else, until she'd finally never get her degree. Janice had more than enough money to finish her education. Because she'd continued to live at home, and there was so little to buy anyway, Janice had saved almost all of her pay during her time at the airfield.

Still, soon after her return to college; more because she couldn't imagine not having a job, rather than because she needed one, Janice had returned to the café.

Now she was right back where she'd been when Cynthia Butler had hailed her on the College's grounds over a year earlier. Her shift was to begin at 6 a.m. It was almost time to leave. Once she'd dressed, and after taking a final resigned look at herself, Janice sighed and left the room.

Normally, this shift would have ended at three p.m., but today she was leaving early. Janice had imagined that time would hang heavily on her as she waited for the hands on the six-sided clock on the outside wall of the café to rotate to 2:45 when she would leave for the train station. Instead, she moved with practiced grace through the motions of her job, and almost before she knew it, it was time to go. She said goodbye to Cleo Crawford who hugged her and wished her good luck. Just as she reached the door to the parking lot, Cleo called to her.

"Smile Janice," she reminded her, "this is a good thing, OK?"

She replied with a wan smile, turned and left the café. Janice walked the two blocks to the train station and took a seat on the platform. She would like to have gone home and changed first, but had felt guilty about asking for more time off than the fifteen minutes she'd already had to have.

Almost exactly on time, Janice heard the train from Dallas as it made its way slowly along the tracks. Her breathing became shallow and she could feel perspiration forming on her face that was only partly the fault of the heat. Soon she saw the dimmed headlight and pointed front of the train almost in one dimension. Moments later, the locomotive moved slowly past her and screeched to a halt. On each of the passenger cars, a conductor swung down and placed a wooden step under the doorway. Soon, people began to disembark and almost immediately he was there. The instant their eyes met she knew she'd been right. She followed Cleo's advice and smiled.

He was in his uniform, the same tropical worsted one he'd been wearing the last time she saw him. This time, in addition to his ribbons and the wings of an aviator, there was a small golden eagle in a wreath sewn to the pocket, the symbol of an honorably discharged veteran.

"Hello, Charlie," she said when he got to her, "how was your trip?"

"Long," he answered, "but worth it."

II

Despite the fact that they had been exchanging letters for almost a year, nothing had really been settled between them. Janice had skirted every opportunity to let Charlie know how she felt. Charlie had been patient, using the skills he had learned as a journalism student to keep his letters interesting and appropriate. In the end, it had actually been Janice who finally proposed the visit. Charlie had agreed immediately, by telegram no less. But, before the date of his leave had arrived, an opportunity to be discharged from the army had arisen and they had decided to wait until after his release. He would then stop off in Edmond on his way back to Washington state from his last assignment at Kelly Field down in Texas. Now he was here.

The couple walked towards the Lookabaugh's home. Charlie strained under the load of his heavy Val-Pak suitcase until Janice finally fitted her left hand into the handle along with his right. Between them the load was more easily carried. Once they had arrived, Charlie gratefully dropped the bag into John Junior's room while Janice bathed and changed her clothes.

While he was waiting, Charlie kept Marge company in the kitchen as she began preparations for a welcome dinner in his honor. Like anyone else she'd ever met, Marge accepted Charlie as though he was a long lost family member, and in moments he was talking comfortably with her and munching on an apple she'd given him without his having to ask, and even before he knew he wanted it. When Janice returned dressed in a brown skirt and cream colored cotton blouse, Charlie stood, and looked at her with such a rapt expression, that Marge had to smile and shake her head behind his back.

When John Lookabaugh arrived home from work he kissed his wife and daughter, tousled the hair on John Junior's head and shook Charlie's hand.

"We've been looking forward to your visit, Charlie," he allowed in a friendly voice, "let's go sit on the front porch and drink a beer while the women finish dinner."

"OK!" John Junior agreed.

"That'll be the day," John said.

"Iced tea for me, Mr. Lookabaugh, if that's OK," Charlie said.

"Sure," the older man replied, "iced tea for everybody."

The three males went out on the large front porch of the house and watched the grass grow as John Junior peppered Charlie with questions until Janice finally came and got them.

Dinner was an all-hands family style affair. Marge and Janice did their best to keep things moving conversationally without much success as the men fell to on the food. After the meal, the dishes were cleaned up and the family and Charlie sat in an awkward silence until one of John Junior's radio programs was set to start. They listened to the radio until John and Marge hauled John Junior off to bed and left the young couple alone.

"I have been looking forward to this for a long time," Charlie began when they were alone.

"I know," Janice allowed, "I have been counting the hours for the past few days."

"We need to talk," he continued.

"I know," she repeated, "but not tonight. I got up at 5 a.m. this morning and I'm beat. Let me go to bed. I don't work tomorrow, and there is something I want to show you. Can it wait until then?"

"Yes, of course," he replied reluctantly. Janice arose and disappeared up the stairs. For some time Charlie sat in the darkened living room. He had wanted to end the silence between them. One more delay was onerous to him. Finally he stood and left the room.

III

When Charlie awoke he was in a tangle of covers on the floor next to the bed. He had fallen heavily and thought he remembered calling out fighters to the gunners on the "Scarlet Woman" in a strangled cry. A moment later, a frightened looking Janice rushed into the room wrapping a robe around herself.

"Are you all right?" she asked in alarm as she moved to his side and kneeled onto the floor.

"Sure," Charlie replied sheepishly, "I'm sorry. This happens to me sometimes."

"Are they nightmares?" she asked.

"I'm fine, Janice," Charlie said gently, "I just fell on the floor. Go back to bed, honey, I'll be OK."

At that moment John and Marge appeared at the door.

"Are you OK?" Marge asked.

"He's fine, Momma," Janice reassured her.

"I really am," Charlie affirmed, "I feel just awful for causing such a ruckus. Please everybody, go back to bed," Charlie said quietly.

John Lookabaugh said nothing, but moved to Janice's side and helped Charlie free his legs from the sheet that had become wrapped around them and then helped get him to his feet.

"Come on, Sweetheart," he said to his daughter, "let's let Charlie get back to bed."

"I'm really fine," Charlie promised.

"Of course," Marge said as she took the sheet and chenille spread and smoothed them back onto the bed. When she finished, she put her arm around Janice's shoulder and the two women left the room. Charlie and John faced each other sheepishly until John finally spoke.

"Nightmares?" he asked.

"They don't seem like it when they are happening," Charlie admitted. "You know, when I joined the Air Corps I thought the idea of only having to fly 25 missions before I could come home seemed like a good deal. Now I realize I've been flying those damned things almost every night for the year since I got back. They were pretty scary when we were really flying them, but I actually think they're worse now."

"I was in the 42nd Division during the last war, Charlie," John told him, "we saw some pretty hairy stuff over there in France. After the war they sent us into Germany as part of the occupation forces. At night in our barracks it was like being in an insane asylum. Guys crying, screaming, doing what you just did.

"I was as bad as any of 'em I guess, Charlie. Not just at night either. Them Germans was starving right after the war. Sometimes I'd see a little kid, all skinny and underfed and I'd just start crying like a little girl."

"How long?" Charlie asked.

"Years," John replied.

"Shit," Charlie responded, then looked up startled before he added, "whoops, sorry."

"Don't apologize for calling shit shit Charlie. Sometimes that's the best word for it. Just know it gets better over time," John said gently and then paused for a moment before he continued. "You OK to try to sleep now?"

"I'm fine," Charlie assured him, "thanks Mr. Lookabaugh."

John had turned and walked almost to the door. When Charlie spoke, he stopped and turned back towards him. "I'm getting the impression you're gonna' be around some," the older man responded with a small but sincere smile, "I'd really like it if you'd call me John."

"I'd like that a lot," Charlie replied, "as long as you let me say 'Sir' sometimes as well."

John nodded and chuckled, "Suit yourself, but you were the officer, I was just a sergeant, and not such a good one at that." He hesitated a moment before he continued, "Women don't always know just what it was like Charlie. I kinda' remember. If you ever feel like talkin' about it, I'd really like to listen."

"Thanks," Charlie hesitated a moment before he continued, "John."

IV

By the time Janice arose and emerged for the day, Charlie had been up for an hour and was sitting on the glider on the front porch. She saw him through the window of the front room as she walked from the stairs to the kitchen. Janice filled a cup with coffee and took it to him.

"Good morning," she said as she handed him the cup. She saw he had an empty next to his foot. He had on neither shoes nor socks, wearing only his uniform trousers and a khaki shirt with the sleeves rolled up above his wrists and no tie. The newspaper was on the seat next to him but it was still tied with the string it had on it when the boy threw it onto the yard.

"Tell me about last night," she requested as she picked up the paper so she could sit down.

"It happens sometimes," Charlie replied. "I had a little talk with your Dad after you went back to bed. It may take a little while, but I'm gonna' be fine." He smiled at her and took her hand in his. They sat quietly like that for almost a minute, staring at the empty street in front of the Lookabaugh's home. Then Charlie sighed and turned towards her. When their knees were almost touching, he added his other hand to their joined ones.

"You didn't seem too eager to talk to me yesterday," Charlie observed, "but I sure wanted to talk to you." He hesitated for only an instant before he continued. "I love you, Janice." Charlie paused before he continued. "I actually believe it was love at first sight. When I saw you with Clara that night I remember thinking, 'Oh my God, I've been looking for this girl my whole life.' I was so glad I said 'yes' when Bill asked me to go out with Clara's friend."

Janice gave him a tiny smile, but said nothing.

"I came to Edmond to ask you something," he continued. Janice felt a rush of blood to her face as he spoke. He sensed her reaction and interrupted himself.

"I'm sorry," he said gently, "I should have gotten down on one knee." Charlie proceeded to do just that. He took her hand, but before he could continue she put her fingers to his lips so he wouldn't speak.

"I want to show you something, Charlie," Janice began, "do you feel like going for a walk?"

"What?" Charlie asked, surprised to have her change the subject so abruptly.

"I need to take you somewhere."

"Where?" he wanted to know.

"Just walk with me, OK?"

"Sure," he hesitantly agreed, obviously off balance at this turn of events, "OK, let's go."

They stood and reentered the house.

"We'll be back in an hour or so," Janice told her mother as Charlie disappeared to finish dressing, "just set aside the bacon and toast, and I'll make Charlie something when we get back."

In a few minutes he reemerged in his full uniform. The two of them walked out the kitchen door and across the yard to the sidewalk and headed west towards Boulevard. When they got to the north south running street, the couple turned north.

"It's a long way, Charlie," Janice warned him, "I hope your shoes are comfortable."

"I hope it's ten miles," Charlie answered, "I'm here to spend time with you. In fact, why don't we make a quick trip to the grocery store? I think we both really enjoyed that last time I was here."

216

"Charlie Morgan," Janice replied with a laugh as she recalled the hour long walk to the store they had taken on the day of Clara's wedding, "if you make me go through that nut roll again with everybody we meet, I will personally load your unconscious carcass onto the next train out of here and I won't care where it's going."

"OK, OK," he yielded, "I'll behave."

Charlie had broken the tension created when Janice wouldn't let him ask his question a few minutes earlier. Now relaxed, they walked and spoke of the things they hadn't written about in their letters. Somehow, for example, Charlie hadn't realized how close Janice was to graduation from Central State. When she told him she would be finished in December, he smiled and nodded his head.

"You seem different to me somehow," Janice finally observed after they'd walked silently for a few blocks, "quieter maybe."

Charlie looked down at the sidewalk beneath their feet and smiled self-deprecatingly. "I am a little different," he acknowledged, "for one thing, I'm unemployed, for another I'm not worried that I'm going to die in a spiraling fireball anymore, and finally, I quit drinking."

"You did?" Janice asked. "Well, I wondered about that iced tea last night. I have to confess that I'm surprised."

"I thought you might be," he replied.

"Not that I'm not pleased for you," she continued, "but what prompted this very positive change."

"I was just drinking to get drunk," he replied, "that's almost always a poor idea. It was part of the live fast and die young crap we all bought into in the Air Corps, the spiraling fireball if you will, that I mentioned a moment ago. Besides," he paused as they took several steps in silence, "I wanted to be more worthy."

"More worthy?" Janice asked chuckling, then continued with a tinge of sarcasm, "more worthy than an instrument qualified multiengine U.S. Army Air Corps Aviator?"

Charlie smiled to have his own words returned to him, "Well," he agreed, "that is a lot, bu-u-u-t" he continued dragging out the word, "that was then and this is now. I'm a civilian now, and I have to tell you," and with this he looked at her with a sideways glance, "I have my sights set pretty high."

"Well, maybe," she agreed, "but you may not know all that you need to."

"So tell me," he followed up immediately, "I want to know what's in the way."

"That's what we're doing, Charlie, be patient."

Charlie had made no secret of his desire for her and Janice had known exactly what question he was getting ready to ask her when they'd been sitting on the porch. Since that night in the parking lot of the Tinker Field bachelor officer's quarters, Janice had known and Charlie had never been reluctant to remind her that he wanted to be much more than just friends.

"Surely by now you know that patience is my special gift," he assured her with a small smile.

Janice and Charlie continued walking north on Boulevard until they reached and then crossed Danforth Avenue. A few minutes later they passed under a wrought iron and stone archway. Shortly thereafter, Janice led Charlie to Tommy Morrison.

"This is him," she said pointing at the headstone.

Charlie read:

**"Thomas Aubrey Morrison
Private First Class, USMC
15 May 1921 - 7 December 1941
Killed in Action in the USS Oklahoma"**

"He was only twenty," Charlie remarked absently.

Janice smiled at the irony.

"How old are you there Grandpa?" she asked.

"OK," he acknowledged nodding slightly and smiling ruefully, "maybe we were all a little young for this gig." Charlie paused for a moment before he continued, "Janice, I've known about Tommy for two years. Why are we here?"

"I guess I wanted him to see you," she replied, "and I wanted you to know something and this is a good place to tell it to you. There's a bench over there," she said pointing, "let's sit for a minute." Janice took Charlie's hand and led him to a weathered concrete bench. They sat facing slightly towards each other, knees almost touching. Janice swallowed deeply and began.

"I saw him the very first day I started at Edmond High. I was fourteen, stick woman, no more shape to my body than a ten-year-old boy. He was sixteen, the most popular boy in his class, president of everything, star of the basketball squad, wide-receiver on the football team, short-stop on an all conference baseball nine. I was so in love from the moment I saw him I just couldn't believe it. I had always been so practical about everything. Suddenly, I couldn't make it through a single day without doing something goofy. Whenever I was in the same room with him I became a complete moron.

"It was awful," she paused and gave a tiny little smile, "except for my daddy, I guess. He loved what a sports fan I had suddenly become. We went to every game for every sport.

"I felt like such a hypocrite. I couldn't tell a field goal from a hangnail, but watching him was so wonderful. He could light up a room like an incandescent bulb. When he was on the football field it seemed like a spotlight followed him wherever he went.

"The funny part was, I was so sure he knew what an idiot I was, and in truth, he didn't even know that I existed." Janice paused for a long moment before she continued. "When he graduated and left for the Marines I felt like somebody had turned off all of the lights.

"After a while, I was pretty much OK. The old practical Janice came back. But, then one day when I was seventeen, suddenly there he was with his little brother right there in the café, staring at me!" Janice shook her head at the memory before she continued.

"At first I didn't even believe it. I kept glancing over my shoulder to see who he was looking at. He wasn't at my table, so I didn't get a chance to talk to him, but the very next morning, there he was again. He still didn't know me at first, but he was flirting with me," Janice's voice cracked, and she hesitated for a moment and looked skyward before she continued, "I felt like Cinderella.

"Tommy's leave was only twenty days long," Janice continued after a pause, "you could say we had a whirlwind romance, but it wasn't true in my case. I'd been imagining it for years." She turned to him and put her hand on his elbow to insure she had his attention before she pulled it away.

"Charlie, this is the part I need you to know," she then averted her eyes from him and looked downward. "We committed to each other. We were going to share our grandchildren. After Pearl Harbor, I was in a daze for almost three weeks before we finally knew for sure. It was like God had played some horrible joke on me. All that time of being infatuated with him and suddenly I was his girlfriend, and he . . .he was even more wonderful than I'd dared to hope. Then after such a short time together, he was gone - gone forever as it turned out."

Charlie was looking at his shoes. He felt like a ghoul because he knew he'd have never even met this girl if Tommy Morrison had survived and it made him ashamed to be so jealous of a boy who'd been dead for four years.

Against his will, Charlie's mind wandered as he considered all of the black humor in which the flight crews had engaged during his tour in Europe. Guys didn't die; they "augered in," or "went south," or "bought the farm." They didn't lose six hundred men when they went to Schweinfurt; it was 60 planes.

There was so much death it had to become depersonalized or none of them would have remained sane at all. There were too many bunks suddenly empty at the end of the day. Too many aircraft flying in formation one moment and smashed to a fiery hell the next. Death, the airmen knew, was what war cost and if any emotion accompanied it, it was just gratitude that it wasn't you. "The stakes" they called it. It was the reason the men of a particular aircraft were closer than brothers to one another, and practically strangers to the men of the other planes with which they went to war. There was just too much at stake for it to be any other way.

As he listened to Janice tell about the death of this Marine he never even met, Charlie realized she was also tearing away the veil he'd kept forced down over his own memories of the war.

Janice's words personalized all of the losses and all of the heartbreak suffered by every family and ever town that would never again see the young men they'd sent to carry rifles, sail ships, and fly combat aircraft. In Janice's face he saw those losses in a way he'd been unwilling to consider before. The weight of it was too great, and Charlie forced those images from his mind. He knew he would have to deal with them someday, but it just couldn't be today. Today was too important, his window of opportunity to change his life too narrow. He brought his mind back to the girl next to him.

"I was certain I was never going to be OK again," she said in a tiny voice, "I don't know how I stood it, except that I shut down every bit of that part of me. Afterwards, I was terrified of that kind of pain ever coming into my life again. It isn't emotional when that happens Charlie, it's physical, and it hurts, it hurts a lot. You can't even breathe when you're crying like that - and you think you're going to die."

"I'm sorry Janice," Charlie said, "I can only imagine how hard all of this is for you to say." *And how hard it is for me to hear,* he thought.

Janice gave a tiny nod of agreement before continuing, "I've never said one word of this to anybody before, but I want you to know." She hesitated for a moment before she continued, grabbing his sleeve as she did, "I - I did my widow's walk, Charlie. I grieved, I cried, I screamed, I cursed God, I did it all. Nothing helped. Eventually, I was able to settle into a routine I could live with, the sad little girl who wouldn't go out on dates. But that wasn't really me, Charlie, it was just easier to be that person than the real me.

"But I couldn't keep it up, and finally, one day, my loss wasn't all I thought about. I had my schoolwork, my job at the café, my friends and family. A few months before we met, I began to realize that my sorrow wasn't going to kill me. At first I tried to force myself to continue grieving. I wanted to do it, but the pain was leaving me. I felt horrible about it, like I was disloyal or something. Tommy was dead, and nothing I could ever do was going to change that.

"To make matters even worse, even if I had wanted to move on, I didn't know how. Everybody had been so nice to me and put up with my moods and sadness. How could I just pick up the pieces and act like nothing had happened? I couldn't, I just couldn't do it.

"Then suddenly this wild card wise guy pilot plops down into my life, and lo and behold, he likes me AND he won't go away." Charlie smiled slightly at the memory. "It was terribly aggravating, and I guess a sort of life saver at the same time. Everybody else I knew was just leaving me alone with my grief and I kind of liked it that way. Only you and Clara wouldn't let me sit and brood indefinitely.

"I could tell how you felt about me, Charlie, almost from the very first night. God help me, on the day Clara got married, I was looking at you with almost as much interest as you were looking at me. I couldn't deal with that and I was determined to shut you out. You were getting ready to go to the same war that had taken Tommy from me. Not only didn't I want someone or something from outside to remind me that life was trying to go on, but I couldn't risk going through that pain again. You were dangerous to me, Charlie, not in the way men always want to be dangerous, but dangerous just the same."

Charlie looked at her, "I'm not sure I understand," he began, but she put her fingers to his lips.

"This is the part I need for you to know, Charlie, don't stop me or I'll never get it out. Since I wasn't going to drown in my tears or die of a broken heart, I was going to have to live instead. It was about then that I realized there were consequences associated with loving Tommy the way I had.

"We," and at this point Janice paused for such a long time that Charlie thought she might have changed her mind and decided not to tell him. Until she continued, he had no idea where she was leading him. Finally, in an almost breathless spurt she continued, "we were intimate, Charlie. I - I didn't get pregnant or anything like that, but I could have. I never thought for one moment that I wouldn't marry Tommy someday, and I loved him so much I couldn't even imagine waiting. After he died I was happy that we'd done what we did. I was glad he'd died knowing how much I loved him.

"Eventually though, I began to worry that I had burned all my bridges behind me - that I was now unfit. I'm not like some girls, Charlie. I can't just go from guy to guy. I figured that nobody who knew would ever want me and if I kept it a secret, whoever I finally did marry would know immediately and feel betrayed. I know the war has changed a lot of things, Charlie. It is no more the same as when my mom was a girl today than it was for her generation or the one before that compared to their mothers. But I live in Oklahoma. I think guys still value . . . what I don't have, I guess, and before we go any further, I wanted you to know."

Charlie waited silently until he was certain she was finished. When she didn't say any more, he allowed his hand to creep slowly across the bench until his fingers covered hers. In his mind, like the flickering images of an old silent movie, a riot of casual flings were examined and discarded. English shop girls, clerks, barmaids, even a noblewoman, and one in the doorway of a London apartment building during a bombing raid that had caught him on the street and too far from any other shelter. That night, he'd been with a girl whose name he didn't even know, who showered him with kisses and sex so frantic that neither of them had even removed their clothing. When the all-clear had sounded she had straightened her skirt and left without even saying goodnight. Charlie had no more considered those experiences "life changing" than he would have a particularly good meal, or a ride in a roadster. Like most of the men of his generation, Charlie had been taught that there were two types of girls: those you, well, went with, and those you married. Charlie had seen plenty of the former and until this very moment the idea that he should be ashamed of those relationships hadn't even occurred to him. Janice's talk of death and her sexual experiences had overloaded his senses, and he didn't know what to think.

"I have to confess," he began after a long pause in which his hand rested on hers, "I wasn't expecting to meet Tommy when we left your house, nor to learn quite so much about the two of you.

"When you started to tell me about him I was scared to death. I thought you were working up to tell me that he was the only man you would ever love, that somehow your life was going to be spent lamenting his. I didn't know how to get past that, Janice. If you'd stopped talking two minutes earlier than you did I'd have caught the next train out of here and pledge or no pledge, I'd have been drunk the whole way home to Washington. I didn't know what was holding you back all of this time. Maybe it's best that I didn't, but if I had, I like to think I know how I would have reacted."

Charlie paused for a few moments and gathered his thoughts. While he was silent, Janice glanced at him and when he saw her face, it had the look of a prisoner awaiting sentencing.

"The war has changed a lot of things, Janice, maybe not everything, but a lot. It brought me here. It sped up the process so I could meet you. It scared the hell out of me so I knew I was going to have to act. Now it has brought me back to this little town. For two years I have been jealous of a dead guy, somebody so wonderful that he could make someone like you love him, and keep loving him even after he was gone.

"Every minute since we met I have been terrified that I would never get through to you. Sometimes, in the hours before dawn I'd awaken in a cold sweat with the fear that I would sit someday in the far distant future, and recall that girl from Oklahoma and wonder where she was, and how her life turned out. Now, I realize the toughest obstacle hasn't been just overcoming your romance with Tommy, but your own image of . . . what . . . some irredeemable level of purity and innocence, I guess.

"We all have pasts, Janice. They are peopled with the ghosts of every person, living and dead that we've ever known and everything we've ever done. Most of us, hell Janice, maybe all of us, are a little cracked and chipped and worn around the edges after all we've been through. But we're still here, Janice; we still have lives to live. I don't love some mythical version of you; I love you - cracked, chipped and dented. I know that you always will love Tommy in a way. I don't want to take his place in your heart; I just want one of my own. I'll make a deal with you. If you'll forgive me my past, I swear I'll never let you worry about yours."

There was a long pause. Finally, Janice's free hand crept slowly across the bench until it came to rest on top of his.

"Yes," Janice finally told him.

"What?" Charlie asked.

"Yes," she replied again. "I will marry you."

Charlie stopped breathing for a moment. He looked at the girl next to him and tears came to his eyes.

"I still can't believe it," he said softly. He got down on his knees in front of the bench and took her hand in his. He stared into her face for a moment and swallowed deeply. He then took his right hand and put it on her cheek.

"You are so lucky," he finally said.

"I know," she replied with a smile and then finished with a hint of sarcasm, "but it's good of you to say so."

"I'm serious," he countered. "There is nobody on earth that is happier right this moment than me. Nobody luckier, and nobody more committed to deserving it. You have always made it impossible for me to be the sarcastic, sardonic and jaded bastard I thought I wanted to be. No matter how ugly reality was, every time I thought of you I would hear birds singing and I'd be back in a Disney movie. I know it kept me from going crazy and however today had turned out, I would still have always been grateful for that. Thank you."

Janice's eyes filled with such rapidity it almost seemed a physical impossibility. She looked through her tears into his eyes for a moment before she spoke. "You're a good man, Charlie Morgan," she said gently as she placed her hand back on his cheek, "and there's one more thing I need to tell you."

"What's that?" he asked.

"I love you."

Charlie spent a moment basking in the words he'd been waiting for two years to hear. Finally he turned his face slightly and said, "Is it always going to be this tough to get you to tell me?"

Janice smiled, "I still love you."

"I want to know since when," he replied.

"Since the night I saw you at the O'Club with Cynthia and Larry."

"Damn," he said facetiously, "I knew if I pressed my case I had a chance that night."

"Don't be so confident, hot shot," Janice smiled at him, "it wasn't until you were walking away from the car that I was sure," Janice hesitated for a moment before she continued. "I almost honked the horn to get you to come back."

"I wish you had." He paused for a moment before he continued, "So, how are the Princess and the Major?"

"Married, and living in Washington, D.C. the last I heard."

"Well," Charlie acknowledged, "somebody had to run the Air Force, I guess. I wonder what Larry has been doing while Cynthia keeps ol' Hap from making a mess of things?" It took Janice a moment to realize that "Ol' Hap" was General Henry H. Arnold, the commander of the American Air Forces during the war. Charlie always surprised her with comments like that and she laughed before she continued.

"It's amazing when you think about it," she observed softly.

"What?" he asked, "Cynthia running the Air Force? It's not surprising to me."

"No silly," she chuckled, "it's surprising how the texture of your life depends upon things like agreeing to go meet somebody's boyfriend, and then there you are, face to face with your own destiny."

"It's not that big of a miracle," Charlie said, "I hadn't given up. If I hadn't seen or talked to you that night, I would have kept right on trying. There probably wasn't a flight scheduler in the entire Air Corps that didn't know I was looking for hops to Tinker. You could have taken book that I'd have been back. I'm nothing if not tenacious."

"I'm awfully glad," Janice said. She was looking down at their hands when she continued, "Promise you'll be tenacious in our marriage, Charlie. It isn't always easy. Especially for people who don't know each other that well. I know I am going to be."

"You have my word," he promised.

When Charlie raised her face, her eyes were gleaming and overflowing with tears that ran in a crazed pattern across her cheeks and collected in the corners of her mouth. In deference to the cemetery, their kiss was gentle, soft, and quick. She tasted of salt and the departure of loneliness and Charlie had never been so happy in his life.

About the Author

Award winning writer Curt Munson was raised in Oklahoma. He has collected the stories of older Americans since he was a teenager and this passion is evident in his work. Best selling author, Chaz Allen (Extraordinary Women) says of him, "No one of recent mind captures the passions, hopes, dreams and spirit of everyday people like Curt Munson. His book is pure reading joy." Munson's writing crackles with authenticity, putting the reader amidst the people, places and stories he is telling. If you've been looking for a writer who can make you care, really care what happens to his characters, look no further. A former Marine, Munson has lived in Edmond, Oklahoma with his wife and two sons since 1993.

Made in the USA
Lexington, KY
10 November 2012